Perimenopausal Women with Power Tools

by

Karen Buley

Perimenopausal Women with Power Tools

Cover Art by *Kristian Norris*

The Wild Rose Press, Inc.
PO Box 708
Adams Basin, NY 14410-0708
Visit us at www.thewildrosepress.com

Publishing History
First Mainstream Women's Fiction Edition, 2020
Print ISBN 978-1-5092-3037-2
Digital ISBN 978-1-5092-3038-9

Published in the United States of America

Beth pulled out the stack of Christmas cards, breaking the rubber band in her haste. Flipping the cards onto the desk, she trembled, her pulse pounding in her temples. She uncovered the pale gold envelope postmarked Rockville, Maryland. Her heart stutter-stopped then resumed its wild tumble. She wanted to tear open the envelope and read more of the handwriting she memorized minutes before. But having guarded her secret with such fierceness, she hesitated. Guilt stilled her fingers in her story's unravel.

She clutched the envelope, shielding the words. Eager but afraid and ready but not, she carried the card into the kitchen. *Make a cup of tea.* She yielded to the emphatic voice. Robotic, she heated water, rummaged for a chamomile teabag, and sifted through mugs. She chose a burnt red cup customized with her initials—*EGJ*—a Secret Santa gift untouched by Reid.

Throughout the years, she wanted to tell him about the baby. The shame of deceit held her back, and then she was an impostor for so long, she couldn't—*ever*. Carrying her card and tea into the living room, she skirted his recliner, propelled by guilt into her own butter-soft chair. She sank into the cool leather. The card on her lap bore a weight of combined hope and joy and sorrow and regret.

Dedication

To My Friends
New, Old, and In-Between

Chapter One

Beth pulled into the parking lot of Home ReSource with ten minutes to spare. The previous week, she forced herself to register for "Beginning Woodworking for Women." She waited until the last minute, and the single opening seemed a confirmation the spot was meant for her. Yesterday, she almost looked forward to class. Now, a storm raged inside, and she wanted to flee.

Out of touch with Missoula, Montana, traffic and travel time, she drove across town faster than anticipated. But she refused to go inside early. She shifted into Park—pausing in Reverse—then turned off the ignition to minimize her carbon footprint. Thoughts tripped over one another with the urge to blast out of the parking lot fighting for top billing. She *could* leave. A departure wouldn't be her first and probably not her last. She could call Adult Ed in the morning and say she had a conflict, which would *not* be a stretch.

Nothing about her being here made sense. Reid, her husband of thirty-two years, had been gone barely a year and she enrolled in a woodworking class? After holing up the entire time, this class was supposed to be her reentry into the land of the living? She had supported his solitary woodworking, never joining him in his shop and now here she was, signed up for power tools? Nothing about this pursuit made one bit of sense, but at exactly five fifty-nine, Beth Jorgennson let out a ragged breath, abandoned the comfort of her car, and walked inside.

A handwritten sign directed her right: past rows of recycled appliances and cabinets, rolls of linoleum and carpet, and assorted collectibles like a pastry case and vintage sewing machine. Window frames—with and without glass—and two old school desks faced the center aisle. The jam-packed building served as a testament to the city she loved. A second sign arrowed left, past a pair of brass headboards propped on their sides, and shelves of putty, plaster, silicone, and tile. Propelled forward by tunnel vision, Beth hardly noticed any of the treasures along the way.

She stopped in front of a closed door. A lopsided, yellow-and-black notice announced, "Caution: Safety Glasses and Hearing Protection Required." Dizziness bubbled in her core, and she clutched a nearby shelf, her fingertips grazing a box of mismatched tile. She focused on an ecru wooden cutout, its flowing letters kitty-corner from the warning—*peace. As if.* She sucked in a breath, her heart tripping, too. *Go.* She took another deep breath and pushed open the door.

A man, his brown hair fading to gray, turned and smiled. "Welcome." He glanced at a sheet of paper and extended a hand. "You must be Beth."

"I am." Her handshake cursory, she pulled away, hoping he didn't notice her palm's dampness.

"Have a seat"—he signaled toward the lone, unoccupied chair to his left—"and we'll get started."

She didn't look at the others as she joined them around a long folding table sandwiched in front of the room. *Please don't ask why I'm here.* Draping her jacket and bag over the metal chair, Beth closed her eyes, long enough to steel herself but short enough—she hoped—that no one noticed her hesitancy.

"My name is Miles Gillette," the instructor began, "and I'd like to thank you all for coming. You might've noticed this class is new, so thanks for being here." He looked around the table.

Beth did, too. In addition to her, four classmates rounded out the group.

A dark-haired, thirty-something flashed a dimpled smile.

Beth managed a slight nod in return.

"I've taught at Sentinel High School for twenty-five years, but this class is my first Adult Ed—"

The door behind him opened. "Sorry. I forgot to give you these refund requests." A wiry man set the forms on the table. "Okay to leave them here?"

"Sure. A quick pitch. Starting next week, Dave would like to take pictures to use for advertising and post on social media." Miles gestured toward the newcomer. "If you don't want your picture taken, just let me know."

"Please do, and thank you." Dave brushed a two-fingered salute and headed out the door.

"Adult Ed offers a one-hundred-percent money-back guarantee. If you decide within the first hour this course isn't for you, grab one of those requests and slip out." Miles' eyes glinted. "You don't need to say anything, except I hope you'd say goodbye."

Beth glanced at the clock. *Fifty-six minutes.* She squeezed her hands into fists, the sharp dig of her nails quieting the roar in her head. *What am I doing here?* She wanted to morph into vapor and float home then burrow into Reid's recliner.

"…introduce yourselves. Tell us your name and woodworking experience. You can say 'zero' or 'a little bit' "—Miles moved his fingers from goose egg to index finger and thumb millimeters apart—"or more." He nodded. "Start us off?"

"I'm Beth—" Words caught in her throat.

Eyebrows raised, Miles held her gaze.

He wants more. Beth wrangled her words. "Woodworking and attending a class are new to me," she said in a small voice.

"I'm Corrine." The platinum blonde one seat over leaned in. "I used to watch my dad work in his shop." She moved her hands apart. "A long time ago."

Forty-five, tops. Beth took another look around the table and confirmed her first impression. *I* am *the oldest one here.*

"My name is Zoe Dail." The dimpled thirty-something shifted in her chair. "I helped our neighbors rebuild their deck last month."

"What kind of tools did you use?" Miles hovered a pencil above the class roster.

"Sander, grinder, chop saw, and an electric screw driver." Zoe ticked her fingers then smirked. "I didn't use them—I was in charge of drinks and snacks."

Her easy banter made Beth want to bolt. She signed up to learn a skill, not engage in small talk. The refund requests captured her gaze.

"I'm Therese," said a sinewy brunette seated across the table. "I putter but want to learn more."

Forty-something. Beth forced herself to guess ages and avoid looking at the clock.

"What do you putter with?" Miles tilted his head.

Therese grinned and folded her hands. "A drill."

He looked from her to the class roster and back. "Are you related to Kate?"

"I'm her mom."

Miles gave a single nod. "She has huge talent."

Therese steepled her fingers against her lips.

Her classmate's eyes were caked with regret. Beth studied her face. *What are you hiding?*

The final woman scooted her chair closer to the table. "My name's Maria. No experience, but I want to help my husband with a project."

"Great." Miles rested a forearm on the table. "What kind?"

Maria glanced down and tucked a strand of hair behind her ear.

Beth contemplated her unlined skin and thick, dark lashes brushing her cheeks. *Twenty-something?*

"A cradle."

"Congratulations." Zoe gave a single clap.

Lifting her gaze, Maria shook her head. "Not yet."

Her words were a breath above a whisper, and sorrow bit Beth's heart.

"Well, thanks for being here." Miles opened his palm. "Do any of you know each other?"

"We do—since college." Corrine flicked a manicured finger between herself and Therese.

Therese crossed her arms. "Yes, but we haven't done any puttering together."

Corrine snorted. "At least not in a woodworking shop."

"We'll do more than putter." Miles slipped two fingers into a large book, opening to a marked page. "Tonight, we'll talk about wood, I'll show you some tools, and we'll take a tour." He turned a color pictorial toward the class and launched into a comparison of hard woods versus soft.

Forty-seven. Beth unfolded her hands and glanced at the clock, surreptitious as she dried her palms on her jeans.

When the woods lesson ended, Miles stood and waved an arm. "We'll go outside before we lose sunlight. You might want your coats."

Goodbye rolled around inside Beth's mouth. Gathering her jacket and bag, she glanced at the refund requests but refused to take one in front of her classmates. *I'll come back.* She edged beside Zoe to tell Miles she was leaving.

Zoe flashed a grin. "I love field trips."

Her words forced a shadow of a smile. Beth shifted her bag and zipped her fleece. *No guts, no glory.* Getting out of the car had been the first step... She slowed and followed Miles out a back door. Cool autumn air caressed her cheeks. She glanced to the west where the sun dipped from the gauzy blue sky. *I'll stay.* Resignation took hold, and mindfulness wrestled sadness for years of missed opportunities she could never recover.

Miles snaked the class along wide dirt rows lined with shower frames, bathtubs, windows, and doors. He stopped midway down an aisle loaded with wood. "You have two options." He pulled scraps from a bin and handed one to each woman. "Oak flooring. Some pieces have stray remnants of shag carpet. I can't imagine why anyone would cover a hardwood floor."

Therese tugged at two orange tufts. "What would we do about these bits?"

"Cut a thin layer off the top." He dug five remnants from a neighboring bin and passed them around. "You'd cut off a layer from this bowling alley maple, too."

"Bowling alley maple?" Frowning, Zoe dragged out the words.

"*From* a bowling alley."

She grinned and tapped maple against oak. "Gotcha."

Beth ran her fingers over the scuffed finish. Her mind rewound forty-nine years to her inaugural bowling excursion. She had rolled eighteen gutter balls and struck five pins with one roll and three with another. Jimmy Nelson teased her about her score, but she discarded his words. She celebrated her birthday the day before and to bowl her age—eight—meant she had been *lucky*.

Maria studied the wood. "Do we have to decide tonight?"

"Next week. We have plenty of each, so you all can use the same kind if you want. Hang on to those scraps, and we'll loop around and head inside." Miles routed them past shelves and bins filled with PVC pipe, ducting, gutters, and siding. "Forty percent of what ends up in landfills is old construction material. Home ReSource works hard to help people reduce, reuse, and recycle." He gestured toward a bin filled with mop handles, brooms, and shovels, and then pointed out shelves of potting containers and garden supplies.

I have stacks of pots in our garage. My *garage.* Beth winced at the singular pronoun's sting. She saved pots for years, big and small, unsure what to do with them. Now she knew. *Worth the price of admission.*

Reid's expression hurtled through her mind.

Back inside, Miles arranged four pieces of wood into a rectangular shape. "Picture frame or mirror, and you'll add trim to give your work a more professional look…" He cinched four narrow strips around the outside of the frame.

Beth stopped listening, her thoughts hostage to Reid's craftsmanship and pride. *You could have taught me so much.* Tightness rose in her chest.

"…cut diagonal corners?" Zoe ran a hand through her hair.

The question mark in Zoe's voice reined her back. She blinked hard to quiet the memories.

"Yes, but I'll cut glass and mirrors, so you'll need to decide by week three. Grab your ear protection, and I'll show you around." Miles swept an arm toward his right.

Grateful for a task, Beth rummaged in her bag for Reid's cushioned orange earmuffs.

The women followed him across the room.

"Workbenches…sander…miter saw…" He pointed toward each. "Plus a dust collector and two table saws." Placing a palm on one saw, he motioned toward the other, nestled front to back.

Sliding beside Zoe, Beth glanced around the workshop. Neat, handwritten labels adorned cabinets and drawers and overflowing bins and shelves. Assorted clamps hung from wooden racks and pegboards. Wood of all sizes filled shelves and stood propped against the back wall. Some boards towered feet above her head. *Reid would have loved this shop.*

Miles launched into an explanation about the table saw and accompanying safety features—featherboard and push sticks—and directed the class to protect their ears.

Snugging Reid's earmuffs, Beth braced a hip against the edge of the table.

Then he fired up the dust collector and saw.

The hooked teeth transformed into a solid circle. Beth stiffened, primed for fight or flight as the oak passed through the blade. The saw's whine whirred an assault despite the earmuffs. When the saw stilled, the subsequent quiet was both welcome and not—she wanted to remember, but she wanted to forget.

"I'll make one of these for each of you so your fingers will be far from the blade." Miles held up the push stick. "The saw automatically shuts off if it touches flesh—you can watch online."

"Not me." Therese scrunched her lips and backed away from the table.

"The video's eight seconds—give it a look. They use a hot dog, which conducts electricity just as our fingers would. You can also scout around the Internet for a saw and finger video if you'd like."

"No thanks." Corrine tapped her index fingers into an *X*.

Words clotted in Beth's throat. *No way.*

"Next week you'll need eye and ear protection, a tape measure, and a pencil." He glanced at the clock. "Any last-minute questions?"

Head shakes and "no's" circled the group.

"Thanks for coming." Miles lifted a hand in a wave. "I'll see you all next week."

Beth slipped on her jacket and grabbed her bag. She avoided looking at him or her classmates on her way out. When she passed the refund requests, she slowed, uncertainty washing over her. *I might not be back.*

Thirty minutes later, she brewed a mug of licorice spice tea and carried it into the living room. Light from the hallway spilled in as she set her mug on a coaster. She turned on the lamp then settled into Reid's recliner. Chestnut brown and butter soft, the chair had been her refuge for the past twelve months. After he died, she cocooned in his spot and hunted his scent. Even after every hint of his cologne disappeared, she wrapped herself in his leather's warm embrace.

She glanced at their matching side tables—two of his works of genius. Her recliner and table were long abandoned. Slipping a hand into the magazine holder, she pulled out her journal. A ribbon and pen marked her spot. She tugged the purple ribbon to the right, under a fabric cover of matching irises with golden centers. Only a handful of times had she penned an entry since AR. *After Reid.*

A chill coursed through her. Beth shivered and laid the journal in her lap. Wrapping her hands around the mug, she inhaled anise, cinnamon, and orange. The aroma of Reid's favorite tea was a bittersweet reminder of shared winter evenings in this cozy room. She sipped until she warmed from the inside out. Then she returned her mug to the table and picked up her pen.

October Sixteenth

Dear Darling,

Tonight, I plunged into "Beginning Woodworking for Women"—my high-dive stunt to learn to live again. Can you believe I signed up for a woodworking *class? Good thing you're not in the ground, or you'd be rolling over in your grave right now.*

She paused, pen in midair. One night out and she wrote *good thing you're not in the ground*? Did what she wrote really matter? Sometimes, she felt as though Reid knew her every thought, as though he were beside her, his voice quiet and clear. Other times, the premise of presence and omniscience seemed absurd. But if he were all-knowing, she could write freely and uncensored—mostly. She took another drink of tea then set pen to paper.

Going to class was harder than I expected. Not just because everything about woodworking reminds me of you…jumping into a jewelry making or kick boxing or hot yoga class would have been hard, too.

They say things get easier after the first anniversary. Anniversary—why haven't they come up with a better word? Like deathiversary. Walking into class was easier than it would have been six months ago or even three. But not the easy I'd hoped for with one year down.

I have about thirty years on my youngest classmate, and ten to twenty on the others. Miles taught high school shop for twenty-five years, but this Adult Ed class is his first rodeo, as you'd say. I've dubbed the class Power Tools One-O-One. Next week, we're diving in to the table saw.

"If I go." Her words rang in the empty room.

Have I told you lately how much I miss you? I think about you every day, though not every minute, which is a spit of progress. Instead of dwelling on what we'd be doing if you were here, I'm struggling with the reality I was forced into. I sometimes think about what we might be doing, though. We could be planning our cruise right now.

Longing ballooned in Beth's chest, and she leaned back, surrendering to the memories.

"You were born in fifty-seven." A grin had skipped across Reid's face.

"I was, and you were born in fifty-eight." She smiled at the tease in his voice. "Your point is?"

He pulled her into a side hug. "My point is when you *turn* fifty-seven, we'll have a grand celebration." Beaming, he whisked a cruise catalog from behind his back. "Winter or early spring might be a better time to get out of Dodge. Wait 'til our anniversary, though you'd be knocking on the door of fifty-eight by then. How old would I be?" He furrowed his brow.

She answered with a kiss.

For the next hour, they sipped Cabernet and had lusted over the catalog.

The words blurred as she stared at the page. A tangle of anger and remorse squeezed her lungs. *You weren't supposed to drop dead at fifty-five.* Had there been forewarning, they would *never* have waited to plan their cruise and sail the seas. Guilt, regret, and memories of sharing a nice red tempted her to pour a glass. Instead, she drained her tea, read what she had written, and picked up her pen.

I wish. Tonight, we might take that coveted vacation in my dreams. I miss you and love you more.

Shifting her gaze across the room, she imagined them side-by-side on the couch—he perusing a finance magazine, and she, nestled next to him, devouring a library book. She wrapped her arms across her belly, longing to feel him beside her. Memories from junior year in college tiptoed through her mind.

She and her roommate, Lucy, had gone from zero

to ninety the day they moved into Sawyer Hall together, bonding over their red hair.

Beth's thick, copper-colored locks contrasted with Lucy's wispy, auburn curls.

Dubbed "The Gingers" one week out, they cherished their nickname. Over spring break, they travelled to Lucy's Boston home. For hours, they had sat on the sofa watching TV with a pair of cats warming their laps.

Images of Lucy and Reid faded into darkness. Staring at her empty couch, she ached, bone deep. Would she ever again experience such tender moments of joy?

****

Six days later, Beth sat in her office, steadying herself on the pink exercise ball that doubled as a desk chair. She scanned her email then opened the one she both anticipated and dreaded.

The following item(s) are now available for pick up and will be held for one week.

She used to delight in those words. Today, that sentence knotted her stomach. She should have paid postage to have the book mailed from Whitefish. But she was able-bodied, owned a car, and had time—more time than she knew what to do with—so delivery seemed extravagant. Skimming the title that sucked her in last week, she lamented her decision *not* to have the book transported to the privacy of her mailbox.

More than a year had passed since she visited the library. She hadn't been anywhere really, except for an occasional dash to the grocery store and a trip to the mortuary to pick up Reid's ashes. The library would ship the book back to Whitefish if unclaimed, but she refused to let it linger, uncollected. She drew in a quick breath, vowing to borrow the book today. *I don't want to fret for a week.*

Opening the link, she browsed the library catalog. She jotted down one more title then hurried to get ready before losing her nerve. Aside from the first night of class, she hadn't worn makeup in months. She applied blush to accentuate her high cheekbones and glanced at her upturned nose. In grade school, she longed for a straight nose like her friend Sari's. Then a new girl, Gail, joined their fifth-grade class midyear and told Beth she *loved* her nose. Jumping from a swing that winter day, she decided her nose was perfect.

She brushed on mascara and stared into her green eyes—wide and questioning. *I'm going.* She didn't waste time choosing the perfect lipstick to offset her olive green sweater. Instead, she closed her eyes and rummaged for a tube in the old candy box. A familiar, scalloped tube rushed memories of her retirement party, and she plucked the lipstick and opened her eyes. *Coral bliss.*

Her mind whirring, she painted her lips. Today's visit would not be one of the long, luxurious ones she treasured in the past. This foray would be surgical-strike quick—get in and get out. She thought having gone to class the previous week would make this trip easier. *I should have known better.*

She grabbed her keys and purse and hurried to the car. The rattle in her head drowned out the radio's murmur. She drove on autopilot, only glancing at the autumn cloak of yellows, oranges, russets, and reds she used to revel in while traversing Missoula streets. Tears pricked her eyes—a visceral reaction to the singer's words even before they sliced into her consciousness. "For a thousand years..." Struggling to clear her vision, she blinked hard. *Keep driving.* She stifled the urge to pull over, melt into the song, and weep. If she stopped the car, she would *never* reach the library.

Lowering the volume, she continued toward her destination, preferring the whisper of words over silence. She drove down Higgins Avenue and turned onto Front Street then parked in the lone lot at the rear of the library. Butterflies stormed her stomach. Entering the basement foyer, she rehearsed her steps. *Fiction then Holds.* She glanced at the table brimming with recycled magazines but did not browse as usual. Instead, she strode through the double doors, past Web Alley and the espresso bar, up the tri-level staircase, into the main room, and straight to Fiction.

Beth found Lolly Winston's book on a bottom shelf, twelve rows back. She snagged the hardback and turned it swift and deliberate, its front cover brushing her leg as she backtracked to Holds. Staring at the rows of books, she stepped side to side. She used to know her fourteen-digit number by heart. Now, she only needed to recognize the last five numbers to find the volume that had traveled one hundred thirty-six miles. *I can't remember...*

Tucking Lolly's book under her arm, she cursed herself for not slipping her library card into her pocket before leaving the house. She flipped through her wallet and removed the card, checking the number then the shelf. Her requested copy sat mere inches away. She snatched the paperback and hurried to the front, grateful for the anonymity of self-service checkout. When she slid her books across the counter, she did *not* want to interpret the expression on a librarian's face. All three stations were busy, but she was next in line.

A mother and preschooler parked a shopping cart filled with books and DVDs at "two o'clock"—Beth's name for the first station at the circular kiosk.

"Six o'clock" had her back toward Beth. Two books peeked from the crook of an arm.

The older man at "ten o'clock" scanned left to right. He finished first then gathered a short stack of books and CDs and turned to leave.

Swooping in, she set her card on the tray, poised for a fast finish.

"Beth?"

Butterflies collided in her gut. Not recognizing the voice, she glanced up.

"Please remove your library card and place your first item on the center of the tray." The machine's robotic voice joined its roving red light.

Number six stood kitty-corner, clutching her books to her chest.

Her smile faded as Beth searched for a name.

"Maria"—the woman slipped a strand of hair behind her ear—"from woodworking."

"Please remove your library card and place your first item on the center of the tray." The voice repeated its command.

"Hi." She shifted her body to shield her books then returned her gaze to the searching light. From the corner of her eye, she focused on Maria's motionless feet, willing her to leave. *But the machine won't stop.* She grabbed her card and replaced it with Lolly's book, its bar code and title face up. *Good Grief* overlaid the cover photo—pink bunny slippers, slender ankles, and the bottom of a filmy, polka dot dressing gown.

"Remove your item and place your next item on the tray. Or select Done."

A rush of heat burned her face. She lifted one book and positioned the second—*I Wasn't Ready to Say Goodbye: surviving, coping and healing after the sudden death of a loved one.* The moment the light registered the bar code, she grasped the book with one hand and pressed Done with the other.

"Thank you for visiting Missoula Public Library. Please take your receipt."

Ready to bolt, she ripped hard and fast, tearing the receipt in her haste. She debated leaving the jagged bit behind. Conscientiousness overruled, though, so she snagged the remaining remnant.

Narrowing her blue eyes, Maria held Beth's gaze.

A slide show of the emotions Beth hoped to avoid flitted across her classmate's face—pity, concern, and sympathy. Beth started toward the door, her heart thumping.

Maria fell into step alongside. Exiting the main room, she slowed. "Are you out back?"

"Mm-hmm." She pursed her lips, her tone neutral.

"So am I."

They started down the steps.

Beth forced herself to take the stairs one at a time, her gait quickening on the second landing. She turned toward the third flight. Within view of the exit, she wanted to sprint.

"Do you have time for a cup of coffee?" Maria rearranged her books.

No. She swallowed hard, searching for an excuse.

"It's okay if you don't." Maria flicked a hand.

"I do." The answer slipped out. *What?* She wanted a do-over. Approaching the overflowing espresso bar, she was filled with relief. "Some—"

"We could walk to the Catalyst." Maria's eyes shone.

Some other time. Beth glanced away from her expectant expression. *I wasn't fast enough.* "I—" Digging past the sour taste in her mouth, she met Maria's gaze. "I'd like to drop these books in my car."

"Good idea." Outside, Maria gestured with her elbow. "I'm over there. Where are you?"

She tilted her head in the opposite direction.

"Be right back."

Hurrying to her car, Beth unlocked the door. She wanted to hop in and holler an apology about a forgotten appointment—*with Reid's recliner.* Maria's face hinted at questions she was not ready to answer—not today and maybe never.

But then Maria was behind her car, smiling.

She stacked her books face down then straightened and steadied her breath before locking the door.

They zigzagged through the parking lot and turned onto Front Street, their feet shuffling through the kaleidoscope of leaves blanketing the sidewalk.

"I love these autumn days." Maria unbuttoned her cardigan.

Tipping her face toward the sun, Beth closed her eyes. She slowed, soaking in the warmth she had hidden from for months. Sighing, she opened her eyes. "Did you grow up here?"

"Seattle. We moved here a little over two years ago. How about you?"

"San Diego, but I've lived here for over thirty

years." *Almost half my life.* She wasn't sure which description made her sound older.

Their chat was hometown-weather cursory until they reached the Catalyst. Weaving through the café, they ascended the staircase near the back and chose an upstairs table overlooking the first floor.

A sandy-haired server arrived and greeted them with a smile. He dropped off menus and left with their drink orders.

Maria glanced at the menu. "Are you hungry?"

Yes and *no* volleyed between truth and dishonesty. But words were a struggle, and she did *not* want to prolong this conversation. *The shorter the better.* "Are you?" She hoped for a swift *no.*

"Mm-hmm. Do you have time?"

"Mm-hmm." The echo made her feel foolish, and she busied herself with the menu. Certain her stomach's rumbles carried when she climbed the stairs, she was glad to order food. Part of her wished, though, she waited a day or even an hour to go to the library. Out of commission for a year, she grappled with small talk. *If I do the asking, I won't have to answer.*

Their server returned with a two-shot hazelnut latte and a pot of hot water and an orange spice herbal tea bag.

Maria ordered first.

After Beth talked eggs and toast, she unfolded her napkin. "What do you do?" A tingle swept up her neck and across her cheeks. "I mean, do you work outside the home?"

Lifting her teapot, Maria smiled. "I'm an OB nurse. What about you?"

"I'm retired." She shifted in her seat.

Maria held her gaze. "How's retirement going?"

She glanced away. *My husband dropped dead seventeen days after I retired, and I've been hibernating for a year.* Though her story was more than twelve months old, she could *not* spill her gut-punching truth. She hoped to find words in the upside down books on her passenger seat. Unable to read grief books before, she wasn't sure she was ready now. She met Maria's patient gaze then swallowed past the lump in her throat. "Retirement is hard."

"I noticed your library books." Maria leaned in. "Did you just lose your husband?"

Her tone matched the gentleness in her eyes. "No." Beth bit her lip. *Tell the truth or slog through lies?* Neither sounded appealing. She steeled herself through a deep inhale and exhale. "I lost him last October." Her words were whisper soft.

"I'm so sorry." Maria extended a hand then brushed the tabletop with her fingertips.

Say something. But Maria's simple gesture, almost reaching for her hand, hollowed Beth's mouth, leaving it wordless and dry.

"Do you want to talk about losing him?" Wrapping her hands around her mug, Maria traced tiny circles with her thumbs.

Beth took a drink of her latte, hoping the warmth, mouth to belly, would inform her words. "I haven't ever. Last week, I talked myself into putting that book on hold. When I got the email..." She shrugged. "I forced myself to sign up for class, too. Then Miles gave us an out..."

Unspoken words hung in the air.

"Are you glad you stayed?" Maria rubbed her jaw.

More or less. She rotated her wrist, saying with a hand what her voice could not.

"I am." A smile inched up Maria's face.

"Thank you." She managed a small smile in return.

Their breakfasts arrived, and they tucked into their food.

Maria picked up a piece of toast. "Do you have any kids?"

"No." Beth readied herself for the evasive version she had perfected years ago. She cupped her mug and took a long, slow drink, hoping the questions written all over Maria's face wouldn't come.

Chapter Two

An hour later, Beth dug in her desk drawer for a red pen before nesting in Reid's recliner. Her journal at the ready, she opened her library book, prepared to devour its words and copy snippets for quick rereads. She paused in the introduction and started to write *we* but stopped midway. The color was all wrong, reminiscent of checkmarks and a C+ on an eighth grade social studies quiz.

She found a blue pen instead and retraced the word. *Much better.* Her own words were mourning black, but she couldn't remember blue's symbolism. *Hope or peace or comfort.* She wanted to memorialize these long-overdue words, so she read and wrote into the night. But deep-rooted words about deceit, betrayal, and guilt besieged her dreams.

The following morning, she fought to shoo the old tapes from her head. "Be kind to yourself." She spoke in a gentle voice, and then repeated the tender mantra after breakfast. Refilling her coffee cup, Beth returned to her library book, journal, and Reid's recliner. As she read, she recorded more passages and stayed put until reaching the end. She flipped to the beginning of her notes. Brushing a fingertip across her script, she closed her eyes, transporting the words from the page to her soul.

She dozed, and then woke with a start thirty

minutes later. Looping through the kitchen and office, she collected paper grocery bags and a marker and headed to the garage. Old potting containers filled two entire shelves. Shaking out cobwebs, she stacked the larger pots and bagged the smaller ones. She penned FROM A WOODWORKING STUDENT in permanent black ink, covering one side of the final bag before filling it to the brim.

A hot wash of satisfaction flowed over her. Though temporary, *woodworking student* was a status she chose, unlike the *W* word thrust upon her. Retirement was not yet real, and she felt as if she were in the midst of a vacation when she received the call…

Beth sidestepped the bags and opened the garage door. Sunlight streamed in. After rounding her car, she unlatched the trunk then circled back, trailing fingertips along Reid's maroon hatchback. *I should do something with his car.* But she didn't know what. She loaded the pots and shut the trunk—the clang of steel assaulting the quiet. At the door, she glanced back, and sorrow pinched her heart. She could *not* imagine a gutted space in place of his car.

I miss you, Reid. She pressed the overhead button then shifted her hand to the doorknob. Inky darkness invaded the garage. She drew in a deep breath, standing still through a slow inhale and exhale before entering the house.

Ignoring the stab of hunger, she stopped in the bathroom to wash her hands then routed to his recliner. She removed a comforter from the back of the chair and cocooned herself in its softness. *I'm not going back.* Serendipity had completed its circle.

Class led to Maria, whose tenderness uncovered

the truth. Her questions asked and answered gave Beth permission to step back and regroup.

She wanted to flee—twice—but hadn't.

Now, with her bravery tested and mastered, she could stay home, hunker in, and read Lolly Winston's book. Tightening the fleece around her, she gave herself a four o'clock deadline to call Adult Ed. *Ample time for the secretary to get a message to Miles.* She would say she had a conflict, which would *not* be a stretch. *I hope Maria doesn't blame herself.* She repositioned in the chair. Maria's questions had in fact done the opposite— empowered her to stay home.

At three fifty-two, she took baby steps: finding Adult Ed's phone number, writing it down, picking up her cordless phone, dialing six numbers, hanging up, and then attempting and pressing End twice more. *What about the pots?* She could deliver them another day and hope she wouldn't run into Dave or sputter an excuse if she did. *But I already loaded the car.* She decided to drop off the containers tonight—slip in early and tell Miles she couldn't stay. The kicker was she didn't know what she'd say.

Less than two hours later, Beth drove into the Home ReSource parking lot and eased into the donation drop-off lane. She parked her car and opened the trunk.

"Looks like you're clearing out." A female voice came from behind.

She turned and looked into the employee's hazel eyes. "A little bit." Her words sounded stilted and dishonest. The day before, she asked herself when she'd be ready to go through Reid's things. "Maybe never" had been her reply.

The two worked side by side to unload the trunk.

"You're in the class." The worker removed the lettered bag.

Not for long. Heat seared Beth's face. "I am."

"Nice." She threaded her fingers through another handle then tilted her head. "Would you like a receipt?"

"No thanks." Beth pulled out the last of the gallon containers and added them to a flatbed wagon.

"Thank you." Gesturing toward the pots, the woman smiled. "Enjoy your class."

I'm ducking out. Beth manufactured a single nod before folding into her car. She made a U-turn out of the donation area then parked opposite the front door. *Be kind to yourself.* Gathering her woodworking bag to busy her hands, she crossed the parking lot, grasping for words.

"You're early, too."

She slowed and looked toward the enthusiastic voice coming from her left.

"I couldn't wait to get here tonight." The classmate joined her on the sidewalk and flashed a dimpled smile. "You, too?"

"Mmm…" Beth opened the door and waved her inside. *Bree? Laree?* She had no idea what her name was.

"Don't you love all this stuff?" The early bird waved a hand toward a credenza topped with a cut glass pitcher and vintage-looking china.

"Mm-hmm." *Now what?* She hadn't envisioned a spectator. Following one step behind, she hugged her bag to her chest and entered the shop.

Miles greeted them with a smile. "Oak's on the right, and maple's on the left."

"I'm all about the bowling alley." The woman ran

a hand through her dark curls. "Do you know which one?"

"No…" He glanced at the wood.

"Fun to think I might have thrown a gutter ball or two over this. Who would've thought?" She turned to Beth. "Which are you using?"

Neither. Beth slung her bag over a shoulder and lifted remnants of each. She tapped oak against maple, losing her resolve. *One more night.* She tapped harder. "Maple." Her choice didn't matter because she was *not* coming back. *Three hours until my reprieve.* Her stomach pitched in reply.

The college friends and Maria arrived and sifted through the wood.

"Take four each, and then have a seat." Miles gestured toward the table.

You can do this. Beth sank into a chair.

"I'd like you all to say your names again before we get started." He glanced from face to face.

"Therese." The woman to his right leaned forward.

Mother Therese. Tonight, she'd relearn their names then discard them on her way out the door. She glanced at the clock. *Two hours and fifty-seven minutes.*

"I'm Corrine." The platinum blonde grinned and thrust a thumb toward Therese. "We go way back."

College friend Corrine.

"Zoe." She flashed a dimpled grin.

That *was her name. Bowler Zoe.*

"Maria." Meeting Beth's gaze, she smiled.

Nurse Maria. Beth forced a small smile then glanced away. She would tell Miles she wouldn't be back but hadn't decided whether to tell Maria, too. Having bonded a bit over breakfast, she felt a niggle of responsibility. She exhaled long and slow.

Miles raised his eyebrows.

"Beth." *Soon-to-be dropout.* She scrunched her toes inside her shoes.

"Thanks—and I'm Miles." He distributed handouts around the table. "Tonight, we're starting with terms and measurements."

A flush started in Beth's core. The inferno spread to her chest and neck and settled on her face and scalp. She laid down her paper. Using both hands, she wiped her brow to obliterate the glisten's reminder that her hormones flip-flopped, too. *I hope no one is watching.* Studying her sheet, she didn't look up until the hot flash completed its exit.

Miles explained width, length, and depth before showing the class how to measure and mark their wood. "Did anyone watch the hot dog video?"

"Five times." Zoe splayed her fingers.

"How was it?" asked Maria.

"Amazing." Zoe held her hands to her cheeks. "Hence, four replays."

"These will keep your fingers away from the blade." Miles slid a push stick toward each of them. "Bring them over"—he tilted his head—"and your eye and ear protection, too."

The first across the room, Beth stood beside him at the head of the table.

He demonstrated how to raise and lower the blade and turn the saw on and off. "But first, I want you to do a dry run. Get the feel of the wood between the fence and featherboard before you use the saw." Miles forced a piece of oak through the narrow channel. "You'll need some strength. When the back of your board reaches the edge of the table, grab your tool to drive the wood the rest of the way." He reached for a push stick and demonstrated the finishing touch. "You'll rip each piece twice—along the top and bottom to get your depth. Eight rips, and then the next person will go." He glanced up. "Who's first?"

"I am." Beth spoke without thinking. Instead of reneging, though, she reached for a board and leaned in. Grateful to practice with the saw still, she muscled the maple through the glove-tight featherboard and fence. *Strength is right.* She donned her safety goggles and earmuffs, glad now to be first. Since this was her last hurrah, she didn't need to strive for perfection, nor watch the others and model their work. She raised the blade, positioned her push stick, and readied her first board. Sucking in a deep breath, she turned on the saw then steered the wood through the blade. When the board neared the table's edge, she grabbed her push stick and thrust hard and fast. Splinters sprayed backward, and the ripped board skittered across the table. The saw's final whirr muffled her noisy exhale. She switched off the saw and glanced up.

Camera in hand, Dave stood to the side.

Not me. She averted eye contact.

"Slow and steady will reduce chip out." Miles tipped his head.

Her earmuffs softened the words. Following his gaze, she looked down. Maple shards, like tree ornaments, clung to her sweater. Heat scorched her cheeks. She positioned another board, her heart pounding as she eased in. Seven rips later, she glanced at her sweater. *Chip out zero.* She rocked back on her heels then gathered her wood and stepped to the side of the table.

"Thanks for paving the way." Zoe scooped her maple and met Beth's gaze. She sashayed to the head of the saw and worked through her rips.

Moving around, Dave angled his camera for a series of photos.

Watching out of the corner of her eye, Beth wanted to pull Dave aside and ask him to ditch any pictures of her. But how could she without calling attention to herself? *Maybe Miles will after he hears I'm leaving.* Still, she would do all she could to stay away from the camera's eye. She had always been a fierce protector of her privacy and in her opinion, social media was a landmine waiting to explode.

Miles summoned her and Zoe to start on their measurements.

The pair followed him across the room to a workbench.

"Look at the grain before you pencil your marks." He ran fingertips along a strip of maple. "You want to see what your inside and trim pieces will look like once you make your cuts."

Beth arranged and rearranged her wood, inhaling its scent. Her touch featherlight, she examined the grain. *I miss you, Darling.* Spotting Dave's approach, she tucked her head, resisting the urge to duck under the workbench.

Two hours later, she clutched her bag. Her courage to talk to Miles hanging on by a thread, she stared at the back of Zoe's head. *Go.*

Zoe gesticulated, her feet unmoving.

Her lingering presence cut into Beth's nerve. *I'll call Adult Ed in the morning.* She gave a superficial wave and headed toward the door.

"You didn't have any chip out when you cut your lengths." Zoe followed her out of the shop.

"Good thing. Getting rid of these slivers will take ages." Passing an aisle of peeling, white cabinets, she plucked at her sweater with exaggerated difficulty.

"I'm glad you paved the way." Zoe tossed back her hair. "Just sayin'."

Beth chuckled. The laugh felt foreign, and she hesitated before exiting into the cool evening air.

Their classmates huddled on the sidewalk.

Corrine turned and smiled. "What's so funny?"

Zoe tilted her head. "Miles told Beth she's the queen of chip out."

Therese widened her eyes. "He did?"

"Just kidding." Zoe brushed her hand across Beth's back.

"He might have if I hadn't slowed down." She slung her bag over a shoulder.

"I forced myself to go slow after watching you—" Maria pulled a strand of hair across her lips.

Beth worked a splinter from her ribbed sweater. "What not to do and what not to wear."

"Gotcha." Therese's smile shifted between the newcomers. "Would you like to go to The Depot for a glass of wine?"

"I'd love to, but I'm making a break for the grocery store." Zoe grinned and zipped her jacket. "Are you issuing rain checks for next week?"

Beth stepped closer to her car. *I'm making a break, too.*

Corrine gave a single nod. "I could handle two weeks in a row."

Eyebrows raised, Maria met Beth's gaze.

The invitation behind her expression gave Beth pause. She glanced away, and then shifted her gaze to Therese. "Sure." She feigned enthusiasm.

"Great." Therese gave a little wave. "See you there."

Beth shuffled to her car. Wishing she said she couldn't make The Depot, she waited for the others to leave. She should have told Maria she wouldn't be back though didn't want to wreck her night. If she bagged out, how would being a no-show look? Her absence wouldn't really matter since tonight had been the end...

Alone on the sleepy side street, she loitered at the stop sign. She stared at the dashboard clock. The minutes advanced once then twice. *Go.* Resignation ruled, and she turned left and drove downtown. As she approached the Russell Street Bridge, she eased off the gas pedal.

Three years earlier, an Environmental Impact Statement recommended replacing the then-fifty-four-year-old bridge.

Learning she and the bridge were the same age, Reid teased her about *her* life expectancy.

Her declaration about having a lot of good years left had made him laugh.

Crossing the bridge for the first time since picking up his ashes, she gripped the steering wheel. "Your years were numbered." A burn coursed through her belly. *But we didn't know.* Battling the urge to circle home, she turned east onto Broadway. She continued to Orange Street then Alder and parked in The Depot's back lot. After slipping her keys into her purse, she checked her reflection in the rearview mirror. *You are a master of deflection.* When she entered the building, she slowed. She scouted for her classmates in the enclosed Deck, which offered a more casual dinner menu than the dining room.

They weren't there.

The aromas of shrimp won tons and buffalo wings wafted into the hallway. Straight ahead, she paused inside the bar, spotting her cohorts on the coveted couches in front of the fireplace.

Corrine chatted with a server.

Beth crossed the tiled floor and ascended the pair of carpeted stairs. *I miss you, Reid.* Memories of date nights filled her with longing and prickled the nape of her neck.

The server smiled. "I can give you a few minutes."

"No…" Bypassing memory-laden wines she enjoyed with Reid, she gazed at the chalkboard hanging beside the door. "I'll have your Pinot Noir." She waved a hand toward the specials. Sinking beside Maria, she curled a thumb and index finger around her wedding ring. *I miss you.*

Corrine shifted a hip toward Therese. "What's the deal with Kate?"

"She's talked about becoming a bone doctor ever since her friend Abby broke her leg in kindergarten." Therese glanced at Beth. "Kate is my soon-to-be-eighteen-year-old daughter. She was obsessed with Abby's cast and crutches and spent hours doing surgery on her stuffed animals and making casts out of magazine pages and cereal boxes. In middle school, she announced she would become 'the best orthopedic surgeon ever.' " Therese spoke through scrunched lips. "Now, she wants to study woodworking."

"Quite a switch." Corrine stretched an arm on the back of the couch. "What changed her mind?"

"Miles."

Corrine snorted and drew back her head. "*Miles*?"

"She's had him all four years." Therese ran a hand through her hair. "She used to say, 'I'll be using tools on bones, so I'm gonna practice on wood.' This semester, she's designing furniture. She told me if she fixed bones, nobody would see her work…'but if I build custom furniture, families will treasure my creations *for years*.' "

Like yours, Reid. Gazing at her wide, gold band, Beth flickered her eyes closed.

"Miles thinks she's really talented." Maria smiled.

"He's her favorite teacher, and she's right— nobody can see your bones. 'Before or after' like she says. But she's wanted to be a doctor for so long…" Therese shrugged. "I worry about regret."

Maria leaned in. "How do you feel about the switch?"

"I feel…" Therese pulled in her lower lip with an accompanying rise and fall of her chest. "I feel like this decision should be about her, but it's a little bit about me, too." Holding her palms in front of her, she raised one and dropped the other. "Maybe eighty-twenty. My fear is Kate will regret this little detour and switch to orthopedics down the road." She straightened her shoulders. "I told her she could always do wood-working on the side."

Like you. Did you have regrets, Reid? Beth picked at her sweater. *I do.* She removed one maple shard then another. *I'm sorry I never told you what happened in New Hampshire…*

Their server returned and set a tray on the coffee table. After distributing cocktail napkins, she lifted a glass and met her gaze.

Beth extended her hands, intercepting her wine between the tray and the napkin. She took a long drink, savoring the rich flavors of berries and spice.

"...Portland's Oregon College of Art and Craft." Therese cupped her glass with both hands.

The city's name garnered her attention. Years earlier, she and Reid visited Portland. They had talked about going back. *We should have followed through...* Heaviness wrapped around her chest. *Be present.* Sipping her wine, she vowed to embrace her age-old tenet. She studied Therese, wondering if mother and daughter shared the same sinewy build and chocolate brown eyes. *Ssshhh.*

"I can't bite my tongue." Therese sighed and scrunched her lips. "I know I should listen and give her time before adding my eight cents—two cents times four." She glanced at the fireplace. "I just want her to be sure."

Corrine rubbed Therese's neck. "The more I micromanaged the twins, the more they fought back."

"*I know.*" Therese looked at Beth. "Do you have any kids? I need some stop-nagging advice..."

Struggling to hold her gaze, Beth gripped her glass and shook her head.

Therese narrowed her eyes.

Unable to peg envy or empathy or a combination, Beth quaffed a longer drink.

"College plans must sound so far into the future for you." Therese waved a palm.

"Mm-hmm." Maria twisted a strand of hair

between her fingers.

Beth glanced away from the ache in Maria's voice and the pain in her eyes—certain the latter mimicked her own.

"Have you been trying very long?" Corrine repositioned, shortening the gap between her and Maria.

"Six months. I haven't had a period since I stopped the pill in April." Maria cupped her elbows. "Stop me if I'm saying too much."

Both anticipating and dreading Maria's story, Beth nestled against the couch.

"We're here to listen." Therese scooted in, her knees brushing the table.

"I had an appointment with my OB-GYN last week." Maria's voice caught. "Some of my blood work was abnormal." She turned to Beth. "That's what I was doing yesterday—getting books about infertility and early menopause."

"What did your blood work show?" Corrine raised her eyebrows.

"Possible primary ovarian insufficiency." Maria flashed finger quotation marks. "Not for sure but if I do have POI"—she folded her hands around a knee—"that could mean an eight percent chance of getting pregnant." She twisted her lips. "Or fifty percent with in vitro and a donor egg."

I'm so sorry. Beth forced a drink past the words clotted in her throat.

Corrine lowered her chin. "When will you know?"

"I'm having an ultrasound and repeat blood work next month." Maria reached for her glass. "Virgin Mary." A wry smile flickered across her face.

Beth managed a small smile in return.

"Sorry I was so whiny." Therese tilted her glass. "I hope you get good news."

Maria tipped her mocktail. "So do I."

In the parking lot, Beth wanted to give her a hug and a reassuring vote of confidence. But having buried the heartache of her own shattered dreams she couldn't—afraid years of hidden grief would be written all over her face.

****

A week later, Maria's words troubled Beth as she debated her planned departure. Lolly Winston's character Sophie Stanton gnawed at her, too. She had twenty years on Sophie in age and marriage longevity. Widows and childless both, she—unlike Sophie—had never tried to have a baby. *Eight percent chance. Fifty percent with in vitro and a donor egg.* She couldn't stop thinking about Maria. And although every waking minute was no longer governed by all-consuming grief, fretting about her friend did not feel any better.

Enmeshed in "to go or not to go," lunchtime escaped unnoticed. Hunger pecked in late afternoon. She steamed broccoli and heated leftover chicken and rice, her thoughts whirring through dinner and cleanup. *Okay—I'll go.* She ceded to the voice fighting on Maria's behalf and wandered into her bedroom. Having learned sweaters and wood chips were not a good combination, she shed her cable-knit sweater and donned a royal blue Henley.

Foregoing the evening news, she sank into Reid's recliner and removed her journal from the magazine holder. *I almost ducked out.* But he didn't need to know. Sliding the purple ribbon to the right, she opened the book and uncapped her pen.

October Thirtieth
Dear Darling,
Tonight, I have to tell Miles whether I'm making a
picture frame or mirror. I'm thinking a frame with an
eight-by-ten of us at Butchart Gardens or one of you at
Logan Pass or Pike Place Market. I love all three of
those pictures, though... End of debate, I'll make a
mirror. When I see my reflection, I'll remember this
class as a baby step in learning to live without you. I
miss you and love you more.

Ten minutes later, she backed out of her garage.
The autumn air was cool and welcoming, and she drove
with the window down. When she approached the
twenty-five-miles-per-hour sign on Lower Miller Creek
Road, she slowed. Reid had been ticketed on that
stretch. "How long ago, Darling?" The date didn't
really matter—his ticket had been a lesson for them
both—but grief's sabotage erased patches in her
previously sharp memory. She had read recall could
improve as mourning lessened, and she hoped that fact
was true.

Turning left onto Reserve, Beth batted at the
sadness flickering through her. Mountain Daylight
Time was nearing its end and the following week her
drive would be masked in darkness. The trees dotting
Larchmont Golf Course were a mixed bag. A few, still
sprinkled with yellow and green, gave way to the gentle
breeze as rogue leaves fluttered to the ground.
Neighboring NSTs made her smile. Dubbed "Nervous
System Trees" by her former colleague Ben, their
stripped branches resembled lonely bundles of nerves.

Two boys kicked a soccer ball outside C.S. Porter
Middle School. Blue and white paper cups cinched in

the school's chain link fence announced its mascot—COUGARS.

Farther north on the right, Benson's Farm lay barren save for decomposing pumpkins. *Tomorrow is Halloween.* Memories of Reid scratched at her throat.

He had loved dressing up and applauding trick-or-treaters' costumes as he distributed candy. His yearly delight wrenched her heart and hinted at an unspoken truth—he would have been an amazing dad. Their sparse block drew only a handful of kids each year, so he stopped dressing up years ago. But he continued to buy three bags of candy "just in case," and then they had taken leftovers to work—two full bags plus change.

Last Halloween, she turned out the lights and burrowed into his recliner. She hadn't bought candy this year either, though she planned to hunker in and read by lamplight. "You would have loved being a dad." Sorrow colored her voice. *I would've loved being a mom.*

As she strolled into Home ReSource, Beth relished the sunshine's gentle caress. Thoughts of Maria tiptoed into her mind. *Tonight, I'll ask for her number.* She wound through the store, and the lopsided *peace* cutout coaxed a smile. *I'm glad I came.* She pushed open the door.

Squatting in front of a back cabinet, Miles glanced over his shoulder. "Welcome."

"Thanks." She looked around the shop. The table and chairs were tucked away. Eyeing an office chair, she set her bag on the seat then draped her jacket over the back.

"How's class treating you?" He unloaded a pile of push sticks onto a workbench.

"O-kay, once I got the hang of the table saw." She straightened her shirt.

"*Go slow*." Laughter edging his voice, he tapped a two-beat drum fill. "That lesson will be my takeaway for next time—*before* someone does a Danica Patrick."

Grinning, she grabbed a push stick. "Good idea." She tapped twice, punctuating her words. Then she helped retrieve maple and oak from the cabinet, unearthing her pieces last.

Her classmates trickled in, offering greetings and claiming their initialed piles of wood scattered around the workbench.

"Tonight, your frames will start taking shape. First, you'll cut your inside pieces to width..." Miles described rabbets and half-lap joints, holding up examples of each.

Beth listened to every word.

"I've set up both saws: you'll cut your boards to width, use the second saw for rabbets, and go back to the first for half laps. Then you'll come here to glue and clamp." He cradled a piece of oak between his hands, its rabbets facing the class. "Do you have any questions?"

"Nope." Zoe shook her head.

The others did, too. They gathered their wood and protective gear and reassembled at the table saw.

Dave arrived and waved hello, but his greeting was buried by the dust collector and saw.

Beth moved from saw to saw, and the wood shavings' aroma spurred memories of Reid. *You could've taught me so much.* Her usual camera anxiety did nothing to soften the ache. Skirting eye contact, she masked her melancholy, concentrating on the tasks at hand. When she passed Dave on her way to the workbench, she glanced away, hoping he'd get the message. *I do not want my picture on social media.*

Miles silenced the dust collector and tuned the radio. "Not too loud?" He raised his voice over the music.

"Perfect." Zoe sang along, showcasing side-to-side hip thrusts at the artist's "no treble."

When the song ended, Dave nodded at his camera. "Fair to post?"

Zoe raised her eyebrows. "Did you take a video or photos?"

"Photos."

"Go for it." She grinned and popped her hips right then left.

"Will do. Check out the pictures I posted last week." He gave a goodbye salute before heading out the door.

Beth focused on her rabbets, debating whether she wanted to scout for photos of herself. By the time she carried her frame to the back counter, she confirmed her final answer. *I do not.*

"So..." Zoe gave a single clap. "Are we on for tonight?"

"You bet." Corrine answered with a pair of hips thrusts.

"Let's fast forward to next week. Who's making mirrors?" Miles held up a fist.

"I am." Grateful to have decided hours earlier, Beth smiled and slipped on her jacket.

"So am I." Maria raised her hand.

"Three, please." Therese nodded at Miles' rabbit ear fingers.

He added a third finger then looked from Zoe to Corrine. "Picture frames for you two?"

"Please." Corrine slung her bag over her shoulder.

Zoe waggled a thumbs-up and herded the women toward the door.

Beth didn't loiter in the parking lot as she had the week before. At the corner stop sign, she idled behind a baby blue convertible. *PRTYOF2*. Studying the backlit personalized plate, she tightened her abs against a gut-punching memory.

She had felt shoved out of her skin—zombie loneliness when she picked up Reid's ashes from the mortuary. The simple act of setting the mahogany urn on the passenger seat engulfed her in numbness. She debated fastening the seatbelt, and then nearly forgot to buckle her own. Everything about this trip felt otherworldly. Pulling out of the parking lot, she turned away from the Russell Street Bridge. The urn beside her seeming to weigh a thousand pounds, maybe even a million, she feared its weight would plunge them through the aging bridge into the darkness of the Clark Fork River. But then driving west on Mullan Road, she cursed her decision to avoid a nosedive. *Joining Reid would be okay.*

Slowing, she almost rerouted. A car horn behind her propelled her forward, but she drove below the speed limit the entire way home—her cargo both weighty and ethereal. Before lifting the cremains from the passenger side, she bent her knees and grunted in anticipation. Hugging the urn to her chest, she straightened. The urn weighed pounds less than in her imagination. *I'm going crazy.* She carried the cremains through the garage and laundry room without stopping to shed her coat and keys and purse.

Her steps leaden, she trudged down the hall and into the living room then lowered into Reid's recliner. Sinking her forehead to the wood, she locked her arms around the urn. Her emptiness gave way to silent screams. She didn't move for three hours—maybe four. Finally, she loosened her grip and carried the urn into the bedroom.

Their king bed cavernous in his absence, Beth nested in his recliner each night. She chased sleep, often without success, in his boxers and T-shirts. But exhaustion ruled. *Delusion, too.* She arranged the urn on his nightstand. Gathering extra pillows from the guest room, she reclaimed their bed. She tucked the pillows behind her and cocooned onto Reid's side. Burying her face in his pillow, she hunted his scent.

The following day, she considered buying a body pillow but nixed the idea, fearing questions if she ran into someone she knew. She had *not* wanted to face an interrogation—then or now.

Chapter Three

A break in traffic paused grief's ambush. Beth considered ducking right and escaping to the comfort of Reid's recliner. But with two classmates idling behind her, she eased forward and turned toward downtown. She drove with intention, silencing memories and holding her breath as she traversed the Russell Street Bridge. When she pulled into The Depot lot, she parked nose forward in the middle row. Opening her car door, she cast a sidelong glance at her woodworking bag centered where the urn had been. *I miss you, Darling.*

Therese's voice carried across the parking lot. "You're driving Sheldon's convertible? What gives?"

"My car's in the shop, and he refused to be my chauffeur." Corrine dropped a key into her purse.

"Joyride later." Therese grinned and wiggled her eyebrows. "Do you want to arm wrestle to see who goes first?"

"The pleasure will be all yours." Beth waved a palm.

"Deal." Therese ran her hand over the hood. "Convertibles are sporty but impractical, in my humble opinion."

Corrine snorted. "No argument there."

Men and their cars. Reid hadn't been into flash or speed. He'd been all about usefulness. She wondered if his fourteen-month old gas was still good.

Therese circled Sheldon's car, caressing the steel.

A pang of loneliness gripped her chest as she imagined her own touch on maple and more.

Maria eased into an empty parking place bordering the sidewalk.

"Shotgun!" From the center of the lot, Zoe hurried toward the group huddled around the convertible.

"I have first dibs." Therese wagged a finger.

"Story of my life—a day late and a dollar short." Zoe looped to the front of Sheldon's car. "You know what else I always say? No time like the present." She flicked her head. "Shall we?"

The cohorts strolled inside and claimed a table kitty-corner from the occupied couches.

Beth slid into a chair facing away from the chalkboard. On the drive over, she decided on a huckleberry martini. *Maybe two.*

Their server arrived to take drink orders.

Last in line, Zoe gestured with an elbow. "I'll have what she's having—a huckleberry martini, please." She tapped a hand on the table and looked from face to face. "So, what did I miss last week?"

"I grumbled about my daughter wanting to become a woodworker instead of a doctor." Therese toyed with the menu.

"Whoa." Zoe jerked back her head. "That's quite a switcheroo."

Maria folded her hands in her lap. "I haven't had a period since stopping the pill…"

"You're preggers?" A dimpled grin blossomed across Zoe's face. "Congratulations."

"I'm not. I had an appointment a couple of weeks ago—"

"Sorry," Zoe blurted. "Open mouth, insert foot."

"You didn't know. Seems reasonable..." Maria wound a strand of hair around her finger. "You want to have a baby, so you stop using birth control, and you get pregnant."

Zoe pinched her bottom lip.

That's what happened to me. Zoe's swallowed words, real or imagined, wrapped themselves straightjacket-like around Beth's chest.

"What did your doctor say?" Zoe leaned in.

"I might have primary ovarian insufficiency."

Frowning, Zoe kneaded her forehead. "You heard that right off the bat?"

"No. I had some abnormal lab results." Maria shifted in her seat. "I'm having an ultrasound and repeat blood work in two weeks."

Their server returned with a trayful of drinks.

Contemplative quiet settled over the group.

After the tray was emptied, Beth sipped her martini. Relishing the taste of the fruity, boozy cocktail, she silently applauded her drink choice.

"So, if you *do* have an issue with your ovaries then what would that mean?" Zoe placed a hand low on her abdomen.

"I'll have a hard time getting pregnant." Maria reached for her glass.

"But she said might, right?" Corrine laid an arm on the table.

"Mm-hmm."

"So, might's the operative word." Zoe steepled her fingers under her chin. "You might rock your blood work and ultrasound and get good news."

Maria gave a slight nod.

Muting the memories swirling through her head, Beth reconsidered asking for her number. Though she was eager to grow their friendship, she did not want to bulldoze her way into Maria's life.

"Do you have any kids?" Maria opened a palm.

"Two girls. Erin's four and Hope is two. I told Nate I hoped our second would be as easy as our first." Zoe crossed her arms and gave a slow nod. "Hope. That sounds like a perfect name." She beamed a deep, dimpled grin. "We decided on the spot…"

Beth took another drink. She wondered if this conversation was hard for Maria and if she asked about kids just to be polite. Getting-to-know-you chats often included questions about kids, spouses, and jobs. For over thirty-five years, she dreaded the kids question. Now, she dreaded all three.

"Was she as easy as her sister?" Therese trailed a finger along her cocktail napkin.

"No-o." Zoe shook her head and pushed back in her chair. "If she was our first, she'd be an only child."

"Ha." Corrine chortled. "If Sophia wasn't a twin, *she* would be an only child."

"So, your twins are the 'party of two'?" Zoe's smiled tipped into a laugh. "Funny."

"No. Sheldon used to joke he couldn't wait for Hunter and Sophia to fly the coop and hear a hostess say, 'Schmitter—party of two'?" Clutching the drink menu, Corrine looked around the table. "They ordered those plates last year."

"Creative." Maria glanced up from her napkin where she had written PRTYOF2 in large print. "What are they doing now?"

"Hunter's studying architecture at MSU. Sophia's

at Seattle U. She started in anthropology but switched to communication studies this fall."

"Twins." Zoe widened her eyes. "I cannot even imagine... How old are they?"

"According to Hunter, they're a year away from MIPs—Minors in Possession." Corrine raised an eyebrow.

"Has drinking been a problem?" Zoe tilted her head.

"They've never been arrested." Corrine raised her glass. "Not to say alcohol and weed have never passed their lips."

Maria clinked glasses with Corrine—Virgin Mary to Cabernet. "How does Sophia like Seattle?"

"She *loves* Seattle. When I called last Sunday, she and a group of friends were walking to the International District for dim sum."

"My old stomping grounds..." Maria tapped a fist against her heart.

Beth didn't add she had fallen in love with the city twenty years prior during her and Reid's first visit. Rather than share highlights and risk questions she sat back, savored her martini, and listened. Leaving the bar, she lingered in the hallway.

"Who was serious about going for a ride?" Corrine reached in her purse.

"I'll catch you next time." Therese zipped her jacket. "Hit me up on a warm, sunny night."

"You think Sheldon will let me drive his baby again?" Corrine dangled the key.

"Absolutely." Therese draped an arm around her friend's shoulder.

Corrine turned to Zoe. "Are you in?"

"When the sun is shining and the top's down, I'll be all in." Zoe grinned and pinged the key.

She flashed an OK sign. "I'll work on a rain check."

"Sounds good. I'm stopping here." Maria gestured toward the women's room. "I'll see you next week."

Beth slowed, debating whether to accompany her or wait in the hall then ask for her number. *Either might be awkward.* "Have a good week." She waved a hand and followed the others into the cool, inky night.

Driving home, she replayed the evening. The snippets about getting pregnant, naming babies, and raising children unleashed a visceral tug deep in her core. She wanted to give Maria a goodbye hug but couldn't—afraid old wounds would crumple her face.

****

A week later, Beth ran her hands over her sleek maple frame, examining its joints with her fingertips. *Snug and flush.* She straightened, feeling a wee bit taller as she brushed against the workbench. *I wish you could see my work, Darling.*

Coming to Home ReSource had been unsettling in the beginning. Everything about class reminded her of Reid. Whether guilt-ridden or sad or prideful, her thoughts soared and plummeted like a rollercoaster. Strapped in, she was along for the ride—sometimes less willingly than others. She was grateful for her classmates and their companionship, though, and for giving her something to think about besides Reid and guilt and grief.

"Tonight's all about trim." Miles held up a demo piece and outlined the evening's agenda.

"I've been waiting for the miter saw." Therese

grinned and rubbed her palms together.

"Kate's a whiz with one." He smiled, turning the demo's angled corner toward the class.

Therese's smile melted as a pensive expression flitted across her face.

Her ambivalence feeling like a mirror image, Beth glanced away.

"Any questions before you get started?" Miles looked around the workbench.

The women shook their heads then gathered their safety gear and reconvened at the table saw.

En route, Miles flipped on the dust collector.

Beth snugged her earmuffs. An attentive observer, she stood to the side while three classmates cut lengths and widths. Then she took her turn. She maneuvered the saw with a slow, steady motion and completed her cuts without a *single bit* of chip out. Meeting Zoe's gaze, she grinned.

Zoe raised both thumbs in reply.

When Therese finished her final cut, she silenced the saw and uncovered her ears. "No Dave tonight?"

Miles glanced up. "No, he'll be back the last night of class."

"He posted some great pictures." Zoe swung her hips right. "Did anyone else see them?" She smirked and swung her hips left.

Beth flicked her head.

"You look so focused in all of your pictures." Therese smiled and waved a hand. "Home ReSource has a link if you want to check them out."

"Thanks." *I don't.* Her stomach knotted. *I hope he didn't use my name.* She cherished her privacy and was resolute about avoiding social media. *I'm not diving in to online photos of me now.* Fiddling with her earmuffs, she joined her cohorts around the workbench and hung back, wanting to be last with the combination squares.

Corrine and Zoe took the lead.

Beth studied their hands. She pictured Reid's hands—strong and warm—and longed for his touch. The memories made her throat ache. She stroked her wedding band with her thumb.

Zoe finished first. "Next?"

Her voice interrupted Beth's musings. She stepped sideways and folded her hands.

"Hang on... C'mon over here." Miles beckoned from the miter saw.

Thankful for a break, Beth followed the group to the saw, mounted on a recessed countertop at the back of the room.

He explained how to operate the saw and demonstrated changing its direction. Then he stepped aside. "Who's first?"

"I am." Zoe deposited her maple on the counter. "Ten digits—wish me luck." She waggled her fingers.

"Luck with a capital *L*." Corrine grinned and shaped her index finger and thumb into an uppercase *L*.

Gesturing toward the workbench, Beth looked from Therese to Maria. "You two go." She scooted to her left, choosing a vantage point between the miter saw and combination square action.

When Maria finished her measurements, she handed the square to Beth. The saw stilled, and she motioned for her to lower her earmuffs. "Would you like to get together for lunch sometime?"

"I would." A smile tugged at the corners of Beth's lips.

"You, too?" Maria asked Therese.

"Getting away is hard. I could do another—" The saw buried her words.

Beth scrambled to cover her ears. She measured and marked her wood, contemplating Maria's question and Therese's answer—straightforward and easy both. Throughout the years, she had been a player in similar conversations. But the week before when she planned to ask for Maria's number, she felt like an excavator digging for buried social skills. Now, a flush of gratitude warmed her core. *We're scheduling a lunch date.* She completed her measurements then stayed at the workbench to help Zoe and Corrine with glue and clamps.

Zoe finished and bumped Beth's hip. "I'm on duty now." She picked up a clamp and twirled it between her fingers.

Edging toward the miter saw, Beth studied Miles. *Are you married? Divorced? Widowed?* Questions replaced the instructions looping through her mind. She doubted the latter, but then told herself he could be widowed as easily as she—married one morning and widowed by afternoon. Her heart hadn't seized, nor had her pulse quivered or skipped as Reid's fluttered then stopped. *Did you know?* For the thousandth time, maybe the millionth, the question crowded her brain.

Up from his desk, on his way to get a drink of water they'd thought…

Heat rushed to her cheeks, and she glanced away. She wasn't interested in Miles—interested in his story, yes. *Everyone has a story.* Maria's revelation kept her coming. This class was a giant leap, not the baby step she dubbed it at first. Her presence here was a big deal.

But dating? *Not* on her radar.

"All yours." Therese mouthed the words over the dust collector's din.

She set her wood on the counter. Clamminess overtook her palms. She dried her hands on her jeans then moved from the knob to her board to the handle and back, focusing on her breathing as she had years earlier. Changing the angle, she eased the saw through the maple for her final four cuts. When she released the trigger, she ran a thumb over her last piece. The forty-five degree angle was smooth and warm.

"Good job easing in." Miles smiled, gesturing with a palm.

"No more Danica Patrick's for this gal." Beth grinned and collected her trim.

At the workbench, Therese glued one side of her frame.

The other classmates stood standby within grabbing distance of the clamps.

"You can go." Miles tilted his head. "Just put your frames on the counter before you leave."

"Question." Zoe lifted her frame portrait style and held it around her face. "Depot encore next week?" She bugged her eyes.

"A repeat works for me." Corrine grinned through her horizontal frame.

"I'm down." Maria tucked her glasses and ear-muffs into her bag.

Reaching for the wood glue, Beth nodded.

"Maybe." Therese glanced up.

"*Excellent.*" Zoe lowered her frame then carried it to the counter.

After the trio tidied up, they waved their goodbyes.

"Kate said you're her favorite teacher." Therese reached for a clamp.

Her matter-of-fact tone captured Beth's attention as she snaked a thin line of glue along the bottom of her frame.

"We-ell…" Miles snugged a second clamp. "She's one of the most talented students I've ever had."

"She loves woodworking." Therese outlined her frame with a fingertip.

He leaned a hip into the workbench. "She's a natural."

Like you, Reid. Beth hushed the memories and returned to wood glue, maple, and clamps. When she carried her frame to the counter, she stood back and admired her work, congratulating herself again for having shown up and stayed.

Driving home, she contemplated her conversation with Maria. A cauldron of doubt bubbled in her head. *She didn't say where or when…and I don't have her number.* Even if she did, she feared she could not wrangle her voice if she picked up the phone.

****

The following week, Beth wound through Home ReSource. "Tonight, I'll ask for her number." She whispered her three-day-old mantra and opened the workshop door.

Her classmates congregated around a workbench and greeted her with smiles and hellos.

"You'll work on three things this evening"—Miles waved an arm—"drilling, sanding, and oiling."

She concentrated on his hands. His care and reverence reminded her of Reid, and his hands became her focal point. She slowed her breathing, yearning to reclaim time and corral lost opportunities.

"After you choose the top then turn over your frame and mark the middle." He signaled toward a model clamped on the workbench. "You'll use two F-clamps so you have both hands to drill. The settings are ready to go, and masking tape will be your depth guide." He circled a finger around a taped drill bit. "Gently pull the trigger and stop when the tape touches your frame. Cover your ears."

Snugging her earmuffs, Beth eyed her frame with a satisfied smile. *Either could be the top.*

Miles demoed the drill, and then lowered his hearing protection. "Drills and sanders…are you ready to jump in?"

"I love to drill." Therese wiggled her eyebrows.

"Sounds like Kate is her mother's daughter." He laughed and slid the yellow tool toward her.

Therese nodded once in reply.

She seems proud tonight. Beth hoped Therese embraced Kate's change of heart—surgeon to furniture maker. Turning over her frame, she considered drilling holes in the top and bottom. *Reversible, Reid.* She measured and marked the top then reached for a pair of clamps. *I can prop my mirror upside down later.* Her interchangeable craftswomanship made her smile.

Zoe gave the "earplugs" command.

Beth repositioned her earmuffs and gripped her drill. *Slow and steady.* Drawing in a deep breath, she pressed the trigger and eased the bit. When the tape met the wood, she released the trigger and spluttered a breath—its noise muffled by sanders and drills. Appreciative of the underwater quiet of Reid's earmuffs, she reached for a sander. She unclamped her frame and started on the top left corner. Intent on sanding, she barely noticed the drills turning on then off. A flash of orange caught her eye.

"Olly olly oxen free." Corrine mouthed the words as she cupped orange ear plugs in her hand and swept them into view.

The radio and sanders were the lone accompanists when Beth uncovered her ears. Curling her fingers around the sander's handle, she imagined Reid's hand atop hers. Remorse knotted her gut. She knew *nothing* about his sandpaper, tools, and wood. Leaning in, she pressed her belly against the workbench. In the last thirteen months, she visited his shop once. Surgical-strike fast, she slipped in then out—leaving with eye and ear protection and a tape measure in hand. *Did you lead me to the sherbet tub?* Her question piercing, she looked up, wondering if she spoke out loud.

No one met her gaze.

After his death, his presence had been tangible. The first time, less than one week out, she was curled on top of their bed midafternoon having cried herself dry. She thought she imagined his hand on her chest. "So I can feel your heartbeat," he used to say. Then he curved his body into hers, and his pulse beat slow and steady against her back. Ephemeral in its return, his failed heart beat as though one with hers.

The second time happened a month or so later as she nested in his recliner. With the pads of his fingertips, he skimmed her temples and traced her ears. She melted into his touch. He caressed her neck—a lingering wisp of pressure then the lightness of air. Her echo of loneliness was tempered through a single inhale and exhale, and she had sobbed, willing him back without avail.

Despite her best efforts to conjure his being, she hadn't felt his physicality since. Too-numerous-to-count times she talked and wrote to him. Sometimes, she sensed his presence, but memories and his intangible spirit provided only a splash of solace as she navigated her aloneness.

"Soft as a baby's bottom." Corrine grazed her palms across her frame.

Her voice wheeled Beth back. Instinctive, she brushed a fingertip along her frame. *I've never felt a baby's bottom.* She glided her sander across the maple and wrote loopy letters in cursive. *B-a-b-y. M-a-r-i-a.* Smoothing the wood beneath her script, she wrote fast and sloppy, desperate to change the subject and protect her friend.

"I love the smell of newborn babies." Maria in-haled and exhaled through her nose.

"So do I," said Therese.

Therese's words were soft and low, but her smile was palpable. Beth kept her head down, fighting the quivering in her lips. She ached, bone deep. *S-o-f-t.* She covered every millimeter of her frame then silenced the sander and stroked the smooth, warm wood. Once the oiling station was ready at the neighboring workbench, she was first to secure a spot. Pouring a puddle of oil onto her frame, she released its nutty fragrance into the air.

An Adele song murmured in the background.

"Could've had it all…" The phrase looped through her head, drowning out the rest. *But we didn't, Reid.* She pressed hard, massaging oil into the maple's thirsty grain. When she finished, she sandwiched her frame between a pair of clean cloths and carried it to the newspaper-draped counter.

Her cohorts arranged their frames alongside hers.

"Remember your photos next week." Miles glanced from Zoe to Corrine.

"Gotcha." Zoe pulled a bottle of hand sanitizer from her bag.

Corrine nodded and extended a palm.

After sanitizer around, the women donned jackets and called their goodbyes.

Beth drove downtown on autopilot, her thoughts muddled. She enjoyed spending time with her classmates—her new friends, really. But slivers of their conversations scratched at her thirty-five-year-old secret. A sharp pain squeezed her lungs and tightened as she traversed the Russell Street Bridge. *Ssshhh.* Pulling into the parking lot, she muted old memories. When she entered the bar, she spotted her friends on the coveted couches. The fireplace glowed warm and welcoming.

"Score." Zoe scooted closer to Corrine and patted her vacated seat.

She sank beside her then shifted her smile to Maria and Therese on the opposite couch.

The five wasted no time placing drink orders—four glasses of wine and one Virgin Mary.

"Can you believe next week is our last hurrah? Meeting you all was my lucky day." Zoe dragged out the words. "Maybe we could get together sometime?"

Maria smiled. "That'd be nice."

"You could come to my house." The moment the words left her lips, goosebumps prickled Beth's skin. *What the hell?* She crossed her arms, hoping no one noticed her shiver.

"When?" Zoe reached into a back pocket.

"I…" She rubbed the back of her neck. *I spoke too soon.* "I'm flexible." The words transformed in her mouth.

Her friends pulled out their cell phones then tapped and swiped.

She sank back—her lungs half empty and refusing to fill.

"How about Thursday the eleventh?" Zoe glanced up. "Would we chase away your husband?"

"No…" Words caught in her throat.

Maria leaned in and gave a slight nod.

"I lost him last year." Beth's voice was soft as dew.

Her words hung in the air.

"I'm so sorry." Corrine turned sideways, bumping Zoe's knee with her own. "I babbled on and on about Sheldon and Hunter and Sophia…"

"Maria found out by default. My library books were a dead giveaway—" Heat rushed to her cheeks.

Their server's return offered a welcome reprieve.

Beth extended a hand, and then gripped her wineglass as though it were a lifeline. She took a long, slow drink. The wine's warmth from her mouth to her belly fueled the desire to withdraw her reckless offer. *But what would I say?* She could say the eleventh wouldn't work, which would postpone but not withdraw. *All or none.*

"What happened?" Zoe met her gaze.

"She asked if I wanted to have coffee. I consented then wanted to bolt…" She brushed a thumb across her glass.

"I meant"—Zoe glanced at her hands—"what

happened to your husband?"

Her words untested, Beth swallowed past the boulder in her throat. "He collapsed at work." She sipped her wine. "According to the doctor, he probably died before he hit the ground."

"I'm so sorry." Zoe slid closer and rested a hand on Beth's leg.

Reflexive, she nested Zoe's hand in her own. "I holed up for more than a year. Then I almost bailed the first night of class...but you shot me a grin on our way to the yard. 'Field trip. I love it.' " Tilting her head, she smiled. "Your declaration made me stay."

Zoe let out a soft breath, her eyes glistening. "Your story gives me chills."

"You cooled my hot flash, too." She squeezed Zoe's hand.

Gentle laughter rippled around the couches.

"I'm glad you stayed." Corrine tipped her glass.

"So am I, but do you really want us to come to your house?" Therese wrinkled her brow.

"To be honest, I wanted a do-over the moment I offered." She took a deep breath and wrangled her words.

"Let's meet at my house." Therese scooted forward.

"No." Beth's reply was swift and certain. "I want you to come to mine."

"Are you sure?" Maria folded her hands under her chin.

"Yes. The eleventh or whenever." She gave an emphatic nod.

Silence blanketed the group, and their attention returned to cell phones and calendars.

Beth breathed in, inhaling her wine's bouquet. She reflected on her offer, sincere and less frightening since her truths were out. Her jumbled emotions swung like a pendulum, she was all alone, and she was an unreliable narrator.

They settled on the eleventh at six o'clock with a potluck at her house.

She gave them her address and phone number. Pulling a pen and mini notebook from her purse, she jotted down the others' phone numbers and email addresses. Her old flip phone served her well, but after Reid died, she cancelled their coverage.

The conversation transitioned to potlucks, favorite dishes, and menu planning—where it remained until the five said their goodbyes.

Thirty minutes later, Beth turned on the kettle before changing into Reid's boxers and T-shirt. Donning her terry cloth robe, she wondered whether she would ever again wear her own pajamas. *Doubtful.* She couldn't imagine a single night without the comfort of her makeshift sleepwear.

The whistle called her to the kitchen. She brewed a mug of licorice spice tea and carried it to his recliner. Hunkering in, she dug out her journal—words at the ready.

November Thirteenth

Dear Reid,

I told my classmates what happened to you. All of them—right after I blurted out we could get together here next month. I wanted to rescind my offer a second later... Once my truth was out, though, having them come seemed like it would be okay. Good actually. I don't know if my head or my heart is nudging me forward but it's one or the other. I didn't say the W word—not sure I'll ever be ready to own that one.

Zoe asked if they'd be chasing away my husband. Little does she know you'd be the life of the party...makes me wonder if you were the force behind my words.

Mystery solved—I believe you were. Thank you. I miss you and love you more.

She slipped the purple ribbon alongside her words and closed the journal. Sipping her tea, she glanced around the living room. "I moved the pictures, Reid." After he died, seeing his smiling image pulverized her into specks of dust whenever she burrowed into his recliner. A month ago, she contemplated peppering the house with his photos. Then she recalled her friend Rachel's home, with every picture showcasing their happy family of three. A truth she had never allowed pierced her core. *Photos of the two of us remind me of what's missing.*

****

Throughout the next four days, Beth picked up the phone numerous times, never making it past six digits before hanging up. When her phone rang Monday afternoon—caller ID displaying Maria's number—her pulse quickened. She answered before voice mail clicked on. "Hello?"

"Beth? It's Maria. I was wondering if you'd like to go to lunch on Wednesday."

"I would." She smiled, certain Maria could hear the lilt through the phone line.

"How about Romeo's at noon?"

"Romeo's sounds perfect." She was still smiling when she hung up the phone.

Call and cancel. Crawling into bed that night, she acquiesced to the command she had battled for hours. She enjoyed spending time with her youngest classmate. But Maria's gentleness, compassion, and pregnancy quest threatened to shatter the promise to her twenty-one-year-old self. *I'll call her tomorrow.*

Chapter Four

You are a master of deflection. Beth woke to her old mantra looping through her mind. Reid's death had chipped at her armor, but years of resilience tipped the scale. She liked Maria and was honored to be her confidante. Turning from the urn, she ignored the stab of guilt regarding her years-old secret. *I'm going.*

The following morning, she arrived at Romeo's at eleven fifty-five. When she opened the restaurant door, the sounds of "Volare" spilled into the vestibule. Looking past the hostess stand, she spotted Maria near a window. "My friend's over there." She gestured and hurried across the room.

Maria stood, her face breaking into a smile as she drew her into a hug. "Glad we could get together today."

"I'm happy you called." She slid into the booth. Driving over, she considered confessing her failed phone attempts but nixed the idea when she exited her car. "Smells delicious."

"Mm-hmm." Maria inhaled through her nose and exhaled a soft sigh. "We love this place."

Their server delivered menus and departed with drink orders—waters for both.

Beth decided on chicken parmesan. She placed her order, and then new arrivals across the room, two women and a baby, captured her attention. *Three generations.* She examined the trio.

Maria and the server talked salmon and shrimp.

Dipping her chin, the older woman submerged her smile in the baby's flyaway hair.

The grandmother's palpable love tugged at Beth's heart. She glanced at Maria, wanting to spin a cocoon around her friend and shield her from the pain of empty arms.

The server smiled. "Your lunches will be right out."

"Thank you." Maria reached for her glass and met Beth's gaze. "I had my ultrasound last week." She swallowed hard. "My ovaries looked shriveled, and my blood work was abnormal again…" Her voice caught. "I have good chromosomes, though."

"Nice." Beth wanted to take back what felt like a feeble echo, but she didn't know how.

"Yeah. I asked for the chromosome analysis." Maria twisted a strand of hair between her fingers. "I asked for another FSH in a couple of months, too, though I've read high levels a month apart confirm POI."

Words scratched at her throat. She downed a long drink. "If your FSH stays high, then what?"

"Then I'll have a hard time…"

Getting pregnant. The weight of old memories crowded Beth's chest.

Maria unrolled her napkin. "FSH stimulates ovaries to produce estrogen, so when ovaries slow down, our bodies pump out more FSH. Levels less than ten are good but higher than twenty usually mean you're marching toward menopause." She took a breath. "If you're my age, twenty or higher could mean POI. Some books call POI premature ovarian failure—POF—which sounds even worse." She tightened her lips.

Say something. But the voice didn't tell her what. Beth took another drink.

"My first level was eighteen point eight and my second was nineteen point one. Sixteen or higher is problematic." Maria flashed finger quotation marks. "Plus, I haven't had a period since April."

"I'm so sorry." She had hidden from those words for months, but they were the best she could do.

Their meals arrived. "Fresh parmesan?" The server held out a mini cheese grater.

"Please." Beth spread her napkin on her lap while tiny ribbons of cheese peppered her chicken and pasta. "Perfect—thank you."

The server shifted her gaze.

"I'm set." Maria shook her head.

She smiled and picked up her tray. "Enjoy."

Beth plucked a breadstick from the basket and took a bite, savoring garlic, butter, and oven-fresh warmth.

Sticking her fork in the middle of her bowl, Maria twirled strands of angel hair pasta. She glanced up. "You and Anthony are the only ones that know."

"Your husband?"

She nodded. "He doesn't like to talk about fertility stuff with me or anyone else. You know how guys are…" Pink crept across her cheeks. "Sorry." She circled her fingers around her glass. "I think meeting you at the library was serendipitous."

A soft cry rang across the room.

The mother stood and gathered her baby then returned to the booth. Raising the hem of her shirt, she drew the infant to her breast.

Her tenderness and ease filled Beth with the desire she denied for years. She studied her friend. "Is working around babies hard right now?"

"Sometimes." Maria sighed and waved her fork. "Whenever I have a rough night, I always hope it's because of hormones and PMS...hasn't been so far."

"How much are you working?"

"I work two nights a week from seven to seven-thirty. Every third weekend, I work four nights in a row—two weeks' worth back to back."

"Four nights in a row sounds hard." Beth widened her eyes.

"I have nine nights off before and six after, which is nice." Maria cut a bite of salmon. "Plus, I sleep okay during the day."

They tucked into their food. A lively instrumental tune played over the speakers.

Two bites later, Maria repositioned in her seat. "Did you ever try to have kids?"

Beth gulped a long drink and swallowed the truth caught in her throat.

"Sorry." Maria pressed a hand against her lips then pinched her chin. "Whether you did or didn't is none of my business."

She set her glass on the table. "We didn't."

"Okay to talk about?" Maria tilted her head.

Slipping her hands under her napkin, Beth dug her nails into her thighs. Bracing herself for questions, she gave a single nod.

"Did you always know you didn't want any?"

She looked out the window. The nearby mountains, Mount Sentinel and Mount Jumbo, lay bare. To the north, snow blanketed Rattlesnake Wilderness' Stuart

Peak. Gazing at the cloudless, azure blue sky, she wished she could change the subject from babies to blues—cerulean to teal to ultramarine. She squeezed a kneecap and met Maria's gaze. "Reid was terrified to have a family. His brother had spinal muscular atrophy and died when he was fourteen."

Maria's expression sobered. "I can't imagine."

I can. She pleated her napkin. "Losing a brother was horrible, but his grief paled beside his parents'. So he vowed never to fall in love, get married, or *never ever* have kids." She gazed at her napkin, accordioned in her lap. "He idolized Jake and his fighting spirit. Jake had been in a wheelchair ever since Reid could remember, so the chair seemed normal. But he hated to see him choke and fight to breathe." She softened her voice. "He had pneumonia twice before…"

"How old was Reid?"

"Twelve and a half. He always added the extra six months." Beth smiled a little. "Their mom was pregnant with him when Jake was diagnosed. She said they wouldn't have had a second baby had they known."

Maria winced. "Poor thing."

"Never *to* him, but he overheard that comment a few times. He felt guilty for being born and for being healthy, and he was always compensating—helping Jake and wanting to make him better. Then Jake died, and his guilt skyrocketed." She stumbled over her words. "He was alive, but his brother wasn't."

"That story breaks my heart." Maria bit her lip. "I'm guessing he was the last?"

"He was. His mom got her tubes tied the day after he was born. I thought he was an only child—we dated five months before he told me about Jake. So…" She gave a rueful smile. "I do know how guys are."

"Five months?" Maria leaned forward and rested an arm against the table's edge.

Guilt and grief seizing her lungs, Beth managed a single nod. She pulled in a deep breath, her exhale quiet and prolonged. "He cried and told me he couldn't survive losing a child. Staying together wouldn't be fair, so he wanted me to find someone else. Get married. Have kids. Be happy." Her pain reflected in Maria's eyes, she glanced away. "We were both miserable. I sent him a card that read, ' 'Tis better to have loved and lost than never to have loved at all.' " She patted her chest. "We got back together the next week, and then married two years later."

"One part bitter and two parts sweet." Maria wound a forkful of pasta. "Was genetic testing an option?"

"Testing wouldn't have mattered. Whether our kids were sick or not, he would have worried about them *every single day*." She rotated her wedding band with her index finger and thumb. "When I try to make sense of his death, that's my one consolation…"

"Your heart broke instead of his." Maria lowered her chin. "Do you—or did you—ever wish you had kids?"

She slid her fingers away from the ring. "Yes." The word clawed up her throat.

Maria answered with her eyes.

In the quiet space between them, Beth could feel her embrace.

When they returned to their food, the friends shifted their conversation to the upcoming class finale.

Her appetite banished by memories, Beth picked at

her chicken and pasta then asked for a box. Exiting the restaurant, she was first to open her arms. The hug was firm and lingering. When she parted, she melted at the tender look in her young classmate's eyes.

She set her leftovers on the console and buckled her seatbelt. "When did we last eat at Romeo's, Reid?" The entire drive home, she searched her memory. The month he died, she resumed journaling, following a forty-year hiatus. *Had I known you'd be gone so soon, I would've jumped in a long time ago.* She owned her current journal for years but had used her keen memory as an excuse not to plunge in. *That thinking was misguided.* Even so, she was certain that absent perimenopausal brain fog and the gut punch of grief, her razor-sharp memory would reign supreme.

Pulling into the garage, she cast a glance at his car. A chill of sadness ran down her spine. She shivered. *I miss you, Darling.* Scooping up her leftovers, she hurried inside, circling to the refrigerator then straight to his recliner. Without shedding her coat, she pulled out her journal and uncapped her pen.

November Nineteenth

Dear Darling,

Maria and I just finished a delicious lunch at Romeo's. When did we last dine there? So much I don't remember… Anyhow, I was glad she called. Maybe you saw my failed attempts. Glad she *followed through.*

She wants a baby… When she asked about us, I told her about Jake. You'd like her. She's wise beyond her years. Speaking of, I'm old enough to be her mom.

You're old enough to be her dad. Beth stared at her penmanship, and her words morphed into the nothingness of a black hole. *If ifs and buts were candy and nuts, we'd all have a mighty fine Christmas.* The old chant whispered its regret. Memories of the days she had been desperate for a baby scrolled through her mind. *But we had a good life.* She and Reid shared the same fierce love he had with Jake. On days when sadness seized, she convinced herself falling in love with him was karmic confirmation she would *not* have been a good mother.

She righted her pen.

We're having lunch in two weeks at Tamarack. I didn't suggest Biga. Might sound silly, but I think of Biga as one of our special places. I'm not ready to forge new memories there.

Tomorrow is our last class, which is hard to believe. Thanks for giving me the nudge to sign up, and then the boot to exit my car. Seeing my classmates each week has been nice, and I'm grateful we'll be getting together here next month. Wish you could meet them—and they you. I miss you and love you more.

As Beth entered Home ReSource the following evening, she recalled her reluctant arrival weeks earlier. *I'll miss this place.*

Therese, Maria, and Zoe huddled around a photo on the workbench.

"Come see." Zoe waved an arm.

Beth slid in beside her.

"Nate. Erin. Hope. *Moi.*" Zoe tapped the air four times, pausing a finger millimeters from the photo.

"Two Mini-Mes." Maria shifted her gaze from Zoe to the photo and back. "Erin's the spitting image of you, and Hope looks just like Nate."

"So says the word on the street." Zoe smiled and stroked the front of her neck.

A yearning bubbled in Beth's core. She studied Erin, whose amber eyes, dimpled smile, and dark curls mirrored her mom's. Hope resembled her dad with steel blue eyes, smooth cheeks, and lighter, wispy hair. The family snuggled together—the girls in matching red taffeta dresses and black patent leather shoes and Zoe and Nate in black and white—all four radiating joy.

Corrine arrived, manila envelope in hand.

Questioning whether or not she could look at another happy family photo, Beth took a single step backward. She hoped no one noticed.

"Let's see." Zoe signaled toward the envelope.

"An original." Beaming, Corrine removed a water-color and cradled it in her hands.

Maria widened her eyes. "You are so talented."

"Pretty enough to smell…" Inhaling through her nose, Beth bent toward the peach rose and glistening droplets.

"Raindrops on roses…" Steepling her hands under her chin, Therese broke into song.

Corrine joined in. She slid her painting onto the workbench and threw open her arms. When she trilled the final note, she smiled and bowed. "Thank you for the standing ovation."

"You know I would've jumped up if I'd been sitting." Zoe flashed a grin.

"So would I for your singing *and* artistry." Clapping punctuated Therese's words. "I didn't know you could paint."

"After the twins left for college, I promised myself I'd take at least one Adult Ed class every year." Corrine gestured toward her painting. "Hence, watercolor last year and woodworking this fall."

"Speaking of, clear glass is here and mirrored there." Miles tipped his head from one workbench to the other.

The class retrieved their frames and staked out their respective places.

"C'mon over." He beckoned Zoe and Corrine. Lifting a tube, he turned its label toward the group. "Silicone is one of the strongest adhesives there is…" He showed them how to use painter's tape to protect the insides of their frames and explained applying silicone to rabbets. "Beads, not globs. If you get squeeze out then use a razor blade to clean it off."

He ushered them to the neighboring workbench and placed a pair of tiny metal triangles in his palm. "Glazier points are great for window panes and frames." Miles swept his hand in a semicircle. "You'll do two on the sides, three on the top, and three on the bottom. Then you'll cut a piece of craft paper to tape on the back. Does anyone have any questions?"

Maria raised a hand. "Do we put paper on the backs of our mirrors?"

"Not tonight. Silicone takes a while to dry, so when you get home, put a book or two on top of your mirror to seal it. You can cut a piece of paper to take if you'd like."

Beth nodded and returned to her frame.

The shop door opened. "I couldn't miss the grand finale." Dave grinned and shed his coat.

Avoiding eye contact, she focused on her work. She wouldn't look online for tonight's photos, either. After cinching blue painter's tape along the inside of her frame's perimeter, she shifted her gaze across the workbench.

Maria dotted beads of silicone, its aroma wafting overhead. She positioned her mirror, snugging it in before flipping it over.

No squeeze out. Beth knitted her brow. Matching Maria dot for dot, she situated her mirror then turned over her work of art. A warm flush of satisfaction coursed through her. *I wish you could see this, Reid.* She studied her reflection, wondering if he could see her new worry lines and hints of gray.

"You two set a high bar." Therese dabbed precise dots of silicone then righted her mirror. The glass captured her single nod.

"Mirrors three and squeeze out zero." Miles smiled and handed them evaluation forms and pens. "This class was my first for Adult Ed, so your feedback is important. I expect honesty—warts and all."

Beth gave the highest marks—*excellent* and *strongly agree. Miles is a wonderful teacher. This class exceeded my expectations, and I'm grateful for everything I've learned. Thank you. Beth Jorgennson.* She set down her pen. *When I sat outside Home ReSource the first night of class, I needed every ounce of courage to get out of my car. I'm glad I did and so very glad I stayed. Sometimes, life unfolds in ways we neither predict nor expect. Thank you, Adult Ed and Miles, for adding this class—this fall.* She read her original comment and held the rest in her heart.

Therese slid her evaluation to the center of the table. "I vote dessert at the Mustard Seed tonight."

"Motion carried." Grinning, Zoe turned her frame front facing and tapped it on the workbench.

"Okay to gather your creations for a couple of photos?" Dave uncapped his camera.

The women chorused their consent.

Corrine and Zoe freed their workbench for the photo shoot and joined the mirror trio.

"Head down, and tail up." Zoe flashed a dimpled grin and picked up a pen.

After staggering the painting, photo, and mirrors, Dave angled his camera. "You each get an A plus."

"Thanks to Miles' crackerjack instructions." Zoe didn't look up.

"The credit belongs to my ace students." Miles swept his hands toward the group.

I'll miss this place. Beth looked around the workshop, and gratitude filled her core.

Dave signaled his finish.

A round of thank-yous followed, and the cohorts gathered their treasures and exited the shop.

Last in line, Beth scanned new offerings on her way out: bookcases, an entertainment center, matching vanities, a pair of corner cabinets, wooden frames, and a vintage pram. *Each has a tale to tell.* Her story sealed in her heart, she carried her mirror into the chilly darkness.

Ten minutes later, she wound around Southgate Mall and eased into a parking place outside the Mustard Seed.

Her friends waited near the hostess stand. Several barstools and tables were occupied, and the hum of conversation filled the high-ceilinged restaurant.

The hostess escorted them to a U-shaped booth in the corner.

Beth stood back and was the last to slide in from the left.

"Is anyone else having wine with dessert?" Corrine

shrugged off her jacket. "Red wine and chocolate are an unbeatable combination. I'm just saying."

"Sold." Zoe slapped her thigh.

"I second the motion." Therese grinned and held up two fingers.

Beth's agreement was silent and reflective as she set aside memories of wine, chocolate, and Reid. Pulling her coat around her shoulders, she rested her hands against her chest. *Tonight is all about new memories.*

Their server arrived and took drink orders—four glasses of wine and one pot of tea.

The dessert specialist followed. She carried a tray laden with artistic replicas and presented a description of each.

Listening to the choices, Beth changed her mind three times then decided on Montana mud pie.

Last in line, Zoe finalized her order as their drinks arrived.

"Cheers to women with power tools." Corrine raised her glass.

"And cheers to a wonderful class." Maria poured a sip of tea.

Beth clinked and smiled then extended her arm toward the center of the table. *Here's to rebirth.* She toasted herself, too, and then inhaled the wine's earthy bouquet before taking a drink.

"Miles was great." Maria turned to Therese. "I see why Kate loves his classes."

"Is he married?" Zoe squinted and leaned in.

"I don't know." Therese shrugged. "Kate's never seen any married-looking pictures anywhere."

"No wedding ring, which doesn't mean much."

Maria filled her teacup. "How's Kate doing? Is she still set on woodworking?"

"She is. Last week, she finished her Portland application. So, we'll see."

"What does Vince say?" Corrine puffed out her chest.

"Not much. I don't think Kate would listen to what he had to say anyway. She might act like she's listening—"

"Is Vince her dad?" Zoe interrupted.

"He's her sperm donor." Therese pursed her lips. "He left when she was two."

"Eww." Zoe wrinkled her nose. "Does he live in Missoula?"

"Anchorage. He comes to see her once a year."

"Are you kidding?" Zoe cocked her head. "He visits only once a year?"

"Works for all of us." Therese tipped her wineglass.

Maria scooted forward. "Does she ever go to Anchorage?"

"We went when she was seven. She didn't like his new wife and didn't like their girls—a one- and a three-year-old. Kate was incensed her dad left her, and then had two more. She announced she was 'never going back.'" Therese put her hands on her hips. "I thought she'd change her mind, but she hasn't so far."

Corrine gave a thumbs-up. "I say good for her."

"She has a mind of her own." Therese waved a hand. "My dad's been saying that since she was a toddler."

"Really?" Corrine raised an eyebrow. "I wonder where she gets her stubbornness."

The comfortable banter between the longtime friends made Beth smile. *I'm glad you're coming to dinner at our house. My house.* The words scrunched in her throat.

"Do you think Dave's photos will drum up business for the next class?" Zoe asked. "I wonder when he'll post the new ones."

"They might." Maria unfolded her napkin. "Your rock star photo was my favorite."

"Talented photographer and talented subjects…his pictures could become recruiting beacons." Zoe grinned and rested her hands alongside her face. "Do any of you follow the *Humans of New York* guy? I *love* his pictures and stories."

"So do I." Corrine rubbed her cheek. "Did you see the one a few days ago with the nanny…"

Beth sipped her wine. She remembered being fascinated by the photographer's work. For an entire week, she contemplated joining social media for his pictures and stories. *I'm glad I didn't.*

The server returned and distributed their desserts.

"Tastes around?" Therese picked up her fork.

"I was thinking the same thing." Maria replenished her tea.

"My germophobe sister would say 'cut a bite with your knife.' " Corrine straightened her silverware. "She refused to let me touch her food with my fork or spoon."

"Pass to the right." Zoe slid her dessert to Corrine. "And you can use your spoons for my parfait."

Beth worked her way through chocolate mousse pie, poppy seed rum cake, chocolate almond parfait, and coconut layer cake. The flavors burst in her mouth.

She and Reid had loved sharing "a bite for a bite"—a throwback to his tender years with Jake. *I thought my sharing days were over.* Tingling warmth flowed through her veins when her pie circled back.

Zoe turned to Therese. "Excellent idea."

"I aim to please." Therese gave a single nod.

"Soooo." Zoe cast a sidelong glance. "I better save my next question for Beth's house."

"You can't leave us hanging." Corrine wagged a finger.

"Well…" Zoe twisted her lips. "I was about to ask if you're dating anyone."

Therese picked up her fork. "Saving that question why?"

"Because asking about dating after 'I aim to please' seemed…" Zoe opened a palm.

"Inappropriate? You're so funny." Therese laughed. "But no, I'm not. I had my hands full when Kate was little. That"—she flicked her fork—"was a play on words. Anyway, I wasn't interested then, and after she met her stepmother, she swore she'd run away if I ever brought home a stepfather."

"She benched you?" A frown flitted across Zoe's forehead.

"Not really. I was enmeshed in parenting and work, so adding another guy to the mix was *not* appealing."

"Hard, though, being a single parent?" Maria nested her teacup in her hands.

"Sometimes. My parents live in Polson, and they've been great." Therese raised a forkful of cake. "What else shall we talk about?"

"Did you see the stars on your way in?" Maria smiled and glanced around the table. "The Big Dipper was *glorious*."

Beth *had* seen the stars. Gazing at the night sky, she whispered the verse she had guarded in her heart for more than half a lifetime.

****

A week later, Beth rolled over in bed and blew a kiss to Reid's urn. *Happy Thanksgiving, Darling.* After debating for five days whether or not to cook a holiday dinner, she had braved the grocery store that Tuesday. Her fridge well stocked and with untethered hours ahead, she untangled from her covers. She brewed a pot of coffee, cocooned herself in the comfort of Reid's recliner, and pulled out her journal. Sliding the ribbon right, she opened the book and straightened the pen.

November Twenty-seventh

Dear Reid,

Happy Thanksgiving. What a difference a year makes. Last Thanksgiving, I couldn't find a single thing to be thankful for and didn't eat the entire day. I'm glad this year will be different. Remember the card I sent you in college—" 'Tis better to have loved and lost than never to have loved at all"? A year ago, I would've argued that sentiment until I was blue in the face. Wishing I were blue in the face and working my way to your side. Morbid perhaps, but I struggled in those days and weeks and months without you—in the seconds and minutes and hours truth be told.

Now, I can breathe those love and loss words without argument. Though I miss you desperately, my heartache has softened some. I'm able to appreciate the love we shared, wrap myself in sweet memories, and even talk about them a bit, like with Maria. She and I are having lunch next week, and then the gang's

*coming for dinner two weeks later. I'm thankful for my
new friends, and I predict—hope, really—our dinner
will be the first of many.*

*Rachel called and invited me to join them today.
Talk about tried and true. Even though I never answer
her calls or call back, she keeps trying. I miss her and
am thankful for our friendship but moving forward
without old friends on board is easier. For now, I need
to be guardian of the memories—the one who decides
what and when to share. Selfish? Perhaps. I'm sure
they miss you and would love to reminisce, but I'm
aiming for survival. With new friends, I don't have to
worry about old memories slipping out when and where
I least expect them.*

*I'm thankful for my health and relative youth,
though there's the sad irony of losing you when you
were relatively youthful. But as we know, life isn't
always fair. I'm most thankful for you—for giving me
space, for loving me without condition, and for the joy
and happiness and laughter we share. Written in
present tense because in memories and in dreams what
we had continues. On this Thanksgiving Day, I'll set a
place for you and blanket myself in your love. I miss
you and love you more.*

Beth closed her journal and rested it in her lap.
Encircling her hands on the mug, she leaned back into
the leather's warm embrace and surrendered to
memories.

When her six-year-old self stood on a chair next to
her mother in front of the stove, she had felt as tall and
important as an eighth-grader. The aroma of turkey
gravy filled the kitchen. Together, they held onto the
strainer, and her mother's wedding and engagement

rings served as a tether between them. Standing in a too-big apron with her mom's hand nesting hers, Beth had felt *huge*. Like a grainy, old movie, scenes scrolled through her mind. When her junior year in college tiptoed into consciousness, she slipped her journal into the magazine holder and pushed out of Reid's chair. She carried the mug into the kitchen, and her heart ached.

Chapter Five

Unlike her usual MO of preparing the dining room hours before holiday dinners, Beth waited until five o'clock to set the table. Folding a pair of burgundy napkins, she reminisced about her and Reid's first night of china and crystal and candlelight.

They had inaugurated their wedding gifts with Cornish game hens, champagne, and chocolate mousse. Afterward, he lifted her into his arms, stumbling a little as he sashayed around the table in their cozy Garfield Street apartment. But he steadied her with his chest and arms, and she felt so safe in his embrace—his wobble and instinctive recovery had seemed symbolic of what lay ahead.

"Thirty-two years, Reid. Can you believe it?" Her words were soft as cotton. "When was the last time for our dishes?" Their last lovemaking seared into memory, she wondered in hindsight if he had had a premonition. "When did we last use our china?" Her words were louder now as she felt a frantic hunger to venerate the last time just as she had the first.

She remembered their last kiss.

A goodbye kiss like any other, its finality declared itself hours later. CPR and an AED and nine-one-one's army of paramedics couldn't save him and though she knew thoughts that *she* might've made a difference were crazy, they invaded her mind at night under the cover of darkness.

"I would have never let you go." Her words echoed in the empty room. Beth completed Reid's place setting then the oven timer sliced through the silence. The turkey breast's aroma beckoned, and she hurried to quiet the timer. She balanced the roaster on a pair of burners.

"Let the turkey sit for ten."

His voice choreographed the dance, just as his signature peppered the menu: Sauvignon Blanc, pumpkin cheesecake, and jellied cranberry sauce. She liked whole berry, but he had preferred jellied. They made a compromise early on and alternated year to year. More than once, she bought jellied when she should have bought whole berry. This year, too, she bought the kind he liked—just because.

She had changed a couple of things—swapping asparagus and baked sweet potato for green bean casserole and mashed potatoes with gravy. "Would a better diet have helped?" Waiting the requisite minutes before she transferred the turkey breast to the awaiting platter, she paced around the kitchen. *Would a treadmill have gifted you with extra years?* She harbored her question, unwilling to give voice to the pleading in her head.

Her eyes burned when she picked up his beloved carving set. "You should be slicing this." She blurted the words—loud and mournful. Cursing herself for foregoing a boneless breast, she carved without stopping until the bone lay bare. Then she wiped her face with her apron, crumpled into a heap in his recliner, and wept.

Returning to the kitchen, she had no idea how

much time passed. According to the oven clock, she had cried herself dry in ten minutes, which felt ten times longer. She covered the turkey with foil and headed into the bathroom, shedding her apron along the way. Three times she filled her hands with icy water to splash away salt and tears. Then she buried her face in an ivory towel's fluffy softness and inhaled its lavender scent. As she replaced the towel on the rack, she took a deep breath of the aroma wafting from the kitchen. The turkey's scent summoned like an old friend.

She backtracked to the kitchen and debated dishing up in there as she opened the Sauvignon Blanc. *But the table is set, and the serving dishes are out.* After acquiescing to the little voice, she filled the dishes partway and carried food and drink into the dining room. She poured Reid's wine first and then her own. Standing beside her chair, Beth served her plate and left his empty as air. A bone-deep chill coursed through her. She shivered and sank into her seat, wrapping her arms across her chest.

When she stilled, she raised her glass and tipped it toward his chair. "Happy Thanksgiving, Darling." The words scraped at her throat. She took a long, slow drink and willed the wine's warmth to soften the flood of loneliness and sorrow. Returning the glass to her lips, she drained it dry. She retrieved his glass and took a sip before carrying it to her place. Then she stared at her food. She sawed a bite of turkey and placed it in her mouth, chewing without a bit of satisfaction. The asparagus and sweet potato tasted flavorless, too—her taste buds crushed by grief. *This meal is not the same without you, Reid.* She finished his wine, leaving the rest of her food untouched. *What about Christmas?* She cleared the table, unwilling to give voice to the question swirling through her mind.

****

A week later, Beth stepped up to the parking meter at Caras Park. When the command appeared to enter her license plate number, she tapped four-A then hesitated. Hovering her index finger in front of the keypad, she glanced toward the Clark Fork River, imploring muscle memory to kick in. *As if the water will help.* Heat burned her face as she turned from the meter and avoided eye contact with the woman behind her. She hurried to her car, only four spaces away. "Four-A-five-seven-three-one-two." She murmured the number, repeating the sequence as she hustled back.

The woman that leapfrogged ahead stood alone at the meter. She retrieved her receipt and gave Beth a slow, single nod.

Without acknowledgement, she stepped forward. She did not waste time wondering if the nod and compassion in the woman's eyes meant she had been thrust into the same gut-punching-scatterbrained-grief-club as Beth. Nor did she waste time breathing—she held her breath almost without thought until the machine asked for money. Spluttering a breath, she vacillated between one hour and two then opted for the latter—just in case.

A hint of sun peeked from behind a tumble of billowy clouds as she unlocked her car and placed her receipt face up on the dashboard. No snow had fallen to date, and the air was a temperate forty-three degrees. She hoped the weather would hold for weeks. Though she didn't mind the snow, she was not a fan of winter driving. She crossed the lot and entered Tamarack

Brewery through the downstairs sports pub then climbed the back staircase. A blend of appetizing aromas wafted in the air. When she reached the top of the stairs, she spotted her friend at a table near the windows.

Maria greeted her with a hug. Reclaiming her seat, she flicked her head toward the window. "Have you ever ridden the Carousel?"

"I have." Squelching the memory, Beth followed her gaze across the parking lot. "Have you?"

"Mm-hmm." Maria smiled and hitched in her chair. "It's fast."

Their server arrived to take drink orders.

Grateful for the distraction, Beth requested a glass of water. Sunlight streamed onto the table, and she rested her hands in its warmth while she perused the menu. She decided on fish tacos then readied a question to change the subject. After placing her order, she leaned forward. "How was your Thanksgiving?"

"We had dinner with our neighbors." Maria laced her fingers under her chin. "Their boys are three and six—fun ages."

Childhood memories flashed through her mind. "Did they make finger puppets with black olives?"

"No." Maria laughed then glanced at a couple beside them. "Anthony rocked his semen analysis last week." A smile tugged at the corners of her lips. "He was thrilled to learn he has stellar sperm." She flashed finger quotation marks. "We both were. He wants to keep trying—he thinks if I do have POI, we'll be in the eight percent. His MO is 'some is better than none.' "

Beth cocked her head. "I like his MO."

"I do, too. He lifted that saying from his mom."

"What about you?"

Maria sighed and opened her napkin. "I'd like to be hopeful, but I still haven't had a period, which isn't promising."

Words of comfort or hope eluded her, over-shadowed by decades-old memories. *Be present.* She toyed with her glass.

"Fertility drugs don't have a good track record with POI either, so for now..." Maria glanced out the window. "Have you gone through menopause yet?"

"I'm going through." Beth wrinkled her brow. "My last period was five or six months ago. So, I hope I'm in the home stretch."

"Do you mind if I ask how old you are?"

"Fifty-seven." She pressed her palms to her cheeks. "I haven't said that age out loud before."

Maria tipped her head. "I pegged you for fifty or less."

Halfway to a hundred. She held Reid's words in her heart.

"I've been reading a lot of alphabet soup: POI, FSH, IVF, ART... So, I'm changing our toast to PWWPT—Perimenopausal Women with Power Tools." Maria raised her glass, her eyes twinkling.

"Your toast will be a hit." Beth grinned and lifted her glass. "To PWWPT." She clinked and drank, cementing the friendship with ice cold water. When her lunch arrived, she tucked into her food.

Conversations hummed around the room.

Beth savored her first bites of fish, cabbage, chipotle, and cheese. *Good choice.*

"I've learned more about menopause and perimenopause than I ever thought I would at this stage of the game." Maria speared a forkful of spinach and brie. "For example, the average age for menopause is fifty-one… I thought it was older."

She twisted her lips. "That means I skew the average."

"I think I do, too." Maria glanced at her hands.

"How old was your mom?" Beth softened her voice.

"Forty-nine. I remember thinking she was the Wicked Witch of the West." Maria slipped a strand of hair behind her ear. "WWW—I hadn't computed that alliteration. She told me later she didn't realize her explosions were hormone related. I squirreled away that little heads-up."

"Does she know what you're going through?" She crossed her ankles.

"No. Anthony's mom would be crushed if my mom knew before she did, and he's not ready to say anything yet…" Maria stabbed at her salad.

Returning to her taco, Beth wondered if the subject was paused or closed. She met Maria's gaze. "Did Anthony ask you not to tell your mom, or would you rather talk about something else?"

"No. He didn't ask me not to, but he's really private and didn't want to tell anyone. I decided I wouldn't either." Maria rubbed her ear. "Then you reminded me of my mom, so I just blurted out about the cradle."

"I reminded you of your mom?" Her words were a clot of regret.

"Mm-hmm. You closed your eyes, just like my mom does whenever she arrives someplace new." Maria's eyes shone. "Seeing you at the library and going to The Catalyst was so nice. Then sitting next to you at The Depot, I spilled the rest of my story."

"Does Anthony know?" She wrapped her hands around her glass.

"Yeah. He didn't really say anything." Maria shrugged. "I'm not planning to tell anyone else, though."

Beth held her gaze. "Anytime you need to talk, I'll listen and hold back my two cents' worth."

Maria turned over a palm. "You sound just like my mom, which is a compliment."

Heat rushed to her face. *I'd like to be your mom.*

"What about your parents?" Maria lowered her chin.

"They're both gone." She stared at her hands that bore the strength of her father and the softness of her mother. "I lost my dad seventeen years ago from colon cancer." She looked up. "Mom had a stroke five years ago. She died a week later."

Maria rested a hand on her chest. "I'm so sorry."

"Thanks." Her tenderness tugged at Beth's heart. *So am I.* She took a bite of her taco and shifted her gaze to a neighboring table.

A thirty-something man talked with his hands, his eyes sparkling.

The older woman seated opposite had a softness around her eyes. When she leaned in, her face tipped into a smile.

A mother and son. The love on the woman's face was palpable. Beth forced the bite past the thickness in her throat then reached for her water. She met Maria's gaze.

"You miss them." Maria pulled in her eyebrows.

"I do." She spoke in a whisper-soft tone. *All of them.*

Forty-five minutes later, Beth stood and pushed in her chair. "Are you out back?"

"No." Maria waved a hand. "I'm across the street." She wrapped her arms around Beth, smiling when she pulled away. "I'll see you next week for the Perimenopausal Women reunion."

"Sounds good." She held on to her smile all the way down the stairs. When she traversed the parking lot, she glanced at the Carousel. The old memory of her single ride worked its stealth. Being around all those kids had delivered a gut punch she did not want to revisit. *Ssshhh.* She shifted her gaze toward the river, this time asking the swirling water to help her forget.

****

Three days later, Beth hunkered into Reid's recliner. She removed her journal from the magazine table and uncapped her pen.

December Seventh

Dear Darling,

Last December, I was haunted by memories of the day I lost you. This year is easier, but easy *will never be the operative word. I miss you. I'm able to remember our good times and celebrate what we shared, though living without you will never be easy.*

I feel you prodding me to get on with my life, saying "morning has broken" and the time has come to reconnect with old friends. You might be right. For now, though, I want to be the driver of my memory bus. Crazy? Perhaps. But I'm not yet ready to relinquish control.

My woodworking friends are coming next week. I

thought having them here would be good, but now I'm regretting the invite. All week, I've struggled to harness Pollyanna's outlook to no avail. I am decorating a bit when I finish writing this entry. Hopefully, my efforts will spur some Christmas spirit. Last year, I could barely get out of your chair, so decorating feels like another giant leap. I'm not sending cards, but I'll read the ones we get. I get. Last year's cards went straight into the garbage—recycling be damned. I couldn't catch up on old news even if I wanted to. I miss you and love you more.

Beth put away her journal. Her commitment memorialized in ink, she shuffled into the office. She crossed to the computer desk and picked up a photo. *I loved that dress.* Reid had snugged her close—his arm around her waist as he circled his thumb atop her emerald green chiffon. He wore his favorite black suit and new red and green paisley tie. Posing in front of the enormous Christmas tree aboard the Enchantment of the Seas, they had looked stunning.

She examined his nut-brown eyes and espresso-colored hair, fighting to remember when hints of gray peppered his temples and Monday morning shadows. *What would you look like now?* She brushed her lips millimeters from the glass, and a wave of sadness gripped her chest. Replacing the photo, she eyed the closet, just steps away. "You always unearthed our decorations, Reid." She had offered to help, but he had "a system." Slogging to the closet, she opened the double doors and studied his arrangement: long tub on the bottom, two stacks of three atop, and each one labeled in his careful handwriting.

Sucking in a deep breath, she hoisted *NATIVITY.*

She encircled the tub with her arms and hugged it close. Exiting the room, she paused. Her maple mirror captured the determination of her set jaw. "Another giant leap." Her reflection mouthed the words. She carried the tub to the dining room and set it in front of the credenza. Then she rerouted with resolve.

The other two tubs lay buried at the bottom. Peeling back layers of memories, she hefted containers up and out and uncovered *FAKE TREE ORNAMENTS*. She hauled the ornaments into the living room, grunting as she sidestepped the coffee table to deposit the tote onto the couch. When she returned to the office, she surveyed the tubs scattered around the floor. For a New York minute, she contemplated putting up all their decorations. *They're already out.* But putting back tubs would take less time and energy than decorating and un-decorating their entire home. *My entire home.* And though she didn't want a bare house for her friends, she wasn't feeling *that* festive. An-entire-house-decorated festive.

"I'll do the tree and Nativity—period." Beth freed *CRUISE TREE* and slid the container into the middle of the room. She piloted the tote, twice the length of the others, through the doorway and down the hall. Wielding the entombed tree into the living room, she parked it near the picture window. She stepped back and propped her chin in her hands, her throat tightening as she contemplated what lie ahead. *Start with the manger.*

She drifted to the dining room. After laying the burlap runner on the credenza, she centered the stable. Then she unwrapped the pieces one by one. Their order was always a surprise. *Our first Christmas decoration.*

Remember, Reid? An ache crowded her lungs when she placed the baby lamb beside its momma.

Reid had loved to rearrange the animals. Many mornings, she found a sheep or cow or both perched atop the stable. She rescued the strays and returned them to safer footing. Whether in truth or in imperfect memory, her accompanying laughter always seemed an auspicious start to an excellent day. In the early years, they had a running argument about whether or not to have baby Jesus MIA until after midnight Christmas Eve.

"He wasn't birthed until then." Reid lobbied hard, dismissing assertions Mary didn't look pregnant and photos of an empty cradle were nonexistent.

Beth humored him one year and waited to add baby Jesus until the wee hours of the twenty-fifth. She couldn't bear the vacant crib, though, so she cut a swatch of red velour and made a tiny blanket. Ever since—she didn't remember how long—the babe had lain swaddled as he gazed at Mary and Joseph.

She covered baby Jesus with the tiny blanket and stroked the plush softness. "I didn't know decorating would be so hard." Her words were soft as air and gratitude infused because nixing the entire-house-decorating idea was wiser than she had anticipated.

Needing a break before round two, she retreated into the kitchen. She brewed tea in Reid's favorite mug, Mount Rushmore, and carried it into the living room. Sinking into his recliner, she wrapped her hands around his mug and longed for his touch. She gazed across the room. His careful writing drew her in, and she closed her eyes. *Seven years.*

She had returned from a lunch date with Rachel

one Saturday afternoon.

Reid greeted her in the hallway and looped an arm through hers.

"What's up?" She shot him a quizzical look.

"You'll see." He steered her through the house then stopped outside the living room. Slipping a hand over her eyes, he nudged her from behind with the other hand—his touch gentle. He inched forward then stopped and slid an arm around her waist. "Keep your eyes closed." Skimming his other hand from her eyes to her belly, he pressed against her and kissed the back of her neck. "Now."

Beth opened her eyes. A Christmas tree stood in front of the picture window. Its maroon and silver bulbs—University of Montana Grizzly colors—reflected twinkling white lights. "Beautiful, Reid." She clasped her hands over her heart, noticing what she missed when she pulled into the driveway. "You closed the curtains."

"I didn't want to ruin the surprise."

His breath tickled her skin. Unfolding her hands, she covered his arms with her own and relaxed into him.

He twisted to kiss her cheek, and then her lips. "I wanted you to come home to a Christmas tree after our cruise, but I had to settle for artificial." He twirled her toward him.

She answered with a kiss.

They tumbled to the floor and made love by the tree's soft glow. When they returned home on the seventeenth, they had an encore, vowing they would take another cruise someday. Hunting trees in the years that followed, they had savored memories of their cruise and the promise of another.

Now, she stared at the tote, and Reid's script muddled under her unblinking gaze. A tangle of emotions fought with her breath: a messy medley of anger, sorrow, and regret. "You weren't supposed to die." A snappy tone laced her words. Crippled by a rush of sadness, she told herself the tree could wait. She drained her tea, not stopping until the mug's emptiness matched her own. *The pain will be the same tomorrow.* Swift and sharp or prolonged and aching—neither was a declarative winner. In the end, *just finish* prevailed.

She blinked hard against the burn in her eyes and removed two sections of the pre-lit tree. Sweeping a hand under the remaining two pieces, she searched for paper or plastic—instructions to tell her *what to do.* Though she was a whiz at trial and error, right now, anything beyond breathing felt insurmountable. Rummaging around, she heard the paper crinkle before she curled her fingers around an edge. She retrieved the directions and confirmed what she already knew. *I need the other pieces first.* She freed the final two sections. Her grief thicker than oil, she steadied her trembling hands and put up the tree alone.

After plugging in the lights, she draped herself in a fleece comforter. Cocooned in his recliner, she glanced around the room. The empty tubs looked like castaways. "I feel like a castaway." *Castoff or survivor...* she felt neither and both as she stared at the tree. Her guests were coming in ninety-six hours. "I thought I was ready for company, Reid." *I'm not.*

****

For the next day and a half, Beth debated calling off dinner. She finally gave herself an ultimatum—

cancel by tonight, or you're on. Already Tuesday, her guests were scheduled on Thursday. She wrote out a list, numbering the order in which she'd call, and then changed it twice.

After the five-thirty news, she picked up the phone. Maria now being Number One, she dialed six numbers then stopped. *I'll call in fifteen.* But then fifteen turned into twenty then thirty then forty, and the knot in her stomach refused to unravel. She glanced at her watch. Six forty-three. *She might be on her way to work.*

Though she wasn't a quitter, she positioned herself to quit either Plan A or Plan B—dinner or her withdrawal. That word carried some baggage. But no one knew Plan B was even a whisper. She carried the phone into the kitchen, and a shiver seized her shoulders. *I'll run with Plan A. Hopefully, I won't fall flat on my face.*

****

Two days later, Beth sank into Reid's recliner and sipped a mug of chamomile tea. Then she opened her journal and put pen to paper.

December Eleventh

Dear Reid,

My woodworking friends will be here in two hours. Tonight will be the first time we've—I've—hosted a dinner since, well, since you know when. Wish I wasn't so nervous. The burn in my belly feels over the top for only four guests. Wish you could meet them and they you—you'd preside over a mutual admiration society, I'm sure.

I bought our favorite tequila yesterday, and I'm certain your margarita recipe will be a hit. Since Maria's on a mission to have a baby, I'm making a virgin batch, too. Wish you were here to work the blender. I miss you and love you more.

She tucked her pen inside the journal and slipped the iris-covered book into the magazine table. Then she routed to the entryway and stashed the unopened Christmas cards in the Shaker table drawer. Removing them from sight felt cathartic. When the first cards arrived two weeks prior, she scrapped her resolution to read them this year. As more trickled in, she tossed them in a pile, telling herself she'd read them Christmas morning.

Her stomach fluttering on the cusp of her classmates' arrivals, she turned on the porch lights then continued her walk-through. She was not planning a tour but would oblige if asked. Her home had always been tidy and though months had passed when dirty dishes filled the sinks and countertop, she had pulled herself from a speck of grief's wreckage. Her recovery—if even the right word—remained a work in progress, but having guests tonight felt huge.

She plugged in the tree lights and closed the living room drapes, leaving them open enough for the tree to wink a greeting. Most nights, she secured the drapes and every other window covering, too, insulating herself in the comfort of home. Tonight, the tree lights would be a welcoming beacon for her friends. Axing her inspection, she wove to the garage for the outside lights.

On her way back, she acquiesced to the niggle she'd ignored all day. She gathered Reid's urn and carried it into their walk-in closet—its weight magnified by the depth of her loss. Sliding his sport coats and suits left and his slacks right, she tucked the urn in between on the shelf above his shirts and ties.

She made it to the end of the bed before turning. Undetectable in the shadow, the urn was just as she had envisioned. But burying Reid in darkness seemed wrong, so she moved the mahogany vessel to the top of her dresser. Then with a what-the-hell shrug, she returned his ashes to the nightstand where they belonged. "Will I ever feel comfortable with your urn out of sight?"

The empty room swallowed her words.

Chapter Six

When the doorbell chimed an hour and a half later, Beth sucked in a deep breath. Her stomach tangled in a knot of anticipation and nerves. She plodded to the front and opened the door. Seeing Maria centered on the long-neglected welcome mat made her smile. "Hello." She ushered in her friend from the frigid evening air.

"Thanks for having us." Maria tipped a shoulder and nodded toward a lush plant in the crook of her arm. "This poinsettia's for you."

Beth juggled past a casserole dish and freed the plant. "I didn't put up many decorations, so this red and green will add some color…" She quieted the apology in her voice.

Maria narrowed her eyes. "How are you doing?"

"I feel like I need a double dose of antacids." She slowed as they walked down the hall. "What about you?"

"Still no period, and I haven't had any slippery mucus…" Maria met her gaze. "Sorry. TMI. The short answer is I'm planning to have a margarita tonight."

"Ah. Are you ready for one now?"

"I'll wait."

Beth led the way into the kitchen. "Over here." She skirted around the counter to the breakfast nook and centered the poinsettia in the middle of the table. *I wish*

I'd pulled out my Christmas dishes.

"Your table looks nice." Maria waved a hand toward the fan of blue and yellow plates, matching plaid napkins, margarita glasses, and salt rimmer. She set her dish atop a trivet then slipped a bag from her shoulder and removed a package of tortilla chips. "Shall I put these in a bowl?"

"Sure." Beth backtracked to a cupboard and retrieved a canary yellow serving bowl from above the microwave. "Trade you." She set the bowl on the table then gestured toward Maria's jacket. "I'm a little slow on the uptake tonight."

Maria moved her lips into a wordless *O* and slipped off her jacket and scarf.

She carried the pair to the hall closet. When she opened the door, she gasped. *Reid's coats.* She forgot all about them. His were on the right and hers were on the left—with empty hangers in the middle. She buried her face in his navy fleece and hunted his scent as one moment turned into two. Then she slid his coats into the corner and hung Maria's jacket in the center. The doorbell beckoned, and Beth edged to the front, rallying her game face before opening the door.

Zoe shivered on the porch. "Hoo. Tonight is colder than Jack Frost's balls." Exhaling a noisy breath, she scooted inside. "Your house feels nice and toasty, though."

"I'm glad." Beth reached for her clay pot. Halfway down the hall, she slowed. "Closet's there, or I can grab your coat in a minute." She gestured with an elbow.

"No time like the present." Zoe grinned and shed her jacket then draped it on a hanger. She pulled a small orange box from a coat pocket. "I brought some Posh

Chocolat for our chocolate connoisseur."

"Yum." Beth smiled all the way to the kitchen.

Maria and Zoe exchanged greetings.

"Something smells delicious." Zoe slipped the chocolates onto the counter. "Can I help with anything?"

"Are you ready for a margarita?" Beth opened the refrigerator door.

"I've been ready all day." She tucked her elbows against her sides and splayed her hands—thumbs and index fingers touching. "Zoe Dail moves into position and is ready for the pass…"

Beth grinned and handed her the spiked drink before sliding the virgin batch to the back. *Maybe we'll close the night with mocktails.*

"Three—"

Chimes interrupted Zoe's words. "Bartender." She chortled. "Make that four."

"I'd like salt on mine, please." Beth flung the words over her shoulder and hurried to the door.

Corrine and Therese waited side by side.

"Welcome." She signaled them inside. "May I take something?"

"I'm good." Therese flicked her head.

"So am I." Corrine stepped aside. "Lead the way."

She escorted the newcomers into the kitchen.

They unloaded salad and flan and gifts—a pine-scented candle and a bottle of Pinot Noir.

Beth collected their jackets, her stomach softening as she added them to the closet. She glanced at Reid's coats, now shrouded in darkness, and offered silent thanks for her newfound friends.

The women congregated around the table.

"Seven-layer fiesta dip." Maria placed a serving spoon in the appetizer.

"Dig in." Beth waved an arm.

Once the five had food and drink in hand, they segued to the living room.

"You're Grizzly fans?" Zoe claimed Reid's recliner and nodded toward the tree.

The plural tugged at Beth's gut. *This is hard, Reid.* She lowered into her recliner that was untouched for months. "Yes," she managed. "Are you?"

"I'm a Montana Tech Digger." Zoe set her glass on the table. "I cheer for the Griz, though."

"You went to school in beautiful Butte?" Corrine hovered a loaded tortilla chip halfway between her plate and mouth.

"Yep—I majored in Environmental Engineering." Zoe rested a hand on her chest. "I love Butte."

"What are you doing now?" Maria leaned forward.

"Taking time off—AKA sequencing. Love that word, too. I'll ramp up again after Hope starts school." Zoe took a drink. "Most days I love being home, but once in a while, I'd go back in a flash. What about you?"

"I'm an OB nurse at CMC." Maria tipped her head. "Next?"

Therese raised her glass. "I'm the librarian at Lewis and Clark Elementary. I know what you do, Corrine…" She snapped her fingers then gestured to her left.

Beth wiped her mouth. "I retired from the Forest Service last year." Her months-old story sounded untested and new. She shifted in her seat. "What about you?"

"I practice family law, but I say work talk stops here." Corrine tapped her index fingers into an *X*.

"Family talk, too, except I have one question for Beth—maybe two." Zoe waggled her index fingers. "Were you a forestry major?"

"Mm-hmm." Beth leaned back.

"Didn't you have to use chainsaws and stuff?"

"We used chainsaws and crosscut saws, but those days were long ago." She exhaled a shallow sigh. "I liked the crosscuts better."

"Whirrrrr." Zoe twisted her lips. "I'd be all about chainsaws."

"Not me." Corrine scooped a bite of dip. "What's in this deliciousness?"

"Refried beans, sour cream, taco seasoning, cheddar cheese, guacamole"—Maria took a breath—"tomatoes, green onions, and black olives."

"Seven-layer dip?" Zoe frowned. "I counted eight."

"Sour cream and taco seasoning are one. We're one, too." Maria smiled a little and extended her glass. "Here's to the *Perimenopausal Women with Power Tools*."

"Lo-ove." Corrine chortled and clinked with Therese and Maria.

Beth tipped her glass in solidarity.

A grin plastered across her face, Zoe raised her glass above her head.

When the timer rang its symbolic approval, the five friends erupted in laughter.

Beth drank a quick toast. "We can finish our appetizers in here or move to the table." She motioned toward the adjoining dining room and hustled to quiet the timer.

"We're making a move," called Zoe.

The women reconvened in the kitchen then ferried food and a replenished pitcher of margaritas to the dining room table.

"Cheers to our hostess." Therese lifted her glass.

"Hear, hear, and to Perimenopausal Women with Power Tools." Zoe flashed a dimpled smile.

Grinning, the group toasted themselves and each other then filled their plates with chicken enchiladas, stuffed peppers, and southwestern salad.

Zoe turned to Maria. "How was your ultrasound and blood work?"

"Not good." Maria chewed her bottom lip. "We're still hoping I'll ovulate, but I haven't yet. Hence, I can enjoy a cocktail or two without fretting."

Glancing down, Beth inhaled savory spices and straightened her napkin, fearful her eyes might reveal her veiled longing.

Maria tapped a knife against her glass. "This margarita is the best ever."

"Tell us about our new name." Corrine steepled her fingers.

"For the last several weeks, I've read a ton about perimenopause, menopause, and a plethora of acronyms…" Maria took a deep breath. "So, I added PWWPT to the mix."

"I think I might be one P short—WWPT. Tell me everything I need to know." Zoe speared a bite of enchilada.

"How old are you?" Therese leaned forward.

"Thirty-eight." Zoe cocked her head. "What about you?"

"I have eight years on you." Tucking her thumbs,

Therese held up eight fingers.

"Same. AKA forty-six." Corrine turned to her left. "Do you mind saying your age?"

"I'm fifty-seven." Beth glanced at Maria. *Old enough to be your mom.* She drank long enough for the boozy cold to soothe the burn in her throat.

"And I'm thirty-one." Maria set down her glass.

"I'm the *queen* of PMS." Zoe tapped her chest with her thumbs. "So, what's this perimenopausal stuff?"

"Peri means around. Some women have changes fifteen years before menopause, but the average is about four." Maria brushed the back of her neck. "Sorry. The nurse in me can talk about anything— anytime and anywhere. Not sure about the rest of you."

"Fifteen?" Zoe grimaced. "*Gross.*" She turned to Beth. "Are you having any symptoms?"

"Trouble sleeping which could be from…" She scratched her head. "The insomnia started last year. And I've had a few hot flashes."

"What are the symptoms?" Corrine sawed a bite of stuffed pepper.

Maria reached into a pocket. "Should we wait until we're done eating?"

"Go for it, and we'll cut you off if we need to." Therese raised her eyebrows. "Deal?"

The others nodded.

Tapping open her phone, Maria typed and scrolled then cleared her throat.

"I don't know if I'm ready for this." Zoe hugged her shoulders and tucked her head.

"Sorry." Maria set her phone on the table.

Zoe flapped her hands. "*Just kidding.*"

"This list is long." Maria refreshed her screen.

"Bloating, cramping, breast tenderness, irregular periods"—she took a breath—"headaches, migraines, forgetfulness, weight gain, insomnia—"

Therese whistled. "No wonder I'm a wreck."

"Plus dry skin, dry hair, joint pain, crying jags, mood swings"—she downed a quick drink—"heart palpitations, irritability, stress incontinence, decreased libido, and hot flashes. AKA per-i-men-o-pause." She dragged out the word.

"Ugh. Sounds like P M S on steroids." Zoe sputtered a breath. "I am *so* in the club." She looked at Therese. "How long have you been?"

"About a year. My mom was fifty-two." Therese shuddered. "I hope I don't have six more years."

Beth shifted her gaze to Mary and Baby Jesus— covered in red velour. Sadness scraped her throat. She knew her mom had "gone through the change" at fifty, but they never talked specifics. *We didn't talk about a lot of things.*

"Is that what they say?" Zoe widened her eyes. "You'll be the same age as your mom?"

Beth twitched her head, so slight she hoped no one noticed.

"You *might* be. One of my library books says it's the essential book for every woman over thirty-five." Maria fluttered finger quotation marks. "But the average age for menopause is fifty-one, so not everyone needs to dive in that early."

Like me. Preferring to listen, she kept her words to herself.

"Judging from the way I'm going, I have one thing to say." Zoe rested her forearms on the table. "I Better Borrow That Book."

"Ditto." Therese grinned. "Speaking of, what are the rest of you reading?"

"I'm in the middle of the best book." Corrine rested a hand high on her chest. "*Everything I Never Told You...*"

Beth had been to the library once in the past month. She had transitioned from grief books but had nothing to say. When the conversation segued to movies, she was pierced by a stab of loneliness regarding her solitary life. Slipping to the kitchen, she brewed a pot of coffee.

She concentrated on dessert, savoring every bite of melt-in-your-mouth flan. Reluctant to say so out loud, she was ready for her guests to leave so she could change into her makeshift pajamas and curl into Reid's recliner.

"Dinner was great." Zoe folded her napkin. "Let's get together again soon."

"You could come to my house." Corrine raised her glass.

"Would we be banishing Sheldon?" Maria leaned in.

"No." Corrine shook her head. "I'm sure he could find something to do."

"Come here." Beth's voice was soft—her emotions see-sawing as she sampled the words. She took a deep breath. "Having you here has been great." Her words felt convincing and clear as she glanced around the table.

"I'd like that." Maria clasped her hands.

The others chorused their agreement. They tossed around menu ideas and settled on an appetizer theme in January.

Zoe lifted the last of her margarita. "To PWWPT."

The women clinked with a beverage smorgasbord—coffee, tea, and margaritas, both virgin and leaded—and toasted their blossoming friendship.

After nipping offers to leave the leftovers and help with the dishes, Beth accompanied her friends to the door.

"Thanks again for a delightful evening." Corrine gave her a one-armed hug.

Beth squeezed back. "Thanks for coming." *This dinner was huge.*

"Is this table a Shaker?" Therese skimmed a hand across the sleek entryway table.

"Mm-hmm." She stroked the table's edge with a thumb. "Reid made this—" *For our anniversary.* The words caught in her throat.

"He was a woodworker?" Therese tipped her head.

She nodded. "He loved his shop. Kate's welcome to come over and use the wood and whatever. You could come with her if you'd like."

Therese met her gaze. "I'll tell her."

"Back out into the cold." Zoe nested her pot with one arm and hugged Beth with the other. "Thanks again for your toasty home and warm hospitality."

After thank-you hugs around, the four guests exited into the frosty air.

Shivering, Beth locked the door. She trailed her fingertips over the Shaker and bowed for a gentle kiss. *I miss you, Reid.* Then she sidetracked to the living room and closed the curtains. The tree stood sentry over the deafening quiet. She rummaged through their CDs and pulled out his favorite Christmas jazz. Wrapping herself in a fleece throw, she collapsed into his recliner, pulled out her journal, and uncapped her pen.

December Eleventh

Dear Darling,

Dinner was a success. The meal was great and the company was delightful, but I missed you. I didn't put on Christmas CDs—they would've made me miss you even more—so we dined without music. "Boogie Woogie Santa Claus" is playing now though. Once the gang left, I couldn't stand the quiet.

Pouring cream and sugar reminded me of opening our wedding gifts. Remember how thrilled I was when I unwrapped the shamrock sugar and creamer from your great-aunt Mayme? I love that set, but it's been squirreled away since...you know.

No one asked for a tour, and I didn't offer one. I put your urn in the closet for thirty seconds then on my dresser for ten then back on your bedside table. Not that your ashes are a secret...I just wish you were here instead of an urn. Like hiding your ashes would change anything. Finding your coats in the hall closet about put me over the edge.

Beth ran her fingertips over her words. A part of her wanted to untangle from the chair and beeline to the closet to swap the comforter for Reid's navy fleece. Instead, she let out a slow breath and righted her pen.

The crew liked your tree. I didn't tell them the story—I struggled with words all night. Therese complimented the entryway table, and I wanted to say you made the Shaker for our anniversary but couldn't. Will talking about you ever get any easier?

I offered your leftover wood to her daughter. Did I tell you about Kate? She's wanted to become an orthopedic surgeon since kindergarten. Now, she wants to make furniture. Therese fears Kate might regret her decision but is acclimating to the idea her daughter will craft wood instead of bone.

Do you have regrets, Reid? I do. I wish I would've spent some time with you in your shop—learning from you and watching you work. I'm not even sure what kind of wood you have. Had. Neither sounds right. I just know you left a lot.

Thank you for making your earmuffs, glasses, and tape measure so easy to find. Going into your shop was a challenge, and I'm not ready to go back. Why did I say Kate could have your wood? I wish I could rewind... Therese didn't jump on the offer, so maybe they'll pass. I hope they will. I miss you and love you more.

After closing her journal, she stared at the irises until they blurred into a shapeless mass. She did *not* want to return to his shop. Plus, being around kids was *too damn hard.* But she had never told him that sliver of truth. How could she start now?

****

A week later, caller ID displayed Therese's number. Beth reached for the phone then drew back her hand. Her stomach clenched. *I spoke too soon.*

The ringing stopped, and the outgoing message clicked on.

Just tell her. Bracing herself against the counter, she picked up the phone. "Hello?"

"Hi, Beth. Two things—actually three. Thank you so much for the lovely dinner. I'd like to reciprocate on Christmas and have you join Kate, my parents, and me."

While Beth waited for number three, she grappled

for an excuse.

"We'll eat about five, but you'd be welcome anytime in the afternoon...unless you already have plans."

I don't. "Thanks but I—" She let out a soft sigh. "I'm planning a quiet day at home." *Like last year.*

"Would you mind coming over? You could eat and run. Kate is interested in the wood, which is the third reason I'm calling—I don't want to barge in when she's never even met me." Therese took a breath. "She's a dandy... Anyway, holidays have got to be so hard. Could you manage an hour?"

No thank you. The countertop's edge dug into her hipbone, but she didn't budge. Saying *no* seemed harsh, though, as if she were nixing dinner *and* Kate. *Which is what I'd like to do.* She cupped a hand over her eyes. "Tell Kate she's welcome anytime."

"Forty-five minutes? I don't mean to nag, but we'd love to have you."

She pinched the bridge of her nose. "Okay." Her mouth rearranged itself—*I'm sorry* morphing into the solitary word, almost inaudible.

"Wonderful. Kate will be thrilled."

The smile in Therese's voice did little to untangle the knot in Beth's gut. "What can I bring?"

"Do you have a favorite Christmas dish?"

Reid loved candied yams. "Baklava and au gratin potatoes." Beth straightened and shrugged. "Not very traditional, so tell me what you'd like."

"Au gratin potatoes would be great." Therese gave her the address and directions. "I'm glad you're joining us."

So am I. She swallowed her lie.

****

Five days later, Beth settled at the kitchen table with a pen and notepad and a steaming cup of coffee. Sunlight streamed in through the large window and warmed the breakfast nook. Yesterday, she shoveled snow three times—seven inches, according to the newspaper—but today's forecast was sunny and dry. She was thankful she didn't have sidewalks. Shoveling the driveway and walkway had always felt like plenty of exercise, more so since she was alone. She had put off shopping—self-preservation to avoid holiday music and Christmas cheer—but with dinner just three days away, she buckled down and jotted her list. Then she added three bullet points: bookstore, grocery store, and HOME.

Hopeful the streets would be packed or plowed by then, she didn't leave until early afternoon. As she traversed the city, covered in a meringue of snow, she offered thanks for snowplows and their operators, for conscientious drivers, and for all-season tires. Muscle memory directed her downtown and across the Higgins Bridge—her favorite of the four Missoula bridges spanning the Clark Fork River.

She parked in the Central Park Garage. Already thirty-one degrees, working toward a predicted high of thirty-three, the sunshine warmed her face as she strolled one block to Fact and Fiction. Instead of stopping at the counter to buy the planned gift cards, she meandered through the store. Perusing the shelves, she slowed, focusing on books marked F AND F BOOKSELLER FAVORITE or MONTANA AUTHOR.

Circling past Fiction, Collections, Poetry, and

Mystery, she read the back covers of some books and gave cursory glances to others. A small book with a green dinosaur and melancholic title gave her pause. *All my friends are dead.* She picked up the book for a quick look. The milk jug's morose "All my friends expired on Tuesday" caused her to laugh out loud.

A woman beside her smiled.

Beth smiled back and wanted to share the picture that forced a laugh. She contemplated buying the book but decided not to do that either. On her way to the front, a book cover captured her gaze—*Wood Work: A Step-By-Step Photographic Guide to Successful Woodworking.* She stiffened. *Reid has that book.* Had. *Reid* had *that book.* As she remembered the intimacy of a summer afternoon months before he died, sorrow wrapped itself around her chest, strangling her breath. They had sat side by side on the patio with glasses of Cabernet. His delight was tangible, and he had turned every single page.

"Give the book to Kate."

I'll give the book to Kate. His words overlapped hers. Thickness rose in her throat. She stood, taking a moment before using both hands to lift the tome. She balanced the book on her forearm and palm and browsed its pages, debating whether to buy this copy or resurrect the one from home. *How would she feel getting a dead guy's book?* The words and their speed surprised her. *Must be the dinosaur book.* Reid's voice replayed in her mind. *His book* was the one she was thinking of, and she was certain he was, too. She returned the store's copy to the shelf.

Reconsidering gift cards, she continued her surveillance of highlighted books. She added a new filter, though, recent copyright dates, hoping to select a title Therese hadn't read. Beth chose a FAVORITE, *All the Light We Cannot See*, and picked up a second copy for herself before heading to pay.

A customer slid three picture books across the counter then pulled a canvas bag from his pocket.

The infant in his front pack gurgled and cooed—flapping and wriggling bright pink arms and purple legs as though primed for takeoff.

Since hearing Maria's story, Beth was on heightened alert and noticed babies and baby bumps everywhere. She stepped to the side and studied the baby.

"How old is your little helper?" The bookseller slid *My Grandfather's Coat* into the bag.

"She was eight months old yesterday." The dad stroked her cheeks. "We've been reading to you since before you were born, haven't we?"

His singsong voice and loving touch spurred a yearning she had battled for years. Beth scooted behind him so his body created a shield between her and the baby. Her heart ached—for herself *and* for her friend. While she completed her transaction, she was quiet, and her parting "thank you" was laced with sadness. *One more stop.* She trudged to her car then drove less than a mile to Orange Street Food Farm, which she hadn't visited for nearly two weeks.

On the cusp of Christmas, the store bustled with customers.

Some maneuvered overflowing shopping carts.

Others had baskets slung over their arms.

Their faces encompassed an array of frowns, smiles, arched brows, parted lips, and blank stares.

Stress, joy, and in-between. As holiday music played in the background, she worked on maintaining a neutral expression. Mercifully, the songs were upbeat. "I'll Be Home for Christmas" or another like it would drive her out the door—groceries be damned. She scored everything on her list, including walnuts and phyllo dough for the baklava she planned to take to Therese's. Browsing the wine selection, she added bottles of Pinot Noir and Sauvignon Blanc then navigated to the holiday aisle for gift wrap.

She wheeled to the front and angled her cart so customers could get by while she waited her turn. Third in line, she scanned the magazines. One cover story announced "Twenty-five Most Intriguing People." A single word opposite—"Farewells"—and its accompanying photo sucked her in. She had loved Robin Williams and been crushed by his death. Words from August replayed in her head. *RIP Robin and Reid.* She inched forward and was thankful to reach the conveyer belt. "Rudolph the Red-Nosed Reindeer" played over the speakers. Emptying her cart, she started with dairy and ended with wine.

The cashier hummed as she worked. As she skimmed Beth's Greek yogurt across the scanner, she smiled. "Are you ready for the holidays?"

"Almost." Beth forced a half-smile. "Are you?"

"Getting there." She resumed her humming then paused again to hand the receipt. "Have a good one."

"You, too." *I'm dreading every holiday minute.* Beth glanced away, hoping her expression didn't reveal her unease. Driving down Stephens Avenue, she scarcely noticed the light-strewn trees and holiday decorations dotting porches and lawns. When she arrived home, she gathered her books and groceries, three reusable bags in one hand and two in the other, then deposited the lot onto the kitchen counter. She didn't waste time unpacking her bags before circling to the entertainment center and freeing Reid's book.

As she flipped through *Wood Work*'s front pages, she held her breath. *Not a single mark.* Spluttering an exhale, she carried the book to his recliner. Part of her hoped she would find a trace of him—something written somewhere. If she did, though, she wouldn't part with the book. She scoured the tome. Four hundred pages later, she reached the end without evidence of Reid having devoured them.

A mixture of regret and relief churned through her. Beth shifted her gaze from the book to the tree. One she would keep, and the other she would tuck in her memory bank. She clutched *Wood Work* to her chest and carried it to the coffee table then returned to the kitchen to put away the groceries.

The following afternoon, she measured and cut sheets of gift wrap, regretting her haste in grabbing the paper off the shelf. Sprigs of holly wove through scripted words—*Have a Holly Jolly Christmas. As if.* She wrapped Therese's book then flipped through *Wood Work*, giving it one final caress before enveloping it in holiday cheer. Tendrils of loneliness corkscrewed around her. She placed the gifts under the tree and retreated to Reid's recliner. Hunkering in, she immersed herself in the story of Marie-Laure and her sightless world.

She waited to make baklava until the next evening. "Today is Christmas Eve, Reid." She pulled the chopper from a bottom cupboard, and memories swirled through her mind.

Months after she had bought the chopper at a cooking party, Reid diced onion and green pepper. "This kitchen gadget is my favorite." That December, having chopped veggies numerous times, he had helped make baklava for the first time ever.

How many years ago, Reid? I don't remember. Her soliloquy was silent while she unrolled the phyllo dough. *I'm forgetting a lot…grief's whammy? Maria would say perimenopause is causing my amnesia. I hope she's right. Not sure I'll regain my memory once I'm through the peri part, though.*

She wanted him to talk. He did in her dreams and sometimes, when she was awake, she felt his words bone deep. But she didn't now. "I want to hear your voice." Her plea pierced the throbbing silence. Overcome by the hush, she detoured to the living room and combed through their CDs. She put on one of his favorites, "Blue Christmas," and then plodded to the kitchen. Chopping with a vengeance, she drowned in Elvis's words and swatted away her tears.

On Christmas morning, Beth teetered between wake and sleep. She willed herself back to Reid, Glacier Park, and Avalanche Creek. They had just passed Avalanche Gorge on their way to the lake: the creek roared, cedar permeated the air, and Reid ambled beside her—his Indiana Jones hat bouncing with every step.

She struggled to return to her dream then acquiesced to dreamless sleep instead. The harder she tried, the wider awake she felt. Cocooned on his side of the bed, she opened one eye and peeked at the clock. Seven twenty-four. A crush of loneliness replaced the rush of the creek, and she squeezed her eyes shut. Desperate to postpone the inevitable, she fought for slumber. Ten minutes passed then fifteen. Finally, her pursuit hopeless, she sat up and hugged the urn to her chest. "Merry Christmas, Darling." She leaned her head against the smooth, cool wood. *I'm not going.* Absent Reid, she craved solitude and the warmth of memories. *Not* dinner at Therese's. *But seven forty-five is too early to call.*

Chapter Seven

An hour later, Beth returned the urn to the bedside table. *I'll call in a little bit.* She trudged to the kitchen and operated on autopilot: grinding beans, retrieving a coffee filter, and filling the pot half full as she had for months. While the coffee brewed, she slipped her coat over her robe and headed outside.

The morning was sunny and crisp, and the yard and trees glistened like diamonds. Though yesterday's snow cemented a white Christmas, she was grateful she did not need to shovel. The arctic air was a welcome respite as she removed the newspaper from its delivery tube. She tucked the paper under her arm then checked the mailbox she neglected the day before. Sandwiched between a credit card offer and a nonprofit newsletter was a pale gold envelope postmarked Rockville, Maryland, with no return address. *No one I know.* After entering the house, she dropped the card into the entryway drawer. She had ditched her plan to read Christmas cards. *Not today and maybe never.*

She retrieved a pair of unread newspapers from the top of the refrigerator and poured herself a cup of coffee. Then she gathered the papers and mug and carried them to the living room, setting the collection on Reid's table before plugging in the tree lights. She caressed a silver ornament and a wave of sadness crashed over her—its icy nip driving her to burrow under a fleece comforter in the warmth of his recliner. She wrapped her hands around her mug then sipped her coffee to quell the chill.

Once her body warmed, she started with the oldest newspaper, skimming its headlines. "Joe Cocker Dies at Seventy of Lung Cancer." Air stilled in her lungs. She tipped back her head against the yielding leather and surrendered to the memories.

Newlyweds, barely four months in, she and Reid had strolled to World Theatre to see *An Officer and a Gentleman*. When Richard Gere swept Debra Winger into his arms, she sobbed. "Up Where We Belong" encored during the credits, and tears pricked at her eyes.

That night, Reid carried her into their bedroom, crooning the chorus in a raspy voice. He gave her the movie soundtrack that Christmas, and she still had the LP thirty-two years later.

Joe had fifteen years on you, Reid. "You promised…" Her words rang angry and loud. But how could he know they wouldn't dance to David Bowie's "Golden Years" when they were old and gray? She spread her fury between him and Life and Whoever took him away.

When she was young, she had trusted in God's goodness and attended a Methodist church with her parents. But her heart shattered in college and she stopped believing, certain a loving Father would *not* allow such agony. Learning about Jake reinforced her conviction. Driven by memories of setting up the family manger with her mom and dad, she bought the Nativity set after she married. But nostalgia prompted her purchase—nothing more.

Beth tossed the newspapers onto the floor. She curled into a fetal position, tumbling into the recliner's warm embrace. "I miss you, Darling." She stroked her wedding band with her index finger and thumb. *I miss you.*

An hour later, she woke. She straightened, raising her hands overhead and stretching her neck side to side. Her temporary slumber was a welcome reprieve, and she contemplated her decision to ditch dinner. A solitary evening still felt right. *I'd be miserable company anyway.* She made a piece of toast and opened then closed the refrigerator door, leaving the butter unclaimed. Since baklava would be her entire Christmas dinner, she ate her toast dry.

All morning and into the afternoon, she avoided the telephone. At one o'clock, she slogged into the kitchen and picked up the handset. Carrying the phone to the silent backing of Reid's recliner, she rehearsed her words. She scrolled through the history and her stomach twisted as she tapped past Rachel's number.

Rachel's tender tone and words were always the same. "Just wanted to let you know we're thinking of you. I'd love to talk or get together when you're ready. Love you," plus "we'd love to have you come for Christmas" added last week.

The four of them had had so much fun together— she and Reid and Rachel and Jeff. True-blue friends…she knew that separate or together, they would bathe her in comfort and envelope her with love. But the thoughts of their stories, either silent or spoken, were still too hard. *She* wanted to be the driver of the memory bus.

Call Therese. She looked at the lone gifts under the

tree—the bottle of Pinot Noir adorned with red and green ribbon and the pair of books. Sauvignon Blanc and baklava chilled in the refrigerator. She'd deliver them tomorrow or the day after—minus the baklava.

"Go."

The word rocketed through her. She longed to hear Reid's voice but not now. "I don't want to." She stared across the room. Her vision blurred, and the books and wine morphed into one. She and Reid stopped exchanging gifts years ago, making donations to organizations in each other's honor instead. Donating to their passions became more pleasurable than unwrapping shiny packages. She made donations this year, too, "in honor of" as before, unable to transition to "in memory of."

"Shit or get off the pot."

"You." She wanted him here—not old words that used to make her smile. Shifting in the chair, she turned away from the gifts, unwilling to glimpse even a speck of *Holly Jolly*. The telephone screen faded to black, concealing Therese's number. *Maybe a sign.* She glanced at her watch. One twenty. *A sign of procrastination.* She ran a hand over the leather armrest.

"Go."

His voice was a breath above a whisper. She folded her hands and tucked them under her chin. "Okay." Resignation colored her voice. "I'll go." Beth unrolled from the recliner and crossed to the tree. Butterfly soft, she cupped a maroon ornament and stroked it with her thumb. Ignoring her urge to plant a kiss, she stepped away then turned and blew one before hurrying to the kitchen.

Wishing she set out the slow cooker the previous

day, she opened the cupboard and grabbed the cookbook. Once she finished the baklava, though, she collapsed into his chair, telling herself she'd have something to do in the morning. Now, she regretted the decision that seemed so sensible the day before. She always cooked au gratin potatoes on low. Holding her breath, she flipped to page twenty-nine and shifted her gaze to the recipe's end. *High: three hours.*

She spluttered an exhale and glanced at the oven clock. One twenty-eight. She had seventeen minutes, plus cooking time, to prepare the potatoes and leave by four forty-five. Not her usual MO, getting by by the skin of her teeth, but today she had no other choice. She gathered the ingredients then scrubbed, sliced, shredded, layered, and plugged in the pot before rechecking the time. One forty-nine. Weighted by melancholy, she headed to the shower—unconvinced she should heed Reid's nudge.

Three hours later, she backed out of her driveway. Four days past winter solstice, the inch toward additional daylight had just begun. Last year, December twenty-first passed without notice. She applauded the solstice this year, basking in the promise of brighter nights ahead. Holiday displays and Christmas lights illuminated the evening.

At Therese's house, she exited the car then paused before removing the potatoes. *This dinner will be good. I'm where I'm meant to be.* Affirmations looped through her mind. She brushed a hand across her knotted belly, willing it to relax. Tiny white lights twinkled from the porch railing. A Christmas tree, hung with novelty bulbs like the ones boxed in her closet, cast a multicolored glow through the picture window.

She lifted the potatoes from the car floor, and then forced one foot in front of the other on her way to the house. When she rang the doorbell, she exhaled a noisy breath that hung in the air like a wispy cloud.

Behind one of the frosted panes bordering the door, a shadowy figure approached. The door opened, revealing a brown-eyed teen. "C'mon in—I'm Kate." The aroma of baked ham wafted onto the porch.

"Beth." She handed her the slow cooker. "I'll be right back." A hodgepodge of emotions flowed through her veins. Working slow, even breaths, she hurried to the car. She packed the rest for a single trip—the books and baklava snugged in a rectangular cardboard box and the wine bagged and cushioned with newspaper. Sliding an arm through the strap, she shouldered the bag then gathered the box. She shut the door with a foot and lumbered up the walk.

Kate reopened the door and welcomed her inside.

Therese greeted her in the living room. "Thanks so much for coming."

"Thank you for having me." She shifted her smile from mother to daughter.

"Nice to meet another perimenopausal woman." Kate grinned and scooted past—slow cooker in hand.

Therese gave a single nod. "That's my baby..." She extended her hands. "Let me help."

My baby. Sorrow nipped her heart. Shushing old memories, she slid the bag from her shoulder and handed it to Therese. Then she reached into the box and removed the foil-wrapped plate. "Here's a Christmas tradition, plus something for you and Kate." She nodded at the gifts.

"Thank you." Therese gestured with an elbow.

"You can put the presents under the tree."

Grateful for the breather, she stepped to the right. *Douglas-fir*. She squatted and placed the gift-wrapped books atop the red-and-green plaid skirt, and then slid the empty cardboard box to the back. A cluster of craft-stick creations commanded her attention: a snowman, a Christmas tree, Santa, and Rudolph. The handmade decorations added a burst of color to the array of ornaments and gold garland. She stood. "Your tree is lovely."

"I help, but Kate's the director. I don't know what I'll do when—"

Kate swept into the room with her grandparents in tow. "Helen and Frank..." She waved an arm. "And Beth."

Greetings and coat shedding followed.

Then Therese tipped her head.

Beth followed, taking in the home that shouted *Christmas*. Every surface and wall was adorned with a symbol of holiday cheer: reindeer, Santas, elves, carolers, a miniature train, nutcrackers, angels, and a bowlful of glass bulbs. *Lovely*. Though she enjoyed her friend's festive displays, she doubted if *her* Mr. and Mrs. Santa and all the rest would ever again see the light of day.

In the kitchen, Therese set the wine beside a cinnamon-scented candle with plastic holly leaves encircling its base. She met her gaze. "How are you doing?"

"Am I an open book?" Beth ran a hand over her face.

"No-o, but you'd mentioned a quiet day at home..." Edging closer, Therese narrowed her eyes.

"Yeah." She glanced at the candle. "I almost bailed."

"I'm glad you didn't." Therese drew her into a hug.

She melted into the embrace. *The jury's still out.*

"Is Grandpa's wine ready yet?" Kate's voice preceded her into the kitchen.

Therese gripped the bottle of Pinot Noir with a wine opener and depressed the lever down and up—swift and fluid.

"Smooth as silk." Therese and Kate's voices blended as one.

Therese poured a glass and raised her eyebrows.

Kate shook her head. "She'll wait until dinner."

"Tell them dinner will be on the table in ten. Then come back and help."

"Gotcha." Kate flashed a smile and turned toward the door.

You look like your mom. Their likenesses, chocolate brown eyes and sinewy builds, twisted Beth's gut. Therese's silent question and Kate's easy answer did, too. A tug of war ensued as part of her delighted in the tenderness, while the other part pined for the solitude of home.

"Would you like a glass?" Therese raised the red wine.

"Sure." She smoothed her sweater. "What can I do?"

"Get the salad out of the fridge, please. Top shelf—and dressings are inside the door."

She opened the refrigerator and removed the salad. Its crowded shelves dwarfed her own. The table was worthy of a magazine photo shoot: red-and-green plaid napkins and tablecloth, gold chargers, and holly china and glassware. She set the salad beside the centerpiece—an arrangement of pinecones, red ribbon, and a trio of green tapers. Juggling the salad dressings, she made a second trip.

Kate returned and arranged the rolls on a cookie sheet then slid them into the oven.

"You can use that dish and spoon for the potatoes." Therese interrupted her carving and flicked the fork toward the counter.

"Thanks." Beth uncovered the slow cooker and set the lid upside down. "Where are—"

"I'll help." Kate handed her a pair of pot holders and picked up the serving spoon.

Beth lifted the crock from its base and tipped it toward the dish.

As Kate scooped the potatoes, she took a deep inhale. "Cheesy potatoes—they smell delish." She filled the dish then started toward the oven. "Will you please grab my pretzel salad out of the fridge?"

A smile tugged at the corners of Beth's lips. She retrieved the glass dish showcasing the tricolored salad and carried it to the table. "Looks luscious."

"World famous…" Kate shot a grin over her shoulder.

Frank and Helen strolled into the kitchen, arm in arm.

"Did we stay away long enough?" Frank's eyes twinkled.

"We wanted to help…" Helen placed a hand high on her chest. "Therese banished us to the TV room to watch *White Christmas*."

"Speak for yourself. I like being treated like a king. But don't let these two fool you…" Frank wagged a hand between Therese and Kate. "They always manage to come and watch the good parts."

His eyes were the color of his daughter and granddaughter's. Beth shifted her gaze to Helen, whose eyes were robin's egg blue. Memories of holidays with her dad and mom floated into consciousness. A familiar ache filled her chest, its edges laced with regret. *You would have loved a grandchild.*

"Will Your Majesty please carry the wine to the table?" Therese smiled from her dad to her mom. "You earned your get-out-of-the-kitchen-free card a long time ago."

Helen straightened her pearls, fiddling with them as she stepped away from the counter.

"Your favorite, Grandma." Kate lifted a green bean casserole.

Beth wanted to hand Helen the potatoes so she could help, too. Instead, she carried the serving dish to the table. Her heart hurt—her sorrow floating between memories of her parents and Reid. *You would have loved this gathering.* She sat beside Helen and unfolded her napkin.

"Let's pray." Helen bowed her head. "Bless us O Lord and these thy gifts…"

Childhood words learned by rote, she joined in.

"Now, time to eat." Kate speared a slice of ham.

They circled the food around the table.

When Beth returned the beans to their starting position, she surveyed the meal. The tossed salad was reminiscent of a bejeweled tree, and Kate's pretzel salad duplicated the colors of reindeer and candy canes. She gazed at the potatoes, ham, and rolls—the entire feast a kaleidoscope of color and love. *Unlike my planned baklava-for-one.*

Frank rallied their glasses for a midair huddle. "*L'chaim!*"

To life. Absorbing the words, Beth took a long, slow drink. She coasted through the meal—participating in the conversation some but more so savoring each bite, sitting back, and listening.

After dinner, Kate directed them to the living room. "Sit there…" She motioned toward a burgundy glider then handed Beth two gifts. "You first."

She ran a hand over the shiny paper, covered with gingerbread people. Arms splayed, the cookies looked posed to smother her with hugs. The gift tag read *To Beth, From Therese and Kate.* With care, she freed the tape then smoothed out the gift wrap. She opened the box and uncovered a sheer scarf with swirls of black, beige, teal, and rust. "Thank you." Draping the scarf around her neck, she luxuriated in its silken caress.

"You're welcome. FYI, I wouldn't wear that scarf with red." Kate swiped her hand under her chin.

"So says the fashion queen." Therese arched her eyebrows.

"I'm just being helpful." Kate scooted forward. "I do like your sweater, though. Now open your other one."

Beth glanced at Therese. *You'll miss her.* She unfolded the gift card. "Merry Christmas and Happy New Year to Beth from Kate." Reading aloud, she smiled then plucked tufts of red and white tissue from the Santa bag. Inside were two Posh Chocolat bars. "Crushed Brazilian Coffee Beans and Apricot Pumpkin Seed—*yum.*" She held one in each hand. "Would anyone like some?"

"They're all yours. I got hints from her." Kate smiled and flicked a thumb. "Your turn, Mom."

"You—"

"I'm last." Kate folded her hands on her chest.

"Okay then." Therese balanced her gift on her lap. Running a finger under the seam, she loosened the tape. She revealed the back cover, and a smile blossomed across her face. "ESP—this book is on my TBR list."

"She means To Be Read, Grandpa." Holding her palms parallel to each other, Kate moved them left, center, and right. "Momma's rocking the acronyms."

Momma. A memory of Beth's college roommate's term of endearment flashed through her mind. She bit her lip, fighting its quiver.

"What's the title?"

Helen's question pulled her back. She repositioned her scarf and eyed Therese.

"*All the Light We Cannot See*—this book received stellar reviews." Therese turned the cover toward her parents, seated on the couch. "Plus it's an NBA finalist—National Book Award."

"Second dibs." Helen raised a hand.

Frank curled his hands around his mouth. "Third."

His makeshift megaphone made Beth smile.

"Not if I get my hands on Momma's book before you do." Sitting cross-legged on the floor, Kate rubbed her palms together.

"Whatever you have there might keep you busy, missy." He gestured toward her lap.

Kate tore a zigzag line between *Holly Jolly* then parted the paper. She righted the book, and a smile filled her face. Skimming her fingers over the cover art, she met Beth's gaze. "*Thank you.*"

The reverence in her hands and face were palpable. Beth swallowed hard. "You're welcome." *Reid loved that book.*

"Let's see." Frank leaned in.

"Hold your horses, Grandpa." Kate flipped through the pages.

Watching Kate devour Reid's book like he had unfurled a mishmash of joy, longing, and regret. The reactions collided in Beth's chest, squeezing her breath.

Frank gave a loud sigh. "My horses are getting tired."

"Check out this garden bench." Kate tipped the book. "Beth said I could use…" She parted her lips in a tiny *o*.

"Reid's shop." She took a deep breath. "You can use the wood and tools and whatever's out there." His words flowed from her mouth. A current of electricity shot down her spine. She grazed her wedding band with a thumb.

"This one is a woodworking wizard." Frank extended an arm.

Red and yellow tree lights reflected off Beth's ring. *You were stellar, too, Reid.*

"A wizard?" Kate gave a little laugh. "That's a first, Grandpa."

"Well you are." Helen toyed with her pearls.

"Yep." Frank clapped his hands. "You are."

"So, cards now?" Kate turned to Beth. "After dinner, we usually play cards."

She glanced at her Santa bag.

"Honey, Beth didn't sign on to play cards. Unless you'd like to?" Therese tilted her head.

"I appreciate the offer, but I'm heading home." She

tucked her scarf inside her red boiled wool cardigan. "Tonight only—no color clashes in this gal's future."

Kate nodded a grin. "Gotcha."

Frank unfolded from the couch. Extending a hand, he assisted Beth out of the glider.

"You're such a gentleman, Grandpa." Kate untucked her legs, stretching them on the carpet. "Hoist me up, please."

"I'll hoist you up all right." He circled to her and reached for her hands.

"Frank, bend your knees." Helen frowned and crossed her arms.

Straight legged, he grasped Kate's hands.

"Your poor back." Shaking her head, Helen dragged out the words.

Letting go of Kate's right hand, her grandpa spun her under his arm. "Dance or play cards?"

"Play cards." Laughing, she spun in the opposite direction.

What am I rushing home to? Tightness gripped Beth's throat. But her book called, and the comfort and solitude of Reid's recliner beckoned as well. She gathered her gift bag. "Dinner was lovely. Thank you for inviting me."

Goodbye hugs and more thank-yous followed.

Therese retrieved her slow cooker and escorted her to the door. "Thanks again for coming and for everything you're doing for Kate. I knew you two would be fast friends."

"She's darling." Beth gave a final hug and slipped into the frosty night. She gazed at the sky—clear and bursting with stars. A silent verse filled her soul, and she leaned a hip against the car to steady her knees. She clasped the pot and Santa bag and snugged them against her. Both morphed into the memory of a wadded flannel blanket in her empty, aching arms.

The evening's chill returned her to the present. She shivered and chirped open the car then started the engine before fastening her seatbelt. Cinching the buckle into place, she cast a final glance at the house. The multicolored tree shone in the window. Somewhere in the background, the happy family continued their night without her. She blinked hard against the burn in her eyes and pulled away from the curb. "Children laughing, people passing…" The lyrics filtered into her consciousness. She muted the radio and completed her drive in stillness.

Only seven o'clock, winter darkness offered permission to hunker in. She shed her clothes and changed into a pair of Reid's long underwear. The cuffed bottoms ballooned at her ankles. She pinned the waistband then topped the makeshift pajamas with her terry cloth robe. Smoothing her scarf, she tucked it inside the thermal top. The silk against her skin created a visceral reminder of Christmas dinner and her new friends.

Hours earlier, the idea of anything other than baklava-for-one had been beyond her comprehension. No one except Reid knew, though, so no one could consider her fickle, capricious, or an unreliable narrator. She had admitted as much to Therese, but her responding hug was an empathetic acknowledgement of the rollercoaster of grief. Therese suffered heartache of her own then rallied via resilience and grit.

Beth had owned those traits, too, until Reid's death plunged her into a pit. Her budding ascent was slow and sometimes sideways. She drifted into the living room and plugged in the tree lights. Cloaked by the soft glow of the memory keeper, she draped herself in the comforter and dropped into his recliner. Then she opened her journal and set pen to paper.

December Twenty-fifth

Dear Darling,

Thank you for coaxing me out the door today. Goading me, I should say. You needed a big stick to push me across town... I'm glad I joined her family, though. Her parents are delightful, and Kate is a firecracker. She loved the book. I love that the book was yours. Thanks for not writing on the pages, though I did have a moment of regret gifting your tome to her. She's coming in five days. I'm not sure I'm ready.

Regrets? I've had a few... Remember that old Frank Sinatra tune? Wish I could redial and spend some time in your shop with you. What should I do when she comes? Is it safe for her to be out there alone? I don't plan to turn her loose at the onset, but I don't want her to feel as though she's under constant surveillance either.

Beyond regrets, I have much to be thankful for. Hugs and kisses for nudging me this afternoon on my second Christmas without you. I miss you and love you more.

She closed the journal. *What card games are you playing?* She could have stayed and probably should have. Reid had been gone almost fifteen months, but she still navigated the messiness of grief. *I miss you, Darling.* She pulled the journal to her chest. The suffocating ache of solitude gripped her core. She stared at the tree, and the branches, lights, and ornaments blurred under her gaze. *Will my heartache ever lessen?*

****

During the next four days, Beth contemplated visiting Reid's shop. On the morning of the thirtieth, she vowed to go in by noon. Kate would arrive at one.

For days, she practiced "the shop" because she didn't want Kate to feel...what? How *would* an eighteen-year-old feel if she called the room "Reid's shop?" *I have no idea.* But changing the shop's name would *not* change the facts: the shop had been his, everything in it belonged to him, and he was dead. Her glumness made her wonder for the hundredth time if she should call and rescind her offer. Either make up an excuse, or tell the truth, though the latter was too convoluted and private to put into words.

"And how would a broken promise make an eighteen-year-old feel?"

Reid's words pulsed through her.

"Suck it up."

Ignoring him, Beth frittered away the morning. At eleven fifty-nine, she crept toward his shop, her heart skittering.

Three months earlier, everything she needed was within grasp, as though he expected her. His earmuffs and safety glasses poked out of a rainbow sherbet tub on the counter. Beside them—in the shell of an old metal ice cube tray—lay a tape measure, carpenter pencils, pens, and a notepad. She needed the first three plus a pencil, though a number two would have been fine. Finding one of his carpenter pencils had felt golden.

"Thank you." She spoke whisper soft. Pausing in

135

the garage, she cycled through an inhale and exhale before opening the door. A glow from the back window broke the darkness, and she switched on the light. "It's freezing in here." Her words rang loud and critical in the neglected shop. Looking for a space heater, she circled the room. "How did you stay warm?"

She crossed to a tall metal cabinet. Tools…hardware…clamps…*like he'd keep a heater in a cabinet.* She bit her lip. *Kate can't work in this chill.* She needed to call and cancel. Then she'd have time to decide if she wanted to withdraw her offer for good.

"Look up."

His voice unleashed a wave of dizziness. Beth grabbed for the cabinet door. When her vision cleared, she settled her gaze on an electric heater mounted in the opposite corner. "Gotcha." She sensed Reid's applause. *You don't know the rest of the story.* Her pushback was reflexive and silent. Scanning the shop, she zeroed in on a stepladder propped at the counter's end. She carried the ladder to the corner and secured its legs.

Years ago, he had scolded her when he discovered her, paint scraper in hand, balanced atop their old wooden ladder. "Never the top." He gripped the ladder until she had descended one rung.

Remembering the quiver in his voice, she climbed to the top then pressed her shins against the cushioned handle and stretched for the heater. *This ladder is different.* Spinning the heater's dial to high, she exhaled at the first blast of warmth, aware only then she held her breath. She climbed down and glanced around, wondering whether to survey the goods and fake familiarity for Kate's sake. A quick debate ensued. *NO. Wait until she gets here.* She yielded to the emphatic voice and closed the door against the cool garage air. Escaping the reminder of love and loss, she hurried past their cars and into the house. She trudged down the hall, wishing she invited Kate for lunch—a gentle lead-in before entering Reid's shop. *The shop.* She couldn't convince herself either was right.

Chapter Eight

The doorbell chimed at twelve fifty. Expecting ten more minutes to rally her game face, Beth sucked in a deep breath. *Help me.* She sputtered a noisy exhale and plodded to the front. As she opened the door, she forced a smile. "Welcome."

"Thanks." Kate stopped in the entryway. "My mom told me about this table." She skimmed her hand over the sleek wood.

Like mother like daughter. A tsunami of longing gripped her chest.

Pausing at the knob, Kate cocked her head.

She nodded.

Kate opened the drawer, and the Christmas cards shifted inside.

Bracing for pity, she balled her fists and stepped back.

"Gorge." Burying her hands in the drawer, Kate met Beth's gaze. "I'm sorry about your husband. I bet you miss him."

"Thank you. I do—"

The tea kettle's whistle interrupted her words.

Beth gave a "follow me" head tilt. She slowed near the closet. "You can hang your coat in there, and then the kitchen is on your left." A snarl of anticipation, sorrow, and remorse surged through her core, propelling her to the stove. She turned off the burner and struggled to quiet her thoughts.

"Nice house. Can I see the rest? I mean…" Kate dipped her chin. "Sorry. Mom told me not to be bold."

"I'll show you the house in a minute. But first, would you like hot chocolate or tea?"

"Hot chocolate, please. Can I help?"

"Mugs are on the second shelf." She flicked her head then rummaged in a drawer for a tea bag.

"Do you have a favorite?" Kate sifted through the cups.

"Too many, which is why I haven't parted with any." She pinched her upper lip. "I should…" With her household reduced to one, the excess was magnified.

Kate chose mugs from a coffee shop and a chocolate company and turned them face forward on the countertop.

"Perfect." Beth gazed at the selections. *Seattle, two decades ago and Christmas, eleven years ago, or was it twelve?* Refocusing, she removed an orange spice teabag. *Be present.*

"Where's—"

She motioned toward the corner cupboard, feeling a flush of satisfaction at the unfinished question and her swift answer.

Kate dropped to one knee and opened the cupboard door. Two quarter turns later, she found the mix on the top shelf. She opened the plastic lid then tipped the shiny foil seal. Cocking her head, she wrinkled her brow.

"I bought the cocoa for you." A prickle of heat spread from her neck to her face. She brushed her cheek with the back of her hand, uncertain whether hormones or emotions or both set her face on fire.

Peeling the foil, Kate smiled. "I love the marshmallows." She scooped two heaping tablespoons then separated out more marshmallows and added them to her cup.

Beth filled Kate's mug first. From the stove, she watched out of the corner of her eye, waiting until the chocolate was mixed. "We'll let our drinks cool." She waved an arm in a sweeping arc. "The kitchen…"

They looped through the breakfast nook then circled to the dining room.

Kate crossed to the manger and cradled the animals one by one. Cocooning the tiniest lamb in her hand, she bent to give it a kiss then placed the lamb beside its mother, nose to flank. She sidestepped the table and surveyed the Nativity set from a distance.

Thoughts of mommas and babies tiptoed through her mind: lambs and ewes, Jesus and Mary, and Kate and Therese. Beth gripped the back of a chair. *Ssshhh.*

"Where did you get your set?"

The softness in Kate's words and tone suggested the question was a repeat. "The Bon Marche." *The year we were married.*

Kate gave a slow nod. "Maybe some Christmas I could come and visit and draw a blueprint."

"Anytime." She wanted to pat her shoulder and confirm with a touch. Instead, she took a step backward and gestured to the left. "Here we have the living room."

"You're a Griz." Kate beelined to the tree and adjusted a maroon bulb.

"I am." Beth plugged in the lights. "Your mom said you want to go to school in Portland?"

"She did?" Kate widened her eyes.

The surprised expression made her want to retract her words. "She mentioned some school…"

"I don't think she wants me to go there." Kate started toward the door. "What's next?"

They swung through the bathroom and guest room.

In the office, Kate sat on the exercise ball. She bounced a little then rolled sideways and reached for the photo. "*Gorge*. Where were you?"

"On a cruise seven years ago…" Beth placed a hand over her heart.

"Bet you have cool memories."

"I do." Grateful *we* morphed to *I*, she studied the picture over Kate's shoulder. *I miss you, Reid.*

Kate gave the photo a final look before replacing it on the desk. Another bounce and she was up. "I'd like to go on a cruise someday."

We were supposed to go again. She swallowed her words.

"Your mirror." Kate stopped and traced fingertips over the frame. "Good job."

"We had an excellent teacher." The mirror reflected her smile.

"The best." Kate gave a single nod.

She routed to the combination mud and laundry room. Reid called the room the former and she the latter. The washer and dryer were on the left with cupboards and a generous countertop opposite. Her ironing board stood in between, which had made the room her mother's favorite.

Kate claimed Reid's side. "Did he make this bench?" She sat and leaned forward, examining the boot and shoe cubbies underneath.

"Mm-hmm."

"He was a craftsman." She straightened and ran hands along the seat.

Beth gazed at the cubbies and all the rest: the wardrobe, vintage bronze hooks, utility sink, and three-compartment recycling bin. "He loved this room." She tipped her head. "The garage and shop are through that door. We'll head out after we finish our drinks."

"Gotcha."

She saved the master suite, *her* favorite, for last. Through the window, she glanced into her backyard. Beautiful up until months of neglect, she pledged to do cleanup this spring.

Kate scooted to a patch of sunshine streaming through the skylight. She closed her eyes and gave a contented sigh, her palms forward and fingers splayed.

Wanting to strike a Mountain Pose of her own, Beth settled for vicarious living instead. Recalling Therese's words—*Kate's the director*—she imagined the void of her forthcoming absence. A lump rose in her throat.

"That sunshine felt great." Kate crossed to the dresser and picked up an eight-by-ten photo, sun-kissed and faded throughout the years. "Adorbs. Everyone looks so happy—like you really liked each other. Did ya?"

We were happy. She examined the photo: one bride, one groom, and two pairs of parents. "We did like each other, which was nice. Can't imagine otherwise…"

"I don't think Grandpa ever really liked my dad." Kate met her gaze. "How old were you? You look so young."

"Twenty-three and twenty-four." She caressed the

frame with a thumb.

"You went for an older man." Kate winked.

"Younger."

"*Cougar*." She covered her face with a hand. "Sorry—so much for not being bold."

Beth laughed. "Every year we were the same age for six weeks, and then I'd lap him on my birthday."

"Bet he liked being the same age." Kate replaced the photo. Gazing around the room, she moved to Reid's nightstand. "Did he make this piece?"

"No." The question sucked the moisture from her mouth. She glanced at the skylight. *Help me.*

"This is…" Encircling the urn with her hands, Kate drew her eyebrows together.

An urn. "Mahogany." He guided her answer, as light as air.

"I thought so." Kate caressed the wood from top to bottom.

Overcome by her tenderness, Beth wanted to ask if she knew what the urn was. But she didn't.

They returned to the kitchen and carried their drinks to the table.

Sitting across from the brown-eyed beauty rekindled the fierce yearning she battled for years. She hurried through her tea, struggling to soften the ache and silence old memories.

Twenty minutes later, Kate turned a slow pirouette in the middle of Reid's shop, scanning floor to ceiling. "This place is amazing." She stopped in front of the lumber cart. "What was he planning to do with the wood?"

Beth fiddled with her sleeve. *I wish I knew.* Guilt stabbed at her gut.

"Sorry." Kate rubbed the back of her neck. "Talking about him might be hard."

"You're welcome to come over anytime and use whatever you'd like. I could help a little." Unspoken regret peppered her words.

"I'm a wizard, remember? Actually, I was wondering if Grandpa could come with me?" Kate held her gaze.

"Having you both would be lovely." She leaned against the counter. "I bet you make a good team."

"He'll *freak out* when he sees this shop." Kate threw open her arms.

Her enthusiasm made Beth smile. "Seeing him again will be nice."

"We might not come for a while…" Kate sifted through the wood. "I'm not sure when he and Grandma will be down."

"Anytime. Poke around now if you'd like." She motioned toward the cabinet and cupboards. Parallel pulls of wanting to end Kate's visit *now* versus wanting to prolong their time together coursed through her. *You can't have both.*

Kate dug a pad and pencil from the vintage ice cube tray, its levered divider long gone. She opened doors and drawers, revealing jars of hardware, an assortment of clamps, paint and primer, and more. She jotted notes then returned to the lumber cart, moving from the wood to the pencil and paper and back.

You would have loved being a dad, Reid. Beth ran her fingertips over the table saw. *I would have loved being a mom.* Biting the inside of her cheek, she muted the phantom of what might have been. She glanced across the shop. *Will Kate's visits get any easier?*

****

Throughout the following week, Beth was gripped by images of Kate. Taking down the Nativity, putting away Christmas ornaments, and embracing Reid's urn all rushed memories of her spirit and the palpable gentleness in her hands. If she *did* know what the urn housed, she had a comfort with death many adults did not.

She missed her. Blankets of gray and white skies had replaced vicarious basking in sunlight, exaggerating her aloneness. The previous winter, she welcomed isolation. Woodworking class transformed her need for seclusion—somewhat. Time with Kate pecked at a longing she had stifled for years, threatening her very core. But on most days, she wanted more.

****

Two weeks after Kate's visit, the telephone jarred the evening quiet. Beth unfolded from Reid's recliner and wandered into the kitchen to check caller ID. *Sheldon Schmitter. No one I know.* The answering machine clicked on, and she turned from her cheerful voice, recorded years earlier. She recalled hearing about a former coworker who didn't erase his deceased wife's outgoing message. After Reid died, she understood why. On countless days, she yearned to click a button and hear his voice.

"This is Corrine. I was hoping you'd be home—"

She punched a button to intercept the uneven voice. "Hi, Corrine. Sorry, I didn't recognize the name."

"Is it all right if I pop over?"

"Sure." With Corrine's angst tangible, she beamed a hug through the phone line. "When?"

"Be there in fifteen." She hung up without saying goodbye.

Replacing the phone, Beth glanced at the oven clock. Six forty-eight. She contemplated making a pot of decaf or opening a bottle of wine but decided to wait and follow Corrine's lead. After adjusting the thermostat, she turned on the outside lights. Then she did a cursory walk-through, knowing the only thing out of place was the comforter she tossed aside before screening the call.

She set coasters on the coffee table and returned to Reid's recliner. *What's up?* She attempted to read, but the question looped through her mind, blurring the words. When the doorbell rang, she hustled to answer, checking the thermostat along the way. Sixty-seven. *I'll offer her a sweater.* She opened the door.

Corrine bolted inside, and a gust of cold air accompanied her. "I come bearing gifts." She thrust forward a bottle of wine with one hand and enveloped Beth in a hug with the other. "Thanks for letting me bust in."

"Anytime." Beth dangled the wine away from the embrace—power she had never felt from her friend. "You might want to wear your coat until it warms up, or I can give you a sweater."

"I'm so hot right now…" Corrine narrowed her eyes. She shed her jacket, passing the closet without a glance. "Wine time." She strode into the kitchen.

Words muddled in Beth's head. She dug in the utensil drawer and freed the wine opener then retrieved a pair of wineglasses.

Tossing her jacket onto a chair, Corrine grabbed the opener. She popped the cork and poured two generous glassfuls.

Beth threw together dishes of almonds and grapes.

The bottle snugged in the crook of her arm, Corrine lifted a glass with each hand and headed out the door.

What happened? A chill ran through her core. She juggled napkins, plates, almonds, and grapes then joined her friend in the living room.

Corrine sprawled across the couch. She clutched her glass, which was already a quarter empty. "Party of two—that asshole." She spat her words and took a drink.

Her gulp sounded noisy and angry, too. Beth sipped past the thickness in her throat.

"I had to take Gilly, our cat, to the vet this afternoon. Saw a car that looked like Sheldon's at the motel next door, so I did a drive-by when I left." She quaffed another drink. "Dumb schmuck. Thinking he could hide his little convertible between the buildings…I refuse to say the name." She flicked her wrist, palm forward. "Motel hopping? What the hell? I nailed him when he got home. You should've seen his face—all twisted and defiant. 'The first time…blah, blah, blah.' " She gripped her glass. "I don't believe *one word.*"

"I'm sorry." Beth's stomach clenched. *I cannot imagine…* She wanted to maneuver past Corrine's white-knuckled hold and give her a hug.

"The only thing I'm sorry about is marrying the cheap bastard. Except then I wouldn't have Hunter and Sophia."

"You're welcome to stay." She rested a hand on Corrine's leg.

"I told him to pack a bag and go back to his No-

Tell Motel. Or go to his little gold digger's place. Who knows? She might have roommates. Live with her parents. Sleep on a daybed in a tiny studio. *Daybed.*" Corrine snorted. "Young barista banging the boss...I wonder what she thinks that'll get her. Not much, I'll tell ya." She cackled and reached for some almonds. "The end. I told myself driving over, just the facts, ma'am."

"My door's always open. Not literally, but you know what I mean." Beth tipped her glass. "If you ever want some wine or a place to stay..."

"Your home is a haven." Corrine answered with a clink. "So-o, how was your Christmas?"

"I went to Therese's..."

Their conversation cycled through holidays, books, and the upcoming gathering of Perimenopausal Women with Power Tools.

"Thanks again for letting me barge in." Corrine carried the empty bottle and glasses into the kitchen. "I didn't want to call Therese. Kate didn't need to see my vitriol." She pulled on her jacket. "I didn't want to call anyone who knows Sheldon either. Not sure which would be worse—seeing a flash of pity or hearing 'what took you?' I don't mean you were second string..." She linked Beth's arm. "I knew I'd be welcome here."

"Anytime." She snugged close and escorted her friend to the door.

"Thanks." Corrine drew her into a hug then exited into the frosty night.

What would I have done? Beth leaned her head against the doorjamb. The deceit and betrayal...she couldn't go there. Losing Reid by death might have been easier. *Might have.* Her years of deceit rushed through her mind. Could she ever reconcile her guilt?

****

Nine days after Corrine's revelation, Beth added the finishing touches to her dining room table. She considered calling her friend in the ensuing days but hadn't wanted to impose. Had she known on the first night of class the relationships that lay ahead, she would *not* have had to dredge every ounce of courage to exit her car. "Thank you." Her words were as soft as dew as she thanked herself and Reid and her newfound friends.

She was eager to see them and hear about their holidays. Filling the water glasses, she wondered if Maria had any news and wondered if Corrine would share hers. *Maybe Therese already knows.* If Sheldon had cheated before, Therese might not be surprised. But whether the hookup was his first or his fifteen, Corrine's solitude would be no match for hers. *At least she has Gilly and her kids.*

Zoe was first to arrive. "I looked forward to this soirée all afternoon." She extended a towel-wrapped serving dish, keeping four fingers threaded through a wine tote. "Chili relleno cheese squares."

"So have I…" *For days.* Beth smiled and took a deep inhale of the dish warming her forearms and palms. "Your cheese squares smell fabulous."

"These CRCSs are delish. I just made up that acronym." Zoe grinned and stopped at the closet. "Hold this for a sec." She eased the tote handle over Beth's outstretched fingers. Then she peeled off her jacket.

Her smile and familiarity—*with my closet*—flooded Beth's veins with a burst of warmth.

Ding-dong.

"Allow me." Zoe hung her coat and did an about-face. Bobbing her head and hands, she strutted toward the door. "Way-oh-way-oh…"

Smiling, Beth continued to the kitchen. She peeked under the foil, releasing the aroma of chilies, eggs, and cheese. Her stomach growled.

Zoe entered the room with a covered cake pan in hand.

Therese and Corrine followed.

"This dessert needs to go in the fridge. I'm all about food right now." Zoe opened the refrigerator door. "Food and friends, I should say."

Therese thrust a bottle of Pinot Noir in her direction.

"I'm all about *wine*, friends, and food." Zoe gesticulated.

"I have red and white open." Beth gestured toward the table.

After taking orders, Zoe poured. When the doorbell rang, she grinned. "You're up."

"Gotcha." Beth hurried down the hall. She wondered again if Maria had a story to tell. *No fretting about your friends.* She cared about them. But wondering—worrying, really—did nothing. *But if they bring things up…* She opened the door.

Maria greeted her with a smile. "Thanks again for having us."

She drew her into a hug. "Thanks for coming." Starting down the hall, she brushed her hand against Maria's back. Memories unfolded of Reid tracing soft circles on her back. The question mark on Maria's face reined her in.

But then they were at the kitchen door and a song wooed them in.

"Hail, hail, the gang's all here…" Zoe swung her arms back and forth.

The timer interrupted her serenade.

She gave a single clap. "Where shall we dish up?"

"The dining room…" Beth opened the oven door. "Trivets are on the table."

"You don't have to tell me twice." Zoe retrieved her dish from the stovetop and led the exodus next door. "Looks delish." She hitched in her chair. "I want the names, please."

"Shrimp and cheese dip." Corrine ladled a heaping spoonful. "Sophia's favorite."

"Mmmm." Maria unfolded her napkin. "I bet they miss your cooking."

"They seem to." Corrine gave a half-shrug. "Taking requests while they were home felt good."

Averting eye contact, Beth straightened her scarf. *I don't want to make her uncomfortable.* So far, Corrine hadn't dropped any clues about whether or not she was playing the Sheldon card close to her chest.

"The Asian meatballs are mine. The pot holders are yours." Maria tilted her head, her eyes shining.

Beth smiled her thanks.

"Crocheted? I wish I knew how." Zoe waved a hand. "I made the chili relleno cheese squares. The girls helped, which made everything take twice as long. I'm not complaining, though."

"My only help was a request for one of these veggie pizzas. This stone is hot, so pass me your plates." Therese slid a spatula under a pizza slice. "Kate has a lot of homework…"

"She's a hard worker." Beth slid her plate to the right. "You'll have to take her some curried chicken and almond rolls." *Reid's favorite.*

"Will do. She *loves* curry." Therese smiled then tapped the table. "Now, no work talk. But I propose family and holiday rundowns are in order."

Beth nodded, grateful she didn't spend Christmas alone.

"Santa was not a hit." Zoe cleared her throat. "Hope screamed bloody murder when we put her on his lap, and she lasted less than five seconds. I used to think parents that forced their kids on the jolly guy's lap were nuts." She rubbed the back of her neck. "Then we joined the club."

"One of my former coworkers *loved* her kids' ugly-crying photos with Santa." Maria leaned in. "Did you get a picture?"

"Of Erin. Hope points to the photo and says, 'Santa scare me.' " Zoe spoke through puckered lips.

"The twins were afraid at that age, too." Corrine gave a single nod. "Hunter cried whenever he saw Santa, unless he was on TV."

"Are they back at school?" Therese rested an arm on the table.

"They are." Corrine speared half a meatball. "Sophia left on the fourth and Hunter on the eleventh."

"Quiet now?" Zoe lifted her glass. "I could use a little quiet now and then."

"Mm-hmm." Corrine pursed her lips.

Beth wondered if her expression meant *end of story*, or if she stifled words fighting for release. If words hovered on the tip of her tongue, she contemplated coaxing the truth.

"Therese, tell Kate she has good taste." Maria lifted a forkful of pizza. "Has she heard anything from Portland?"

"Not yet. She's looking forward to doing some woodworking here with her grandpa, though."

"I told her she's welcome anytime…" Beth wiped her mouth with her napkin.

"She knows, but she wants some bonding time with him." Therese tipped her head. "He's looking forward to seeing you again, too."

The conversation flowed into Christmas and New Year's celebrations.

Beth applauded her decision to go to Therese's. Had she bailed, she wouldn't have anything to say.

After dinner, Zoe stacked the plates on the counter. "Everything was delicious. Plus, we covered a lot of territory while we ate."

"Good thing we are a party of five, which kept us from talking with our mouths full." Therese set her baking stone on the stovetop.

"Erin has a hard time, no matter how many are present." Zoe transferred the silverware into the sink. "When she wants to say something, she gets so excited she can't wait—food or no food."

"I used to wonder if Kate would have been more civilized had it not been just the two of us. Trade you…" Therese gestured to the leftover pizza.

"Doubtful—made no difference with Hunter." Corrine opened the refrigerator.

Beth crossed to a cupboard and retrieved a pair of glass dishes. She handed one to Therese then filled the other with chicken and almond rolls.

Therese slid a piece of pizza into the dish. "I

worried Kate would never learn to chew with her mouth closed, but for the most part she has."

"She's lovely now." Beth glanced at Maria. Worry the conversation proved too hard for her friend clamped her stomach.

Rinsing the dinner plates, Maria stood with her back toward her friends.

Corrine uncovered the dessert, revealing a layer of crushed candies and whipped cream.

"Your dessert looks decadent." Zoe led the migration to the dining room.

"BTS cake." Corrine picked up a spatula and knife.

"An acronym meaning…" Therese smoothed out her napkin.

"Better than sex." Corrine's eyes twinkled.

"Eww—water up my nose." Zoe snorted. "Cut me a hunk. Or should I say, cut me a double?"

"How big?" Corrine raised the spatula.

"Are we talking inches?" Zoe grinned and raised her eyebrows.

"We could. Or you can show me." Corrine separated her index finger and thumb.

"That's puny." Zoe held up her index fingers, her other knuckles touching. "This big"—she flashed her dimples—"and I'm talking dessert."

"Glad you specified—if you get my drift." Therese stood her spoon on the table. "Been a long time…"

"I get your drift." Corrine sliced cake to order.

"Fi…nal…ly." Zoe raised a heaping spoonful. "BTS for PWWPT."

"Hear hear," seconded Corrine.

The women dug in.

Beth chewed with her eyes closed, savoring the

flavors of chocolate, caramel, toffee, and cream. *Reid would love this.*

"Hands down better—pun intended." Therese licked her lips. "Though it's hard to remember the other."

"I'm working on forgetting." Corrine set down her spoon. "I gave Sheldon the boot last week." She thrust her palms toward the center of the table.

"Whoa." Zoe widened her eyes. "*Spill.*"

"Do you want to talk about what happened?" Maria tucked a strand of hair behind her ear.

"Yeah, my bad." Zoe cupped a hand over her mouth. "Sorry—"

"I'm glad to be rid of the sorry schmuck." Corrine pursed her lips, her nostrils flaring. "Only two things to tell… He's screwing one of his little baristas, and I'll be better off without him."

"The dirty dog." Zoe huffed a breath.

"What did your kids say?" Maria propped a forearm on the table.

"They don't know yet. I'm so angry right now, plus it's his story to tell." Corrine gulped her wine. "The little weasel needs to own what he's been doing. I don't think she's much older than they are."

Scooting her chair sideways, Beth slipped an arm around Corrine's waist.

She tipped her head in reply.

Beth lingered with her head against Corrine's— silky copper to platinum blonde.

"I'm sorry." Maria toyed with her napkin.

"Shithead." Zoe shook her head then turned to Maria. "How are things going for you in the sex department?"

Zo-e, Beth wanted to say. She liked her, but sometimes her social filter seemed clogged. *Maybe she needs to get out more.* She reached for her water glass. *Look who's talking.*

"We're still trying…'doing it for science' as Anthony says." Maria ran a fingertip along the edge of her plate. "Not all the time. I mean, you know…"

"Must be hard." Therese rubbed her jaw.

"Better be hard." A grin flickered across Maria's face.

"You're funny." Zoe shoveled a spoonful of cake. "What's in this deliciousness?"

"Devil's food cake, sweetened condensed milk, caramel ice cream topping, toffee bars, and whipped cream." Corrine ticked her fingers. "Better than sex."

Smiling a little, Beth waggled a hand in a "maybe, maybe not" gesture.

"Could be a tie but that's all I'm saying." Zoe held out her spoon.

"I'd like the recipe." Therese squared her shoulders. "That's all I'm saying."

"Anthony's not big on sweets, and I'm watching what I eat, so this dessert would last ages in our house." Maria picked up her mug. "This cake is delicious, though."

Therese sighed. "I wish I could say the same. Sweet and salty—I love them both."

"If you had to pick one, would you choose salty or sweet?" Zoe asked.

"Sweet, with a handful of honey roasted peanuts every now and then." Therese looked around the table. "What about you all?"

"Salty." Maria brushed a hand across her cheek.

"Same." Beth nodded.

"This is my final answer." Corrine dipped her spoon in the middle of her cake.

"Right is sweet, and left is salty." Zoe held up her hands. "Eenie meenie miney moe…" She ended on her left middle finger then furrowed her forehead. "Perimenopausal brain fart."

"Salty." Four voices blended in unison.

"Winner winner, chicken dinner—salty PWWPT." Zoe shot an arm into the air. "Though I would've pegged Maria for sweet and Corrine for salty. No offense."

"*Moi?*" Corrine pressed hands alongside her face.

Zoe leaned forward. "You're sassy, which is a compliment in my book."

"Compliment accepted." Corrine tipped her wine-glass.

"I'd say we're all a little of each." Therese alternated her palms up and down.

"*Sweet and Saasssy* Perimenopausal Women with Power Tools." Zoe dipped her chin. "SSPWWPT. *S*s silent."

Beth laughed. "Silent *S*s accepted."

"What's on tap next month?" Zoe scraped the last of her cake.

"We could get together at my house." Therese folded her napkin and set it beside her plate.

"Do you mind coming back here?" Beth looked from face to face. "These gatherings feel like our little routine."

"I concur." Maria smiled. "Coming to your cozy home is a treat."

Settling on February twenty-third, Beth agreed a

Mardi Gras celebration five days late would be perfect. *We talked about going to New Orleans for Mardi Gras, Reid.* A dull throbbing crept into her chest. So many dreams she could never recover... She pushed back her chair, fighting to quiet the secret nipping at her heart.

Chapter Nine

Two weeks later, Beth meandered to Reid's shop and turned on the heater. She gave up calling his shop anything else—it had always been and would continue to be exactly that. *Reid's shop.* In the kitchen, she brewed a pot of coffee and heated the kettle. The mugs Kate chose were front and center on the shelf. She removed the pair and added Mount Rushmore to the mix. When the doorbell chimed, she hurried to the front, her pulse thrumming. She threw open the door. The cool air confirmed Punxsutawney Phil's prediction—six more weeks of winter.

"Hello." Frank wiped his feet. "Thanks for having us."

"Like I told Kate, you're welcome anytime." Beth smiled and stepped aside.

"Caramel rolls from Bernice's." Kate handed her a brown paper bag, turned sideways. "Grandpa and Grandma picked up rolls on their way into town."

"Yum." When she reached the kitchen, she peeked inside the bag. "Are you ready for one now? I have coffee and—"

The tea kettle cut her off.

"Time to get to work." Frank raised a pair of canvas bags. "We'll take a break in a bit."

Not now? Lowering her head to hide her disappointment, she removed the kettle from the burner.

Then she met Frank's gaze. "Would you like something to drink?"

"Therese fixed us a couple of water bottles." He lifted a hand and nodded toward the bag. "A cup of coffee will be just what the doctor ordered in a while—coffee and a roll."

"I doubt a roll is on your doctor's orders, Grandpa." Kate slipped an arm through his.

He winked in reply.

Beth led the way down the hall, through the laundry room and garage, and into Reid's shop.

Kate assumed the lead and guided her grandfather around the room. "We can use whatever we need, right?"

"Yes." Beth cupped her elbows. A tangle of envy and regret wrestled pride and delight, wrapping tendrils around her lungs. She sucked in a breath. "Looks like you're set." She lifted a hand then lowered her arms to her sides. "Let me know if you need anything."

"Will do. I'll send in the boss if we need you." Frank jutted out a thumb.

"Aww—I've never been anyone's boss before." Kate put her hands on her hips. "Let's get cracking, Grandpa."

She started toward the door. Half of her wanted to be a mouse in the corner and listen and watch. The other half considered that impulse intrusive and unfaithful. Her mind whirring, she shuffled through the garage and into the house. What was the draw now for hanging out in Reid's shop? Recapturing his essence? Mourning her loss? Absorbing the bond between Frank and Kate?

Yes. Yes. Yes. She poured the coffee into a carafe

for herself then readied the coffeemaker for a fresh pot before placing salad plates, silverware, and her favorite yellow-and-blue plaid napkins on the table. Her solitude magnified, she routed to the living room and buried herself in the comfort of Reid's recliner. A desperate hunger consumed her, and she closed her eyes, yearning to rewind time and recapture missed opportunities.

Two hours later, the laundry room door opened.

Beth hurried to the kitchen to turn on the coffeemaker and kettle.

Kate's voice carried from the hallway. "He always says, 'measure twice and cut once'…" She backed into the kitchen.

Frank followed.

"How are things going?" Beth met his gaze.

"Going well, though I'd forgotten how bossy my granddaughter can be." He slipped an arm around Kate's waist.

"I learned from Mom, and I'm pretty sure she learned from you, Grandpa." Kate gave a wide-eyed wink.

"Well, I'm pretty sure I'm ready for a cup of coffee and a roll." He winked back.

"I'll do the rolls." Kate crossed to the counter. She reached into the bakery bag and paused, her hand half in and half out. "My hands are clean."

He chuckled. "We know…"

"Beth didn't know, Grandpa." Kate removed a pastry. "I didn't want you to think my hands were full of sawdust."

"You're conscientious, Kate." She handed her a dinner plate.

"Thanks." Kate arranged the caramel rolls—all

three spilling over the plate's edges. "How long?"

"Thirty seconds."

"Gotcha." She loaded the plate and punched in the time. As the microwave whirred, she ran a palm over the countertop.

Overwhelmed by an ache bubbling in her core, Beth rummaged in a drawer for a spatula. She knew karma led her to fall in love with Reid. Throughout the years, she struggled to suppress her desire for a child. Now, she quelled the hunger she would not—*could not*—allow.

The timer rang, and Kate opened the microwave door.

An oven-fresh, buttery aroma filled the room.

Frank inhaled. "Those rolls smell divine."

"Divine, Grandpa?" Kate raised the plate. "You make me laugh."

"You've had me laughing since you blew your first raspberry. At me, remember?"

Kate steadied the plate with one hand and tapped her forehead with a free finger. "I have a mind like a steel trap, right?"

"Right. And I have a memory—"

"Like a pig." Their voices blended in unison.

Beth smiled from one to the other before handing Kate the serving utensil.

Frank grinned and waved a hand. "But she's never convinced me she knows a single thing about pigs and their memories."

"One of the wonders of the world that doesn't get the credit it deserves." Kate hip-bumped her grandpa and carried the snack to the breakfast nook.

Melancholic whispers nagged while Beth poured

coffee. She enjoyed the tender bantering, but her company's shared memories, quips, and palpable love were bittersweet reminders of what she had lost. The kettle puffed a cloud of steam, and she turned off the burner. *Reveling in their love beats another day alone.* She poured water into Kate's mug, atop cocoa mix plus extra marshmallows.

"Yum." Kate stirred her drink then was the first to the table.

Beth brought up the rear. Sinking into a chair, she eyed the roll centered on her plate. "Smells like pure deliciousness." She settled in and popped a taste into her mouth, savoring the flavors of butter, sugar, pecans, and *love.* "These rolls are fabulous." She leaned forward. "What are you two working on?"

"A coffee table…" Kate raised a hand in front of her lips, talking with her mouth full. "Don't tell Mom, okay?"

"Mum's the word." Beth flattened her lips.

"Good one—mum for Mom. She thinks we're making a garden bench, but I wanted something to remind her of me every single day." Kate speared a bite of her roll. "If we made a bench, she'd have to go in the backyard… So, we decided to make an indoor piece. Right, Grandpa?"

"Right…to remind her you'll be the finest furniture maker in the Pacific Northwest. This one used to say she wanted to become an orthopedic surgeon." He tipped his head. "Until last fall, Kate? I don't remember you talking about woodworking before then."

"Yeah. I didn't say anything until I needed to work on college apps." She shrugged. "I didn't know what Mom would think—or Dad."

The latter sounding like an afterthought, Beth recalled Therese's words. *He comes to see her once a year.*

"I think your new plan is brilliant." Frank rubbed his jaw. "Why waste your craft on bodies? Your patients would be asleep, and nobody could see what you were doing under all those drapes. Then you'd cover up your handiwork with skin and stuff." He turned to Beth. "You should see her creations. Her talent belies her youth."

"Miles said you're one of the most talented students he's ever had." She cleared her throat. "Not sure I was supposed to tell you…"

"Mum." Kate zipped an index finger and thumb across her lips. "And thanks for letting us use Reid's shop."

The two words she fretted about rolled off Kate's tongue. Swallowing past the lump in her throat, she managed a small smile. "You're welcome."

Kate led the remainder of the conversation. When she finished eating, she carried the dishes to the sink then steered her grandpa to Reid's shop.

Beth wanted to follow them out the door. Instead, she covered the dirty dishes with hot, sudsy water, plunged in her hands, and scrubbed. Later that afternoon, she escorted her company to the front door.

"I kind of like working with my Grandpa." Kate rubbed his arm. "We'll probably need three more days. Saturdays, but we're not sure when. Sundays are his sacred days…"

"The taskmaster will keep you posted." Frank shifted his bags. "Thanks again for everything."

"Yeah." Kate gave her a quick hug. "Thank you."

The embrace released a flood of longing. Beth wrangled her voice. "Anytime." Once the car engine faded into stillness, she strolled to the mailbox and back, relishing the twenty-degree temperature rise. Despite the pesky groundhog's prediction, the fifty-degree afternoon hinted at spring. Inside, she scanned the mail, flipping past a hand-addressed envelope postmarked Rockville, Maryland. No return address. *Some nonprofit.* She dropped the pile on the entryway table and continued to Reid's shop.

Aside from coffee table pieces and the leftover scent of sawdust, the shop was as tidy as it had been that morning. She shut off the heater and put away the ladder. Then she brushed her fingertips along the table saw and countertop, stopping at the rainbow sherbet tub. She encircled the tub with her hands, invoking sweet memories of eating ice cream with Reid. Her thoughts segued to Kate and Frank. She imagined their family sharing ice cream and stories and *love*. Would she ever again experience such tenderness?

****

The following week, sunlight warmed the breakfast nook as Beth sat at the kitchen table. Days of unopened mail confronted her. Throughout her marriage, she had been the gatekeeper. Reid rarely opened anything, even mail addressed to him. By default, she became the bill payer and money manager. She hadn't minded. Her banker husband hadn't minded, either. Weeks after he passed away, when she finally tackled a mountain of mail, she was grateful bill paying was a lesson she would *not* have to learn.

After sorting the mail into two groups, she attacked the bills first. She had never done online banking.

Inputting account numbers on the Internet made her
nervous. She wrote out a trio of checks: for the water
company, electric utility, and the credit card company.
Then she slid her letter opener through each envelope in
the second pile and dug in. A dark pink rose graced the
front of an off-white card. Wondering which nonprofit
stepped up its game, she opened the card.

Dear Beth,

*I hope you'll read to the end... At Christmas, my
sincere intent was to stop after a single card if I didn't
hear from you. Please don't think this second card
means I can't be trusted. I can be. But as I count the
days until I give birth, I am overwhelmed by thoughts of
you. I say a prayer of thanksgiving every day for the gift
of life you gave me. As Valentine's Day approaches, I
wanted to send a final note of love and thanks. Unless
you ask me to, I won't write again, but I'll think of you
with appreciation and love all the days of my life.*

Truly,

Emma

Beth clutched the card, her hand shaking. *I had a
baby girl.* Thick sobs permeated the air. The sound
plummeted her back as her mind spiraled in an out-of-
control nosedive.

She had begged Doctor Ziegler not to tell her
anything about the baby. But when the hospital elevator
closed that day in May and whisked her to the medical
floor, she was certain she left behind a baby boy, along
with a million tiny bits of her heart. She cordoned off a
piece of her soul back then, too, barricading memories,
emotions, and a thousand questions she refused to ask.

He was a she. Rereading Emma's words, she
struggled to contain the twist and tangle of all she

stuffed away. She hadn't read Emma's Christmas card, nor any other. Like the previous year, she almost pitched every single one. After Kate discovered the cards' hiding place, Beth gathered the cards that afternoon and carried them into the kitchen. When the garbage can opened, she paused, remembering Reid's pride the day he presented the motion sensor can. The forester in her kicked in, and she rubber banded the cards and put them on top of the Christmas totes to sort for recycling. He used to tease her about her obsession with saving trees. She knew old habits died hard but this year, unlike last, something—or someone—stopped her from tossing the cards.

Thirty-six years of sorrow and shame broke open as she admitted her truth. Reid didn't nudge her from the garbage can that day. He never knew about the baby. No one did, except Lucy and Lucy's mom.

When she had started her exchange year at the University of New Hampshire, she didn't know she was pregnant. Then she missed her period but blamed her cross-country move and the newness of the East Coast. Even though she was tired, she didn't worry when a second month went by. But when she didn't have a period in November, she knew. Three weeks later, she summoned the courage to find a Family Practice doctor. She called for an appointment while Lucy was at bio. On the cusp of finals, the only opening for a new OB conflicted with her Economics of Forestry exam. Beth considered that a good omen. She might have a miscarriage—her mom had had two—and the January appointment would be a moot point.

All fall, her boyfriend, Ian, wrote mournful letters about how much he missed her. About how the fact his family trip to Italy would fill his entire Christmas break was the shits. Then he wrote that he would change his flight so he could see her before she returned to school.

She was firm in her reply. *This is a once-in-a-lifetime opportunity, and I forbid you to cut your trip short because of me.* She knew *forbid* would make him smile. *We'll be together in our hearts, and after a few short months, we'll be together for infinity. I'll think of you every minute, and I know that, between ogling Italian beauties, you'll think of me, too.*

The last sentence would crack him up. What she didn't say was she was glad they wouldn't see each other. She wasn't sure how things would progress and with Ian gone, she could pretend they didn't have anything to worry about.

When she filled out her health history that January, she left one section blank. *Father of baby.* She looked at Doctor Ziegler—his blond crewcut and steel gray eyes carbon copies of her high school geometry teacher's—and told him she didn't know who the father was. Heat burned her face when she swallowed her lie and said she couldn't keep the baby.

He didn't press.

In the ensuing months, she agreed to a private adoption. She always used *I*, never *we*, burying her fib even deeper. Whenever a part of her argued she needed to tell Ian about the baby—nighttime debates were the worst—she refused to listen.

Three weeks before her due date, Ian sent a letter. *I don't know how to tell you this.* His opening line mimicked what she rehearsed. *I met someone in my finance class. We started out as friends.* The next words were blacked out. *I'm sorry. Ian.* Not *Love, Ian.*

Angry tears mixed with tears of relief, and Beth wept until she was dry as sawdust. When she gave birth nine days later, the week before finals and eight days before Mother's Day, she cried big, fat crocodile tears for her and her baby. *Garrett or Genevieve.* For the names she never shared and the baby she had never met.

Leaning elbows on the table, she unfolded her napkin and wiped the ribbons of salty tears. She examined Emma's handwriting, searching for any hint of her own. *What do you look like? How did you find me? What did you write in your Christmas card?*

She traipsed to the office and the urgency of her heartbeat belied her staggering pace. *Did you send a picture? Are you married? What's your due date?* She assumed Emma was married and planned to keep her baby. But as she could attest, both of those presumptions could be wrong.

Beth pulled out the stack of Christmas cards, breaking the rubber band in her haste. Flipping the cards onto the desk, she trembled, her pulse pounding in her temples. She uncovered the pale gold envelope postmarked Rockville, Maryland. Her heart stutter-stopped then resumed its wild tumble. She wanted to tear open the envelope and read more of the handwriting she memorized minutes before. But having guarded her secret with such fierceness, she hesitated. Guilt stilled her fingers in her story's unravel.

She clutched the envelope, shielding the words. Eager but afraid and ready but not, she carried the card into the kitchen. *Make a cup of tea.* She yielded to the emphatic voice. Robotic, she heated water, rummaged for a chamomile teabag, and sifted through mugs. She

chose a burnt red cup customized with her initials—
EGJ—a Secret Santa gift untouched by Reid.

Throughout the years, she wanted to tell him about
the baby. The shame of deceit held her back, and then
she was an impostor for so long, she couldn't—*ever*.
Carrying her card and tea into the living room, she
skirted his recliner, propelled by guilt into her own
butter-soft chair. She sank into the cool leather. The
card on her lap bore a weight of combined hope and joy
and sorrow and regret. Desperate for the tea's warmth,
she wrapped her hands around the mug and sipped until
draining it dry. Her lungs emptied, too, and she inhaled
long and slow.

Quivering, she opened the envelope and removed
the card. *PEACE. LOVE. JOY.* She gazed at a cobalt
blue sky, sprinkled with twinkling stars. The air
seeming too thin to breathe, she opened the card.

Dear Beth,

*I've written so many drafts, none of which seemed
right. Writing this letter is important, though, so here
goes.*

*When I feel the rolls and kicks of my unborn baby,
I can't help thinking of you. Of the woman who gave me
life and the woman I know so little about. So much I'd
like to know and much I'd like to share, but I'll
understand if my card goes unanswered. In the event
this note is the beginning and end of our
correspondence, I want you to know three things.*

*I was so sorry to learn about the loss of your
husband. Holidays can be especially hard. Please know
I'm showering you with love.*

*Bennett and I are expecting our first baby in April.
We've decided not to find out the sex, though most of*

our family and friends can't understand why. I can't understand why anyone would want to ruin such a wonderful surprise.

Finally, adequate words don't exist to express my gratitude. Thank you *feels so slight, but it's the best I can do. I hope you realize the depth of my appreciation.*

Now comes the hard part. I would love to hear from you, so I am enclosing my address. Unless you ask me to, I won't write again, but please know I will hold you forever in my heart.

Love Always,

Emma

Holding the card to her chest, she hunkered into the leather's embrace. A memory swam into consciousness.

Thirteen days postpartum, she had slogged through finals in a fog. Grief's unrelenting force pounded her every molecule. Now, packed and ready to go, she glanced around the dorm room, her throat throbbing. "I'll miss you so much." The words clawed their exit.

Curled in a heap on her bed, Lucy sobbed. "I'm gonna miss you, too."

She looked away, the rawness in Lucy's voice and face unbearable. "I can't stay in touch. Too many memories—"

"Good memories." Lucy swiped at her nose, her voice breaking.

Her mournful whimper pierced Beth's core. "Plus sad…"

Lucy tucked her chin. "You own a piece of my heart…"

Beth crumpled beside her and gathered Lucy in her arms, her tears wetting her friend's curls.

Lucy bawled then her sobs followed Beth out the

door. But she didn't look back.

Years later, Lucy sent a card to Beth's old California address.

The forwarded greeting with a Boston postmark and no return address appeared in her mailbox on Christmas Eve.

Dear Beth,

Merry Christmas. A quick note to say I think of you often. Some days, the year we roomed together in Sawyer Hall feels like yesterday. Other days, our time together feels a lifetime ago.

I hope you're doing well. All is well with me. I'm married and have three kids who keep me on my toes. As we enter a new decade, I just wanted to say I hope you found the happiness you deserve and have the passel of kids you always wanted.

Love,

Lucy

She committed the words to memory. Then, afraid Reid might find the card, she had buried it in the trash.

Tears pricked her eyes. Beth pressed Emma's card to her nose. She breathed in the night sky then Emma's handwriting, searching for her daughter's scent. A whisper of lotion or hand soap or something—*anything* to bring her closer to her baby. *My Emma.* The words filled her with wonder. Sniffing nothing but paper—not even dried ink—she skimmed fingers across the handwriting then slowed when she reached the end. *Emma.* She traced the signature with a single fingertip. Blanketing the words with her hand, she closed her eyes, her soul awash with thick sorrow.

The following morning, a hot flash drove her out of bed. Then guilt returned. *Happy Valentine's Day,*

Darling. Everything felt muddled. Since learning about Emma, knots of anguish and remorse battled pride and delight. *Maybe he knows.* At times, she sensed Reid's presence, bone deep. If he did have a window into her world, yesterday's ocean of tears would have sounded an alarm. *What a way to find out.* Had she known Emma would find her, she would have told him the truth—exposed herself for the phony she was and risked losing his love. He deserved to know. She pulled on her terry cloth robe. *He deserved better.*

She spent the day in fits and starts, searching for words. That night, under the cloak of darkness, she armed herself with pen, paper, and an ultimatum. *You can't go to bed until you finish.* Like Emma, she drafted her words. Crafting and molding and crossing out and inserting, she started and stopped. A riptide of emotions, sorrow and joy and all the others in-between, knocked around inside her chest. She could write volumes but wouldn't. Not now. She wrote, rewrote, and then rewrote again, allowing the feelings to course through her. Emptied and exhausted, she smoothed out her draft and put pen to stationery.

Dear Emma,

One thing we have in common is our struggle to find words. Like you, I've written numerous drafts, but I'll start with this admission. I read your Valentine's Day card first. Not intentionally. I didn't read any Christmas cards until yesterday. Thank you for writing not once but twice. Thanks, too, for your kind words about Reid. Your wisdom makes me wonder if you know the agony of losing a loved one. If so, I'm sorry for your loss.

Sorrow shattered my heart the day you were born.

I didn't see you or hold you or even know you were a baby girl—I knew if I said hello I could never say goodbye. Ever. I couldn't give you the life I wanted, and a loving couple longed for you. Letting you go without a hello was the hardest thing I have ever done. Hearing from you and learning you and Bennett await the birth of your baby filled me with joy. I am eager to learn more about you and am happy to answer any of your questions. One I have for you is how did you find me?

Today is Valentine's Day. Thank you for making mine so special. I hope yours was lovely, too, and I wish you and Bennett much happiness in the coming days. Your handwritten cards are treasures, but if you'd rather email, my address is elvijo923@bresnan.net. I look forward to hearing from you again.

Much Love,

Beth

She skimmed a fingertip along the inside flap of Emma's envelope and brushed her lips to the dried adhesive where her daughter's might have been. Then she sealed her envelope and added a butterfly-soft kiss. *What questions will you ask?* At the thoughts of one query she did *not* want to answer, Beth placed an arm across her abdomen, her stomach roiling.

Chapter Ten

Five days later, Beth browsed the Mustard Seed menu. Aromas of garlic, ginger, teriyaki, and grilled meats filled the air.

Maria slid an arm around her shoulder and leaned down for a cheek-to-cheek hug. "Sorry I'm late." She folded into an empty chair.

"I'm perusing options." Beth smiled and slid aside her menu.

"Mmmm. I was thinking about plum wine with a slice of lemon on my way over." Maria toyed with her silverware. "I didn't have any on our dessert run, but a glass sounds good today."

Her smile faded. *You're not pregnant.* She laced her fingers in her lap.

"You know what that means. We're not at the end of the road, though…" Maria gave a half-shrug. "On the bright side, a glass of plum wine sounds delicious."

"I love your attitude." She squeezed her hands and hushed the news consuming her thoughts.

Their server arrived.

Beth ordered a glass of wine then turned her attention to the menu. She sighed. "I can never get past chicken osaka. Do you have a favorite?"

"A few, but today I'm all about shrimp ginza with brown rice." Maria closed her menu.

"I like brown, too. Reid always ordered white."

She glanced out the window, slowing her breathing at the easy slip of his name.

Maria hitched her chair closer to the table. "I thought of you on Saturday."

Valentine's Day. She nodded.

A companionable silence followed, broken by their server's return.

After ordering lunch, Beth clinked her glass—plum to plum.

"I was scoping out Mardi Gras recipes, which is why I was late." Maria dug a notepad out of her purse. "Tell me what you think..." She placed the pad sideways between them.

Hurricanes, fruit kabobs, muffuletta crostini, Mardi Gras slaw, margarita shrimp salad, jambalaya, gumbo, king cake, and creole bread pudding. Beth scanned the page. "Looks like a feast."

"We'll have hurricanes for sure, but I listed two choices for everything else." Holding an index finger and thumb parallel, Maria moved her fingers down the list. "I might not be drinking, but I can bring the rum and other ingredients if you'd like."

"Send me the recipe and I'll make them, plus mocktails if need be." Beth straightened her napkin. "Okay to talk about?"

"Yeah. My FSH was eighteen point nine. The one before was nineteen point one, so this was a smidge better. No period or slippery mucus, though, hence..." She tipped her wineglass. "Anthony hasn't said anything lately, so I haven't either."

"Which means your families still don't know?"

Maria nodded. "I remind myself we haven't even been trying a year. Since I'm under thirty-five, I'm not considered infertile until one year of unprotected intercourse." She fluttered finger quotation marks.

"Would you like to tell your mom?" Beth leaned forward.

"Sometimes. Anthony hasn't asked me not to, but…" Maria tucked a strand of hair behind her ear. "Knowing I can call you anytime helps."

"Mm-hmm—anytime." *I had a baby girl.* For days, she rolled those words around in her mouth: silent and spoken, soft and loud, half laughing and crying, but overwhelmed *every single time.*

"NO."

A child's emphatic voice garnered her attention. She shifted in her seat and looked to her left.

A curly-haired boy in a youth chair crossed his arms and shook his head. "No-no-no."

Beside him, a thirty-something dad slid a bowl toward an empty chair.

Beth pinched her bottom lip. *Are you having a boy or girl, Emma?* She wanted to shout her news. Instead, she ran a thumb along the edge of the table.

"I'm ready for the good, the bad, and the ugly." Maria tipped her head. "Toddlers' diapers—those are the worst."

I've never changed a diaper. Kneading her thighs atop her napkin, she braced for a question.

Maria glanced his way. "I'm ready for diapers and beyond…"

She rested a hand on Maria's arm. "Whenever you need a pair of ears, give me a call."

"Thanks." Maria lifted her glass.

Beth answered with a clink. She took a drink, allowing the sweet, fruity wine to wash away her words. *Maria's* story deserved a voice, not hers. When her lunch arrived, she tucked in with gusto.

"So, do you think it would be okay to email this list to everyone?" Maria waved her fork. "Tell them you'll make hurricanes, and I'll do *crostini*. Ask them to pick a salad, main course, or dessert. Will I sound bossy?"

"I don't think so."

"Yeah. Plus, I'll tell them the menu's not set in stone." Maria glanced at the list. "They can make something different if they want."

Beth raised a bite of chicken and rice. "Who could argue?"

"No one." Their words overlapped.

Grinning, she popped the fork into her mouth. She sat back, relishing the flavors of the gingery dish and the companionship of her young friend.

When she exited the restaurant, she lingered in the sunshine.

"Thanks again for being my sounding board." Maria enveloped Beth in her arms.

She swallowed past the stone in her throat. "You're welcome." *I'm having a grandbaby...* She wanted to blurt out her story but hugged Maria instead. Walking to her car, she quieted the thoughts rolling through her head. Could she keep the secret she tucked away more than half a lifetime ago?

****

Four days later, Beth stepped back to survey her dining room table. *Perfect.* Aside from Christmas, she rarely decorated. The previous day, though, she popped into The Treasure Chest and bought a package of fleur-de-lis confetti. Backing out of the room, she admired the light's reflection on the tricolored flowers sprinkled around the table. She donned the Mardi Gras ensemble she assembled the day before: hunter green pants, gold blouse, and purple cardigan.

The sweater had been a hit the first time she wore it to the office.

Her coworker Fran delighted in the purple cardigan. During morning break, she entertained the staff with an exuberant recitation of a poem about aging, the color purple, and learning to spit.

Weeks from retirement, Beth looked forward to keeping in touch after she was gone by partaking in monthly lunches and occasional happy hours. Rain or shine, she knew exactly what to wear the first time she reconnected—her purple cardigan and a red hat. She hadn't planned to retire and become a widow less than three weeks later.

Widow. She hated that term and its subsequent crush of grief. True, she *had* discarded her desire to entomb herself in her crawl space never to be found…but more than sixteen months out, she still didn't want to reunite with friends from before. That word, too, carried new weight. *Before Emma.* She glanced at her watch. Her guests were due in ten minutes. *Did you send an email?* She could steal a moment to look, but even if her inbox harbored a reply, she needed untethered time to read and absorb the answer. *How did you find me?* She had instants she was sorry she asked, followed by the incredulous *how could you not?*

Quieting her mind, Beth brushed her hair with long, luxurious strokes. Then, because she was senior member of the Perimenopausal Women with Power Tools, she dug out a tube of cherry red lipstick and painted her lips.

Ding-dong.

She gave her reflection an approving nod then hustled to answer the door.

Therese and Corrine stood side by side, sporting cat eye glitter masks.

"*Laissez le bon temps rouler!*" Gold glitter outlined the flecks in Corrine's hazel eyes.

"AKA let the good times roll." Therese's brown eyes twinkled behind glittered green.

"Good times await—courtesy of Emeril Lagasse." Beth smiled and ushered them inside.

Corrine passed her a slow cooker and led the way, peeling her coat en route. She stopped at the closet.

"Low?" Beth tipped her head.

"Please."

Continuing to the kitchen, she plugged in the pot beside the coffeemaker. Lifting the lid, she inhaled the savory aroma of jambalaya, reminiscent of the neglected Cajun seasoning in her spice drawer. *You loved that peppery blend, Reid.* A blast of stifled laughter interrupted the stab of nostalgia. She glanced up.

Someone stretched an arm into the doorway. Three glitter masks dangled beneath. "Which one?"

"Purple, please." She matched the falsetto voice, pitch for pitch.

Corrine carried in the masks then leapfrogged the lone purple one over the others. She shook loose the remaining pair and propped them against the punch bowl. "Spill targets?"

"I don't plan to spill one drop of Emeril Lagasse's hurricane cocktails." Beth lifted the ladle and gave a contented sigh. "Who's ready?"

"*Moi.*" Corrine raised a hand, shoulder high.

"*Laissez le bon...*" Therese stopped, open-mouthed.

"*Temps rouler.*" Corrine extended her fist into the air.

Beth grinned and filled three tall glasses—iced and ready—then garnished each with an orange slice. Distributing the drinks, she tipped her glass toward the others. "*Laissez le bon temps rouler.*" She clinked and rested a hand on her chest. "My one-off."

"One fell swoop—"

The doorbell interrupted Therese's words. "Ladle another. I'm guessing whoever is at the door will be ready to roll the good times..." Her voice faded down the hall.

Returning to the punch bowl, Beth filled another glass. She knew Zoe would be ready for a cocktail. Plus, Maria called that afternoon to say she was looking forward to a hurricane, *not* a mocktail.

"Smells delicious." Zoe's words preceded her into the kitchen.

Maria followed, carrying a platter.

"Allow me." Scooting beside her, Therese reached for the dish.

Corrine drew wide circles with her mask-draped arms. "Green or gold?"

Watching the pair of masks twirl like anemic toy hoops, Beth sipped her drink.

"Gold for me, unless you'd rather." Zoe shifted her weight.

Maria straightened her collar. "Green's great."

"The colors will complement our eyes." Zoe

flashed a dimpled grin and lifted her bowl. "Where do you want this salad?"

"On the counter for now." Beth raised a glass. "Are you ready for a hurricane?"

"Is water wet?" Zoe snickered. "I've been ready all day. You in?"

"I am." Maria snugged her mask and dug in her purse. "Five strands in each—these beads called our name." She draped purple and gold beads over an arm then tore the cardboard fastener from the green bunch.

"Take one down, pass it around, green, gold, and purple beads 'round our necks." Zoe sang and slipped a green strand over her head.

Beth accepted the beads, one color after the other until a shiny triad hung from her neck.

"*Laissez le bon temps rouler.*" Corrine rallied a toast.

"*Oui Oui.*" Zoe clinked glasses. "That's all I know—plus 'Frère Jacques.' "

"Kate loved that song. *Frère Jacques, Frère Jacques, Dormez-vous? Dormez-vous?*" Therese extended a palm.

Zoe joined in, singing in round.

Corrine did, too.

Tapping her foot to the beat, Maria smiled.

After the final "Ding, ding, dong," Beth burst into applause. "Bravo. Might not be French…"

"Hear, hear." Zoe raised her glass. "Let's eat."

Hurricane in hand, Beth brought up the rear. Settling at the dining room table, she filled her plate with muffuletta *crostini*, Mardi Gras slaw, and jambalaya. The spicy aromas made her stomach growl. She dove into the culinary delights of New Orleans and offered silent thanks for her friends. Relishing the easy flow of conversation, she joined in once in a while but was happiest to listen. What she most wanted to talk about, but knew she could not, was Emma. Chewing a bite of *crostini*, she savored its blend of olives, peppers, and garlic while she studied her classmates' eyes: Maria's sapphire blue, Corrine's flecked hazel, Therese's chocolate brown, and Zoe's amber. *What do your eyes look like?* She wondered if Emma's eyes mirrored hers or Ian's. *Or maybe they're a color of your own.*

"Do your kids know?"

Zoe's question interrupted her contemplation. Beth glanced at Corrine.

"No. They'll speed dial me after he tells them." Corrine tapped an index finger on her palm.

"You're giving him control?" Therese pointed with her fork.

"I'm making him squirm. Dumb schmuck." Corrine scowled. "He needs to own his story. When he tells them about his little barista, I don't know what they'll say."

I never told you my story, Reid. Her appetite stripped by the grip of deceit, Beth cut a sliver of shrimp.

"How long will he wait?" Zoe rested her chin in a hand.

"As long as he can…" Corrine swigged her hurricane. "I'm not letting him off the hook. 'You dink, you pay,' as one of my law school chums used to say."

"I'm guessing she, or he, didn't go into criminal defense." Maria set her knife on her plate.

"Kathryn. She used to work in a county attorney's

office." Corrine rubbed an ear. "I'm not sure what she's doing now. She was a live wire."

"Two questions..." Zoe leaned forward. "Where is he living, and have you talked to your kids since you kicked him out?"

Beth grimaced then covered her mouth with her napkin. *I hope no one noticed.*

"He's in a duplex in the Rattlesnake. I've talked to the kids, but they didn't ask about him. When they do, I'll tell them he has some news." Corrine steepled her fingers. "Then he can't weasel out."

"Wouldn't you like to be a fly on the wall?" Therese hovered a forkful of jambalaya.

"No-o. I have no interest in hearing what he has to say. *Asshole*." She dipped her chin.

Beth's heart tugged for her friend.

"You do hold the power." Popping the fork into her mouth, Therese flashed a thumbs-up.

"Say what?" Zoe lifted her mask and wrinkled her brow.

"I'll explain in a minute." Therese pushed away from the table. "Who's ready for a hurricane refill?"

"I am." Straightening her mask, Zoe grinned.

Corrine held up her glass.

"Thanks, but I'm set." Maria sipped her drink.

"I'll help." Beth reached for Zoe's glass and followed Therese into the kitchen.

"Kate sure enjoyed her woodworking day with her grandpa." Therese plunked ice cubes into a glass.

"She's darling." Beth glanced up, holding the ladle midair. "I told her she's welcome anytime, but I know she likes working with your dad."

"They're two peas in a pod..."

You'll miss her. She wanted to draw Therese into a hug but tipped her glass instead and drank a silent toast. When she returned to the dining room, she set down Zoe's drink with a flourish.

"Thanks, barkeep. So…" Zoe snapped her fingers. "What's our lesson?"

"One Corrine had to beat into my head years ago. I might have been her most bullheaded client—"

"Client and friend…" Corrine waved a piece of *crostini.*

"Both?" Therese put her hands on her hips.

"Most pigheaded friend? Ab-so-lute-ly." Corrine enunciated each syllable. "Most hell-bent client?" She waggled a hand. "That's a toss-up. You're definitely in the top ten."

Half listening, Beth picked at her salad, sensing a special email topped her inbox.

"Damn. I wanted to be number one." Therese tapped her lip with a little finger. "All I could think about was strangling Vince's scrawny little neck. Her words, if I remember correctly, were I was 'consumed by anger.' "

"Mm-hmm, plus 'your anger is killing you.' " Corrine encircled her own neck with both hands. "Does he still have a scrawny little neck?"

"You be the judge at Kate's graduation party." Therese turned to Beth. "You, too."

"What are we?" Zoe flapped a hand between herself and Maria. "Chopped liver?"

"No—you'd be welcome. We didn't order many announcements because Kate doesn't want people thinking she's fishing for gifts." Therese spoke through scrunched lips. "She always asks about my

185

perimenopausal friends"—she smiled—"and she calls her friends 'the PMS-ers.' "

"She's thoughtful." Beth met Therese's gaze.

Zoe huffed a laugh. "I know a few PMS-ers."

"Her friends don't know…" Therese shook a finger.

"Gotcha." Zoe held a hand in front of her mouth. "We'll hold our vote about her dad's neck in private."

If I go. Beth rearranged her beads.

"So…" Zoe squared her shoulders. "What's the rest of the story?"

"Want to hold court and tell them?" Therese rested her forearms on the table.

"You." Corrine interlaced her hands then extended her index fingers. "I'll do rebuttal and closing."

"My perimenopausal brain farts might skew my memory, but between the two of us, we should get things right." Therese ran a thumb along her glass. "After Vince filed for divorce, I had zero patience for Kate's terrible twos. I couldn't eat or sleep…I just wanted to destroy him."

"You blamed everything on 'that asshole.' " Corrine spoke through cupped hands.

"According to this one"—Therese flicked her head—"I was giving him a lot of power."

"Which she denied with every ounce of her being. So, I did this when she wasn't looking." Corrine raised her chin and rolled her eyes. "Oh, you're *choosing* to starve yourself and stay awake all night and let Kate drive you crazy. She didn't like that explanation either."

"No, and then I wanted to strangle your scrawny little neck." Therese wrung her hands. "I don't know who made me more furious—you or Vince."

Listening to the banter of the longtime friends, Beth pleated her napkin. Her friendship with Lucy had gone from zero to ninety the day they moved into Sawyer Hall. Nine months later, she shoved aside their bond. Heaviness crowded her chest. *I miss you, Lucy.*

"People play the blame game and throw the victim card all the time because it's more satisfying…" Corrine turned to Zoe. "All they're doing is giving someone else control."

Therese raised an arm and rested her wrist against her forehead. "Guilty as charged…"

"How long before you rallied?" Zoe brushed back her hair.

"I don't remember." Therese straightened and shrugged. "Blaming him made me feel vindicated, so I wasn't a very fast learner."

"Hence…" Corrine sat back and crossed her arms. "Her tiptop standing in my most-obstinate-friend hierarchy."

"Last week, Erin shook a finger at a friend, complaining about who knows what. I told her to freeze and look at her hand." Zoe pointed at Therese. "What do you see?"

"One finger pointing at me. But when I do this, I see three fingers pointing at you." Therese rotated her wrist.

"See what I mean?" Corrine laughed and threw her hands up. "She worked every angle until finally—just to humor me, I think—she agreed she was in charge, and Vince was not the boss. Every once in a while, though, she'd plummet into victim mode."

"Here's a new visual for the blame game." Zoe tucked her elbows against her sides, fisted her hands, and swayed side to side in her chair. "Now, follow along, class...place your pointers on your chest, raise your thumbs to the sky, and wiggle your other fingers. Ta da." She grinned. "Feel free to use this move with your clients."

Wriggling her fingers, Beth rattled her beads and joined in the laughter.

Zoe swiveled in her seat. She fiddled with her mask then turned to face them—one eyeball visible. "Arrrr guys the worst?"

"*She was bad.*" Whispering, Corrine cast a sideways glance.

"Avast ye, mateys." Zoe rapped her knife and fork and crossed them in front of her. "Ditch ye bloody work talk."

"Overruled." Corrine pounded a fist on the table. "We're talking life lessons, and for the record, guys are the worst. Therese and one other woman, maybe two, rounded out my ten-most-obstinate-clients list."

"Do you do a lot of divorces?" Maria shifted in her seat.

Expecting a quick kibosh, Beth raised her eyebrows. *No one can see them.* Waggling her eyebrows behind her mask, she squelched the smile tugging at her cheeks.

"Yes, but only joint dissolutions—no more messy divorces."

"You represent both?" Therese leaned back in her chair. "I can't imagine."

"Not anymore." Corrine reached for her glass. "I did a couple of times, and then a client looked me square in the eye. 'Our agreement is fair, right?' He and his soon-to-be ex had decided on everything before they hired me, but she was getting a better deal."

"What did you say?" Maria tucked a strand of hair behind her ear.

"I nodded…" She scratched the back of her neck. "They'd already worked out everything and in his mind—maybe in hers, too—all was fair and square." She crossed her index fingers in front of her lips. "The end."

"You know what Marie Antoinette would say?" Therese stood and opened her arms. "Let them eat cake."

"All hands on deck." Zoe clapped five times.

Beth hurried to the kitchen and turned on the coffeemaker and kettle. She drew in a deep breath. *Do you like coffee, Emma?* The hope of an email raised goose bumps on her arms. As the voices from the hallway grew louder, she rubbed her hands along her sleeves.

Her cohorts set their dinner plates and serving dishes on the counter.

Therese unveiled the king cake.

"Me feels a parade a brewing." Zoe raised an eyebrow.

"Gotcha." Beth gathered pots, pans, and spoons then outfitted a drum corps of four, including herself.

"Oh, when the Saints…" Holding the tricolored dessert aloft, Therese led the ensemble.

Beth fell into step and marched into the nook, around the kitchen table, and out the door. She strutted, sang, and drummed down the hall, through the living room, into the dining room, and then back to the kitchen where the singing continued. Breaking out of formation, she quieted the kettle and filled a teapot.

Trading a pan for the rose-covered porcelain pot, she gave it a gentle tap with her spoon.

Maria exchanged her pan for the coffeepot. She played a tune on the pot's plastic lid.

Again hoisting the cake, Therese led the group back to the dining room: one pirate, four drummers, five voices—and an equal number of shit-eating grins.

After a final drum roll, Corrine sank into her chair. "I think we have a musical future."

"But first, let us eat cake." Therese picked up the knife. "How big?"

"This big." Zoe separated a thumb and index finger.

Therese made the first cut then glanced up as she repositioned the knife.

"Aye, Cap'n." Zoe dipped her chin to her chest.

"Be careful when you chew." Therese slid the slice of cake onto a plate and passed it to the pirate. "A surprise is baked inside."

"Yo ho ho." Zoe thumped her fork on the table.

Therese cut the cake to order and was the first to dig in. She pressed the tines of her fork against a bite-sized piece then used her knife and fork to raise the bite to her mouth.

Beth did the same, jiggling a leg as she chewed. *I want to get to my computer.*

"Keep a weathered eye open for the booty, mateys." Zoe raised her glass.

Halfway through dessert, Beth struck something with her fork. Scraping away cake, she discovered a tiny plastic baby—its body and outstretched arms covered in crumbs. *This prize should have been Maria's.* Heat seared her face. *I'm having a grandbaby.*

She wanted to blurt her news but instead lifted her hurricane and sipped past the thickness in her throat.

"Blimey!" Zoe widened an eye. "What's the booty?"

"Eenie meanie. Some say the winner makes the next king cake. Others say she throws the next Mardi Gras party." Therese ticked two fingers.

Afraid her voice would betray her, Beth drained her glass.

"You have the next party, and I'll do the cake." Corrine turned to Therese. "Where did you find the baby?"

"Harrr—The Treasure Chest." Zoe jutted her chin. "I have me pirate ways." She straightened her mask— both eyeballs now visible. "In case you couldn't tell, I've been a pirate for Halloween four years running."

"You don't say." Corrine grinned. "I might have to sign up for tutoring."

"Keep me in grog…"

Acquiescing to the soundtrack in her mind, Beth stopped listening. She was tired of shushing questions about Emma. Anxious for her company to leave, she couldn't wait to rush to her computer.

After the women finished dessert, they cleared the table.

Beth passed her dishes to Maria and veered to the hall closet. Nipping offers to help clean the kitchen, she distributed coats then ushered her friends to the door. She hurried through goodbyes and swung to the sink to scrub the king cake baby. The charm seemed like an omen, so she wanted it close when she fired up the computer. *I might be crazy…*

She hustled to the office and placed the baby on the

keyboard above F-five and F-six—between E and G. *Emma and Genevieve.* While she waited for her email to load, she held her breath. Then she scanned her inbox. *Nothing from Emma.* She dropped her shoulders. *So much for maternal premonitions.*

Maybe a letter was en route between Maryland and Montana. She hoped so. *I should have asked her to email.* With their relationship blossoming, she wanted it to bloom as fast as possible. She logged off and removed Emma's Christmas card from the desk drawer. Then she tucked the plastic baby inside—under the stars and cocooned by her daughter's words. Returning the card to the drawer, she glanced to her right, drawn in by a glimpse of Reid's paisley tie. Her stomach pitched. He should have learned her truth years ago. Telling him now—in death, she argued—seemed a horrible blow.

Since learning about Emma, she tapered off her journal entries. She contemplated jotting something before returning to the kitchen, but the words clamoring in her head could not be shared. Even if she penned an innocuous note, leaving out the king cake baby would be a glaring omission. Could she ever write the truth? Exiting the office, she glanced right, unable to face the impostor in the mirror.

****

Five days later, Beth flipped through several envelopes on her way into the house. The familiar handwriting quickened her pulse and she hurried inside, resenting the one-second pause to close the garage door. She didn't stop to take off her coat. Instead, tunnel vision drove her to the living room, past Reid's recliner, and straight to her own. Dropping her purse, keys, and other mail onto her lap, she held Emma's card and worked a finger under the flap. She brought the envelope to her nose for a hungry inhale then placed a soft kiss. *Did you plant a kiss, too?*

Prickles of anticipation rushed her body, and she removed the contents. *Two pages.* A folded note fell on top of her purse. She shifted her gaze to the letter.

Dear Beth,

Your card affirmed my decision to write again after saying I wouldn't. Thank you so much for your honest words, which bear witness to your unconditional love. Carrying this baby makes me doubt I could ever be as selfless as you. Again, the words thank you *feel so slight.*

A hot flush crept up her face. Countless times throughout the years, she berated her selfishness, chiding that her concern hadn't been for the baby but only herself. She cared about both of them, but *selfless* was never part of her story. Though she breathed words of protection every single day, she battled any other thoughts about what she left behind. Reading Emma's words, she understood why. *Thinking about the baby was too damn hard*—her baby girl she now knew… She exhaled long and slow then refocused on the letter.

The answer to how I found you is twofold. The short answer is when I searched for you last fall, I found your name in your husband's obituary.

The word dropped like lead. Battling a mishmash of emotions primed to explode and tear her apart, she elbowed out of the chair. The letter and note, along with her lap contents, fell to the floor. Slowed by the shrapnel of feelings too big for words, she wove as if through a minefield then slogged outside to escape the truth. The cold winter air bit her cheeks. Circling the yard again and again, she plodded atop the stiff, dead grass of winter. *Your death led her to me, Reid.* But then she wanted to reel in those words, because how could she mourn the first but celebrate the second?

Chapter Eleven

After thirty, maybe forty, laps around the yard, Beth returned to the living room. Torn between wanting to read the rest of Emma's letter and wanting to forget its beginning, she shed her coat and tossed it onto the couch. Digging through the pile on the floor, she collected the letter and note. Then she wrapped herself in a fleece comforter and sank into her chair. She scanned the first page, skipping over the *O* word to find her place.

I don't know the heartache of losing a loved one. Learning you were married more than thirty-one years, though, speaks to grief beyond my imagination. I'm so sorry. The other answer to how I found you is a longer one—and one I hope won't upset you.

So do I. Fighting the urge to bolt, she steeled herself to *just read.*

Doctor Ziegler was my family doctor. More than once, I gave him an earful about wishing I knew the identity of my birth parents. My adoptive parents are wonderful, but as a teenager, I didn't always appreciate them. I didn't know Doctor Z was your doctor, too. He'd just sit back and listen to me vent while my mom waited out front. Enclosed is a copy of a note he sent two years ago.

With trembling hands, she unfolded the paper. The ghost of Doctor Ziegler's penmanship loosened a web

195

of remorse, and she squeezed her eyes shut, drowning in memories. *Breathe in. Breathe out.* As she repeated the mantra, she let the note flutter to her lap. When her mind quieted, she opened her eyes and picked up his words.

Dear Emma,

When I closed my practice, I found your birth mother's file buried in a cabinet. You and your earnest questions always reminded me of her. Much has changed in the adoption world since you were born. At this juncture, I'm taking the liberty of sending you her health history. I hope only good things come out of my actions but if not, I'm prepared to live with the consequences. My bigger regret would be to lament, "I wish I had."

Your mom gave me your address, so I'm sending this snippet of your past with her blessing. She said you're doing well. I never doubted you would as I watched you blossom throughout the years.

Warmly,

Orin Ziegler

Tears sprang into Beth's throat. Picturing Doctor Ziegler caring for Emma with his soothing voice and tender touch, she blinked hard to still the words swimming on the page.

I can't imagine how Doctor Z's words might make you feel. When I first read them, I was overcome with both gratitude and fear. I was thankful for the gift of his trust and grateful to learn a bit about you—especially in your own handwriting. But I was afraid about what your reaction might be if I found you.

For two days, I rallied the courage to search for your name. When I typed the letters, I couldn't breathe.

"No results found" made me heartsick. I debated contacting an adoption registry but then told myself the dead end meant you didn't want to be found.

Beth sucked in a breath. She grasped for a sliver of comfort—confirmation those three words meant Reid was better off not knowing, and her secret was hers to keep. Throughout the years, she hushed a desire to find her child. The thought filled her with equal doses of optimism and terror. *Just like Emma.* She adopted a motto—*que sera, sera*—and hearing Doris Day sing those words in an old movie made her tingle from her scalp to her toes. Glancing away, she steadied her breathing. Then she refocused her gaze.

I didn't show Doctor Z's letter to Bennett or my parents until after I searched for you. Bennett encouraged me to explore adoption registries, but I never did. I buried the letter in a desk drawer then dug it out after I got pregnant. As I mentioned, part two was the longer answer...

You were a healthy twenty-one-year-old, and I'm hoping your good health continues. I'm wondering, too, about my birth father, though I'll understand if you'd rather not answer. I hope my question isn't offensive— my apologies if so.

All is well with Bennett, Bean, and me. I hope you are well, too, and I look forward to hearing from you again. Thank you for sending your email address. Mine is elovkau55@gmail.com. If you'd rather email, no worries, but I loved receiving your letter. At the expense of sounding silly, reading and holding some- thing you've touched makes me feel closer to you.

Much love,

Emma

Shame and guilt wrestled happiness and joy. Years had passed since she thought about Ian. On fleeting occasions when she wondered how his life turned out, she never looked for him. Wrapping her arms around her belly, she tipped back her head and sank deeper into her chair. That night, she lay awake for hours. The prosecution—*tell her*—and the defense—*do not*—volleyed back and forth until she drifted into restless sleep.

She woke firm in her conviction not to tell Emma about Ian. Thirty-six years ago, he deserved to hear about a baby. *Not now.* A letter from Emma—when he probably had a wife, kids, and grandkids—would pack a gut punch no one deserved. The flip side was she did not know what to say.

All morning and into the afternoon, she grappled with her reply. She shunned paper and pen, composing in her head as she added, deleted, rearranged, and then replaced words she axed. After a thorough chastisement followed by sufficient self-talk, she arrived at a truce. Losing Reid and reconnecting with Emma were chapters in her history. Heeding Corrine's words, she would *own* her story, mourning the former and celebrating the latter. She questioned ever absolving her deceit. But knowing her secret was never driven by spite, she sought a thread of comfort.

When the phone rang mid-afternoon, she hurried to the kitchen. Grateful for the interruption, she answered without checking caller ID. "Hello?"

"Hi, Beth, this is Kate. Grandpa's coming Saturday, so we wondered if we could work on"—she paused—"the coffee table."

The final words were a near whisper, and she

strained to hear. "Of course."

"Thanks. See you soon."

Mumbling a cursory goodbye, she replaced the handset and powered on, working in thought alone. Hours later when words remained beyond grasp, she pulled out her hot air popcorn maker. Though her popper was years old, she refused to replace it with prepackaged, microwaveable bags. As the aroma of popcorn filled the kitchen, she poured a glass of Cabernet. She hunkered into her recliner with a book and a two-course dinner—vegetables and fruit—AKA popcorn and wine. *Tomorrow, I have a date with ink.*

Many hours and several diversions later, Beth sank into a dining room chair and twirled a pen between her fingers. Memories of childhood baton lessons competed with the oppressive silence. She sidetracked to the living room and sifted through CDs then wasted more time tuning the volume before returning to the table. *Start writing.* She sucked in a deep breath and forced an exhale—choppy and loud. Five sentences in, she pushed away from the table and circled to the office, her stomach skittering. She snagged a pencil and reclaimed her seat.

Reading Bean's nickname reminded me of yours. I used to think of you as "two."

She reread the end but not the beginning. Despite orders from the critic perched atop her shoulder, she refused to start over. A Mozart violin concerto drifted into the room. *Just write.* Submitting to the voice urging stream-of-consciousness writing, she put pencil to paper.

I feel sheepish writing two, *but that word helped me take good care of you.*

She continued her story without edits. Then Ian's name slipped out. Words taking her where she did not want to go, she dropped her pencil and sprang from the chair. Her heartbeat thrummed in her temples. *This letter is just a draft.* She paced around the house, and a skirmish raged inside her head. Six laps in, she yielded to the quieter voice and returned to the dining room.

I hoped I'd miscarry over Christmas break. Draining her coffee, she refused to write that sentence, even though Emma would never see it. A memory flitted through her mind.

She hadn't realized until days later the tiny flutter on Christmas morning—as ephemeral as the brush of an eyelash—was her baby's hello. When the butterfly-soft somersaults became more insistent on New Year's Day and every day thereafter, she silenced her hope of miscarrying. Then Doctor Ziegler told her he had a lovely couple longing for a baby, and guilt wiped out the remaining whisper.

Censoring the previous sentence, she swore she'd let the next ones rip. Then, as though the draft were a lump of clay, she would mold her words into something tidy and compact. She puffed out her cheeks and sputtered a breath through pursed lips. *Conceived in love...* The Kenny Loggins refrain replayed in her head. Emma had been conceived in love, and now *she* was in love and awaited the baby that would make Beth a grandma... Staring at her words, honest and raw, she was grateful to have scribbled the truth. She owned her story, but this chapter was not meant to be shared with Emma or anyone else.

How do girls hide their pregnancies these days? With open adoptions and more and more single moms and unmarried couples having babies, she supposed concealed pregnancies might belong in the past. The controversy over abortion rights had picked up steam, though. Regardless, loose clothing kept her secret safe, and she empathized with anyone who wanted similar privacy these days. Since meeting Maria, she noticed babies and baby bumps everywhere. Every grocery store checkout lane displayed at least one magazine cover with a baby bump, baby, or happy family gracing its full color, glossy front. *I'm glad I didn't see all those pregnant bellies back then.* She could not imagine displaying her own rounded belly, even if she had nothing to hide.

In the beginning, she hadn't contemplated *boy* or *girl*. Not wanting to refer to the baby as *it*, though, she deferred to male pronouns by default. She remembered mornings when she wakened with both hands cradling her belly. Otherwise, she avoided touching her abdomen to thwart unwelcome attention. Every kick and hiccup rushed a grim reminder that giving up her baby might take strength beyond her ability. In the secret of night, though, she woke to the magnetic attraction between her hands and belly. Skin on skin, she caressed her tummy, massaging her baby even in her sleep. *So hard…so hard…* The words looped through her head. Tears leaked from her eyes and puddled in her ears but removing her hands hurt a thousand times more. She surrendered to the pain, continuing her caresses until her alarm beckoned her out of bed.

I had a baby girl. The words filled her with wonder. Instinctive, she rested a hand over the hollow space that had guarded her baby. Silence filled the room, and she segued to the CD player and pushed Play. Then she resumed her position before the critic convinced her to ditch every single word.

She smoothed a piece of stationery, part of a retirement basket from her coworkers. When she uncovered the linen paper with its purple scrolls, Fran winked and pointed out an accompanying grape-scented gel pen. Beth forgot about the aromatic option tucked inside the desk drawer. She picked up the black pen instead, glancing at the draft that lay catawampus to her right. The words yet to unfold would be easy in the beginning…but in the middle, she had no idea.

Dear Emma,

Thank you for writing. I agree, receiving letters is a treat, and finding yours in my mailbox was the highlight of my day. Thank you. I'm glad to hear all is well with you, Bennett, and Bean. I was a healthy twenty-one-year-old, and I tried hard to take good care of you, too. Once I realized I was pregnant, I stopped drinking. Not that I drank a lot…but after learning I was eating and drinking for two, I didn't touch another drop.

Other than dragging out my perimenopausal years, I'm still in good health. TMI perhaps, but I've learned from a friend who's trying for a child you might go through menopause at the same age as your mom. My mom was fifty, though, and I hope to be done before I'm fifty-eight.

Writing *mom* gave her pause. Her focus had been on her unborn grandbaby and thirty-five-year-old Emma. She could never recapture first words, scabbed knees, teenage angst, or graduations. *I am a mom.* She breathed the words in the quiet of her heart and again out loud.

Unlike my friend Maria, I didn't struggle with infertility. I hope you and Bennett didn't, either.

A band squeezed her chest, leaving only a tiny space to breathe. She dropped the pen. *Tell her the truth.* Combating the voice in her head, she turned the letter sideways then upside down. She spun her words around and around then sucked in a shallow breath and picked up her pen.

Your birth father's name is Ian Boumdett. I loved him, and he loved me. We had sex for the first time the night before I left for a National Student Exchange. He pulled out, and though I knew withdrawal wasn't always effective, I didn't worry.

Her heart pounded a staccato rhythm. Staring at the truth, she debated crossing out the last paragraph—which would have looked awful—or starting over. One CD track followed another, and then she exhaled a ragged breath and righted her pen.

He was overseas during Christmas break, so I didn't see him. I didn't know how to tell him about you, and then during spring quarter, he met someone new… His break-up letter felt like a sign, and we never saw each other again.

Beth rubbed a hand over her chest, willing her heartbeat to *slow down.*

I wanted to bury his name. For the last two days, I wrangled ways to deflect your question. But in the end, I knew withholding his name wasn't fair. I don't know where he is or what path his life has taken. He was a healthy twenty-one-year-old, five-foot-ten, and one-hundred-fifty-five pounds—give or take. His mom, dad, and younger sister were healthy, too. He had beautiful cornflower blue eyes, dark brown hair, and a room-lighting smile.

Do with that information as you wish. Knowing whatever happened was beyond her control, she kept those words to herself. *Que sera, sera.* She would not search for Ian and break the news, but like Doctor Ziegler, she refused to live with the bigger regret—*I wish I had.*

On a lighter note, I'm thrilled all is well with you three. What's your due date? I would love to have a picture of you, Bennett, and your baby bump. Take good care, and I wish you continued happy and healthy days.

She lifted her pen. Though she terminated parental rights years ago, she was, and would always be, Emma's birth mother. But unless or until Emma coined a replacement, she had a single name. She set pen to paper.

Much love,
Beth

"MommaBeth." She thrilled at the sound. *Will I ever have a new name?* The question was too big to ask out loud.

****

Five days later, Beth welcomed Kate and Frank into her home for another woodworking date.

Kate pressed a Bernice's Bakery bag into her hands. "Grandpa says when we do something a second time, it's—"

"Tradition, tradition…" He flung open his arms. "I won't tell you how many traditions have been two and out, though."

"Not this one." Kate winked and led them down

the hall, stopping midway to hang their coats.

Beth marveled at her self-confidence and poise. *Were you like her, Emma?* Countless questions somersaulted through her mind. She accompanied her guests into the kitchen and peeked inside the bag. The sweet aroma filled the air, and she drew in a deep breath. "They smell divine."

"That's what I said." Kate tugged on her grandfather's sleeve. "Shall we eat them now, Grandpa?"

"We'll eat when we take a break." He handed Kate a canvas bag. "I'll be ready for a cup of joe with my roll in a bit."

"You're rocking another one of your rhymes, Grandpa." She grinned and nudged him with her elbow. "We never know when you'll come up with something witty."

"I learned how to be witty from you." He linked her arm. "Lead the way, madam."

"Do you need anything?" Beth gestured toward the coffeemaker and sink.

"We're set." Kate steered him out the door.

Their tenderness tugged at her heart. *I'm having a grandbaby.* She wanted to shout her news but sipped her coffee instead. The Colombian Roast washed away the words. A memory crowded her mind.

When her mom had learned about Jake and heard twelve-year-old Reid's subsequent vow, she was quiet as she shifted her gaze past Beth and brushed a hand across her glistening eyes. "Do you think Reid will change his mind about having kids?" Her question came almost two years later.

She would never forget the hunger in her mother's

eyes and the yearning in her voice the month before the wedding… Pink crept up her mom's face, and she recanted her words. Both of them had struggled to hide their pain.

She remembered her dad's words, too, years after she and Reid had married.

"You'd make a wonderful mother, sweetheart." He wrapped her in his arms and kissed her cheek.

Sorrow and guilt scratched at her throat. His eyes revealed what his words did not—he would have loved being a grandpa. She suppressed the longing in her voice and had stifled any hints of her desperate desire for a baby and beyond.

Routing to the entertainment center, she tightened her muscles, primed for fight or flight on her clandestine mission. She retrieved her knitting bag and removed the tiny alpaca sweater. Exhaling a jagged breath, she willed her body to relax. Nothing made sense. One minute, she wanted to holler her news from the rafters. The next, she proceeded in stealth. *Relax.* Kate and Frank would not arrive in the living room without her hearing them. She caressed the yarn she purchased at Joseph's Coat two days earlier. How long ago had she finished Reid's maroon crewneck? *Four years ago? Five?* She couldn't remember.

I should do something with his clothes. The words surprised her. She told herself numerous times she would never get rid of his stuff. Her rational, reduce-reuse-recycle self argued that decision, but so far, aside from a book and wood, she couldn't part with his belongings. *How long did you wait, Mom?* Two or three years—she wasn't sure… Muting thoughts of her parents, she picked up her knitting. As she focused on the click-click of her needles, she struggled to convince herself her mom and dad were better off not knowing about the baby.

Two hours later, Beth joined her company in the breakfast nook. She savored a bite of the caramel roll's bakery-fresh goodness. The sunlight streaming on Frank's hands awakened childhood memories of her dad, doughnuts, and sun-drenched California mornings. *Ssshhh.* She glanced across the table. "Has your mom asked about your project?"

"She asked how the bench was coming." Kate arched her eyebrows.

"What did you say?" She leaned forward.

"I told her we're making a surprise." Kate patted her cheeks. "I've never been good at telling lies—not that I want to be. I used to have a friend who lied all the time. She thought she was good, but she wasn't."

"Do I know her?" Frank shifted in his seat.

Kate nodded. "Savannah. She has dark hair and always wore cute dresses to my birthday parties. Remember that one?"

"Nope."

"Some of her lies were bald-faced, but a lot were lies of omission. Y'know what I mean? She didn't even think those fibs were lies… I think they're the worst." Kate speared a piece of her roll. "For a while, whenever she'd tell me anything I'd think whatev, but one day I told myself my trust was in the ditch." She grinned. "Remember how I used to say 'in the ditch' when we played cards?"

Lies of omission… A chill ran down Beth's spine. Her shudder was so slight, she hoped no one noticed. She swigged her coffee.

He gave a hearty laugh. "I do—instead of in the hole. What were you—about four?"

"Yep. That was the day you started calling me precocious." Kate winked. "Anyways, I decided life's too short to have a friend you can't trust. I stopped hanging out with Savannah in middle school, but I'm nice whenever I see her."

"Sounds like you learned a lesson you could teach us grownups." Beth encircled her mug with her hands.

"Maybe. Sorry about the life's too short." Kate held her gaze. "But I bet you didn't expect Reid to die when he did."

"I didn't." Surprised and comforted by her candor, she glanced away.

"Have you read *The Fault in Our Stars* or seen the movie?" Kate reached for her hot chocolate. "Talk about life's too short."

She shook her head. "I don't think I could get through either one."

"Yeah—they're sad…"

"With a librarian momma, I bet you grew up with lots of books around your house." Beth studied her young friend.

"Plus grandparents who love books." Kate tipped her head. "He and Grandma always give me at least one book with every present."

"I learned to love to read from your grandma." Frank stroked his chin. "I don't think she would've married me otherwise."

"What about you and Reid?" Kate lifted her last bite.

"Reid read some, not as much as I do. Did. Do…" She waved a hand. "The library was one of my favorite places as a kid. Still is."

"Mine, too." Kate glanced at her grandpa's empty plate. "Time to get back to work." She stacked her plate and mug.

"I'll get those." Beth reached for Frank's dishes. "Your boss is calling."

"She's a taskmaster." He lowered his chin and raised his eyebrows.

"Someone has to be, Grandpa." Kate linked his arm and guided him out the door.

Beth buried her head in her hands. Paralyzed by deceit, she sat without moving, and then abandoned her knitting for the remainder of the afternoon.

That evening, she sank into her recliner and opened her journal. Since learning about Emma, she penned only a few cursory entries. Her words seemed stilted and untrue. Conflicting pleas for truth and charades haunted her throughout the years, but the reality was she was a fake.

After Reid died, she was consoled when she sensed his presence. Now, consumed by guilt, she scrapped the notion he lingered nearby. She talked to him sometimes but stopped believing he could hear her. "I'm so sorry." Her words rang low and mournful. At times, she was desperate to confess the truth. Fear and shame kept her secret intact—the confidence she vowed never to share. *Then my secret found me*. She closed her journal and blanketed herself in fleecy darkness. But how could she tell him in death?

****

The following week, Beth was halfway through a knit-one-purl-one row when the phone rang. She set her knitting on the magazine table and unfolded from her recliner. By the time she reached the phone, the answering machine clicked on. She lifted the handset and pressed Talk. "Hi, Maria, I was in the middle of knitting…" She swallowed hard, wanting to take back her words.

"Nice. What are you working on?"

"An afghan." She leaned against the counter. *Don't ask for whom.*

"I've always wanted to learn. Maybe you could teach me someday." Maria took a breath. "I'm calling to see if you'd like to go to lunch on Tuesday? Saint Patrick's Day, so we could have corned beef and cabbage, or something else…"

Straightening, she smiled. "Corned beef and cabbage sounds great."

"How about dining at the River City Grill? We could meet at the Orange Street exit pullout at eleven, and I'll drive?"

"Perfect." She smiled all the way to the living room. Her knitting tempered the waiting game, but every afternoon she hurried to the mailbox. Though her head told her Emma needed more time, she battled impatience. Skimming her fingertips over the afghan, soft as the mohair cardigan she bought years earlier, she closed her eyes. *Do you look like me? Did you send a picture?*

Chapter Twelve

Two days later, Beth rushed into the house and tore open an envelope, ripping the flap in her haste. She sank into her recliner and removed a letter and *two photos*. Emma's cornflower blue eyes and smile made her gasp. *Just like Ian's.* Her daughter's nose and high cheekbones mirrored hers, and a swell of pride filled her chest. The strawberry blonde hair, swept into an updo on her wedding day, was a color all her own.

Snuggled beside Bennett, Emma was the same height, though her floor-length gown covered her shoes. *How tall are you? Were you wearing heels?* She wanted to know every single detail but would not bombard her with questions. Shifting her gaze to Bennett, she studied his eyes. Green or hazel or gray— she couldn't tell. His wavy brown hair shone in the sunlight.

She slipped the second photo to the front. A quiver tugged at her lips—the gentle pull between a smile and tears.

Bennett stood behind Emma. Dipping his chin to her shoulder, he encircled her and her baby bump with his arms.

Emma rested her hands atop his.

Together, they shaped their thumbs and fingers into a perfect heart.

Beth imagined Little Bean kicking and stretching

beneath their hands. Her stomach fluttered in reply. She recalled cradling her belly, and an ache sprouted in her core. Ian had never been part of that visual, and though she didn't wish she raised Emma—*Genevieve*—alone, seeing the happy family stirred unwelcome melancholy. Their palpable love sparked a flash of joy, too, and she pressed the photos to her chest.

She and Reid had shared such a love, minus a baby. But after she closed the door to motherhood all those years ago, falling in love with someone terrified to have a child was karmic payback.

"Maybe I could have given you a good life." Her words echoed in the empty room. Without a crystal ball, she would never know about the road not taken. *And that has made all the difference.* She turned over the photos. *July Third. March Ninth.* Almost five years in between. Placing the pictures side by side, she looked from one to the other. In the recent photo, their smiles were *for her.*

"I have a son-in-law." Bennett's status was a piece of the puzzle she hadn't comprehended until now. She breathed the words whisper soft then unfolded the stationery.

Dear Beth,

Thank you for your letter. I can't imagine the turmoil my question unfurled... Special thanks for sharing such intimate details and telling me my birth father's name.

Enclosed are a wedding photo and a picture we took the day I received your letter. We got married Fourth of July weekend. Bennett lobbied hard for July third because the month and day added up to the year. He assured me if we were married on that weekend, he would never forget our anniversary. Plus, he said "ten ten" doubled down the month and day of my birth— "five five." Have I told you he has a way with words?

You were born in fifty-seven... Reid's statement edged into her mind. *You would approve, Darling.* Guilt, joy, sorrow, and pride tumbled in her chest. She blew out a long, slow exhale and returned her gaze to the letter.

Our baby is due April twenty-fourth. All is well, and I'm a little over thirty-three weeks in the picture. I plan to work as long as I can then use my twelve-week parental leave once Little Bean is here. I'm moving toward the finish line with an open mind, so we'll see how things go.

What was your labor like? I was an average size— seven pounds four ounces, with a thirteen-and-three-quarter-inch head. How long did you push? Some say your birth experience mimics your mom's.

Filled with wonder, she exhaled a soft breath. *I am a mom.* She ran a thumb over her daughter's hand-writing, drowning in the words.

Others say no correlation exists. I call those odds fifty-fifty, but Bennett calls them a crap shoot. We're halfway through our Lamaze classes and are conscientious about practicing the breathing and relaxation exercises. I'd like to have a drug-free birth, if possible. We're vacillating about having our Lamaze teacher, Jennifer, who's also a doula, with us for Bean's birth. As we get closer to our due date, hopefully yes *or* no *will declare itself for both of us. Next week, we're taking an infant care and CPR class then we're scheduled for a breastfeeding class the week after. Bennett calls our preparation "the trifecta."*

Asking about my birth might be asking you to relive an experience you'd rather not. I spent the last half hour debating whether to tear up this letter... Please don't feel compelled to answer my questions. Just know that as we approach our baby's birth, I cannot stop thinking about you. Penning a thousand thank-yous *would not adequately convey the depth of my appreciation and love.*

Would you mind sending a picture? My friends can't understand why we haven't talked or emailed. I considered calling, but my hormones are so wild, I'd just bawl on the phone. Which means video calls are off limits... Your letters are treasures, and I look forward to more in the future.

With love,

Emma

Beth rubbed her temples. *My friends don't know.* For years, she suppressed memories of her labor. Meeting Maria nudged murmurs into her consciousness, but she batted them away. Now, Emma wanted her to remember.

She set the letter and pictures on her side table and circled to the laundry room. *Mom's favorite.* Shushing that memory, too, she hunted mindfulness as she loaded the washer then wound to the kitchen. She brewed a pot of coffee—no decaf—intent on mustering the courage to revisit the past. Carrying a steaming mug into the living room, she wrapped herself in fleece and curled into her recliner. She closed her eyes. Like an old movie, scenes rolled through her mind.

In the dead of night, an ache, low in her abdomen, had awakened her. Fighting the tightness in her chest, Beth kneaded her belly and didn't stop until she felt a familiar nudge. "You're okay." She whispered her relief. Unable to see the clock in the inky darkness, she chased sleep, but the cramping persisted.

She didn't take childbirth classes, but each night after tucking into bed, she devoured the handouts from Doctor Z's nurse. Then she returned the papers under her mattress and practiced her breathing—quiet so Lucy wouldn't hear. As the pain wrapped around her body, she began slow, rhythmic breathing. She jiggled a foot, too, and the friction against the sheet ebbed and flowed with each contraction.

Lucy rustled her covers. "Are you in labor?"

Her roommate's sleepy voice eased the lonely blackness. A surge of warmth spread from Beth's neck to her face. "I think so." She untangled from her bed and flicked on the desk lamp. The time was only four forty-five—way too early to be awake on a Saturday morning.

"I'll take your notes, plus a pen and paper, please." Yawning, Lucy stretched an arm.

Thank you. She gathered a spiral notebook and pen and rummaged under her mattress for the labor tips. Then she hurried down the hall to the bathroom, certain Lucy would speed-read the handouts she crammed weeks earlier.

Back in bed, Beth breathed through contractions— ten to twelve minutes apart according to her roommate's record. Hiding her nervousness, she stilled her foot. When the pains bumped up to eight minutes apart, Lucy said she was taking her to the hospital. Butterflies collided in Beth's belly. She dressed and made another trip to the bathroom, thankful her neighbor's doors were still closed.

"Please let me stay with you, or at least hang out in the waiting room." At a red light, Lucy waved a hand then gripped the steering wheel. "You might change your mind."

Staring at Lucy's white knuckles, Beth shook her head hard. *I told you* no *a thousand times.* But her throat was too thick and sore to say the word again. When the car pulled up to the hospital, she hooked her canvas bag with a foot. *Go back.* She flicked a hand. Then she lumbered out of the car without a thank-you or goodbye and pretended not to hear her roommate cry.

Slowed by the weight of her belly and bag, she reached the reception desk seconds before a wave of pain returned. She breathed through the contraction, but her rhythm was sloppy and fast. The smell, reminiscent of hydrogen peroxide and her mother's freshly mopped floor, hit her hard. So did the pitying look from the grandmotherly receptionist when she asked if someone was parking the car. Her *no* sounded feeble and small, and she wanted to run after Lucy and beg her to stay, even though she knew her roommate was long gone.

The receptionist asked her name, and then reached for a telephone. "Sorry, we don't have a volunteer to take you there..." She pointed with the phone. "Go straight then turn left. I'll call OB and tell them you're on your way."

She trudged away from the desk and turned at the intersection. A sign at the end of the hall announced OBSTETRICS. When she approached the nursery windows on her right, she stared straight ahead, without even a sideways glance. Her stomach tangled in knots. She pushed open the door.

A middle-aged nurse greeted her with a smile. "My name's Marietta. I'll be taking care of you." She extended a hand toward Beth's bag.

Beth glanced away from the kindness in her brown, gold-flecked eyes. She clutched her duffel to her chest, unwilling to surrender her tether to the outside world. At a pair of closed doors marked LABOR AND DELIVERY, she hesitated, overcome by a wave of dizziness. She squeezed the bag even harder.

Marietta opened one side of the double door, and then brushed a hand against her back.

Buoyed by the gentleness of her touch, she put one foot in front of the other, barely noticing the nurses' station and staff along the way.

"Are you leaking water or bleeding?"

She shook her head and followed Marietta into a labor room, past an empty bed to the far one covered with a sheet and big blue pad. A second sheet lay folded at the foot of the bed.

"I need you undressed from the waist down." Marietta pulled a curtain between the beds. "I'll grab the copy of your prenatal record and be back in a minute."

After the door clicked shut, she set her bag beside the room's lone rocking chair. She removed her shoes, jacket, pants, and underwear then bundled them on top of her duffel. Still wearing her navy knee socks, she crawled onto the bed and spread the top sheet over her rounded belly and thumping heart. A contraction started. She squirmed, making the pad crinkle. She focused on her breathing, reclaiming a bit of the control she feared she abandoned at Sawyer Hall.

When Marietta returned, she washed her hands and

asked about Beth's contractions. Explaining the fetal heart monitor, she slid two wide bands under her back. She felt all around her belly then fastened the contraction sensor up high. "Do you want the volume on or off?" She squirted blue gel on the ultrasound disc.

Her voice matched the warmth and tenderness of her hands. "I want to hear…" *Him.* Beth glanced at the clipboard on top of the monitor, grateful her prenatal record wasn't visible. She remembered Doctor Z underlining she *did not* want to see or talk about the baby. *At all.* The cool goo on her belly made her flinch. Then a strong, steady clip-clop filled the room, and heat rushed to her eyes. Numbers flashed on the screen: 138, 145, 137, 143…

Marietta fastened the second strap and repositioned the sheet. She checked vital signs and pointed to a contraction's rise on the monitor tracing. "The sensor doesn't tell us the strength." Shifting to the bedside, she placed her hands high on Beth's abdomen and pressed with her fingertips.

Pain wrapped around her. She closed her eyes and rubbed her belly, struggling to control her breathing in front of a new audience.

The baby twisted and poked, and his heartbeat sped to a gallop.

When the contraction ended, Marietta patted her leg. "Nice job." She washed her hands again then donned a glove, adding clear gel this time before checking Beth's cervix.

During the exam, Beth stared at the screen. A fist or elbow pushed against her belly—in protest it seemed. The numbers shot up—162, 159, 167, 161—and she traced little circles over the nudge. *We're okay.*

Her knocking heartbeat belied her words.

"You're two centimeters dilated." Marietta pulled off the glove.

Her stomach clenched. "Only two?" She had been one centimeter and completely effaced for two weeks. Gripping the hem of her smock, she twisted, pulling the fabric taut over the monitors and bands.

At the sink, Marietta met her gaze in the mirror. "Ten more minutes…then I want you out of bed. Walking can speed up early labor, or slow or stop contractions if they're false." She dried her hands and collected the clipboard. "I'll bring you some ice chips." Pausing at the doorway, she smiled.

False. Massaging her belly, she felt a tap in reply. She wanted the kicks and turns to last forever, but these contractions were too strong to be fake. A pain started in her back, and her uterus tensed under her hands. *No way you're false…no way you're false…* The words flowed in and out with her breath.

Marietta delivered a cup of ice chips and a spoon. She stretched the tracing between her hands. "Seven minutes apart…everything looks good." She turned off the monitor and unhooked the straps. "Walk inside or out, and I'll recheck you in an hour." She gathered Beth's clothes and laid them on the foot of the bed. "You might not need your coat."

Beth shoveled in a spoonful of ice chips before getting dressed. In the bathroom, pain overtook her breath. Struggling to breathe with her eyes open, she focused on the doorknob. When she passed Marietta at the nurses' station, she fluttered a wave, anxious to get outside before the next contraction. Her heart pounding, she pushed through one set of double doors and then the other, hustling when she reached the hallway.

A tall man held up a dark-haired toddler in front of the nursery windows.

"He's too little…" The boy pressed a hand against the glass.

Out of the corner of her eye, she glimpsed a row of bassinets before turning from his small voice. Continuing toward the front, she avoided the receptionist on her way out the door. Sunshine warmed her face. She yielded to the push-pull of the day and walked at a medium pace. Part of her wanted to carry the baby forever while another part wished labor would hurry. A contraction stopped her cold. She plunged her hands into the pockets of her jacket and focused on a tree branch. *No way you're false…* She rubbed her belly through the fabric and repeated her chant.

When the contraction ended, she sputtered a huge cleansing breath then veered to a parking lot. She ducked between cars to avoid a family of three walking toward the hospital. Stilled by another contraction, she leaned a hip against a white station wagon. As she breathed, she stared at a floral air freshener dangling from the rearview mirror. She dodged two other groups on her way to the lot marked STAFF PARKING. Alone, she braced herself against random vehicles every few minutes, convinced pain this real could *not* be false.

After her stop-and-start walk, she was dilated two and a half centimeters. The day powered on with an enema, shave, and a mixture of blurriness interspersed with bits of clarity. Beth didn't like being in bed, so she sat in the rocker or walked around the room, halted every four or five minutes by another contraction.

Doctor Z stopped by. He pulled up a chair next to the rocker and rested a hand on her arm. "How are you doing?"

"Okay." She held his gaze as she had when she lied about Ian. This time, the ache was too big for her chest. She pinched her leg under her gown.

A wordless understanding passed between them.

"I'd like to check you." He patted her arm then looked at the monitor tracing before circling to the sink.

His exam was gentle. Hearing she was dilated between three and four centimeters, she caressed her belly. The end seemed more real, and her gnawing, hollow stomach flip-flopped at the news. When the labor pains engulfed her body and attacked every single breath, she asked for drugs, grateful Lucy wasn't there to watch her writhe. She had to be at least four centimeters—Doctor Z's orders. During her exam, she gritted her teeth, ready to stifle a scream if she heard "not yet."

"You're four and a half centimeters dilated." Marietta assured her she'd be right back, and then returned with her hands full. She started an IV and administered pain medication.

The drug reduced the pain by half, and Beth dozed for minutes at a time.

Marietta sat on a straight back chair beside the bed. She shifted her focus between the monitor tracing and paperwork. But during every contraction, she set down her pen, pushed aside the narrow table, massaged Beth's legs, and helped her breathe.

Her eyes became Beth's focal point. The baby's heartbeat did, too, though its rhythmic cadence rushed swells of sadness.

A little before three o'clock, Marietta told her another nurse, Cheryl, was taking over. "We picked her especially for you. She's wonderful."

"I don't want you to go." Beth clutched her hand.

"You'll love her." Marietta traced tiny circles on Beth's hand with her thumb.

Don't leave me...don't leave me... The words became her silent plea as she breathed through an ache sharper than before.

Marietta gave her hand a final stroke then stood and drew the clipboard to her chest. "We'll see you in a few minutes."

Squeezing her eyes shut, she refused to watch her leave the room. She battled waves of pain—three or maybe four—then the door clicked open.

"Beth and Cheryl." Marietta gestured from her to the newcomer.

"Nice to meet you." Cheryl smiled.

Beth felt her pulse in her throat. She considered the compassion in the thirty-something beauty's ebony eyes. *Please help me.*

After looping to the sink to wash her hands, Cheryl nested Beth's hands between her own. "I hear you're doing great."

The softness of her warm, cocoa-brown hands and soothing touch added to Beth's tears. She gazed from one nurse to the other then freed her hands to give Marietta a hug. Words tangled on her tongue.

Cheryl massaged her legs and coached her through every contraction.

In two three...out two three...in two three...out two three... As she breathed, Beth focused on her dark eyes. She asked for drugs twice more, though each dose took away less of the piercing ache. In the middle of a contraction, warm liquid gushed from between her legs. "*More…*" Her high-pitched whine sounded other-worldly. The pain smothered her words, and she shook the IV tubing, certain her hips were splitting in two.

Cheryl checked her and said she was almost ten centimeters dilated. "Breathe like this, he…pa…he…pa…" Face-to-face, she exhaled the words, centering Beth's head between her hands.

Stabbing waves seized her body. She thrashed and swore, fighting to breathe.

After a few more contractions, Cheryl checked her again. "You're ready to push." She taught her to tuck into position and hold her breath. Cupping a hand behind Beth's neck, she curled her chin to her chest and counted in her ear. "One two three four five six seven eight nine ten."

Panic merged with the pain. Beth just pretended—puffing her cheeks but fighting to keep her abdominal muscles soft as putty. The pressure *hurt like crazy*, but she did not want to let her baby go. *Ever*. Her uterus tightened and shoved.

Cheryl helped her onto a stretcher then covered her with a warm flannel blanket and wheeled her down the hall.

A younger woman assisted with the transfer and settled Beth on the delivery table.

An icy chill washed over her. As the heat waned from the blanket, she shivered against the table's thin cushion. A contraction gripped, and she placed both hands low on her belly, pulling toward her rib cage to keep her baby inside. Flat on her back, she stared at a giant spotlight suspended from the ceiling. Reflected in the shiny silver light was a warming bed like she'd seen in a magazine at Doctor Z's office. A folding screen stood between her and the bed. *To hide the baby.* Pain consumed her chest, slamming her heart and lungs.

"You're so close." A mask muffled Cheryl's words. She strapped Beth's legs in stirrups then snapped on gloves and washed her bottom.

The cold, smelly cleanser and light—now aimed between her legs—sparked a wave of dizziness. Staring at the warming bed's reflection, she sputtered moist, choppy breaths. *I want my baby.*

Doctor Z arrived through a door that faced the foot of the delivery table. Nearing her head, he met her gaze. "You're almost done." He held his arms bent at the elbows, and drops of water clung to the backs of his forearms and hands. Green scrubs, safety glasses, a mask, and a blue paper cap replaced his street clothes.

The softness in his eyes and voice pierced her core. A quiver pulled at her lip, and another siege of tightness ripped through her body. She fought to hold onto her baby, but guttural grunts escaped her mouth.

He covered her belly and legs with blue paper drapes. "This numbing medication will ease the pain. You'll feel pressure…"

Stinging followed along one side of the baby's head then the other, but she didn't even flinch. Beneath her ribs, her soul exploded. *Please numb my heart…* Choking her breath, the words clawed at her throat.

The door behind her head opened. A tall woman entered the room and slipped behind the screen.

Beth looked away from the newcomer's reflection in the light. Nothing—not even Cheryl's steady counting in her ear—veiled the crackle of paper then the snap of latex coming from the secret space.

With a pink-and-blue baby blanket draped over her forearms and hands, the woman moved toward the foot of the table.

Another contraction hit, and Beth screamed a soundless plea to *stop pushing.* Her words mirrored Doctor Z's—hers overlapping his—but her body took over and pushed out the baby.

He gave one tiny mew then fell silent.

Holding a blanketed bundle, the woman darted behind the screen.

Rustling…shuffling…rubbing… Beth strained to hear more from the concealed spot. Hot tears trickled sideways, collecting in her ears. "Is he okay?" She choked out the words.

Cheryl nodded and stroked her hand, her eyes glistening.

Certain the thin nod was proof he was not, she shook with sobs.

"You need a few stitches." Doctor Z looked past her draped belly to meet her gaze.

His voice was soft and low, but she didn't answer.

Cradling a thick white blanket, the tall woman hurried from the room.

The click of the door reduced Beth to nothingness. Wracked by sobs, she scarcely registered the blob plopping from between her legs or the gushes of warm liquid that followed. She closed her eyes, longing to morph into a vapor and *find her baby.*

Cheryl caressed her hand then reached under a drape to push on her belly.

Placing a gloved hand on top of the drape, Doctor Z pressed straight down on her abdomen. "Give her zero point two…"

The mask dampened his words as he rubbed hard and fast with his fingertips, digging into the fleshy softness of her belly. Pain shot through her, overtaking the place where the baby had been. A steady drip landed somewhere beneath the table. She gripped the hem of her gown.

Behind her, Cheryl rummaged in a cabinet.

"She's giving you something for the bleeding." Doctor Z leaned in and continued his massage. "Redheads can bleed more…"

Don't. The blood had *nothing* to do with her hair. Every drop poured from her heart. No one could stop the bleeding, but that inability was okay because she could *not imagine* living without her baby. The textured ceiling panels blurred through her tears.

"You'll feel a little poke."

Cheryl's voice sounded light-years away. Something cold and wet on her thigh preceded the sting and burn which paled beside the steady kneading on her belly. Beth imagined herself back in her dorm room with her baby inside. She hardly noticed her uterus tightening, more stitches, or Doctor Z and Cheryl returning her to the labor room. Tendrils of sorrow wrapped around every cell. Motionless, she lay with her eyes closed, erasing the world around her. Then soft stroking on her cheeks and the scent of hand soap nudged her back.

"Everything is stable, and I can move you to another room…" Cheryl ran a hand down Beth's arm and caught her hand. "Would you like to stay in OB or go to the medical floor?"

"Go…" The rest clotted in her mouth. She could

not bear to hear babies cry. But knowing the silence of *her* baby, the quiet would be worst of all.

Wheeled past the covered nursery windows, she stared at the curtains adorned with multicolored sea creatures. An ache grew in her chest. When the elevator door opened onto the second floor, she felt as though the oceanic pain would destroy her.

Cheryl rolled her to a private room at the end of the hall and tucked her into bed. She returned with another warm flannel blanket, snugging it around Beth's body and under her feet. Then she straightened the covers and leaned in for a hug. "Take good care."

"Is he okay?" she whispered.

"Yes." Cheryl tightened her hold.

Her breath warmed Beth's neck. *Don't leave me.* She gripped her nurse, wanting never to let go.

When Cheryl wriggled away, she held Beth's gaze. Her eyes shone. Closing the curtain, she sniffled.

Then the wheelchair clattered against the doorjamb.

A sob started low in Beth's body. She knew if blood made a sound, it would sound like that— wounded and raw. The agony of her empty arms seeped to her marrow, and she needed something to hold in the space meant for a baby. *I want my stuffed monster.* She debated about bringing her plush bed partner, a high school graduation gift from Nana, to New Hampshire. Worried a stuffed animal would seem juvenile, she left him home.

I need him now. She wadded the flannel blanket, a reminder of the one that insulated her baby, and curled onto her side. Hugging the warmth to her chest, she buried her face, certain no amount of flannel could absorb her snot and tears.

Her recovery was excruciating—her bottom throbbed and her breasts ached, but the hole in her heart hurt worst of all. She mourned alone.

Returning early from a final, Lucy caught her once. She slid onto Beth's bed and wrapped her in her arms.

Her sobs fell onto Lucy's chest and soaked her shirt.

They had clung to each other all afternoon.

Beth's throat ached. Repositioning in her recliner, she tucked her chin under her comforter then crossed her arms and hugged her shoulders. The memories, more painful than she imagined, wrenched her soul. She did *not* want to tell Emma anything about labor or beyond.

"How are you, Lucy?" Silence surrounded her words. She regretted breaking their bond. With her story stretched between them, though, maintaining a relationship all those years ago seemed impossible.

If she told Reid about the baby, how would things have turned out? What if she spilled the truth while they were dating? Or given in to the incessant voice imploring *tell him* after years of secrecy? Learning he was married to a liar, how would he feel? Some might argue she didn't *really* lie because he never asked if she ever had a baby. Kate's words about lies of omission buzzed in her head. Could she ever shake the shame of her deceit?

Chapter Thirteen

The next morning, Beth drifted between wake and sleep. Ignoring her bladder's insistence to get up, she hugged a pillow to her chest and straightened her legs, willing herself back to slumber. All night, labor scenes bombarded her dreams, but she was no closer to knowing what to tell Emma. After restless minutes, she shoved aside the memories and rolled out of bed.

Happy Saint Paddy's Day, Darling. She wondered what the holiday was like in heaven. Quite a party, she assumed as she slipped her robe over Reid's thermal underwear. She believed the afterlife was all good and hell nonexistent. But even if she were wrong, he would undoubtedly be enjoying a slice of bliss. *Cheers.* She lifted an imaginary glass. *This one's for you.* Two hours later, she parked in the Orange Street pullout and hurried to Maria's car.

"Happy Saint Patrick's Day." Maria stretched to give her a side hug.

"Great idea." She smiled and buckled her seat belt. "How are you doing?" Her question sounded cursory and fast, and she glanced away, wishing for a do-over. She wondered how Maria's fertility quest was going but didn't want to intrude. Nor did she want to blurt out about Emma and her baby.

"Doing well…" Music played in the background. Maria backed up then gazed straight ahead as she eased out of the parking lot and onto the interstate.

"I've been thinking about corned beef and cabbage all morning." Beth stroked her wedding band with her thumb. "I haven't had any for a couple of years."

"What did you and Reid used to do?"

"Go out. I debated whether or not to cook corned beef this year…" She shifted in her seat. "What about you and Anthony?"

"We went to the parade on Saturday and had Reubens afterward. With his tax season and my wonky schedule, our goal is to have corned beef and cabbage or Reubens sometime in March and call it good." Maria shot her a quick smile. "Today's a bonus."

"For me, too." Longing filled her core—more ache than pang. She placed a hand high on her chest and gazed at the Clark Fork River. *I miss you.* Thirty minutes later, she raised her glass, inhaling a multitude of restaurant aromas. She shifted her gaze skyward for an instant before taking a drink of her stout. She savored its rich, dark flavor. *Happy Saint Paddy's Day, Darling.*

"Good?" Maria leaned forward.

"The best ever." She stabbed a forkful of corned beef.

Maria nodded at the glass. "I meant your beer—I've never seen you drink one."

"I don't very often…" Memories of Irish stouts with Reid floated through her mind.

"Mmmm, I love a good beer. Draught Work's Mexican Chocolate Porter is my fave." Maria rested her forearms on the table and lowered her chin. "I had a period eight days ago."

Grinning, Beth tipped her glass. "Cheers."

"Thanks." Maria smiled back. "It only lasted three days, and I didn't have any slippery mucus, so when I saw the blood—" She glanced to her left.

Beth followed her gaze.

Two women and a man engaged in conversation at a nearby booth.

All around them, the River City Grill pulsated with holiday cheer. Beth scooted her chair closer to the table.

"I'm pretty sure I didn't ovulate." Maria tucked a strand of hair behind her ear. "I didn't have fertile mucus or mittelschmerz—mid-cycle pain. Some women have pain every month." She tilted her head. "Did you?"

Beth rearranged her napkin. "I didn't really pay attention…" She hoped Maria didn't notice the catch in her voice.

"Before going on the pill, I know I popped some eggs. When your mucus looks like egg white and you can stretch it this far"—Maria moved her thumb and index finger from an *O* to an uppercase *C*—"then it's time to get busy, if you know what I mean."

Their server stopped to check in and refill their water glasses.

"Everything's delicious." Beth smiled and took a bite of cabbage, holding a hand over her heart while she chewed. Then she met Maria's gaze. "What did Anthony say?"

"Time to pick up the pace." Pink crept up Maria's cheeks. "Plus, you don't need to be telling anyone."

She zipped her fingers across her lips. "What are your thoughts?"

"I've done a lot of rereading the past week. Some say an eight percent chance of pregnancy with POI and no fertility treatment. Others say five to ten." Maria picked up her knife. "I like to think I'll make the cut, so in the meantime, I'm being as healthy as possible…"

Bypassing her beer, she raised her water glass. "Here's to you and Anthony and to a healthy egg and hearty sperm."

Maria smiled and clinked.

I had a baby girl. Glancing away from the hopefulness in Maria's eyes, she slugged a long drink of water, washing away words she could not share.

That evening, Beth nestled on the couch and paged through a photo album. The most recent photos, already a year and a half old, lay entombed in a camera. She planned to work on them post-retirement. Instead, the camera remained untouched in a basket on the computer desk. She didn't have the strength today to browse its pictures. Reliving memories of her final months with Reid, compounded by a swathe of guilt, felt like too big a betrayal. She flipped through the album pages, contemplating whether to send a photo of her or one of them both.

Looking for a photo is hard either way. She paused at a picture taken at Butchart Gardens almost three years ago. The floral perfume seemed to drift off the page. She wore her favorite sundress, black with splashes of daisies. Reid was the center of attention, though, sporting his canary yellow polo shirt and backdropped by a riot of roses. She had two copies, framing the second and taking it to work. *That picture is still in one of the boxes.* She squelched the reminder of another unfulfilled, post-retirement goal—sorting through stuff she hauled home.

Pulling the photo from its sleeve, she examined her

younger self. Aside from a smattering of gray hair, her looks hadn't really changed. She remembered a young coworker who was certain her hair would turn white following the heartbreak of her sister's sudden death. Beth convinced her the myth was false. Had a veil of truth existed, she would have returned from New Hampshire a shattered twenty-one-year-old with hair rivaling Dame Helen Mirren's.

Images from the dorm room and hospital rooms skated through her mind. She closed the album. *I'll write tomorrow.* She'd sum up labor in a single sentence. *Remembering was too painful.* Crawling into bed, she added another line. *I'm sorry.*

She spent the night more awake than asleep, dozing in fits and starts. *I could write an abbreviated version minus the angst.* Telling Emma a bit about labor would be the kind thing to do, but she doubted she could manage even a smidge. This journey crushed her heart and soul. Thus far, the voice clamoring for self-care led the pack.

As the room lightened into the soft shades of morning, she climbed out of bed. Over breakfast, she paged through the newspaper but could not stop thinking about the letter. *Stop fretting and write.* She set her bowl in the sink and refilled her coffee cup. After detouring to the laundry room, she dug through the recycling bin and extracted the Sunday newspaper. She cut out an article about doulas and carried it into the dining room.

Emma's photos lay propped against a cut glass vase centered on the table. Brushing a thumb across the etched crystal spurred memories of wedding gifts and Reid and her favorite California neighbors. She shifted her gaze to the stationery. *This house is too quiet.* She backtracked to the living room, browsed their CDs, and chose a piano instrumental. Hopeful the soothing sound would inform her words, she plucked the picture of her and Reid from the coffee table. Then she laid the photo face up at the base of Emma and Bennett's pictures. Three lives intertwined since their number decreased by one. *I should have told you.* But she rejected that option years ago...

She glanced away. The knot in her stomach spoke the truth. Leaving Reid's picture in the living room was not an oversight but rather self-preservation. *I'm so sorry.* She turned their photo face down and slid it away from the others. Then she reached for her pen.

Dear Emma,

Thank you for the pictures. Bennett is every bit as handsome as you are beautiful. He sounds wise as do you. Reading about your anniversary made me laugh. Seems you both chose wisely, and I wish you many happy and healthy years together.

Glad Little Bean is doing well. I hope the next few weeks will be uneventful, so you can save your parental leave until after Bean's arrival. Practice your breathing—it will carry you through labor...

The words flowed. *No reading. Just keep going.* She straightened her pen.

My memories of labor are spotty but here's what I remember—

Twelve days before my due date and after hours of contractions, Lucy drove me to the hospital. She pleaded to stay but to be honest, I couldn't bear to see my agony and sorrow reflected in her eyes...

She wrote the facts, glossing over the angst. But

her heart ached. She returned pen to paper.

"When you arrive to give birth, you park your modesty at the front door, but it waits there until you leave." I've never forgotten Marietta's words. My vote, for what it's worth, is to have Jennifer on board. I'm enclosing an article from our Sunday paper—serendipitous—about doulas' increasing popularity nationwide. Birth is a powerful experience. I love your attitude of hoping for a drug-free labor but keeping your options open. Employing a doula on your upcoming journey sounds spot-on.

Beth read her last paragraph. A flush of satisfaction travelled up her neck and face at her inaugural, albeit unsolicited, sage motherly advice. Then she reread Emma's letter, mustering her resolve to answer the remaining questions.

Your labor will be different on so many levels. Reading about your trifecta made me smile. Reid loved that word. He would be so happy to learn about you, Bennett, and Bean.

Liar. She buried the pen beneath her stationery and lumbered out of her chair. Then she escaped to the backyard and struggled to quiet her mind. The winter air nipped her face and neck and bit through her clothes. Circling the yard, she hugged her arms tight across her body, not caring that she lacked a coat. The truth was, after thirty-three years of marriage, she had *no idea* how Reid would feel learning about a baby. But Emma did not need to know about her deceit.

Shivering, she returned to the house. She sidetracked to her closet for her wool fisherman sweater. After returning to the dining room table, she ran her fingertips over Emma's closing words. *Yes*, she, too, loved the thrill of handwritten letters and quivered at the thoughts of stumbling through phone or video calls. Even without the rollercoaster of perimenopausal hormones, she knew her voice would betray the years of sorrow she stuffed away. She hesitated to acknowledge the secret wish to hear her daughter's voice and search for any hint of her own. Maybe someday, but for now, Emma's letters were treasures beyond measure. Glancing at the upside down photo, she returned pen to paper.

Enclosed is a photo from one of our favorite places. We loved visiting Victoria, British Columbia, and a trip to Butchart Gardens was always a highlight.

She studied the back of the picture—its royal blue, acid-free ink memorializing the date and place. Righting the photo, she looked from her image to Emma's. Two old pictures tiptoed into memory. Detouring to her scrapbook might mean she would miss the mail carrier's rounds, but she pressed away from the table, stepping into silence. Memories and words consumed her focus, blocking out the quiet that wrapped around her. She stole into the living room. For a nanosecond, she considered browsing for music from the photos' era. She hit Play instead and hurried to the office.

Her mementoes lay buried in the bowels of the closet. As she lugged the old ketchup box into the middle of the room, she grunted. Then, remembering dorm room debates about which ketchup brand was best, she smiled. She worked the ends of the tape and opened crosswise first then lengthwise to reveal the guardians—graduation cards and three copies of her commencement program. Removing the layers with care, she turned reckless as she dug through years of memorabilia.

When Beth grazed something round and cool, she gasped. Lifting her stuffed monster from his cocoon, she smiled at his rattle eyeballs and crooked smile. She hugged him to her chest then turned him so he could survey her work. As she rummaged to the bottom of the box, she proceeded with caution and cupped both hands around her scrapbook's bulging pages. Concert stubs, letters, report cards, photos, and bits of history spilled beyond its edges. After shifting her monster to the crook of her arm, she set the album on her lap then turned its pages with care.

The envelope protruded from beneath a UNH report card. She slipped a finger under the yellowed and lifeless tape then held her breath when she removed the card. The face-to-face photos were the confirmation she sought, and she exhaled long, slow, and deliberate. Her mind spiraled backward.

Willie, the black patch tabby, had glommed onto her lap minutes after she arrived at Lucy's home for spring break.

Ulysses, his blue-cream-calico littermate, claimed Lucy's lap and stretched to rest his paws on her shoulders.

"Their momma got around." Lucy ran her hands from Ulysses' paws to his tail.

"They have different dads?" Beth wrinkled her brow.

"Yep." Lucy buried her face in her kitty's fur.

Remembering the blank section on her own health history, she glanced away. Heat scorched her face. Throughout the next two days, she rearranged Willie on her lap and ballooned her smocks away from her belly. She carried the baby low and wide but with a cat on her lap, she didn't know where to rest her hands.

The following morning, she browsed a bookshelf. While Lucy was in the shower, she curled up on the couch with a copy of *The Chocolate War*.

Willie jumped into her lap, pushing his paws up and down before tucking next to her belly.

Engrossed in the book, she sank a hand into his fur.

Lucy's mom, Diane, joined her. Reaching over to pet Willie, she brushed Beth's fingers with her thumb. "Are you having a baby?"

Her voice was soft as cotton. *No.* She stared at Diane's hand—her olive skin shades darker than Lucy's. She buried *her* hand deeper into the fur, her stomach pitching under the weight of the lie rolling around inside her mouth. Then she gave a single nod.

"When or if you'd like to talk, I'll listen." She nested Beth's hand in hers. "Does Lucy know?"

She shook her head.

"Shall I tell her later?" Diane held her gaze.

Relief washing over her, she nodded. *Then I'll have a friend to talk to.* Hours later, she shared Lucy's double bed and whispered long into the night. Throughout the remainder of the week, Beth didn't worry once whether space existed between her belly and smocks.

Two weeks later, a card arrived addressed to *her*. The name on the address label quickened her pulse. *Diane Spethman.* She hurried upstairs and dropped onto her bed, grateful Lucy was in class. Scooting against the wall, she sat cross-legged which was getting harder to do. Then she tore into the card.

Dear Beth,

Thank you for spending your spring break with us. After hearing so much about you, meeting you was a pleasure. All best as you finish out the school year. Please know I'm only a phone call away. Willie and Ulysses have been moping around since you and Lucy left. Come back anytime.

Truly,

Diane

Two photos lay sheltered between her words. On the back of each picture, her loopy handwriting memorialized the day. *Spring Break March Fourteenth. Beth, Willie, Lucy, and Ulysses—Forever Friends.* A deep, raw ache of longing filled her chest. *I want to go back.*

The baby twisted and kicked inside her.

His gymnastics were stronger than usual, and Beth wondered if he was feeling happy and sad, too, like the weave of emotions zigzagging through her. She sat for an hour, stroking her belly and staring at the photos. That afternoon, she showed Lucy the pictures and note. She had tucked the envelope into her desk drawer, pulling out the photos whenever she was alone.

Since moving to Missoula, she looked at the pictures a handful of times, careful to store them face-to-face as Lucy's mom had. If Reid ever found the card, she was certain he would replace the pictures front to back.

Discovering the photos' familiar position was validation he didn't find them. *As if.* No way would he have sifted through her old college box.

She turned over the top photo as though opening a book. Longing's familiar ache tugged at her core, and she wrapped her arms around her stuffed monster.

Willie had lain curled on her lap, snugging the fabric of her favorite red-and-blue plaid smock against her rounded belly. She smiled for the camera.

Beside her, Lucy beamed and held Ulysses' front paws in her hands.

The girls nestled on the couch, their bodies touching—shoulders to knees.

In the second photo, Lucy sported a silly grin and splayed two fingers above Beth's head.

Oblivious to the rabbit ears, Beth gazed at Willie, cradling him between her hands. She didn't realize Diane snapped a picture. To a casual observer, she looked as though she inspected the cat, but she held the truth. Responding to her baby's kicks, she pulsed her arms against her sides and belly. Then she had squeezed her eyes shut to dam the tears.

The memories of her unborn baby and lap warmer scratched at her throat. She lifted the first photo and closed the album around the second. "Keeping you out would be too damn hard." She gave her monster a final hug then returned him to the box. "You, too." She carried the photo to the dining room and overlapped the images so mother and daughter were side by side. "You look like me." With a featherlight touch, she traced a fingertip over Emma's baby bump then over her own. "I miss you."

But how can you miss someone you barely know? She closed her eyes. *I knew you in every twist and turn. You knew my heartbeat from the inside out.* Yes, she thought Emma was a boy, but that mistake did nothing to dilute the maternal tenderness she buried deep within. Having uncovered her love, she wanted the moon and more.

But Emma was in charge.

She would follow her lead—rejoicing in every offering Emma cast her way and accepting with grace whatever their futures held. Straightening the photo, one of only two confirming her pregnancy, she imagined Emma drawing it close to her heart. She picked up her pen.

This picture was taken the day after Lucy learned I was pregnant—nine weeks before my due date. My smocks did a good job of hiding my belly, and I made sure she never saw me undress after I started to show. Once the cat was out of the bag, though, I relaxed around her. A silly pun I know, but a little aside—Willie sat on my lap every chance he could. He'd purr, you'd kick, and I wished those days would last forever.

Debating whether or not to ask for a baby picture, Beth let out a slow exhale. *Yes* and *no* fought toe-to-toe with equal conviction. A newborn photo might split open the scars far beyond what adult Emma had. She would never regret Emma finding her—*ever.* But reopening memories barricaded more than half a lifetime ago unleashed a fresh onslaught of sorrow. Though her decision was for the best, that knowledge did nothing to soften the ache.

Finally, after nipping the backtalk, she convinced herself she would be better off without a baby picture. She abandoned her vow to avoid reading her letter. "I'm checking for errors." Her words rang hollow in the empty room. She managed a quick reread. Skimming the pain, she reminded herself Emma deserved honesty. Then she returned to her pen.

Thank you again for your letter and pictures. As I

write this, you're closing in on your due date. I wish you and Bennett continued good days as you prepare for, and await, the birth of your baby.

Much Love,

Beth

She turned over the photo of her and Reid, and her throat tightened. She could *not* nest these pictures face-to-face. Instead, she placed the older picture on top—face up. Diane's loopy handwriting on the photo's back served as a thin layer between truth and deceit. She folded the letter around the photos and newspaper article and slipped them into the envelope, already stamped and addressed.

Unable to produce even a hint of moisture in her bone-dry mouth, she carried the letter into the kitchen. She turned on the faucet for a fraction of a second, collected a bead of water with a fingertip, and dampened the flap. Then she sealed the envelope and trudged down the driveway. Opening the mailbox, she sputtered a huge breath. *Mail.* She removed a grocery store flyer and a glossy advertisement for a lawn care service. Sandwiching her letter in between, she carried them into the house. *One more day.* She dug deep for the courage to reveal Ian's name and admit her deceit. But could she ever tell Emma her deception hadn't ended with him?

Chapter Fourteen

A week later, Beth knelt in the living room and sifted through CDs. When she reached the Rolling Stones, she paused, stilled by memories.

The night she and Reid danced in their seats at the Stones concert made both of their Top Ten lists. For weeks afterward, he blasted their Stones CDs, working his best Mick Jagger impressions as he sang along. The weekend before he died, the seventh anniversary of the concert, he clasped her hands and sang along to "Let's Spend the Night Together." After an afternoon of tender lovemaking, she drifted into a deep, blissful sleep, wrapped in his arms.

She hadn't listened to them since. Buoyed by the impending arrival of her woodworking friends, she pulled out a stack of Stones CDs. She selected *Made in the Shade*, tuning the volume to reach the kitchen. As she stuffed the mushrooms, she danced a little— bittersweet reminiscences scrolling through her mind. The doorbell chimed in the middle of "Happy." She considered turning down the volume along the way but answered the door instead.

"I'm down." Zoe's grin matched her own. "Been waiting for six o'clock all day without realizing we'd be rocking to the Stones. My Grammy would call that 'gravy on the cake.' "

Her sultry voice and accompanying hip swivels

made Beth laugh. "Sounds like your Grammy would fit right in."

"She would. San Francisco chicken—I think she'd approve." Zoe passed the dish before shedding her coat. "Whenever we'd visit, she'd let my sister and me choose new recipes, and then we'd shop and cook together."

"Nice Grammy." She stopped midstride. *I wonder what I'll be called.* Her outstretched elbow clipped Zoe in the ribs. "Sorry. Think we should turn down the music?"

"Can we can dance later?" Zoe wrinkled her face and rubbed her side. "This pain should be gone by then."

"Oh, we can dance"—she shimmied—"and if you haven't done any acting then you've missed your calling."

"Good to know. Tonight, though, I'm a rock star goddess." Zoe broke into an air guitar solo, augmented by a one-leg-raised-single-foot hop. She turned toward the living room. "We'll listen to this bad boy from the beginning…"

Beth smiled all the way to the kitchen. She hoped Zoe's wit would rein her in and hush unbidden thoughts of Reid, Emma, and her grandbaby. The music stopped then resumed with "Brown Sugar" low in the background.

"*Love them.*" Zoe danced in and nudged her hip. "What are we drinking? I'll pour."

"Blackberry basil spritzers." She punctuated each word with a hip bump.

"Yum." Zoe rubbed her belly.

Ding-dong.

"Back in a Jumpin' Jack Flash." Showing her dimples, Zoe threw the words over her shoulder and headed out the door.

You will keep me focused tonight. She set a bowl of blackberries alongside the Prosecco, basil, seltzer, and agave syrup. Maria, or any seltzer drinkers, would need the latter, according to the recipe propped against the syrup. She surveyed the table: ramekins, champagne flutes, spoons, and the five muddlers she bought last week were fanned and ready. *Perfect.* Folding her hands, she offered thanks for her friends, the Stones, and sweet memories.

"Basil blackberry spritzers." Zoe's voice carried from the hallway. She led a trio into the kitchen and waved a half gallon of ice cream in Beth's direction. "Big Dipper." Without waiting for an answer, she opened the side-by-side and put the ice cream in the freezer.

"Mmmm." Beth shifted her smile to the newcomers. "Welcome. Hot here, cold there." She gestured toward the countertop. "Can I help with anything?"

"This." Therese proffered a bottle of wine. "Sounds like we're having something better tonight, so save it for next time or drink it in the interim."

"Would anyone like some?" She turned the label toward her friends.

"The night's young. Hear that? Dance party tonight with *the Rolling Stones*." Zoe lowered her chin and swiveled her hips.

Laughter rippled among the group.

"After our feast. Drink ingredients are over there…" She tilted her head. "Plus, a muddler for each of you to take home."

"Gotcha." Zoe gave a thumbs-up.

Beth slid the mushrooms into the oven and set the timer then joined her friends around the table.

"This tool will get more use than my push stick. I'm just saying." Zoe grinned and waved her wooden muddler. "I've always wanted to be a mixologist. What's that song—'Hey Bartender'?"

"Don't know." Corrine poured floral wine charms onto the table. "You mix mine, and I'll wrap one of these beauties around the stem of your glass. The charms are for you..." She looked at Beth. "They shouted *new recipe night* when I saw them last week."

"Thank you." Beth smiled and glanced at Maria's ramekin—already a sea of purple and green.

"Dibs on this one." Therese twirled a green stem, and the bright yellow flower wiggled above her fingers. "I love the smell of lilies."

"I'm not sure which smells better—blackberries or basil." Zoe looked up. "What are our choices?"

"Calla lilies...tulips...orchids...and..." Therese held up a blue charm. "Mystery flowers."

Beth picked up one of the latter. A pair of pale pink petals, reminiscent of playing card spades, and two pink leafy things encircled a dimpled center. *A belly button.* Her mind reeled backward. She had meant to ask Doctor Z to cut the cord so her baby would have an innie—not a half-innie half-outie like her own. She forgot, though, and in the tumult of labor hadn't given her baby's belly button another thought.

Lost in regret for not asking Doctor Z the question that burned in her mind as she lay awake in her dorm room and wrangled sleep, she studied the flower's perfect pink innie. She wanted to blurt her news. As her announcement clawed at her throat, she circled the tiny, pink center with a thumb.

"Do you know these flowers?" Therese tapped Beth's charm with a salmon look-alike.

She rotated the charm and turned it over, slow and deliberate. "No—and that's my final answer." Lilting her voice, she attempted levity.

"Madam?" Corrine swept her hand above the charms.

"I'd like the periwinkle one, please." Zoe sank her muddler into a ramekin. "Periwinkle for perimenopausal, or for *one* of the perimenopausals, I should say."

"Gotcha." Beth handed the blue mystery flower to Corrine.

"Am I popping the cork?" Zoe reached for the Prosecco.

Beth nodded.

"You don't have to tell me twice." She peeled the foil.

"But you have to tell me how to fix this charm…" Corrine wound an orchid around her glass.

"I had to hold my stem at the tip." Therese pinched her thumb and index finger together.

Corrine arched her eyebrows. "I haven't held anything at the tip for a while."

The cork's blast punctuated her words.

It's been a year and a half for me. As she muddled berries and basil, sadness and remorse stacked like weights on Beth's chest. She yielded to the feelings without reprimand because to ignore the ache only increased its power. Exhaling a slow, measured breath, she glanced up and met Maria's gaze.

Maria flicked her head.

Her friend's unspoken words added a new brick of sadness to her emptied lungs. She formed her lips into a silent *O*.

Spooning puree into a pair of glasses, Zoe added sparkling wine until bubbles reached the rim. "Too tall to call, as they say at the craps table. Better take a swig before you pick up your glass."

"Let the wild rumpus begin." Corrine lowered to a squat and sipped.

Zoe did the same. Sporting a purple moustache, she straightened and licked her lips.

"Reminds me of college days, though we didn't drink anything this fancy." Therese tipped her glass and added Prosecco then followed with Beth's glass for two perfect pours.

Maria added seltzer and mixed her mocktail without commentary.

Beth sipped her drink, and the sweet and savory flavors burst in her mouth.

The timer rang.

"Let's eat." Zoe lifted her glass.

Maria lingered in the kitchen and balanced a platter beside the cookie sheet. "Your mushrooms look delicious."

Drawing in a deep inhale of the aromatic appetizers, Beth used a spatula for the transfer. "I hope they taste as good as they smell." She wanted to check in, but Maria's stories were hers to share or not. Collecting their drinks, she followed her out the door. At the table, she filled her plate and recited her recipe name and ingredients.

Zoe raised a bite of mock potato bake. "I think my girls would love this dish, even though Erin dislikes cauliflower. We don't say hate, so dislike gets a lot of use, especially regarding vegetables."

I had a baby girl. Beth pressed a fingernail into her palm, fighting to quiet the words.

Corrine straightened her napkin. "I'll email the recipe. Hunter's not a cauliflower fan either, but he'd like the cheese and bacon."

"I want all the recipes." Zoe turned to Maria. "What are we having with Big Dipper?"

"Blueberry crisp." Maria slipped a strand of hair behind her ear.

"That combo would get some love at my house." Therese smiled and cut a bite of chicken.

"How's Kate doing?" Maria leaned forward. "Is she counting the days until graduation?"

"She's counting the days until spring break." Therese held her fork in midair. "We're going to Portland."

"To see that woodworking school?" Zoe reached for the salt shaker. "What's the name?"

Therese nodded. "Oregon College of Art and Craft. We meet with an admissions counselor Tuesday. I feel like I should be over the no more Doctor Kate by now…" She puffed out her cheeks then exhaled through pursed lips. "For years, she's dreamed about becoming a doctor, so I just want her to be sure."

"She beams when she's here with your dad." Beth stroked her chin.

"Plus, when you visit campus and see how excited she is…" Corrine waved her knife. "I predict your doubts will dissolve."

"I do, too, but excuse me for a moment..." Zoe formed her hands in the shape of a *T* and pushed away from the table. At the entertainment center, she sifted through CDs. "Next up...*Forty Licks*."

"Street Fighting Man" drifted from the neighboring room.

"So, where were we?" She reclaimed her chair.

"Deep in another conversation about Kate..." Therese placed a hand high on her chest. "I'm considering you my anchors after she leaves."

"Always." Corrine patted her arm.

"We're a good crew." Zoe glanced around the table. "How are things going for y'all?"

I have some big news... Beth squeezed her kneecaps between her middle fingers and thumbs. "You're welcome here anytime. All of you."

Corrine smiled and raised her glass. "I can vouch for that." She took a sip. "Sheldon finally fessed up. Hunter told me, I get that marriages don't always last, but Dad should have moved out before he started screwing around. He needs to grow a pair."

"Ha." Zoe slapped her thigh. "You raised a wise one."

"Thanks. He wants some guts DNA from my side of the family. *Guts* is my word, but he used a different one." Corrine's eyes twinkled.

"I hear ya. You know what deserves more respect?" Zoe held up an index finger. "*Ovaries*. Whichever dude said women are the weaker sex was crazy. Know what I mean?"

"Can you imagine if guys had the babies?" Corrine rested an arm on the table. "We'd be marching toward zero population growth."

"Marching? We'd be *extinct*." Zoe swiped a hand across the front of her neck. "Hunter and Sophia are lucky to have you."

Corrine shrugged. "Sometimes, I wonder…"

Beth glanced at Maria, and her heart ached for their friend. *I want you to be a momma, too.*

"Your salad is delicious, Therese. Kate's another lucky one." Zoe spooned more cranberry and apple slaw onto her plate. "How old was she when the scrawny-necked guy left?"

"She was only two." Therese flattened her lips.

"Wow…" Zoe shook her head. "She wouldn't even remember him. What's his name?"

"Vince. But from now on, we'll call him 'Scrawny Neck'—SN for short." Therese clinked her knife against her glass. "His name will be our little secret."

"To PWWPT." Using both hands, Zoe lifted her glass.

Beth clinked and drank, hopeful the interrogation was a wrap and Maria would be spared. She took a bite of stuffed mushrooms, savoring the rich blend of spices and cheese. *You'd love these, Reid.*

Corrine let out a snort.

Following her gaze, Beth glanced across the table. The stem of Therese's wine charm stood phallic in the calla lily's center. "I can't get no…" wafted from the living room.

Therese hummed a soft accompaniment and curled her lips into a half-smile.

Beth tightened her charm—its stem horizontal at the base of her mystery flower—and crooned the chorus.

When the song ended, Zoe slipped a finger under

her stem. "We got cheated, Beth. ED—E…rec…tile Dys…func…tion."

"You need a little blue pill." Therese twirled her glass. "Like I'd know…"

"Hypospadias." Maria dipped her head.

"Say what?" Zoe wrinkled her brow.

"Hypospadias—when the opening isn't at the tip." Pink crept up Maria's cheeks.

"So it'd be way down by the balls?" Zoe held up a forearm and cupped her elbow.

"You mean by the *scrotum*. When I changed Hunter's diaper, I practiced saying 'this is your penis, and this is your scrotum.' " Corrine turned a palm face up then face down. "We didn't say those words in the hood, so I didn't want to choke on them when he got older."

"Yeah, I would've been like 'this is your pecker' and 'these are your balls' or 'this is your schlong' and 'these are your nuts.' We mixed it up." Zoe folded her arms. "Really—the opening would be way down there?"

"I've only seen one. His was closer to the tip and off to the side." Maria pleated her napkin.

"Poor little buckaroo." Corrine crossed her legs. "Did he need surgery?"

"Mm-hmm. Usually they wait at least six months." Maria pressed her napkin to her lips. "Sorry—that info was over the top."

The fabric muffled her words. A pang started low in Beth's abdomen. She rested a palm over the empty space that had supported her baby. *Are you having a boy or girl, Emma?*

"More like over the bottom." Zoe grinned and held

up her glass. Her charm's stem pointed across the table. "Eat up, sailors. Blueberries and dancing are next."

Beth finished round one and stacked her dishes. "You Can't Always Get What You Want" murmured in the background. *Aren't those words the truth...* She pushed back her chair.

Corrine flicked her charm and pinged her fingernail against the glass.

Laughter erupted around the room.

Beth led the exodus and returned with a bowl of blueberry crisp à la mode and a freshly muddled drink. She smoothed her napkin on her lap. "Did any of you go to their concert?"

"Yes." Therese clasped her hands over her heart. "Did you?"

"We did. I…" She glanced at her dessert. "We did. Reid liked to say we partied like rock stars with twenty-three thousand of our closest friends." The memory drew a smile.

"Then we've been friends for years." Corrine tapped the table with the end of her spoon.

"We were close enough to spit." Zoe grinned and turned to Maria. "Were you there, too?"

Maria shook her head. "I saw them in Seattle."

"They're in their sixties and seventies and still touring… I want to rock out when I'm seventy-something." Zoe rolled her shoulders. "Eat up, sailors."

The friends finished dessert, cleared the table, and congaed into the living room.

Emptiness overtook Beth's core during "Have You Seen Your Mother, Baby, Standing in the Shadow?" She hugged her belly, hoping no one noticed.

The Perimenopausal Women with Power Tools

took turns in the spotlight. They danced, shimmied, and strutted, extending center stage clear to the dining room table.

An hour later, Beth pulled out her long-neglected journal. Hungry for a hint of Reid, she reclaimed his recliner and burrowed under a fleece comforter. She didn't tell her friends the rest of the story.

The day after the Stones concert, he explored ticket options for their Seattle venue. They spent several hours giddy at the prospect of seeing them again but reconsidered when they saw the inflated online prices.

Beth tightened the comforter around her shoulders and refused to acknowledge why her entries dwindled. "Miss You" broke through the chatter in her head. She picked up her pen, struggling to ignore the guilt scraping at her throat.

March Twenty-sixth

Dear Reid,

The Perimenopausal Women had a Rolling Stones dance party after dinner. Hands down, I played the best air guitar. Or, if I were being literal, one hand up and one hand down. Everyone had a specialty: Corrine— rooster struts, Maria—windmills, Therese—duck walks, and Zoe—hip swivels. Therese schooled us on their names. Maybe you knew what those moves were called when Mick and the guys danced across the stage...

I learned Corrine, Therese, and Zoe were three of our closest friends the night of the concert. Plus, we were a decision away from befriending Maria at the Seattle venue. After discovering we'd all seen the Stones live, we chose "It's a Small World" for an international-themed potluck next month.

Sometimes, I feel as though you know everything

anyway. Other times, I'm not so sure. I do know I won't have a definite answer until after I join you, which I hope won't be for a long time. A hurdle confronted and cleared. The day you died, a part of me died, too. I wanted to join you that day then the day after then the next day...for days and weeks and months I lived a zombie existence, wishing I were with you. But now I'm ready to stick around for a while, which lifted eight thousand pounds from my chest.

Well, darling, I'm sated and sleepy, and our bed is calling. Wish I were about to crawl in beside you. I miss you and love you more.

P.S. I'm having a grandbaby. She wanted to memorialize her news on paper. Kate would call her censorship a lie of omission. Maybe even call her a coward. Her fib sucked the moisture from her mouth. She closed her journal. Could she ever reveal her truth?

****

The following week, Beth navigated her wheelbarrow to her rose bed—overgrown and in need of pruning.

A choir of robins and sparrows hailed her with their morning serenade. "Where have you been? We missed you."

Imagining their lilting greetings, she smiled. "I missed you, too." She spoke to the flora and fauna, breaking into a monologue as she started with the Madame Hardy rosebushes. Continuing to the neighboring Geminis, she reveled in the April sun shining warm and welcome on her back. She uttered loving words to help the roses grow then confessed she was not avoiding them but rather herself. Had slipping away been possible, she would have wriggled out of her skin, tunneled into the crawl space, and hibernated for an entire year—maybe longer.

The daffodils were next—their tight buds straining to burst. As she weeded, she caressed the plants and recited her life trajectory since emerging from her figurative cavern almost six months earlier. She segued to the crocuses. The purple, white, and gold flowers displayed a burst of color, heralding spring's arrival. Then hunger and the anticipation of another new arrival prompted her to take a break. She shed her gardening gloves and swung inside to wash her hands.

I hope a letter arrived. She hurried down the driveway and opened the mailbox. *The water bill.* She slumped her shoulders and closed the hinged door with an elbow before trudging to the house. The knowledge that Emma's third trimester fatigue might delay her response softened Beth's disappointment a bit. But her eagerness to learn as much as possible about her daughter was difficult to quell. *My grandbaby is due April twenty-fourth...* She spoke those words aloud only once. Her lone audience—the Christmas poinsettia—offered no response, but her heartbeat knocked in her chest. She practiced for naught, though, because her story could never be shared.

The following day, Beth popped into Orange Street Food Farm. She wove around a pint-sized shopping cart jackknifed in the middle of the pasta aisle.

A young customer-in-training tapped two boxes of fettuccine against the cart's handle.

Are you in kindergarten? Steering around the cute little towhead, she cast a lingering glance. For years, she avoided bellies, babies, and beyond, struggling at times to ignore the reason why. Reid never mentioned her avoidance. Whether unnoticed or silenced by guilt—assuming he were to blame—she wasn't sure. After befriending Maria, she allowed babies and baby bumps to inch onto her radar. Once she learned about Emma and Bean, she noticed older children, too.

She turned the corner and navigated toward dairy. Milk topped her list. On the cusp of Easter, eggs were a screaming deal. She added a dozen to her cart, though she had half a carton at home. As a little girl, she loved dying eggs and hunting the Easter Bunny's plastic, candy-filled treasures. Discovering he wasn't real, she worried baskets, candy, and plastic eggs would come to an end. But her dad delighted in hiding eggs each year until she outgrew the thrill of the hunt.

She and Reid gave a cursory nod to the holiday. They bought pastel-colored malted milk eggs then overflowed the ivory scalloped bowl they received as a wedding gift. Plus, he always baked a ham.

Beth slowed at the seasonal display. Deciding zero malted milk eggs were better than an entire bag, she rolled past. She debated buying a piece of ham. Occasionally, she cooked, but many nights she did not. She finally stopped the admonitions. If she wanted bran flakes and raisins for dinner, so be it. She circled left and nosed her cart perpendicular to the deli case.

A white-haired man, the sole customer, ordered quarter pounds of olive loaf and provolone. He loaded them into his basket then turned and winked. "Have a marvelous day, young lady."

His gravelly voice rushed memories of her dad's tender, "Hi, my sweetheart." *You would have been a wonderful grandpa.* Her throat closed, and she managed a nod.

A woman in a flowing caftan approached the counter.

Beth gestured for her to go ahead. When the turn reverted back to her, she ordered a half pound of Black Forest ham—her dad's favorite.

Outside, the sunshine warmed her face, and she lowered the car windows before exiting the parking lot. She drove on autopilot, scarcely noticing the traffic sounds or music blaring from a neighboring car window. Ignoring the voice telling her to pull in *then* check the mail, she stopped at her mailbox at the edge of the driveway. "I'll be fast."

The engine's purr was the only response. She hurried around the front of the car, opening the box with one hand and removing a single envelope with the other. *A card from my Emma.* Leaving her seatbelt unbuckled, she edged the car into the garage. She carried her groceries to the kitchen counter without pausing to refrigerate the perishables. Then she hastened to her recliner and opened the card.

Twin bunnies adorned the front. Inside, Emma's script—*Dear Beth,* and *Love, Emma, Bennett, and Bean*—bookended a simple message.

Happy Easter!
Happy Spring!

Goosebumps covering her arms, she unfolded the letter.

Dear Beth,

Thank you so much for the letter and pictures. The Photos Are Priceless. I couldn't write last night because my eyes were seas of tears. Now, I'm fighting waterworks again...

The picture of you and Reid unlocked the

floodgates. When I studied your college picture, "I look like you" filled my heart.

You do look like me. Beth shifted her gaze to the pictures of Emma and Bennett propped on the entertainment center. Blinking hard against the burning in her eyes, she straightened the letter.

Bennett came home to my ugly crying and was so afraid something was wrong with Bean. I handed him your pictures and letter. Then he cried, too. He said we were ringers, and he can't wait to see my beauty grow as yours has. Calling him handsome and wise was spot-on. Adding compassionate equals another trifecta.

Hoooo. I'm hoping a bit of levity will keep my tears at bay...

You were—and are—beautiful. Special thanks for sending a photo of one of our shared moments.

A throbbing ache bloomed deep and low where Emma had tumbled and swam. *I miss you.* She rested a hand on her abdomen, and then refocused her gaze.

Thank you for sharing the story of my birth. Learning you labored alone, I cannot imagine the pain of reliving that day. Words fall short in conveying the depth of my admiration for your strength, your courage, and your unconditional love. Indescribable awe is the best I can do, yet I long for more.

I'm thankful you—we—had two great nurses. Your words, plus the newspaper article, were the tipping point for Bennett and me. We asked Jennifer to be with us during our labor and birth. Thanks for your wise words which steered us in that direction.

A flush of warmth spread through her body. *They're taking my suggestion.* She reread the last sentence then turned over the letter.

We finish our Lamaze classes tomorrow night. Bennett takes his coaching very seriously, so we're faithful about practicing. I love his involvement and drive. We have infant care and CPR this week and breastfeeding next. Then we'll be ready.

Thanks for your words of support regarding a drug-free birth. I'm approaching labor with an open mind, but I appreciate, and plan to run with, your vote of confidence. Your spring break photo is my new focal point. A memento of you and your incredible strength will be so powerful as I work to meet Little Bean. Thank you.

Jennifer gave us a sheet of affirmations which we read every night. My favorite is "I am safe. I am sound." Bennett likes "everything is going right" and "ride the wave." He's in charge of adding the handout and your photo to our labor bag before we head to the hospital. Our nursery is ready, so we're in good shape as we march toward the finish line. Speaking of end points, I've completed this note without tears wetting the page.

Thank you again for your letter and photos. I wish I could do justice in expressing my bottomless awe, gratitude, and love.

Namaste,

Emma

Beth tipped her head against the back of the chair. She never embraced the courage or altruism of Emma's words. *Ever.* Weighted by guilt and grief and sorrow and shame, she was both prisoner and guard. Her lungs felt titanic as she steadied her breathing. Not because of Emma's praise but because of the beauty of her prose. She wondered if her wordsmith daughter realized her words' charm. Recalling their shared struggles crafting letters, she pondered nature versus nurture. She liked to think *she* was a good writer. But sprinting from her story for so long, she struggled to find purchase when she stopped to script words.

Up until seven weeks ago, she harbored an altered version of this story. She didn't wish to return to those unenlightened days, but the yearning that followed wrenched every cell in her body. Though she could never reclaim the days of baby gymnastics and a purring cat, she longed to meet Emma and Bean and enfold them in her arms. She pieced together her heart four times—after losing her baby, parents, and Reid. But if her secret hunger did not unfold, could her patchwork center survive?

Chapter Fifteen

Beth spent the next afternoon working in her yard. Pulling the metal rake through the dead grass of winter, she freed the scents of soil and new growth. Yesterday's letter lay on the kitchen table. Without questions to answer, she lacked a road map to guide her reply.

Are you religious? Emma could have chosen a secular card for her sake since neither knew anything about the other's religious beliefs—or lack thereof. In an earlier letter, she *had* mentioned saying a prayer of thanksgiving every day. But as she could attest, prayers didn't always equate with religion.

Her church-going days were long behind her. She didn't object to organized religion, though, even after leaving to forge a spiritual path of her own. *What would our lives be like if I kept you?* No one could answer that question. She wondered which of Emma's character-istics might hint at her own. Some did, she hoped, like their shared gift with words.

Sparrows chirped back and forth across the lawn.

She wished letters to her daughter flowed with the ease of birdsong. *Daughter.* The wonder of the word diminished a smidge, though she couldn't imagine thinking about Emma without a bit of awe. An hour later, she peeled off her gloves. A mishmash of words whirling in her mind, she caressed a rosebush on her way to the house, careful to avoid the thorns.

The following morning, Easter Eve, sunlight poured into the breakfast nook. Vowing to write before the mail carrier's rounds, Beth circled to the office for stationery and a pen. She poured a second cup of coffee and returned to the nook. The bunnies stood sentry in the center of the table—two watchmen as she uncapped the pen.

Dear Emma,

Thank you for the card and letter. The bunnies are my new dining companions... I wonder what your household will be like next year with a Little Bean of your own. Writing that makes me smile as, on the cusp of Easter, advertisements for jelly beans are everywhere.

She questioned whether her last sentence sounded silly then wondered if her overreaching restraint was sillier than her words. Exhaling long and slow, she returned pen to paper.

I'm glad you liked the pictures. The photo with Reid is one of my favorites. I debated sending the picture of Lucy and me—and you—so I was touched to read you're using it as your focal point. Learning Jennifer will be with you during labor filled me with joy. Thank you for telling me my letter tipped the scale.

This week, I spent time in my garden and yard after a year and a half of neglect. Digging in the dirt felt good, and I looked around with a new perspective. The buds and new growth reminded me of you, Bennett, and Bean. You have a remarkable spring in store.

By the time you receive this note, you'll be closing in on thirty-eight weeks. Please set aside pen and paper as you and Bennett prepare for one of the most important days of your life. I look forward to finding a birth announcement in my mailbox, and I'd love to hear a snippet about your labor sometime. If you don't write for weeks or months, I'll understand. You will be a busy, wonderful momma. I cherish the cards and letters you've sent, and I'll treasure the ones yet to come. But for now, take good care of yourselves, each other, and Little Bean.

She reread her letter and wanted a do-over. Her selfish self pined to hear from Emma as much and as often as possible. But her wise self—dare she say her maternal self?—scribed the better words. She righted her pen.

You are in my thoughts each and every day, and I breathe words of affirmation for you. You are safe. You are sound. Everything will go right. Practice your breathing, rest up, and no more underselling your writing ability. You are a true wordsmith.

All My Love,

Beth

She transferred a soft kiss from a fingertip to the envelope, recalling the softness and scent of her burgundy sealing wax. A Christmas gift from her grandparents, she wrote to them weekly through the remainder of fifth grade. *Life was simpler then.* A longing to picture Emma as a baby and a fifth-grader and a college coed tightened her throat. The years hidden behind them could never be recaptured, but uncharted territory lie ahead. She closed her eyes, wishing with all her might to be part of even a tiny bit.

****

Two days later, the phone rang. Beth checked caller ID and smiled as she picked up the handset.

"Hello, Maria."

"Hi. I was wondering if you could grab lunch Thursday or Friday."

She glanced at her calendar. "Either would be great." Her entire month was open, other than dinner on the sixteenth and Kate and Frank's visit two days later. She had drawn a kidney bean on the twenty-fourth—Arbor Day and Emma's due date—tiny in hopes her friends wouldn't notice.

"Do you have a preference where or when?"

"No preference when…" She trailed a thumb around the ninth and tenth, drawing sideways figure eights. "How about Biga Pizza?"

"I was thinking the same. Shall we say Thursday at eleven thirty?"

The smile in Maria's voice was palpable. "Perfect—see you then." Beth hung up the phone and returned to the calendar. A chill coursed through her, and she shivered. She enjoyed their lunches. But concealing her truth from Maria made her feel like a fake. *Which I am.* Penciling in the date, she debated spilling her truth, or burying her news under another layer of lies. Neither sounded like a winner.

****

Three days later, Beth tucked into caprese salad at Biga Pizza. Nudged by memories, she savored the aromas and taste of tomatoes and basil, olive oil and sea salt, and mozzarella and *love.* She exhaled a soft sigh. "Reid adored this place. We always shared, too." She waved a finger between their salad and pesto pizza.

"He had good taste." Maria leaned forward. "How does being here without him feel?"

The compassion in her voice tightened Beth's

265

chest. "Being here with you feels nice." She rested a hand over her heart. "Thanks for calling."

"I'm glad you didn't bail the first night of class." Maria's eyes shone.

"So am I." Her words were soft as dew. Airborne pizza dough caught her eye. As the disk hovered overhead, she contemplated the force—if any—that propelled her to sign up for class and exit her car.

The dough fell into the chef's outstretched hands.

Symbolic—dough and life... Though she wasn't sure how.

Maria tucked a strand of hair behind her ear. "You're the only one I talk to about TTC—trying to conceive."

"What's new?" Beth lowered her voice.

"We're still trying. I haven't had fertile mucus or another period..." Maria nodded at their plates. "Sorry. I should wait until we finish eating."

"Sounds rough." A sinking feeling in her stomach spun memories of Emma's butterfly-soft tumbles. She rested a hand low on her abdomen.

"Yeah. Those spritzers were really good. I didn't say anything..." Maria flicked a wrist. "I didn't want mocktails to be a lead-in to my pregnancy quest."

Her story knocked around inside her throat, and she gave a slow nod.

"I haven't had a cocktail since my period—"

Their server stopped by to check in and refill their water.

"Everything's delicious." Beth smiled and took a bite of pizza then savored the flavors of pesto, pine nuts, and goat cheese. An animated conversation at a nearby table drew her attention.

A brunette with a messy updo talked with her hands.

Her three dining companions, thirty-something women, shook with laughter.

"I wonder if they're talking about wine charms." Beth tipped her glass.

Maria wiped her mouth and grinned. "I can't listen to the Rolling Stones without thinking about our dinner. We had fun."

"I hadn't listened to them since before Reid died." The words rolled off her tongue.

"We rocked Zoe's choreography." Maria picked up the spatula and raised her eyebrows.

"Yes, please." The wordless question and her easy answer triggered a memory of Therese and Kate. *I had a baby girl.* Placing her hands in her lap, she dug her nails into her palms.

Maria served them each another slice of pizza then met her gaze. "May I ask you something?"

"Sure." She worked to mask the caution in her voice.

"How hard was knowing you'd never have kids?" Maria scooted closer. "And did a lot of people ask why you didn't have any?"

Gripping her glass, she took a long drink. "The question was always, when are you…" *having a baby*? She twisted her lips.

"More people ask are you these days." Maria fluttered finger quotation marks. "I dislike both."

Memories of Zoe substituting dislike for hate coaxed a small smile. "I keep hoping your period was a good sign." Beth tilted her head. "Can you ovulate without that mucus?" *Did I have any?* She had no idea.

"Mm-hmm. But some women have EWCM—egg white cervical mucus—even when they don't ovulate." Maria separated her index finger and thumb. "Acronyms rule fertility sites."

"I hope you're reading pregnancy sites soon." Beth reached across the table and squeezed her hand.

Maria pressed back. "So do I."

An ache filled her chest. *Are your hands this soft, Emma?* She battled the tiny voice telling her she might never know.

****

A week later, Beth sifted through CDs as she awaited her guests. Kate's words about repetition and traditions drifted through her mind. Doubtful that a second night of Rolling Stones music could outshine the first, she popped in Kenny G's *Heart and Soul*. Stepping sideways, she collected Emma's photos from the entertainment center and studied them for the hundredth time. Not that she was counting… She drew the photos to her chest—over the whisper of the pulse that nourished Emma for nearly nine months. *Can you hear my heartbeat?* She planted two butterfly-soft kisses millimeters from the photos before slipping them between a pair of books. *Our story is safe. Our story is sound.* She didn't know where that affirmation came from, but she planned to run with it.

Are you here yet, Little Bean? She didn't have premonitions about boy or girl but defaulted to female pronouns because she'd used male for Emma. "You are safe. You are sound. Everything is going right." Routing to the breakfast nook, she spoke soft and low. The bunnies stood watch from the center of the table. "You can come back in a little bit." She removed the card and skimmed a fingertip over Emma's words. *Whether you are pregnant or parenting, I envelop you with my love.*

Ding-dong.

She placed the card inside the phone book before hurrying to the front. When she opened the door, the welcome mat lay empty. She stepped onto the porch.

Zoe faced the street.

Standing beside her, Beth surveyed the scene. Buds dotted the pear tree. She didn't see a single deer. To the southwest, Lolo Peak lay shrouded in snow.

"Smell that?" Zoe inhaled through her nose and exhaled through her mouth. "Smells like spring."

"I smell…" She drew in a deep breath. Opening her mouth, she blew out a noisy release, remembering choppy exhales in a hospital parking lot. She wrapped her arms around her belly and took a second, quieter breath. "I smell cinnamon sweetness."

"Accra banana peanut cake." Zoe smiled and nodded toward the pan. "The girls sprinkled cinnamon and sugar right before I left, and I cut them a deal. We're having scrambled eggs and cake for breakfast tomorrow." She shrugged. "This cake is sort of like banana bread."

"They're lucky girls."

"I'm a lucky momma." Zoe led the way to the kitchen and set her pan on the stove. Sliding a bag from her shoulder, she removed a bottle of wine. "This Argentinian Malbec is one of our faves."

"Mmmm… The wine opener and glasses are on the table." She gestured toward the breakfast nook.

"You don't have to tell me twice." Zoe grinned and set the wine on the counter. She peeled off her jacket and draped it over Beth's outstretched arm. "I might have your glass poured by the time you get back."

"We'll see." Walking to the closet, she replayed Zoe's words. She was a momma, too—a birth momma. What would her friends think about that? *They'll never know.* She hung the jacket, quieting her thoughts.

The doorbell rang.

"Told ya!" Zoe called.

Smiling, Beth headed to the door.

A large, covered pot sat unattended on the mat.

"I'm coming…" In the driveway, Maria stooped inside her open car door.

She hurried to help.

"Thanks. Grab the soda, please." Maria smiled over her shoulder and nodded toward the passenger seat. "I went back and forth then decided on spaghetti *bolognese.*" She plucked a dish from the car floor. Walking to the house, she didn't offer any hints about TTC. "I'll grab the sauce in a minute." She pointed with a foot.

Beth breathed in the savory aroma. "Yum. Smells scrumptious." *I'm rooting for you.* She beamed good thoughts all the way to the kitchen.

Zoe greeted them with wineglasses in hand. "Maria?"

"Italian soda." Maria balanced her dish atop a trivet. "Pomegranate, please, if you're pouring. I'll be right back."

"Gotcha." Zoe set a wineglass on the counter. "Your glass is charm-less, Beth, though *you* are not charmless."

Pulling grated parmesan cheese and soda from the bag, Beth grinned. "Good to know." She handed pomegranate soda to Zoe and stowed blood orange in the fridge. "Do your girls share your way with words?" She rummaged through the scalloped bowl. Bypassing the pink mystery flower, she selected a white calla lily.

"They've glommed onto 'dammit.' " Zoe cleared her throat. "I've switched to 'darn it,' but sometimes my old standby pops out."

"What old standby?" Corrine led Therese and Maria into the kitchen. "I know you were expecting Maria, so no look what the cat dragged in." She held up a platter. "I come bearing gifts."

"Hail, hail, the gang's all here," Zoe sang. "Which is better than ding dong the witch is dead." She frowned and cupped a hand over her mouth. "See what I mean? I have to work on what pops out of my trap. 'Dammit' is my old go-to. I've changed to 'darn it,' but that M sound is hard to break…"

"Better than the F-bomb." Corrine arched her eyebrows. "My kids heard a few of those growing up."

Did you, Emma? Beth sipped her wine and leaned a hip into the counter.

"Haven't they all?" Therese turned her wine bottle toward the group and ran a hand down its label. "Shall we brighten this conversation over glasses of a nice Shiraz?"

"Or there's Malbec on the table." Zoe gesticulated.

Beth grinned at her accent, which sounded more Irish than Argentinian.

"Plus, we have Italian soda." Maria raised her glass.

Corrine unzipped her wine tote. "*Mi vino es de Chile.*"

"*Muchas gracias. El fiesta…*" Beth extended her

hands, palms up. Unable to retrieve "awaits," she gave a vigorous clap. "*Salud.*"

"Ditto." Zoe raised her glass and jutted an elbow toward the table. "Wine charms, *amigos*?"

"*Sí, amiga.*" Corrine set her Cabernet beside the Malbec. Searching through the bowl, she removed the periwinkle flower. "From now on, I'm sticking with these." She wiggled the silicone charm back and forth. "Hypo what?"

"Hy-po-spa-di-as." Maria ticked her fingers, enunciating each syllable.

"Time to eat up, sailors." Grinning, Zoe ticked her fingers five times.

"Aye aye, captain." Beth carried her wineglass and salad to the dining room then slipped to the living room to replay the CD. As she claimed the seat at the head of the table, she inhaled the flavorful aromas that filled the air.

"What and where..." Therese served a heaping spoonful of rice and beans. "I'll start. My dish is Costa Rican *gallo pinto*."

"For dessert tonight, we're having Accra banana peanut cake, courtesy of Ghana." Zoe grinned and extended a fist toward Beth. "Just like our first class. Go."

Brushing Zoe's knuckles, she accepted the imaginary microphone. "Nicoise salad from across the pond. *Vive la France*." She spoke into her fist then passed the mic to her right.

Maria reached with both hands. "From the country shaped like my mother's old boot, we're dining on spaghetti *bolognese*." She smiled then delivered a two-handed pass.

"To round out tonight's five, we have Japanese pork *gyoza*. AKA…" Eyebrows raised, Corrine swept her fist in an arc.

Zoe slapped the table. "Alex, what are pot stickers?" She flung an arm to the side and flicked open her fingers.

"With that beautiful mic drop, Zoe is back on the board." Corrine squared her shoulders.

"And here is the host…Alex Trebek." Grinning, Therese signaled to her left.

"Thank you, Johnny…" Corrine glanced around the table. "Tonight's categories are Costa Rica, Japan, Ghana, Italy, and France. Therese, start us off."

In Double Jeopardy, we have Birth Mothers, Lies of Omission, New Hampshire… Her mind straying from recipes and ingredients, Beth unfolded her napkin. When her turn arrived, she gave a cursory rendition of her coworker Fran's favorite salad.

"Kate would love this." Therese tilted a forkful of tomato, olive, and hard-boiled egg.

"Let's email our recipes every month. Not until after we get together, though." Zoe wagged a finger. "I love the surprises."

"I agree." Maria leaned forward. "Speaking of Kate, how was spring break?"

"*Fabulous.*" Therese clasped her hands under her chin. "She was in her element."

"No regrets?" Beth took a bite of spaghetti. The flavors tasted rich and satisfying, and she raised a thumb in Maria's direction.

Therese shook her head. "Not a one. Kate prepped me along the way." She shifted her hands to her hips. "She said if she put hardware in someone's wrist or

273

fixed somebody's knee, that'd be important. 'But I'm gonna make furniture to be passed down through generations. *How cool is that*'?" She spoke through scrunched lips.

"Damn cool." Corrine flicked her knife.

"The campus was beautiful, and we met wonderful people. All of the faculty make art, and some of them even look like art." Therese cut into a pot sticker. "She can hardly wait for school to start."

"Sounds awesome." Maria tucked a strand of hair behind her ear. "Portland's a fun place to visit."

We intended to go again, Reid. Beth brushed her wedding band with her thumb.

"Road trip... *Perimenopausal Women Play Portland*—a made-for-TV movie in the making." Zoe flashed a dimpled grin. "Who's in?" She thrust a fist toward the center of the table.

"I am." Corrine shot an arm into the air.

Therese raised a hand and rocked side to side.

Grinning, Maria did the same.

Zoe lifted one hand and stretched her fist toward Beth with the other.

Extending both hands high above her head, Beth leaned to the right. "Touching me, touching you..." Joining in a rousing version of "Sweet Caroline," she reached out, swayed, sang, and smiled.

"All in." Corrine thrust a double thumbs-up, ending the choreography.

"Kate would be thrilled." Therese's eyes shone.

"Maybe next spring?" Zoe leaned back. "I can ask Nate's mom to babysit. Plus, Kate will have a chance to learn about the city before we turn her into a tour guide."

"Let her acclimate before telling her about five old broads." Corrine placed her hands on both sides of her jaw. "Scratch old. Do any of you remember the Bette Midler quote about a broad having a wicked tongue?"

A band wrapped around Beth's chest. *I have a lying tongue.* She covered her mouth with her napkin.

"I don't usually do this…" Zoe pulled out her cell phone.

"Research is acceptable." Corrine motioned toward Maria's plate. "Are you done?"

"Mm-hmm." Maria crisscrossed her knife and fork on top.

"I'll handle the investigation while y'all clear the table." Zoe waved her phone.

Beth led the migration to the kitchen, and then reconvened over dessert, French roast, and green tea.

"Here's what the Divine Miss M has to say." Squaring her shoulders, Zoe leaned back and cleared her throat. " 'People always love a broad—someone with a sense of humor, someone with a fairly wicked tongue, someone who can belt out a song, someone who takes no guff.' " She set down her phone. "We are *so covered.*"

Beth nodded, both at Zoe's raspy imitation and at Bette's words. *Are you a broad, Emma?* She slid her wineglass aside and took a long drink of water, washing over the story caught in her throat.

"Better than I remembered." Corrine steepled her fingers.

"Kate will fit right in." Therese held her fork midway between her plate and mouth. "Zoe, this cake is fabulous."

"Thanks. So, we'll have six broads rocking

Portland. And unless I clean up my mouth"—Zoe pinched her lips—"my girls will become broads, too."

"Which would be perfect," said Therese. "Raising them to have a sense of humor…"

Beth glanced at Maria who was focused on her cake. She knew parenting talk wasn't intended to exclude, but her heart wrenched for her friend—and for herself.

"…that's good stuff."

Repositioning in her chair, Beth looked at Corrine.

She curved a shoulder toward the table and fisted her hands. "Guff and stuff and scruff and tough—no one will ever call their bluff." Corrine jabbed the air with her right hand followed by her left.

"I'm guessing Sophia follows in her mother's footsteps." Zoe held up two fists then shifted left and right in her chair. "Maybe not in the wicked tongue department—"

"Especially in the wicked tongue department." Corrine threw another pair of punches. "She's strong-willed, which I admire."

"Is anything new with you?" Uncurling her fingers, Zoe rested a hand on Maria's arm.

"I had a period last month, but I'm pretty sure I didn't ovulate." Maria bit her lip. "I haven't had another one yet…"

"Fingers crossed." Therese entwined her index and middle fingers.

Zoe widened her eyes and looked at her nose. "I'm crossing my eyeballs and toes, too." Slipping a finger under her wine charm, she raised its phallic center. "To Maria and Anthony…and stuff."

Beth clinked with the others then sipped the last of

her wine. She flickered her eyes closed, wishing with all her might for a baby for Maria.

"What's on tap next month?" Therese ran a thumb along the edge of her plate.

They tossed around ideas, and then settled on their moms' favorite recipes in honor of Mother's Day.

I'm a mom. Beth gulped her coffee. The burn traveled from her mouth to her belly, searing her words.

Fifteen minutes later, she drifted through goodbyes then stopped at the entertainment center. She retrieved the photos of Emma and Bennett from between *Little Women* and *The Old Man and the Sea.* Propping the pictures against the book spines, *To Kill a Mockingbird* and *Of Mice and Men* added extra support. The irony of the titles, all fiction, did not escape her notice.

The photos spoke the truth. *I'm a mom and soon-to-be grandma.* As she had each evening since receiving the pictures, Beth kissed a fingertip. "Good night." She floated her finger over Emma's baby bump and breathed the words. *Will I ever hold you, Little Bean?* Afraid to give voice to the question haunting her soul, she whispered her query in the quiet of her heart.

****

Two days later, Beth folded laundry midafternoon. Longing to beam herself into Reid's shop with Kate and Frank, she settled for the nearness of the dryer.

Day three of their woodworking project, her company already had hours of work and caramel rolls behind them.

How is your afternoon shaping up? She would see their progress when she slipped in to turn off the heater. Smoothing a hand towel, she imagined baby clothes and linens washed and ready hundreds of miles away. *Is*

Little Bean here yet? Throughout the day, she let her thoughts wander from Emma to Kate and back. Kate's coffee table neared completion and Little Bean did, too. She would see and smell and touch the former, but the latter… *Be present.* Fighting the familiar burn in her gut, she reached for a washcloth.

The door from the garage burst open.

Kate strode into the room, slowing when she met her gaze. "Come see." She threaded her arm through Beth's. "Mom will *love* her new coffee table."

Tugged across the laundry room and through the garage, Beth squeezed Kate's arm with her own. As she entered Reid's shop, she paused. A fluttering sensation swooped through her belly.

Grinning, Frank stood with one hand on his hip and the other extended toward the table.

A medley of pride and regret crushed her breath. Studying Kate's work of art, she silenced thoughts of Reid's creations, Emma, and Little Bean. "Your table is beautiful." The words scraped past her sandpaper throat.

"I told you." Kate snugged her arm. "This Mother's Day will be the best *ever*."

"Until you gift your momma with a custom dining set someday." Frank smiled and slid an arm around his granddaughter's waist. "We make a good team."

"So do you, Grandma, and Mom." Kate's eyes sparkled. "You better come see her once in a while."

Beth met Frank's gaze and gave a subtle nod.

"Your mom might get so sick of us, she'll tell us to *back off*." He raised his chin.

"No, she won't." Kate nudged him with her hip. "I'll be back three more times to varnish, and then we'll pick up the table on Mother's Day. Okay?"

"She's giving me the boot." Frank heaved a sigh.

"The big boot." Kate swung her foot and tapped the back of his shoe.

"You're welcome anytime," Beth said. *I'm having a grandbaby.* Their loving exchange loosened the words rolling around inside her mouth. She wanted to tell Frank she was joining his club. Then ask Kate if she could practice being a grandmother with her—though she had no idea what she'd do. Instead, she tucked in her upper lip and averted her gaze. Could she ever come clean?

Chapter Sixteen

Six days later, Beth busied herself all morning with laundry and housecleaning. *Nesting*. She read only five percent of babies arrived on their due dates. Maria's chance of conceiving could be eight percent, or maybe ten. If she had to choose one, she wanted Maria to rock the odds, not Emma. Little Bean's arrival was certain, though likely not today.

I should plant a tree. But she didn't need a tree to remember this Arbor Day. Restless, she gathered her purse and keys midafternoon and hopped in her car. She drove north on Brooks then pulled into a center turn lane. Other than her two recent visits to the Mustard Seed, she hadn't been to Southgate Mall in ages. She parked near the east entrance, nosing her car toward home.

The sun broke out from behind a billowy cloud. *A sign?* Glancing at the sky, she beamed affirmations to Emma as she crossed the parking lot. Throughout her career, she shopped for clothes twice each year, or sometimes thrice. Reid hadn't been much of a shopper either. *Step lively.* His expression swam through her mind. She was here to walk more than shop so she strode with purpose, turning right at Clock Court. But the play area slowed her pace.

In the past, she stole an occasional glimpse at the recessed wooden train. Today, she gave herself permission to look. Painted the University of Montana Grizzlies maroon and silver, the train hosted a knot of giggling, shrieking toddlers and preschoolers. The kiddos climbed on and around the train and tumbled down its slide.

Adults and more wee ones dotted the plush, wrap-around couch.

A crawling baby in a striped headband planted her hands on the back of the seat and pulled herself up.

Beside her, a thirty-something dad smiled from ear to ear. Shifting his body in rhythm with his baby, he hovered a hand close to her back.

On the opposite side of the couch, a blonde woman wearing reading glasses held a picture book in one hand. She snuggled a rosy-cheeked toddler on her lap.

A grandma. Little Bean's imminent arrival shadowed her every breath. Beth strolled closer to study the pair.

The little guy grinned then turned a page. Pointing and laughing, he cast sideways glances at his grandmother.

When she met his gaze, laugh lines crinkled at the corners of her eyes.

You and me someday, Little Bean? Imagining the warmth of a child on her lap, Beth placed an arm across her belly. She shifted her gaze to the play area's book kiosk. For the first time, she noticed the built-in shoe cubbies below.

Two barefoot young girls eyed each other.

"You wanna be my friend on the train?" The one whose brown curls made her taller by an inch reached for the other's olive-skinned hand.

What color will your hair be? She brushed the nape

of her neck and continued past the trio of steps, carpeted and wide for little hands and little feet. *I'm expecting my first grandbaby any day now…* The words wriggled in her throat. She wanted to say them out loud, casual and anonymous to one of the adults scattered around the play area. But she circled the couch instead and headed back toward Clock Court. She window shopped children's stores, though she slipped into department stores. There, she could feign another purpose if she ran into anyone she knew. She wound through infant departments and caressed the cotton softness of unisex sleepers. *When will you be here, Little Bean?*

Three laps in, she stopped to look for a birthday card for Emma. She planned to buy a present later, though didn't know what. The Mother's Day cards gave her pause. She was a mom. Her daughter was, too, either a mom-to-be or a new mom. *You are safe. You are sound. Everything will go right.* Edging past "Special Mother" and "Funny" and "Any Mother," she stopped at "Daughter." A card with a bouquet of pink roses captured her gaze.

From the moment I held you,
I knew I would be forever changed.

The air stilled in her lungs. She sucked in a deep breath and fled empty-handed past the play train and out a side door. Her heart pounded. Emma's birthday was eleven days away. She sank into her car and rested her head against the steering wheel. Could she ever shop for her daughter?

****

Four days later, after purging the vision of her mall escape, Beth shouldered her purse and returned to the car. *I am safe. I am sound.* Sunshine beat through the window. Forty-three degrees and inching to a high of fifty-one under a cloudless, blue sky, the day radiated perfection.

She wasn't any closer to knowing *what*, though she did have a firm *where* as she traversed Lower Miller Creek Road. Driving to Rockin Rudy's, she rehearsed her plan: gift first, card second, and Mother's Day card third. The latter wasn't an absolute, though she hoped she could manage all three. Approaching the parking lot, she zeroed in on an empty spot right in front. She claimed the space—a good luck beacon—then steeled herself through two long inhales and exhales before exiting the car. Inside the store, the aroma of sweet, earthy incense greeted her like an old friend.

Saul, the resident caramel-colored cat did, too, holding her gaze as he lounged by the front counter. "Where've you been?"

She imagined his words, slower and softer than those of the neighborhood birds. *I've been out of commission.* She slung a shopping basket over her arm then passed truffles and huckleberry delights, journals and magnets, and soaps and crystals. Montana-made products and local artists' wares drew her in. She browsed hats, scarves, and jewelry, and then tried on a slim, silver bracelet. The engraved lettering caught a glimmer of light. *Joy.*

Thoughts of Emma's other mother flitted through her mind. *She* might be the better one to give such a gift. Silly, perhaps, but as Beth removed the bracelet and placed it in her basket, she decided to buy it for herself instead. She browsed bamboo plants, pottery, toys, and gift ideas too numerous to count. Returning to a local artist's ceramic mug, she ran a hand over the rich blend of colors—reminiscent of a mix of honey, cinnamon, and dark chocolate. *I think you'd like this, Emma.* She added the mug to her basket then backtracked to the front.

Do you drink coffee or tea or neither or both? She wished for a crystal ball to unveil the past and future. Perusing beverage options, she chose two bags of her favorite Missoula tea—one for herself and one for Emma. She skirted shelves of incense, some just ten cents a stick, and proceeded to the edge of the room. There, wrapping paper draped long, wooden dowels. Using both hands, she raised a sheet of pink peonies. She rolled the gift wrap and added it to the basket—the generous sheet jutting out the end. Then she continued down the ramp and selected a moss green ribbon and bow. Ignoring the fluttering sensation in her chest, she advanced to the plethora of birthday cards.

She bypassed "Daughter," though she did not rule out a return. Some cards garnered a fleeting glance. Others prompted her to look inside. Without a possible keeper in hand, she looped to "Local Artists." A watercolor of Missoula's old peace sign awakened memories. Slowing her breathing, she led her thoughts from the past to the present and lifted the card from the rack. *Blank.* She added an envelope then slipped the pair between the giftwrap and mug. As she moved toward the front of the store, she held her chin high and relished the warm flush of satisfaction that flowed through her. Months earlier, completing a simple shopping excursion was beyond her ability. Today, she summoned the courage to shop for her *daughter.*

A twenty-something woman and a middle-aged

man browsed the Mother's Day racks.

She slowed. Plenty of room existed for her to join them. But after her choke in the mall, she wanted privacy for her second attempt. She continued on to checkout. *I'll be back.*

After lunch, she settled at the dining room table. Encircling Emma's mug with her hands, she closed her eyes. She radiated love, joy, friendship, and grace, plus health, protection, safety, and peace and willed them all into the clay's every pore. "You are safe. You are sound." She spoke in a whisper. Tightening her grip, she slid her hands up until her thumbs and fingers met. She tented the top and filled the inside with every good thing, too. Beaming love into the paper, tape, and ribbon, she longed for Emma to feel her maternal love. *Birth mother.* Though the qualifier defined their relationship, she refused to submit to melancholy. She gave Emma the gift of life, affording her a better start than she could have offered all those years ago… Beth added the bow then brewed a cup of tea.

Returning to the dining room, she considered the possibility that one day, miles apart, she and Emma might drink Missoula tea at the same moment and reflect on their love. She yearned to picture her in her home. *Where do you sit to drink a cup of tea or read the paper? Do you even subscribe to a daily newspaper? Read one or more online?* She wanted all the answers, but the undisputed facts remained… Her daughter was the driver of the bus, and she was the passenger.

She sipped her tea, and the flavors bloomed on her tongue. Mulling words for Emma's card, she studied its watercolor front. Memories tiptoed back.

For nearly twenty years, she and Reid had

conducted frequent hikes up Waterworks Hill to the iconic peace sign. They always paused to raise their water bottles to the Northside Liberation Front—the legendary originators and keepers of the thirty-foot symbol that embellished the telephone tower overlooking the city. The phone company whitewashed the tower and erased the artwork each year. Then, under the cover of darkness, anonymous members of the NLF returned and repainted the peace sign.

When news surfaced of the company's plan to dismantle the obsolete tower, she and Reid packed a picnic lunch, complete with a bottle of Cabernet and plastic wineglasses. They hiked for a final toast and shared the trail and hillside with an array of adults, kids, and dogs, several of whom had sported glistening eyes or tear-stained cheeks. *Fourteen years ago, Reid…*

The memory scratched her throat, and she took a long, soothing drink of tea. Paper at the ready, she segued to practice prose, striving for words that matched the card's perfection. She wrote and revised then set aside her paper before revising again. Her words lacked the excellence she sought, but they were heartfelt and filled with love. She memorialized the date on the back of the card—*April twenty-eighth*—then she turned it over and straightened her pen.

Dear Emma,
For thirty-six years
I held you close
and loved you with every beat of my heart.
May all your wishes come true
on this, your special day.
Happy, happy birthday to you.
All My Love

"MommaBeth." Her voice was as faint as the name she signed with her fingertip. She drew the card to her lips and placed a soft kiss over the signature visible only to her. For years, she was a hidden presence in Emma's life. Now, her spring break photo would help welcome her grandbaby into the world. *When will I meet you, Little Bean?* Will *I meet you?* She crossed her arms over the ache in her belly, unable to soothe the pain.

****

For each of the next three days, Beth descended on the mailbox as soon as the carrier made her rounds. Flipping through the mail, she held her breath. Then disappointment tangled with the trapped air, and she blew out a ragged exhale.

On Saturday, Kate's impending arrival tempered the waiting game. She wondered how the day would unfold. Though Frank's absence ended their tradition, she was certain Kate would be a delight. When the doorbell rang, she rushed to the door.

Kate pushed a Bernice's bag into her hands. "We're eating first." She shrugged off her jacket. "Did ya hear the big news?"

"No-o." Walking down the hall, Beth inhaled the bakery-fresh aroma. She hoped her tone didn't belie her fib, but she refused to ruin the impending college announcement.

"It's a girl." Kate's eyes sparkled.

"How do you know?" The words came too fast and too harsh. "A girl?" Beth softened her voice.

"Yep. Eight thirty-four London time. The news is all over the Internet. One guy camped outside the hospital for *sixteen days*." She widened her eyes before opening the closet door. "Hashtag Great Kate Wait. She got to the hospital around six, so she went superfast."

"Wow." Beth steadied herself against the wall, shifting her thoughts from Emma to Duchess Kate. "Two-and-a-half hours *is* fast."

"Yeah. No name yet—should be one in a couple of days." Kate proceeded to the kitchen. "Shall I get the mugs?"

"Yes, please." She smiled and gestured toward the cabinet. "Grab the hot chocolate mix, too."

"Deal—and yes, please, I would like mine heated." Kate winked.

"Gotcha." *Be present.* She busied herself with the microwave and coffeemaker. Then, seated at the table, she tucked into her roll. "Mmmm. Your grandpa's missing out."

"His loss." Kate leaned forward. "Will you please give my mom a call once in a while after I'm gone? I know work will keep her busy, but I don't want her turning into a loner."

"Sure." She nodded and shifted her gaze to her plate. *I know all about being a loner.*

"We want you to come to Jakers with us on Mother's Day, too. For a thank you, plus we like your company." Kate waved an arm toward her grandfather's usual seat. "Then Grandpa and I will come for the coffee table. Okay?"

"You're a tough saleswoman..." *but thanks anyway.* She crossed her legs.

"Awesome. We have reservations at noon—for five." Kate grinned and cut a piece of her roll. "Grandpa said to tell you their Prime Rib and Seafood Buffet is *divine.*"

She opened and closed her mouth. *Will you be like her, Little Bean?*

Kate rested a forearm on the table. "If you don't wanna answer that's okay, but did you and Reid talk about having kids?"

"He was terrified to have a baby…" She brushed her wedding band with her thumb. "When he was in seventh grade, he lost his brother." Her voice sounded hollow, and she glanced away. "If we had kids, he'd worry about them every single day." She met Kate's gaze. "Sorry—TMI."

"Dang. *I'm* sorry. That question was none of my business." Kate pinched her bottom lip. "But you'd be an awesome mom."

I am a mom. Beth gulped her coffee, long enough for its warmth to soften the lump in her throat. "I think you'd be an awesome daughter."

"Mutual admiration society." Kate lifted a fist.

She bumped her fist in reply, and a tingle of electricity swirled through her.

"I bet he would have been a good dad, though. Mine left when I was still in diapers…" Kate stabbed a morsel with her fork.

"You have a wonderful momma." She rubbed a hand over her heart. *I'm having a grandbaby.*

"Yep—and you'll get to meet my dad at the graduation party. Grandpa doesn't like him, but he promised he'd rise to the occasion." She puffed out her chest.

"My roommate used to say that before every biology exam. Lucy Spethman…" The flood of memories tightened her belly.

"Did you pick her?" Kate repositioned in her chair.

"Was she nice?"

"I didn't, but we got along great." Beth held her gaze. "What about you?"

"I committed to that Portland school—Oregon College of Art and Craft." Kate grinned and patted the tabletop. "I'll make something for you while I'm there…"

"Congratulations." She punctuated her smile with a single clap. "I'll settle for third in line—after you craft pieces for your momma and grandparents."

"Grandpa already called first dibs…he can be a whiny one." Kate smirked. "Anyways, I sent in my housing application, and the school matches students from these questionnaires. I'll get my roommate's contact information this summer, so we can email and text and stuff." She patted a back pocket. "You can request someone if you want…but I don't really know anyone, except the kids I met on our tour. Plus, waiting to hear is sorta like Christmas, you know?" She closed her lips around her fork.

I'm waiting for news, too. Beth tapped her chin with a little finger. "Do you do video calls?"

Kate nodded while she chewed. "Sometimes. Mom will probably wanna see my smiling mug every day. Grandpa's words…" She placed her palms alongside her cheeks. "She's gonna miss me. Tell your other friends to give her a call, too, but don't let her hear you."

"Will do." She finished the last of her roll, and then washed down its lingering sweetness with a drink of coffee.

"Time to get to work." Kate pushed away from the table.

Beth folded her napkin. "Do you want me to join you?" The words tumbled out.

"I'm good but thanks anyway. Varnishing doesn't take too long." Kate carried her dishes to the sink. "I'll see you in a little bit."

She lifted a hand in reply. The weight of her words tightened around her chest, and she worked to fill her lungs. She never volunteered to join Reid in his shop. *Ever.* Her offer to Kate, even though it was declined, felt like a betrayal. Contemplating her years of solitude, she admitted the truth. Alone, she shed the armor that shielded her deceit. She didn't always like herself, but those secluded hours made her feel pounds lighter and gave her time to *just be.*

She wanted to recant her fib. A lie of omission Kate would say—a lie that suspended her life in ways she didn't realize. She sat, unmoving. By the time she drained her coffee, it was lukewarm.

Twenty minutes later, she sat on the couch and stared at Kate's cell phone screen.

"She's *beautiful.* I hope they name her Diana— Grandma *loved* Princess Di." Kate scooted closer and draped an arm on the back of the couch. "I bet Diana would love being a grandma. That car wreck was so sad…"

The warmth of Kate's leg rushed memories of Lucy, Willie, and baby gymnastics. A gust of grief hollowed Beth's belly.

On the screen, Duchess Kate cradled her newborn. Shifting her gaze between her baby, her husband, and the crowd of onlookers, she smiled and waved.

Prince William nestled alongside. Beaming, he murmured, gestured, and waved then reached for Kate's hand and descended four steps.

Roars, cheers, and the shutter sounds of cameras filled the air.

The infant lay with her eyes closed, swaddled in a white knit blanket and cap.

Silencing the memory of her empty, aching arms, Beth focused on the baby's cherubic face and tiny nose. "I think she needs her own name—not her grandma's." Measuring her words, she spoke in a soft voice. "Diana would be a good middle name."

"Yeah, but having a grandbaby named after her would be an honor... We'll know next time." Kate cast a sideways glance. "Does Tuesday or Wednesday work?"

I'm having a grandbaby. Beth rested a hand on her stomach. "Either one."

Kate tapped off her phone. "Okay. How 'bout Tuesday, and then I'll come back Saturday for the final coat?" She raised her eyebrows.

"Perfect." Beth gave a single nod.

"Thanks for watching the new princess with me— might be too hard for my mom." Kate scratched her neck. "Her baby girl's about to take off, and her and Dad's happy bubble burst a long time ago."

So did mine. Beth gazed at the magazine tables. *Once, and then twice.*

"I hope she'll see the little cutie patootie. Grandpa..." Kate stood. "He teaches me all the good sayings." She retrieved her jacket and draped it over an arm.

In the entryway, Beth drew her into a hug. "I'll see you on Tuesday."

"Deal." Kate smiled then slipped out the door.

She trailed a hand over the Shaker table. Afraid her face would crumple if she discovered a birth announcement, she listened for the car's engine to fade before she headed to the mailbox. She removed a single piece of mail—a glossy advertisement for a pizza company—and slumped her shoulders. *Is news winging its way to Missoula?* Returning to the house, she pondered the royal watchers that greeted the new princess. She was a crowd of one, figuratively camped steps from her mailbox to await the news.

Consumed by a piercing ache of loneliness, she shuffled to the entertainment center. She removed the photos from their hiding place and studied the picture of her growing family. The collective, palpable joy—of Emma and Bennett, Kate and Frank, and Duchess Kate and Prince William—was confirmation life goes on. She could never recapture her past—*ever*. But chastising herself was not the answer. Placing a whisper-soft kiss over Emma's baby bump, she pledged joy in the beauty of the present and in the hope for the future. *Starting now.* She propped the photos on the shelf. Folding her hands under her chin, she closed her eyes and breathed an age-old verse in the quiet of her heart. "Boy or girl, Little Bean?" *I can't wait to find out.*

Chapter Seventeen

Two days later, Beth pulled up to Rockin Rudy's at two minutes after nine. A pair of cars dotted the lot. Longing for solitude, she hoped they didn't belong to likeminded Mother's-Day-card browsers. She was on a mission to find a single card. *Fast.*

She exited the car and grabbed her purse with a draft, pen, stamp, and Emma's address tucked inside. Though she doubted the mail carrier would come around before she returned home, she'd write and mail Emma's card beforehand, just in case. Pushing open the door, she barely noticed the scent of incense. Tunnel vision directed her past truffles, coffee, and tea to the greeting cards.

A ponytailed woman with a stroller browsed the front rack of the Mother's Day section.

No. Beth stopped and turned, focusing on a package of pineapple licorice. Feigning interest in the wide variety of candy flavors, she debated leaving or browsing the store. *Get in. Get out.* She took a deep, calming breath and headed toward the second rack.

After her implosion in the mall, she limited her search to blank cards. A photograph of yellow roses, semicircled by *Happy Mother's Day*, grabbed her attention. *Joy.* Years ago, she schooled Reid on rose colors and their meanings. Throughout subsequent summers, he presented her with single garden roses.

Red and coral were his two favorites—love and desire.

A twinge of regret clenched her stomach. *Be present.* She caressed her bracelet. *Joy.* She opened the card to confirm a rogue poem didn't lurk inside. Less than a minute in, though, and insulated between the racks, she replaced the card. *I'll look a bit longer.* She scouted the rest of the rack then inched toward the back of the other.

Cards and metal separated her from the woman with the stroller. Beth gazed at flowers, hearts, and tea cups. *A good mother lets her kids lick the beaters.* The handheld mixer prompted a smile. Foregoing her "blank only" admonition, she lifted the card. *A great mother turns off the mixer first.* She laughed out loud. Grateful the overhead music masked her laughter, she glanced around.

No one was in sight.

Two spinner racks completed the Mother's Day selection. She edged to the closest one. *Would I have been a good mother?* She hoped so. *A great mother?* She wasn't so sure. After scanning the first spinner, she stepped to the second for a cursory look. On the verge of backpedaling for the yellow roses, she pulled out a card.

You will *Forever*
be in my
Heart

Centered beneath the script were two dark pink hearts—little cocooned inside big. She opened the card. *Blank.* Swallowing past the ache in her throat, she removed the envelope.

The other shopper drifted to the neighboring spinner.

Slowing, Beth peeked in the stroller.

An infant with spikes of dark hair slept beneath a cherry red blanket. Overhead, a black-and-white mobile with geometric shapes dangled from the canopy.

She squatted, needing a moment to wrangle her breath and her voice. *You're precious.* Straightening, Beth met the mother's gaze. "How old…"

"He'll be five weeks old tomorrow." She glanced toward the stroller and back. Her eyes shone. "So far, he's been a dream."

I'm having a grandbaby. Beth smiled and tightened her fingers around the card. "Have a Happy Mother's Day." Her words came out tender and soft.

"Thank you…" She placed a hand high on her chest. "I will."

Beth examined the baby an instant longer, and wistfulness coursed through her. After paying for the card, she considered going to Break Espresso. A latte sounded good but penning her message in public did not. Instead, she drove to the post office and parked in the far corner of the lot. Cushioned in the privacy of her car, she opened her purse and removed the thrown-together correspondence kit. She turned her purse sideways, but her wallet poked through the butter-soft leather, erasing any hint of a flat surface. Rummaging in the console, she found a small box of tissues. *Take two.* She turned over the box, balanced the makeshift table and card on her lap, and picked up her pen.

Dear Emma,
A mother's love for her
child is like nothing
else in the world.
It knows no law, no pity,

it dares all things and
crushes down remorselessly
all that stands in its path.
Agatha Christie
All My Love

MommaBeth. Using her fingertip instead of ink, she traced the letters—beaming love into the signature only she could see. Sliding the card to the right, she straightened her pen.

I expect Little Bean will be out and in your arms by now… You were a toddler when I discovered these words from Agatha Christie. I sheltered this verse deep in my soul and loved you with a quiet, hidden fierceness from afar. Learning the you *of my love has filled me with indescribable happiness.*

*My heart overflows as I share in the love and joy of your first Mother's Day—*our *first Mother's Day. Thank you again for reaching out not once but twice. Words fail to express the depth of my gratitude and delight at the unfolding of our relationship. Let me simply say—*

Thank you
I love you
Happy Mother's Day

She pulled the card to her chest. *I love you with every beat of my heart.* She sat without moving then lifted the card to her lips. Minutes later, she strode inside to the mail slot.

The following morning, Beth slumped at the kitchen table. "Why didn't you call and reschedule?" Her words assaulted the silence. This was her daughter's birthday, and she wanted the day to herself. But now Tuesday was here, and Kate was coming and that was that…

She nabbed a fleece jacket from the laundry room wardrobe then swung into the garage. After collecting her gardening tote, she proceeded to the backyard. Rays of sunshine beat against her face. She knelt on a spongy, fuchsia mat in front of the tulips. "Little Bean was due the twenty-fourth, and I've been waiting to hear for days. Today is my baby's birthday..." Pausing, she caressed a golden petal. "But I don't expect news this day." The latter was whisper soft.

Caw-caw...Caw-caw-caw.

Straightening, she spotted the sleek, black bird in a nearby ponderosa pine. She smiled and raised her chin. "Caw-caw-caw."

"Do you think they understand you?"

Reid's old tease replayed in her head. Guilt thickened her throat. *Maybe.* Her long-standing reply silenced his words. Quieting her mind, she focused on her yard's glorious burst of colors: reds and yellows, pinks and purples, and oranges and whites. She plunged a dandelion digger into the forgiving earth and shook free a clump of weeds, laboring through the tulips then circling to the hyacinths. The grape-scented flowers were last, and she delighted in their sweet fragrance.

After an hour, she shed her gloves. Grateful for a bit of exercise, she strolled through the gate and around the house. She didn't hurry—the chance of finding news on Emma's birthday seemed an unlikely coincidence. Slowing, she inspected the shrubs edging the yard. The rhododendrons' tight, purple buds looked about to unfurl. *Like you, Emma?* She continued to the potentillas, whose blossoms were weeks away. Squatting, she pulled a few easy weeds then dusted off her hands and headed to the mailbox.

She peered inside. *Bills and junk.* Using her cleaner hand, she removed the short stack of mail. Buried at the bottom was news from Emma. Her pulse pounded in her temples. Cursing the locked front door, she sandwiched the card away from her soil-stained fingers and rushed around back. She scrubbed her hands at the utility sink. Careless with the towel, she ignored the remaining drops of moisture and wanted to tear into the envelope *right now.* Her rational side prevailed—she refused to read such monumental news in the laundry room. Starting down the hall, she worked a finger under the flap and removed the card.

Happy
Mother's Day
to my Birth Mom

The words swallowed her in. She sagged against the wall, catching herself before her knees wilted and she slumped to the floor. Trembling, she opened the card. *Emma and her baby.* She turned over the photo.

Olivia Elise—one minute old
April twenty-ninth

"My baby had a baby girl." Her voice echoed in the empty hall. "I have a grandbaby." Soft as cotton, the words filled her with awe. Hot tears pricked her eyes. She nestled the card and photo, and a second one, too, in her lap. Then she wiped the tears with the bottom of her shirt. She uncovered the other photo, and her eyes puddled again.

Bennett and Olivia
April thirtieth

Love and joy and sadness and regret crowded her lungs. Tucked against the wall, she struggled to breathe. She sat without moving for one minute—maybe two.

But the floor was unsuited for these holy words. Clutching the card and photos to her chest, she pushed to her knees and feet. She stopped in the guest bathroom for tissues then skirted Reid's recliner and sank into her leather's warm embrace.

Birth mom. Two heart-shaped red ribbons linked beneath the words. One was complete, and the other had a tiny break at the bottom. Space enough for Emma to slip out and back. Beth blinked away the mist and opened the card.

Happy Mother's Day,

We welcomed Olivia Elise on April twenty-ninth at nine thirty-four in the morning. She's a beautiful, healthy baby—seven pounds fourteen ounces, and twenty-one-and-a-half inches long. Though she's only a drop more than twenty-four hours old, she's breaking us in. We're tired but over the moon in love.

Throughout my labor, I felt your quiet presence. I thought I'd grasped the enormity of your courage, strength, and love. Yesterday, I realized I under-estimated all three. Infinite thanks for gifting me with life and for helping me become a mom. My heart bursts with gratitude and love.

Namaste,

Emma, Bennett, and Olivia

She soaked an entire tissue. Then she wiped her hands on her jeans and picked up the photos.

Olivia lay snuggled on Emma's chest, her shiny hair plastered to her head. Wide-eyed, she studied her momma, grasping a single digit with tiny, blue-hued fingers.

Her cheeks glistening, Emma gazed at her baby.

Imagining the wonder in Emma's eyes and the feel

of newborn skin against her chest, Beth rested a hand over her heart. An ache erupted in her core. She envisioned Bennett's eyes shining, too—both momma and daddy awestruck by their Little Bean. *You had a baby girl.* Unchecked tears spilled down her cheeks. She cleared them with the back of her hand then examined the second photo.

Bennett cradled Olivia in the crook of his arm. He propped the swaddled and sleeping beauty upright for the camera and flashed a lopsided grin.

She drank in her granddaughter's features: her flyaway, light brown hair, dark lashes, pale pink cheeks, button nose, and rosebud lips. A kaleidoscope of emotions too big for her body swirled inside. Shifting the first photo to the front, she bent forward, placing two butterfly-soft kisses millimeters from the picture. "You're thirty-six today…and your baby girl is beautiful." Her voice broke.

Olivia's sweet innocence magnified the rawness of her loss. Throughout the years, she revisited her story in secret thousands of times, maybe even a million. Certain her decision was for the best, she never allowed herself to think otherwise because doing so *was too damn hard.* A crystal ball might tell a different truth but one she would never know. What she did know were two irrefutable facts. Emma, Bennett, and baby Olivia were in her life, and she was determined to relish whatever came her way. She doubted their relationship would grow as fast or as jam-packed as she hoped, but her years of denial were now a whisper of the past.

You're six days old. Beth looked from Olivia to Emma. Struggling to purge memories of her own isolated, turbulent postpartum days, she pondered their first week at home. *You are safe. You are sound.* She planted another kiss. *Everything will go right...*

Three hours later, she plodded to the front door. Words tangled in her throat.

"Charlotte Elizabeth Diana—but you probably already heard." Kate swept into the entryway.

"I did." Beth held her gaze. "What do you think?"

"Diana Charlotte Elizabeth would be better." She flicked a hand. "I'm just sayin'."

"Maybe. Do you know what today is?" So close to spilling her truth, Beth started toward the kitchen.

"A day I'm old enough to have a margarita in Mexico." Kate gave an open-mouthed wink. "Or do you prefer *Cinco de Mayo*?"

"How about"—she let out a noisy exhale—"a day for cheese melts and raspberry lemonade?"

"Good Plan B." Kate tilted her head. "What can I do?"

Beth waved her into the kitchen. "You can start on the cheese melts."

"Gotcha." Crossing to the sink, she washed her hands.

Kate's ease and familiarity with her kitchen tugged harder today than others. Working to bury her story, Beth opened the refrigerator. She removed corn tortillas, shredded cheese, and chopped onions and set them on the counter beside plates and silverware. Then she returned to the fridge for salsa and lemonade. "Ice?"

"Yes, please." Kate held up the package of tortillas. "One or two?"

"One. Start on yours..." She pressed the ice dispenser and gave Kate a sidelong glance.

" 'Kay." Kate arranged two tortillas on a plate, overlapping the edges. She unzipped the cheese bag and shook a mound on each. "How was your day?" Working both hands at once, she spread the cheese.

The jolt of Reid's old question emptied her lungs. She sucked in a breath. "Good…" She poured a glass of lemonade then swigged a long, cold drink. The berry and citrus flavors coated her mouth to her belly. "How was yours?" She topped off her glass before filling Kate's.

"Senioritis is going around." Kate scrunched her lips. "My immune system succumbed a couple of months ago."

Masking a smile, Beth wrinkled her brow. "Is there a cure?"

"They're conducting clinical trials"—she leaned in and dipped her chin—"with diplomas."

"Aah…" Beth gave a slow nod. "I hope you're in the study."

"Meeee, too." Kate slid her plate into the microwave.

Beth uncovered the onions, and the pungent aroma permeated the room. The smell did nothing to awaken her appetite. She forced herself to make a cheese melt then joined her friend at the table.

"I guarantee every senior can tell you how many school days we have left." Kate rolled a tortilla and lifted it with both hands. "Seventeen—plus finals and graduation practice…"

Half-listening, she murmured an occasional reply. *I have a new grandbaby.* She choked down a few bites, barely tasting the savory flavors.

"Time for the baloney layer—get it?" Kate

gathered her dishes. "Probably not, because I just made up that name. I'll tell Momma these three coats are to remind her of my old fave: bread, baloney, and bread. No mustard or mayonnaise for this former eight-year-old." Grinning, she tapped her chest with a thumb. After circling to the sink, she moseyed from the kitchen without a backward glance.

What was your favorite sandwich, Emma? Beth wanted to know everything... Alone and unneeded, she surrendered to memories of glasses of a nice red and Reid's accompanying daily inquiry. "How was your day?" Those four words embodied an intimacy she admitted that afternoon. *Kate makes me feel like a mom.* A web of loneliness wrapped around her chest. Captive at the table, she pleated and straightened her napkin.

"Happy birthday, Emma." She redirected yet again. Before Kate's arrival, she tucked away the photos. But she wanted to shout her news from the rooftops or at least announce it in the privacy of her kitchen. The secret she guarded with her life—a thirty-six-year-old lie of omission—now included a second layer. She was a *grandma.* How could she reveal one without the other? Reid deserved to know before anyone else, but he was gone. Were her secrets buried forever?

****

Thursday afternoon, Beth hauled a warm bedsheet from the dryer. The telephone rang, but she didn't hurry to check caller ID. As an unfamiliar male voice filled the kitchen, she composed a mental note to resubmit her phone number to the National Do Not Call Registry. She turned to retrace her steps. Hearing the caller's name, she froze.

After a flicker of a pause, he drew in a breath.

"Emma's husband." He exhaled the words.

Her stomach lurched. She wheeled around and reached for the phone then pulled back her hand. If he said anything bad, she would run toward silence and hit delete after the quiet returned.

"She doesn't know I'm calling. Sorry…"

At the hesitation in his voice, she leaped for the phone. *Sorry why?* Viselike, she squeezed the handset but the Talk button seemed acres away.

"I was hoping to catch you and not leave a message."

Heart pounding, she stifled a scream. Unable to interpret his tone, she turned toward the door, ready to drop the phone and flee.

"I'd like to surprise Emma with a ticket to Montana for Mother's Day."

Beth crumpled against the counter, bracing herself with her elbows and knees.

"Wednesday, June third, until Monday the eighth looks good, but if different dates work better, that would be fine."

YES… Just listen… Yielding to the quieter voice, she straightened her legs.

"Olivia should be at least a month old—for me— though the airline said she could fly earlier." He took a breath. "Anytime between May twenty-eighth and the end of July would be perfect."

Book 'em, Danno. But she just listened.

"You can text or email me…"

A medley of emotions thickened her throat, making words impossible. Scrambling for paper and pen, she jotted the number and email address, adding a pair of stars at each end.

"I have another present, so no worries if you can't let me know before Mother's Day. But, Beth"—his voice caught—"this gift would be for you, too. *They're beautiful.*"

His whispered adoration was tangible through the phone lines. *Yes.* She blinked away tears.

"Or you can call; I think I forgot to say so. I hope to hear from you, and I hope you'll say yes." He gave a one-syllable laugh. "Hope and hope—I didn't script that. I did this…" He swallowed hard. "If a visit doesn't work, I won't tell Emma I called."

She struggled to decipher the movement in the background.

"Take care—"

His voice broke, and the answering machine clicked off. Waving the phone above her head, she danced down the hall. "Emma and Olivia are coming to Missoula." She reopened the dryer and removed Reid's green KettleHouse Brewing Company T-shirt. Sinking her face in the still-warm cotton softness, she lassoed her joy. *They can't.* She had dug a hole thirty-six years too deep. Desperate as she was to meet Emma and Olivia, could she crawl out and spill the truth now?

The following night, Beth chased sleep. As she watched the digital numbers on the clock creep forward, she had no idea what to tell Bennett. But he deserved an answer before Mother's Day… When the light of dawn seeped into her room, she groaned. She *dreaded* Kate's arrival. Her decision regarding Emma and Olivia was still in limbo, and she could not afford distractions. Which brewed another point of angst— *brunch.* She contemplated calling Therese and feigning illness then bowing out of their date. But Kate and

Frank needed to pick up the coffee table tomorrow. Fibbing over the phone might be manageable, but could she maintain her lie in person? She rolled away from the urn and buried her face in a pillow.

Three hours later, she settled at the table and inhaled the bakery-fresh aroma of caramel rolls.

"I bet you'll be glad when I'm out of your hair." Kate straightened her napkin.

"No-o." Heat rose in her cheeks. "Having you here has been nice."

"Thanks for letting me use Reid's shop and stuff." Kate gestured toward the garage.

"Anytime." She took a bite of her caramel roll. Savoring the rich, familiar flavors, she smiled. "*Divine.* Thanks, Kate."

"I'm just following Grandpa's lead." Kate grinned then cocked her head and looked at the ceiling. "Do you think Reid's up there supervising?"

Sometimes I wonder. Beth brushed a thumb over her wedding band. "Maybe… What do you think?"

"He could be. Especially since you didn't hang out with Grandpa and me. He might figure somebody from the household should cast an eagle eye." She rubbed her neck. "Sorry, but ya know what I mean?"

"If he *was* observing, I predict he watched with a curious eye and not a critical one. He'd applaud your work every step of the way." Beth raised her mug. "That book was his." The words wriggled out.

"Really?" Kate widened her eyes. "Now I love the book even more." She leaned forward and rested an elbow on the table. "Has giving up his stuff been hard?"

Beth glanced away from the compassion in her eyes. "You're the only one I've given anything to." She met her gaze.

"Wow..." Kate talked around a mouthful of roll. As she chewed and swallowed, she pulsed her fingertips against her lips. "I'll tell Mom she better take good care of her coffee table. When I finish today, I'll come get ya." She reached for her hot chocolate. "Do you have a rolling chair?"

"No. I have these chairs or an exercise ball..." Beth motioned around the table.

Kate set down her mug. "I'll figure out Plan B."

She wrinkled her brow.

"Patience is a virtue. Virtue is a grace. Both put together make a very pretty face." Kate placed her hands on her cheeks. "Grandpa..."

I'm a grandma. Her heart hammered in her chest. "He's a wise one." She forced the words.

"Yeah. He's looking forward to seeing you tomorrow. Plus, he's been jonesing for a roll. I told him he has classic FOMO—fear of missing out..." In between bites, Kate wove tales about her grandpa. Stabbing her final piece, she grinned. "The big guy and I can pick up Mom's table after brunch, right?"

"Right." She sipped her coffee.

Flashing a thumbs-up with one hand, Kate popped her fork into her mouth with the other. Then she tipped back her head and drained her mug. "I'll come and get you when I'm done."

"Leave those..." Beth gestured toward her dishes. "I'll get them."

"Thanks." Kate stood and pushed in her chair. "I'll see you in a little bit." Rubbing her hands together, she headed out the door.

Beth propped her elbows on the table and covered

her face with ice-cold hands. The lies hurt her head. She told herself Kate would be a distraction. With a decision to make, she couldn't afford an interruption. *As if.* Since Bennett's call almost forty-eight hours ago, she had nothing but untethered time. She was a pro at evading the truth and reframing her story—trapped behind a lie of omission. *The worst kind.* Echoing like a curse, the lie tormented her sleep for the past two nights. Hell, the past thirty-six years…

Honesty forced her hand, and she acknowledged why she didn't want Kate to come. Her presence reinforced Beth's maternal feelings—the ones she took to the mat—piloting her closer to an answer.

Yes, she ached to reclaim the past and infuse honesty from the beginning. But she was left with water under the bridge, spilled milk, a lie that couldn't be undone, and a hundred other clichés. She had a choice to make, and she would be damned to let regret be the boss. Guilt, too, told her what she couldn't do— undeserving woman that she was. Instead, she would choose the path less traveled. Or perhaps the path traveled by thousands more who, after years of deceit, came clean. Opting for happiness, joy, and truth, she would choose *to live.*

She cleared the dishes and rushed to the computer. As her email loaded, she noticed the time at the bottom of the screen. Eleven thirteen. *No time for practice prose.* She fished Bennett's email address from the desk drawer then placed her fingers on the keyboard.

Dear Bennett,

What a wonderful surprise to hear from you. Your message made my heart sing! A visit from Emma and Olivia June third to the eighth sounds perfect… I am eager to learn their itinerary. I'll arrange for a car seat and baby bed, and please let me know what else I can do to prepare for their arrival. Their presence will be a marvelous, new adventure.

Thank you for filling me with joy this Mother's Day. Emma wrote about some of your virtues. I'm adding thoughtfulness to the list. I look forward to hearing from you.

With love,

Beth

Sputtering a choppy exhale, she pushed Send. The Enchantment of the Seas keepsake tormented her peripheral vision, and she picked up the photo. She studied her and Reid and their palpable love.

After drinking a little too much wine that night, she almost blurted out about the baby. *Neutral territory.* Then, afraid her secret would dwarf their ocean view stateroom or shrink the entire ship if Reid wanted to get away, she reconsidered spilling the truth.

I'm so sorry. She replaced the photo and turned off the computer, her stomach burning. When she exited the room, she avoided the mirror and shuddered at the thought of breaking open her lie. *When should I tell my friends?* How *should I tell my friends?*

Chapter Eighteen

Twenty minutes later, Kate swooped into the kitchen. Grinning, she linked Beth's arm. "Close your eyes when I tell you to."

"Will do." Beth held on, feeling the urgency of the tug down the hall and through the laundry room. In the garage, the varnish aroma wafted from Reid's shop.

The door stood cracked open.

At the doorway, Kate paused. "Time to reconfigure." She grasped Beth's left hand with her left, and then slipped her right arm behind Beth's back. "Now."

Beth closed her eyes.

Hip to hip, Kate shuffled forward.

Extending her right hand, she touched nothing but air. As she inched forward, her senses heightened.

"Stop." Kate dropped her hand. "Keep your eyes closed."

Beth drew in a deep breath and firmed her stance. She squeezed her eyelids tight, fighting the pitch and roll of her eyeballs behind rebellious lids. The air shifted behind her, and she felt Kate's hands on her waist.

"Take one step back then sit."

As she eased backward, she flinched at the cool, hard pressure against her calves.

Kate tightened her grip.

Beth sank, her knees buckling at the intimacy. She flailed her arms. *Keep your eyes closed.*

"Whoa." Kate lowered her then released her hands. "Now."

Opening her eyes, she glanced down. *The stepladder.*

"I told ya I'd find something…" Meeting her gaze, Kate winked.

"You're a genius." Beth smiled and turned to the coffee table. *Gorgeous.* On Tuesday, she slipped in for a quick peek. Seeing the table now along with pride oozing from Kate's every pore made her clap and stand for a closer look. "Your work is *stunning.*" Reverence in her voice, she clasped her hands against her chest, fighting the impulse to stroke the wet, lustrous surface. "Your mom will love her new table."

"She will." Kate's eyes gleamed. "And thanks for the standing ovation."

Beth smiled then clapped thrice more. "You *are* a wizard."

"I wanted to roll you in, but the ladder was a good Plan B." Kate tilted her head. "Did you figure out about the standing O when I asked for a rolling chair?"

"No…" Beth shifted her hands under her chin. "I clapped because you are a master woodworker."

"Thank you." Kate grinned and slipped her arm through Beth's. "So, brunch tomorrow, and then Grandpa and I will swing by." She navigated to the front door. "Thanks again for letting us use Reid's stuff." She drew her into an embrace.

Her breath was warm against Beth's neck. *I have a new grandbaby.* A whisper away, the words knocked around inside her mouth.

"I *love* his book." Kate gave an extra squeeze then flashed a smile. "See you tomorrow." She opened the door and scooted into the spring afternoon.

Beth locked the door and hurried to fire up the computer. A tingle of anticipation shot down her spine. She shivered then leaned forward and scanned her inbox. *Nothing.* Well, not exactly nothing but not the prompt reply she hoped for. She puffed out a long sigh. *He has other things to do.* Turning off the computer, she vowed to wait a few hours before checking again. Not right before bed because she didn't want the screen's glow interfering with melatonin production. Her thinker was challenged enough without a second sleep thief joining the battle.

She lasted until nine o'clock—eleven o'clock Maryland time. If Bennett hadn't replied by then, she figured he wouldn't until the following day. Unless he was burning the midnight oil, which she hoped he wasn't. She preferred that, with a newborn in the house, he and Emma capitalize on sleep whenever they could. *You're parents now.* She didn't begrudge their new role; she was thrilled for them. But letters, pictures, and Bennett's voice mail—which she refused to erase—bore reminders of the past she could never reclaim.

How's parenthood going? Waiting for her email to load, she jiggled a foot. Then *three* emails from Bennett lined her inbox. She opened the bottom one first, her pulse thumping in her temples.

Dear Beth,

Thanks for your reply. Reservations are booked.

She whooped a garbled cry and nearly fell off the exercise ball. Half laughing, she reached to steady herself then refocused on the screen.

313

Emma and Olivia will arrive at one fifty on June third and will depart at eleven thirty-five on the morning of June eighth. My Papa Bear instinct drove me to buy Olivia a ticket, so she'll fly in style in her car seat. Arranging for a baby bed would be perfect.

The only other preparation is to get a Tdap vaccine if you haven't had one. Pertussis has staged a comeback, so the vaccine is recommended to protect our kiddos. I got mine at a pharmacy. Your health department or pharmacy would be good bets.

Thanks again for your graciousness. Tomorrow will be a special day, highlighted by the look on Emma's face when she opens her Mother's Day card. I wish you a Happy Mother's Day, too.

All best,

Bennett

They're coming. She read his words twice more before opening *FW: Emma K Washington June Third. Confirmation code… Flight… Departs… Traveler— Emma Elizabeth Kaulien.* Goosebumps rushed her arms. *She's named after me. Maybe.* Intentional or coincidental, she didn't know. But as she opened the third email, *FW: Olivia K Washington June Third,* she was certain of one thing. "My Emma and Olivia are coming to visit." She turned away from the cruise photo to announce her news. Then she launched off the exercise ball and hooted and danced around the room.

On her way out of the office, she paused in front of the mirror. The glass spoke nothing of the change within. Her friends could look at her without a single suspicion. She had *no idea* how she would break her news.

The next morning, Beth spent far too long sifting

through her closet. She ran her hands over silk, polyester, cotton, and linen. Finally, she decided on a teal dress with black side panels and a skinny black belt. *Casual and comfortable but Mom-ish?* She wasn't going as anyone's mom, nor would she be regarded as such, so what she wore didn't really matter. After sliding the dress over her head, she tightened the belt and mulled its irony. She did not feel like a Master Black Belt this morning. All she wanted was to stay home and be thanked with a caramel roll when Kate and Frank picked up the coffee table.

Throughout the years, she had plenty of experience bucking up, save for her reclusive months following Reid's death. *I'll rally again.* She swung into the bathroom and emerged fifteen minutes later—mascara, blush, coral lipstick, and a spritz of perfume the finishing touches. *Seven months...* As she donned a long, black cardigan and a pair of black heels, she replayed the first night of woodworking class. She reflected on everything that transpired since, and the leadoff seemed ages ago. *Glad I didn't bail.* Had she any idea of the forthcoming friendships, she would have been first through Home ReSource's doors. "You're overestimating." She glanced in the lowboy's mirror and smoothed her dress. Then she strode to the laundry room and gathered keys and purse.

Cool air blew in through the car's open windows. She reached Jakers Bar and Grill in less than ten minutes. Idling in a center turn lane, she waited while a handful of vehicles passed by. When the traffic broke, she turned into the lot as a car backed out of a front-row parking place. *Score.* Easing into the space, she let out a breath, her fortuitous timing summoning a shadow of a smile. *I'm where I'm meant to be.* She entered the building and glanced left, scanning the front tables.

"Welcome to Jakers." From the reception area that separated the restaurant and bar, a thin, college-aged host smiled and opened his hands.

"Thank you. I'm meeting my friends..." She looked beyond the host stand to a cushioned bench. Savory aromas filled the air.

A thirty-something couple with two children were the bench's lone occupants.

She met his gaze. "MacCaffert—party of five?"

He zigzagged a finger down a sheet of paper. "You're the first one here. I can seat you..." He stepped from behind the stand.

"Thanks, but I'll wait." Beth edged past him toward the young family. *Two girls.* She rested a hip against the end of the half-windowed wall that shielded a portion of the restaurant from the reception area. From this vantage point, she admired the preschooler's turquoise dress and her baby sister's fuchsia ruffles. *Where did you get their clothes?* Fearing her question might lead to one in return, she bit her tongue.

"Where *are* they?" The girl sporting turquoise anklets and shiny black shoes wiggled off the seat.

"On their way." Her mom caressed her small hand with one hand and smoothed her dark, glossy hair with the other.

The family's light brown skin was a perfect match. Beth shifted her focus to the dad.

Cuddling the baby on his lap, he nested a hand in his. With his opposite fingertips, he traced figure eights on her chubby leg.

His touch looked feather soft. *Like yours, Bennett?*

Suppressing the urge to close the gap and run her fingers through the infant's auburn, spiky hair, she rearranged her purse then glanced up.

The mother held her gaze.

Caught in her scrutiny, Beth gripped her elbows. "How old are they?" She steadied her voice.

"How old are you?" The mom wrapped an arm around her daughter's waist.

A touch for courage. Her stomach tugged at the tender mother-daughter connection.

Pressing her thumb against her pinkie, the preschooler uncurled three fingers then held out her hand.

"You're a big girl." Wanting to reach for her hair, too, Beth fiddled with a sleeve. "How old is your sister?"

She looked at her hand and freed her pinkie then tilted her head. "Four months."

Beth leaned toward her small voice. "She's a lucky duck to have a big sister."

"She's a *great* big sister." Her mom patted her shoulder. "Do you have any—"

"You beat us." Kate engulfed her in a hug. "Happy Mother's Day."

"Thank you." She brushed her cheek against the teenager's damp hair and inhaled its rosemary-mint freshness. Gazing over Kate's shoulder, she fluttered a wave. "Have a nice day."

The woman smiled. "You, too."

Beth joined Therese, Helen, and Frank and after a quick round of hugs, she followed the host to the table. A flush started in her core—hot flash and yearning doubling down. She sank into a chair, turning to drape her purse over its back. Then she ran a forearm across her brow and dabbed the moisture with her knit cardigan. All around her, the restaurant buzzed with holiday cheer. Straightening, she eyed her napkin and fought the urge to free the silverware and bury her face in the cotton cloth.

Kate drew in a slow breath. "Smells *divine*."

"I told you." Frank squared his shoulders.

Beth shed her sweater then slid her palms under her thighs.

Their server arrived. "My name's Quinn—I'll be taking care of you. How many moms do we have?"

"Three." Kate smiled and waved an arm.

I am a mom. The words leapt into her mouth. She reached for her water.

"Happy Mother's Day." He glanced around the table. "Is everyone thinking about the buffet?"

"We are." Frank patted his belly. "I've been thinking about the buffet all week."

"So have I." Quinn grinned and segued to their drink orders. "Help yourselves." He gestured toward the center of the restaurant.

Kate leaned over and squeezed her hand. "You're like my second mom. Just sayin'."

You're like my second daughter. A riptide of emotions washed over her: joy, sorrow, longing, and regret. An icy chill competed with the scorching heat. She shivered, so slight she hoped the others didn't notice. "I'm honored to be your second mom."

"Mutual admiration society." Kate winked, orchestrating a fist bump before slipping between her mom and grandma. "Ready?" She slid her hands from their shoulders to the chairs.

Beth stood and stepped back, signaling for Helen and Therese to go first.

"Age before beauty." Helen smiled and brushed a hand against Beth's back as she passed.

The tender touch unfurled memories of her mom. *You're a great-grandma.* She smoothed her neckline and rested a palm over her heart.

"Beauty before beauty, Grandma, followed by…" Kate glanced at her grandpa.

"A most handsome devil." He chuckled and winked.

"Whatev." Kate motioned the women toward the buffet, her eyes twinkling.

Taking her place behind Therese, Beth filled her plate with bits and bobs, salivating at the smells. Lobster alfredo… Shrimp scampi… Miso citrus salmon… Almond crusted cod… She raised a spoonful of steamed mussels and inhaled the garlicky aroma.

"Beth?" A female voice came from behind.

She twisted to her left. The mussels clattered to her plate.

An oval-faced woman smiled then shifted her feet. "Nice to see you."

Mary…Molly…Mitzi… She couldn't remember the name of the Forest Service employee that worked at the end of the hall.

"I was so sorry to hear about the loss of your husband." The woman-with-an-M-name leaned forward and lowered her voice.

A band tightened around Beth's chest, flattening her lungs. "Thank you." She spoke in a small voice then swung an about-face and replaced the spoon. Memories clawed their way into her consciousness.

Hiking Mount Sentinel the summer before he died, Reid's remarks had been off-the-cuff. "I don't want a service. Sprinkle my ashes up here. Do a little tap dance if you want." He unfolded from a bench then grinned and shuffle-hopped.

"I'll tap dance the entire way." She punctuated the tease in her voice with a shuffle-hop of her own, adding a pair of heel-toe-heels for the finale. Then she filed away his words for what she expected to be years. Not months. Per his request, she did not have a service. Coupled with her subsequent isolation, she had little practice with condolences. The few times she received sympathetic words, her MO was to acknowledge and duck away. Or thank and change the subject—a master of deflection. A funeral might have eased the aftermath. Instead, she limited herself to clandestine grocery shopping in the ensuing months, choosing a time and place where she hoped to avoid crowds and people she knew. Generally, she had been successful.

Avoiding eye contact with those behind her, Beth stepped away from the buffet—the line doubled and her appetite halved in a single moment.

"Hard?"

Therese slipped a hand under her elbow. Beth managed a nod, her mouth as dry as sawdust. Though her hibernation was not a secret, it did not deserve voice during a Mother's Day buffet. Returning to the table, she dawdled as she positioned her napkin and lifted her silverware. *Be present.* She cut into her salmon and forced a bite then worked through nibbles of each seafood offering. The rich flavors awakened her taste buds.

Kate eyed Beth's plate. "Good?"

"Mmmm." She gave a satisfied sigh. "*Divine*." She tucked in with enthusiasm then, appreciating the meal and the family that made her feel as though she were one of their own. Leaving the restaurant, she pulled Kate aside. "I put a captain's chair in the shop."

"Thanks." Kate grinned and leaned close. "Grandpa might topple off the stepladder…"

"Agreed." She murmured her reply. A round of thank-yous and hugs followed. First out of the lot, she arrived home minutes later and waited outside to greet her guests.

Kate had the passenger door open before the engine stilled. "You go in first." She waved an arm toward the garage. "When I say 'now' then open the door."

"Gotcha." She flashed a thumbs-up.

"I want you to close your eyes before the big reveal for the full effect…I'll tell you when to shut 'em. Okay?" Kate grabbed her grandfather's hand.

He snapped a salute.

Beth wove through the garage and stationed herself inside Reid's shop. Cracking the door, she listened for her cue.

"Close your eyes, Grandpa." Kate's voice carried. *Shuffle…shuffle…shuffle…*"NOW."

She pulled open the door.

Kate led Frank by the hand and eased him into the shop. "Take his other arm." She flicked her head.

Nodding, Beth cupped his left arm between her hands.

Kate sidestepped right, leading the way with slow, choppy movements. "Now, stop. Keep your eyes closed, Grandpa." She let go of his arm and scooted behind him. Then she reached for his hand and placed it on an armrest. "Steady?"

"Yes, ma'am." He took a step backward. Brushing a leg against the seat, he shook free from Beth's hold. Then he grasped both arms of the chair, squinting a little as he sat. He exhaled a long, low whistle. "Bravo." A two-beat clap accompanied the word. He stood and clapped some more before sweeping Kate into his arms. "You are an *ace*."

Pressing four fingers against her tongue, Beth blew a series of long, shrill notes.

"*Thank you*." Kate tipped back her head. "You helped, Grandpa."

"I followed orders." He winked at Beth.

"Whatev—and thanks for the standing O." She patted his cheek before stepping out of the embrace.

You'll miss her. Beth skimmed her fingertips along the coffee table.

"My pleasure. What were you—about seven?" He rested a hand on Kate's back. "This little missy sang a song, and her grandma and I clapped and jumped up and hollered 'standing ovation.' "

"Yeah, and he had to explain those words. From then on, I made him and Grandma sit before I performed or showed them my work." Kate plopped into the chair. "How many standing O's have you given me?"

"Eight thousand, three hundred seventy-two." He stroked his chin. "Sound about right?"

"Minus five thousand, one hundred forty-nine." She patted her legs with each word, adding a rat-a-tat-tat at the end.

"All I know is you always give us something to

cheer about." Frank's eyes shone. "When you're a famous furniture maker, you better scatter some 'not for sale' chairs in your shop. Keep those standing O's coming."

"Good idea." Kate stood and flexed her arms. "Now, let's grab this baby so Mom and Grandma won't wonder what happened to us."

"Aye aye, Boss."

Holding her breath, Beth pushed the button to raise the shop's big door. Unused for almost two years, the door creaked into gear. She sputtered an exhale. *Slick as snot.* Reid's words flitted through her head. Sunlight flooded the room, exposing bits of dust floating in the air.

Frank opened the SUV's hatch.

A lump rose in her throat. *I'd like to tag along.* She stepped outside and caressed her bracelet, imagining Therese's joy at the table's reveal.

Balancing her end of the table, Kate flashed a grin before lowering the furniture into the back of the car.

Frank centered the upside-down table then closed the door. Meeting Kate's gaze, he smiled and gave a single nod.

Kate's smile mirrored her grandpa's. She wrapped her arms around Beth's waist. "I'll miss coming here. Thank you *so much.*"

"Anytime…" *Thank you for opening my heart.* She held on tight, inhaling again the scent of rosemary and mint. "Thanks again for the buffet and *divine* rolls." She gave one extra squeeze before unlocking her arms.

"You're welcome." Frank gave her a quick hug. "Thanks for everything."

Opening the passenger door, Kate turned. "We'll

see you at my graduation party."

My Emma and Olivia will be here. The words scratched at her throat. She raised a thumbs-up then plodded through the garage and pressed a button. The rumbling whirr of the overhead door masked the car engine's fade. Hugging her shoulders, she tucked her chin and pressed against the tendrils of loneliness and regret that uncoiled in her chest.

In the kitchen, Beth studied her Mother's Day card. She covered the broken heart's tiny opening with a fingertip and claimed the heart as her own. *I'll never let you go.* The old ache of what-might-have-been chipped at her gut. She closed her eyes and acknowledged the pain. Then she grazed a kiss over Emma's signature and replaced the card in the center of the table.

Years earlier, she read that Mother's Day generated the most greeting card sales nationwide. Her wound reopened then with *I'll never get one.* But she quickly purged every little bit of sorrow and remorse because to feel the feelings was too damn hard.

Pushing away from the table, she blew a kiss toward the pair of ribboned hearts. *I hope many more cards will follow...*

The next day, she sailed through her shopping excursion, save for a brief debate while examining collage frames. A six-photo family frame caught her eye. Though she held a unique position on Olivia's family tree, she didn't know if Emma and Bennett would include a picture of her or not. She selected her second choice—a nine-photo, oak frame minus an inscription. At home, she set the frame and a handcrafted hat, made by a local designer from pre-owned clothing, on the dining room table. Beside them, she stacked a trio of books: *The Very Hungry Caterpillar*, *Goodnight Missoula*, and *Hello Baby!* Then she added the sweater, booties, and afghan—her hand-knit, natural alpaca creations being the crowning touch.

Beaming love and pride and joy into her hands, she wrapped the gifts in mint green paper adorned with multicolored zoo animals. Once the lot was wrapped and boxed with packing peanuts on all four sides, she examined the watercolor on the front of the card. A downy-haired baby gazed with wide, searching eyes. The expression bore yet-to-be discovered wisdom and grace. She opened the card and reread the verse.

Into your world
this being
Into your life
this gift
Into your arms
this love.

Then she picked up her pen.

Dear Emma and Bennett,

All best as you embark upon a wonderful, new adventure with your sweet baby. I wish you a lifetime of good health and happiness. To Miss Olivia, I add a wish for years of warm laps and good books.

All My Love

NanaBeth. She wrote her name in the quiet of her heart. After driving to the post office to mail the package, she spent the remainder of the afternoon digging for courage. *I need to tell Maria first.* At five o'clock, she picked up the phone. Her stomach burned. Pacing around the kitchen, she tapped in the numbers. *I hope I can leave a message.*

Ring...ring...ring...

"Hi, Beth."

Startled to hear her name, she hardly noticed the smile in Maria's voice. "Hi..." She swallowed hard. "I'm wondering if you'd like to go to lunch on Wednesday."

"Lunch would be great. When and where?"

She gripped the bottom of her shirt and twisted. "Hob Nob at eleven thirty?"

"Perfect—I'll see you then."

The fire in her belly calmed a little, and she penned in the date on her calendar. *As if I'd forget.* That night, a gripping fear hollowed her nerve. She didn't *really* need to tell Maria before the others. *She'd understand. Wouldn't she?*

****

Two days later, Beth eased her car onto Lower Miller Creek Road. Silencing the radio, she reviewed her plan—lunch with Maria first and a Tdap second. She drove on autopilot, and her heart beat a scared, uneven rhythm. *I had a baby thirty-six years ago... My daughter and grandbaby are coming next month... I'm a birth mom...* New words and old tripped through her head. As she passed the three-story brick façade of Hellgate High School, she had no idea whether she'd use any or none of her rambling, choppy story. Two blocks later, she backed in between a motorcycle and a minivan to park parallel in a two-hour-free-parking zone.

Hurrying down Higgins Avenue, she glanced across the street at Big Dipper. *When did we last stop for ice cream, Reid?* Their orders never changed—a one-scoop, salted caramel sugar cone for him, and a one-scoop, half El Salvador coffee half green tea plain cone for her. *A tradition.* They visited the shop the summer before he died…*but which day?* She wanted to remember every detail. The ice cream would have tasted so much sweeter—only one part bitter had they known… She couldn't remember so many things. Ordinary days passed without warning; no red flags alerted their significance. *The last time for…the last time we…* She heaved a sigh. *Would he want to know the end was just heartbeats away? Would she?*

He loved life and was full of dreams. But if he knew his life would be snuffed short, he would have completed a second cruise.

The traffic light changed from green to yellow to red. *Stop.* Reframing her thoughts, she crossed Higgins then Fourth Street. She scouted the Hob Nob's sidewalk tables. All three were occupied. *I hope Maria isn't sitting at the counter.* Her impending news—which might remain a secret—deserved face-to-face conversation.

Maria waved from a window seat.

"Score." Beth murmured Zoe's word of gratitude and pushed open the door.

"I say we order." Maria stood and drew her into a hug. "I'm hungry."

"Sure." *I'm not.* She wound around tables to the end of the line. Aside from three counter seats and a two-top in the center, the small café was full and hummed with conversations. She scanned the chalkboard, grateful for the reprieve and the privacy of their cozy table up front. Her attention leapt between the menu and the multitude of words rolling through her head. Pleasant aromas filled the air, but she couldn't summon her appetite. She ordered a pear and gorgonzola salad and picked at it, scarcely tasting the sweet and tangy flavors. Her story lay scrunched in her throat. Gripping her water glass with both hands, she shifted in her seat. "I received a Valentine's Day card"—she dipped her chin—"from my birth daughter."

Maria leaned in, her lips a tiny *o*.

"She turned thirty-six last week…" Heat seared Beth's core. Pleating her napkin, she glanced out the window then skipped backward and forward in her story's unravel. "Reid never knew I had a baby… Now, I have a grandbaby, and Emma and Olivia are coming next month." She ended with the three most important facts. Silence stretched between them, and the background noise faded into oblivion.

Holding Beth's hands across the table, Maria traced tiny circles with her thumbs. "You thought protecting your story was for the best."

Her words and butterfly-soft strokes delivered a tangible hug. Beth stared at their hands. Memories and Maria's compassion squeezed the air from her lungs. "You remind me of my labor nurses." The words were soft as dew. She looked up. "I thought they were saints."

"I'm glad you had good nurses." Maria's eyes glistened. "Relinquishing a baby is the most selfless thing you can do…"

I always felt selfish. A wave of sadness washed over her. Closing her eyes, Beth surrendered to Maria's words. When she exited the restaurant, she wrapped her arms around her friend. "Thank you for everything…"

Maria nodded. "Thanks for telling me."

Beth tightened her grip. As she stepped away, she

held Maria's gaze, imparting gratitude too deep for words. She trudged to her car. Feeling heavy and spent, she longed to return home. Instead, she drove downtown to the Missoula City-County Health Department. On the first floor, a pair of double doors held neighboring signs—IMMUNIZATION CLINIC and WIC: WOMEN, INFANTS, and CHILDREN. Squaring her shoulders, she mustered her resolve to protect Olivia then opened the door. A right-angled construction wall cordoned off more than half of the shared reception area, creating a hallway to the right. She glanced left.

The sandy-haired woman seated behind an IMMUNIZATION CLINIC CHECK-IN placard smiled.

"I'd like a Tdap, please." She spoke before reaching the counter.

The receptionist nodded. "Have you been here before?"

"Years ago for a tetanus shot…" Beth repositioned her purse.

She assembled paperwork on a clipboard and slid it across the counter.

At the opposite end of the registration desk, a mom with a baby in an infant seat and a preschool-aged boy checked in at WIC.

"Weels on the bus…" As he sang, the child wrapped an arm around his mother's leg.

Focused on the sweet voice beside her, Beth gave a cursory listen to the receptionist's instructions. Then she carried the forms to the empty, downsized waiting area. Hearing the young family's approach, she avoided eye contact and flipped to the consent for care. The words she floundered through over lunch caught in her throat—where she wanted them to stay. After returning the completed documents to the counter, she cast a glance at the baby.

Dressed in a one-piece, green-and-white striped outfit, the bright-eyed infant gurgled and kicked.

"Red...lello...boo..." The sibling pushed beads up and around a maze of brightly-colored wires. "Lello...red..." He grinned.

The gleam in his eye forced a smile. Beth bit her lip. *Will you have a sister or brother someday, Little Bean?*

"Beth?"

A female voice interrupted her musing. Moisture evaporated from her mouth. She approached a tall, slender woman—an RN, according to the name badge dangling from a lanyard.

"Come on back. My name is Phyllis..."

She followed her into an exam room.

Phyllis gestured toward a chair. "You're here for a Tdap?"

"Mm-hmm."

The nurse opened a manila folder. "Do you have any special kiddos in your life?" She passed an information sheet.

Blood surged through her veins. "A new grandbaby." The giant words inched from her mouth. "She'll be here next month."

"Congratulations." Phyllis smiled. "Thanks for coming in, too. Pertussis cases surged a few years ago..."

On the way home, Beth stopped at a red light on the corner of West Broadway and Orange Street. She danced her fingers over the bandage—a subtle badge of honor rising beneath her sleeve. *My Emma and Olivia are coming to Missoula.* When the light turned green, she stepped on the accelerator. Her stomach clenched. *Can I tell the others?*

Chapter Nineteen

Five days later, Beth descended upon her recliner and tore into an envelope. *A birth announcement.* She gasped and pulled out the news. A letter fluttered onto her lap. The vital statistics on the front of the announcement garnered her attention.

Name: Olivia Elise Kaulien
Date: April twenty-ninth
Time: Nine thirty-four a.m.
Weight: Seven pounds fourteen ounces
Length: Twenty-one-and-a-half inches
Head: Thirteen-and-three-quarter inches
Chest: Thirteen-and-a-half inches
Loved by: Emma and Bennett Kaulien

Inside, framed by an oval-shaped cutout, was a picture of her grandbaby. She studied Olivia's untamed hair, her wide, dark eyes, and her rosebud lips that hinted at a smile. A tingle of awe prickled her skin. *You're perfect.* She brushed a kiss millimeters from the photo then unfolded Emma's letter.

Dear Beth,

Since I opened my Mother's Day card, I cannot stop smiling. Bennett's homemade gift certificates did trigger some happy tears… "This voucher entitles the bearer to a round-trip ticket from Washington, D.C. to Missoula, Montana, June third to June eighth." He made one for me and one for Olivia. Learning we will meet each other in a few short weeks was the Best Present Ever.

Isn't Olivia's picture precious? Whoever said newborns don't smile was dead wrong. I can't imagine a sweeter, easier baby... She's already thirteen days old. My parents arrived last weekend. Mom is staying through the week, which has been nice as Bennett and I figure out this parenting gig. We even had a short date night on Saturday. His parents are coming the twenty-second, so we're in good shape.

Sleep deprivation is our biggest challenge. I hope Liv will be one of those babies who sleeps through the night at seven weeks. Hmm, I haven't called her Liv before. Either this pen is a conduit for maternal shorthand, or fatigue has me punchy...

Thanks in advance for getting a baby bed. Otherwise, we're all set. The countdowns to our wedding and due date were two of my life highlights. Adding the countdown until we meet adds up to a trifecta. I Can't Wait.

Much Love,

Emma

Neither can I. She gazed at Olivia's photo. A band of envy and regret wrapped around her chest, squeezing her ribs. Memories of her empty, aching arms stung clear to her marrow. She cupped her elbows across her belly and inhaled a slow, irregular breath. *I couldn't offer you the start I wanted.* But life was messy. Surrendering her baby shattered her heart... Now, knowing she wasn't a grandma on duty deepened the bruise.

Emma and Olivia are coming in sixteen days. Yes, she was grateful for their blossoming bond, but she refused to ignore the hurt. Better, she realized, to acknowledge and accept the pain then move on. Resting her head against the back of the chair, she let herself feel the feelings—*all of them*. Then she leaned in for one kiss and another, skimming Olivia's picture with her lips.

She wandered into the kitchen and brewed a cup of tea. Corralling mindfulness and joy, she carried her mug to the breakfast nook. *Three twenty in Maryland.* She encircled the mug with her hands and bowed into the steam. As the heat warmed her face, she inhaled the aroma of spices, fruits, and flowers. She sipped, and the warmth traveled from the inside out.

Are you taking a moment, too? She left her chair and checked the calendar. Noting with a smidge of satisfaction Emma was between visitors, she closed her eyes. *I hope you're drinking Missoula tea in your Missoula mug and feeling MommaBeth's love.* She routed to the office and returned with a notecard and pen.

Dear Emma,

Thank you for the birth announcement. Olivia's picture is priceless. I noticed the wisp of her smile right away. Wouldn't you love to decode her sweet baby thoughts? I'm glad to hear all is well…

Like you, I can't wait until we're together. Please let me know if any last-minute thoughts come to mind as I await your arrival. Do you have any food allergies? Likes or dislikes? Foods Olivia doesn't tolerate? By the time this reaches you, we'll be within two weeks *of our reunion.*

Much love,
Beth

I'm days away from telling my friends. A chill gripped her. She shivered and dropped her pen. *I don't know if I can.*

****

For three days, Beth wavered about sharing her news. But guilt and remorse whittled at her story, leaving it as fragile as bird bones. *I can't tell them.* With dinner T-minus thirty and her past reduced to dust, she repeated the words over and over. She reconciled two stumbling blocks that afternoon… Maria, she hoped, would feel sheltering her story was best, and she'd *rent* a baby bed. Maybe even buy one, since she predicted more visits in the future. The expected serenity eluded her, though. Instead, apprehension kneaded her gut—its burn consuming her body.

When the doorbell rang at five fifty, she sucked in a deep breath. *Who's early?* Rallying her game face, she lumbered down the hall and opened the door.

"Manhattans in the making." Corrine held up a reusable bag and sashayed into the house.

"We didn't want to be tardy with the drinks." Therese handed her a slow cooker then kissed her cheek. "Thanks, love. I'll grab the rotini."

Words lodged in her throat, and she clutched the pot and headed to the kitchen.

Unloading her bag in the breakfast nook, Corrine hummed.

Beth didn't recognize the tune. She leaned against the counter and plugged in the cooker. Then she rummaged for pot holders, even though Maria's handmade pair and two others lay fanned and ready.

Therese set her dish on the stove then met Beth's

gaze. "Do you need any help?"

Tons. But neither she, nor anyone else, could absolve her guilt. Wrangling a reply, she pulled out a pair of oven mitts.

"Ready for my mom's fave?" Corrine swept a palm in a semicircle.

"I've been ready all day." Therese grinned and rubbed her hands back and forth.

So have I. Beth circled to the table for a better look at the new additions: sweet vermouth, whiskey, bitters, maraschino cherries, and a cocktail shaker set. Coupled with the old-fashioned glasses, tongs, and ice bucket, the minibar beckoned. She wasn't much of a whiskey drinker, but the anticipation of a stiff drink caused her mouth to water.

"On the rocks"—Corrine waved a hand—"four ice cubes in each, please."

"Gotcha." Therese picked up the tongs.

"For my encore career, I'd like to open a distillery." Corrine poured a jigger of whiskey into the shaker.

As the liquor's aroma filled the air, Beth slipped into a chair and folded her hands across her roiling belly.

"I'll be your mixologist." Therese plunked ice cubes into the glasses.

Corrine mixed in sweet vermouth and shakes of bitters then added ice cubes without splashing a single drop. "Stirred, never shaken, according to my sweet mom." She inserted the long, slender spoon and counted from one to fifty.

"Finally." Therese wiggled her eyebrows.

"No shortcuts for perfection." Corrine strained

ruby red cocktails into four glasses. "I'll wait and check in with Maria."

"Deal." Therese garnished each with a maraschino cherry and raised a glass. "Cheers."

Beth clinked and drank one sip then another. The bitter, sweet, and boozy warmth worked its way to her belly. *Could be a long night.*

Ding-dong.

Willing her stomach to soften, she excused herself and headed to the door.

"…busting in." Zoe turned and smiled. "Buffalo chicken dip." She raised a dish and a bag. "I told Maria I have the app…"

She extended her hands. "Your manhattan awaits."

"Winner winner, chicken dinner." Zoe flicked an elbow and scooted past. "I'm set."

Ascending the porch, Maria held Beth's gaze. "How're you doing?"

She shook her head. *Not well.* Fearful her eyes might reveal the truth, Beth glanced down and reached for the bowl.

"If there's anything I can do or say…" Maria passed the salad and slipped an arm around her waist.

Unspoken words swirled all the way to the kitchen.

"Hail, hail, the gang's all here…" Zoe waved her hands in and out.

Maria joined a trio of voices. Before stepping aside, she patted Beth's waist.

Beth set the salad on the counter and sipped her cocktail, swallowing past the lump in her throat.

"What the hell do we care now-ow-ow?"

As her friends' voices faded, she gripped her glass.

"Sparking water…" Maria removed two tall bottles

from her bag. "Limeade—if anyone would like some now or later."

"Lime shlime. No offense, but New York City is calling my name." Zoe turned to Corrine. "NYCs—are manhattans ever called that?"

"Not that I know of." Corrine gave a half-shrug.

"Well…" Zoe cleared her throat. "N Y C. Coined by PWWPT." Gesticulating, she sang and puffed out her chest. "Singer-songwriter—do you think I missed my calling?"

"I do." Maria lifted her glass. "To PWWPT—those who will always be there."

"Amen, sister." Corrine clinked and grinned.

Beth answered with a cursory tap. *You are a master of deflection.* Hooding her eyes, she focused on her cocktail and quaffed a drink.

"Shall we?" Zoe tipped her head.

"Mm-hmm." Beth led the way with the slow cooker and placed it at the head of the table.

Therese claimed the nearby captain's chair. "Rotini…" She gestured toward her stoneware dish. "Then pass your plates for cacciatore."

The savory aroma did nothing to restore Beth's appetite, which was nonexistent since the previous day. She served a spoonful of salad and slid the bowl to the right.

"I'd like the names and ingredients, please." Corrine reached for a serving spoon.

"Oriental cabbage salad." Maria shifted in her seat. "Cabbage, green onions, ramen noodles…"

The clamor in her head drowned out her friends. When she registered the hush, she looked up.

The others studied her.

Beth curled her toes. "German chocolate cake mix, evaporated milk, margarine, walnuts, caramels, and chocolate chips." Her mom's favorite dessert was seared into her memory, and she recited on rote.

"What's the name?" Zoe leaned in.

"Turtle squares." She rubbed her jaw.

"AKA pure deliciousness." Therese smiled and lifted her glass. "Here's to our moms and their recipes."

"Cheers." Maria clinked with Beth then nodded once.

Now. Reading the murmur behind Maria's gaze, she gulped her drink, grasping the glass as though it were a lifeline. "I'm a mom." The words tumbled out. "Thirty-six years ago, I had a baby…" For the second time in the history of the Perimenopausal Women with Power Tools, Beth held center stage.

Her words hung in the air.

"Holy hell." Zoe steepled her fingers under her chin. "You've kept this secret for thirty-six years? I would've combusted after three months—maybe even one."

Corrine exhaled a long, slow whistle. "What a story."

"One I never expected to share." Beth pleated her napkin atop her knotted belly.

"With a happy ending you didn't expect either, except it's not really the end." Maria's eyes shone.

"Mother and grandmother." Therese hoisted her glass.

"Hear, hear." Zoe stood and motioned toward the center of the table.

On her feet, Beth stretched an arm for a verge-of-breaking-glasses toast. Beaming, she glanced around

Karen Buley

the table. *A standing ovation.* The sip tasted sweeter than before and nudged her appetite.

"You'll have to bring Emma and Olivia to the graduation party." Therese flicked her fork.

"If it's okay with Kate—"

"Are you kidding?" Therese arched her eyebrows. "She'll be thrilled."

"But I don't want a fuss... Kate will be the star, and we need to keep a low profile." Beth skewered a bite of tomato, rotini, and chicken. "We have a neck to size up."

"I'll be in charge of Operation Stealth." Zoe bugged her eyes.

Corrine snickered.

"You doubt *moi?*" Zoe tapped a thumb against her chest. "Our mission will be professional. SN won't have any idea we're talking about him and his perhaps-formerly-scrawny little neck." She cleared her throat and turned to Beth. "Are you glad you told us?"

She bit her lip. "I wish I would've told Reid first."

"Not to be blunt, but if he hadn't died"—Zoe dropped her chin—"Emma wouldn't have found you."

Therese rested a hand on Beth's arm. "You lost one love and gained three others..."

Heat traveled from her neck to her face. She closed her fingers around her bracelet. *Joy.*

"And if Reid does know, I bet he's up there cheering." Maria leaned forward.

Holding her gaze, Beth shushed a niggle of doubt. "I hope so." When she escorted her company to the door an hour later, she luxuriated in long, tender hugs.

Zoe lingered in the entryway. "We'll bring the bassinet over next week."

340

"I'd be happy to swing by your house." Beth rested a hand high on her chest.

"Thanks, but the girls love excursions. Erin tells me to have fun with my PM ladies, which she thinks means 'night'…" Zoe flashed a dimpled grin. "I'll give you a call." She gave a final squeeze and slipped into the inky darkness.

A push-pull of regret and relief coursed through her. She turned from the Shaker table. Feeling both heavy and light, she drifted to the kitchen.

The following morning, Beth carried a mug of licorice spice tea to Reid's recliner and opened her journal. Memories floated through her head. *I'm sorry.* Using a fingertip, she airbrushed her apology then picked up her pen.

May Twenty-second

My Dear Darling,

Thirty-three years ago, you made me the happiest girl on the planet. The happiest baby according to your great-aunt Mayme. We didn't listen when she told us we were too young to get married. Your friend Tom loved teasing me about robbing the cradle—which meant you were the baby, not me. We ignored the skeptics, affirming we were "crazy in love." Crazier yet that thirty-three years have passed…

This month would've been perfect for our second cruise. My one consolation is the night we lusted over the Royal Caribbean catalog, we had no idea what was coming down the pike. Our shared delight in dreaming about time on and off the ship and time on and off each other…you know what I mean. Those memories, and others like them, cloak me in comfort.

I miss you, Darling. Thank you for the love,

laughter, and joy we shared throughout the years. I miss you and love you more.

She encircled the mug with her hands. The tea's aroma rushed reminiscences of cozy winter evenings. She took a sip, drawing the warmth from the inside out. "I'm so sorry." The words offered little balm to the emptiness of her soul. She dipped her forehead against the hot porcelain. Could she ever rectify her guilt?

****

Three days later, Beth pulled into the parking lot at the base of Mount Sentinel. Cars, along with a smattering of bikes and a pair of bicycle trailers, packed the lot. She eased into one of the few empty spaces, and a chill prickled her skin. Shivering, she zipped her hoodie though the outside temperature display read fifty-six degrees. She collected her water bottle and the baggie of ashes from the console and exited the car. Her pulse hopscotched in her chest. *I hoped fewer people would be here.* She stuffed the sandwich bag into a pocket of her cargo shorts then climbed the stairs to the trailhead.

Slowed by guilt and grief, she drew in deep, ragged breaths and plodded along the dry, rocky path. At the third switchback, she collapsed onto a bench. *Ten more.* Already, she shared the trail with an infant in a front pack, a well-known, local octogenarian, a dozen or more in-betweens, plus three dogs. She tied her hoodie around her waist and gulped a long, cold drink of water. *You were with me last time, Reid.* He liked to hike side by side, though he was quick to drop back so other hikers or runners could pass by or weave around them.

Now, reduced to a party of one, she resumed her trek, weighted by melancholy. She hiked with laser-like focus, her heart pounding. When the metal signpost at the base of the one-hundred-foot, whitewashed M edged into view, she blew out a labored sigh of relief. She navigated the final switchback to the concrete icon—the symbol of the University of Montana that, to many, represented instead their beloved city of Missoula. Winded after her three-quarter-mile climb, she looked for a quiet place to sit.

Four teenaged girls huddled on one leg of the M.

She looked away from their animated voices and laughter to the M's other leg.

Two thirty-something men sat with a preschool-aged boy between them.

A handful of people milled around, some angling cell phones and cameras over the Missoula valley.

Beth headed toward the guys.

The three of them sat with their legs touching.

A tingling warmth coursed through her. *Dads and their son.*

One sat with his right arm draped behind his family. Sunlight captured the glint of a gold band on his left ring finger.

The other, who sported a matching gold band, rummaged in a backpack then handed granola bars to each. Meeting her gaze, he smiled.

She smiled back. *I hope your son's birth mom or surrogate has witnessed your love.* Thoughts of Emma tiptoed into mind. *Ssshhh.* She continued past, leaving space for two or three others before claiming the edge of the M. Chunks of gray peeked from beneath the peeling whitewash. Repositioning her legs on the cool, coarse concrete, she nested a hand inside her pocket. The baggie was warm.

Clear azure sky stretched for miles, save for strands of wispy clouds above Mount Dean Stone to the south and Blue Mountain to the west. In between, deep in the Bitterroot Range southwest of Missoula, veins of dark blue pushed through the snowpack on Lolo Peak. Beth circled her gaze to the right: from Ch-paa-qn Peak—its trailhead forty miles away—to Stuart Peak, to Mount Jumbo, less than two miles north. She gave each mountaintop a single glance, along with the University of Montana campus, Washington-Grizzly Stadium, and the Clark Fork River. *The view is beautiful, Reid.* Closing her eyes, she yielded to bittersweet memories.

"We made it to the top!" A child's voice carried from the left.

The sweet, happy shout broke through Beth's reflection, and she opened her eyes.

A pint-size girl held hands with an older woman and a younger, tanned one—all three with honey-brown hair.

A mom and grandma. Strands of longing uncoiled inside her chest, squeezing her heart and lungs. She removed her hand from her pocket and rested it over her heart. *You, me, and your mom someday, Little Bean?* Alone now on this leg of the M, she shifted to her left.

The girl tugged the others to the space vacated by the dads and their son.

She didn't hear them leave. Fumbling with her water bottle, she wanted to listen to and watch the newcomers. But the reminder of the past and present pulled at the fabric of her shorts. Beth stood and proceeded right, away from the three generations sharing her seat. She turned right again to hike alongside the M and when she reached the top, she turned right once more. *A...maz...ing grace how sweet the sound...* Her cadence matched her ascent, and each syllable and step created a perfect union.

Reid didn't mention a song, but the lyrics persisted—stronger than their whispered introduction... *And grace will lead me home.* She stopped for a slug of water, searching her memory for the rest.

"Start over."

Loud and clear, his voice filled her soul. Her belly fluttered and she pressed a hand against her abdomen. After the quivery sensation stilled, she resumed her climb. She sang from the beginning and when she reached the end of verse three, she rewound without apology. Turning left, she continued her hymn. As she neared her destination, she finished the third verse for the final time.

"A double trifecta."

The words echoed in her head. She completed her last steps in silence and lowered onto the outcropping rooted in memory. Dangling her feet over the edge, she leaned against the rocky backrest that barely cleared her tailbone. *No one's around, Reid.* She quieted her ragged breathing then removed the baggie and cupped it in her hands. A lump rose in her throat, crowding her breath. *I don't know what to do.* She considered her options— pour out the ashes or sprinkle them with her fingers and direct their descent. Coarser than the "ashes to ashes, and dust to dust" of her imagination, the cremains' grit and substance—the first she'd seen—surprised her. *Now what?*

He didn't want a service...

She respected his wish but lacked a manual to

345

guide this second request. Since he called himself an agnostic, she wasn't sure about a prayer...then she considered the words that accompanied her climb, and silent reflection seemed more than okay. She closed her eyes and spoke in the stillness of her heart.

Mindful and reverent, she stood and buried her hand in ash and bone. In sacred unity, she sifted memories through her fingers then scattered the hallowed ashes where feet would not tread. She continued with quiet dignity. When the bag lay empty, she turned it inside out and slipped it over her hand. Tears spilled down her cheeks. With the baggie as her wand, she made a gentle sweep. "There's no place like home." Releasing the final specks, she breathed the words three times. She righted the bag and tucked it into her pocket. Then she sat—long after the sunshine dried her face.

Plodding down the mountain, she felt bits of her heart disintegrate with every step. Emptied, she silenced the radio before leaving the parking lot. Muscle memory directed her home then she lingered in the garage. An ache bloomed in the hollow of her chest, overtaking her core as she trailed her fingertips along Reid's car. She trudged into the house, its hush heavier than before. The phone's message light promised a balm to the oppressive quiet. She pushed Play.

"Hi Beth, this is Rachel. Sorry I haven't called for a while. I think of you often—telling myself I'll call later then never do. Feeble excuse, I know." Pause. "Anyway, just wanted to let you know I'm thinking of you." Pause. "I love you and miss you and hope we can get together soon. Please give me a call."

The answering machine clicked off.

Rachel phoned last Memorial Day, too. Beth's wound was still raw, and she erased the message without guilt. Today, her friend's voice soothed the silence, so she replayed the tape three times. *I'll call you later.* Right now, recollections and her upcoming visitors commanded her entire focus.

That night, she removed the baggie from her pocket. *Empty as air.* Throwing away the sandwich bag seemed disrespectful, so she set it on the bed. While she washed her face and brushed her teeth, she mulled possibilities. She folded the bag into a little rectangle and tucked it beneath her pearls. *I should have told you, Reid.* His urn and the darkness of her jewelry box magnified her deceit. She buried her face in her hands. *Could she ever tell him the truth?*

Chapter Twenty

Four days later, Zoe arrived with baby equipment and her girls in tow. "This stroller was Erin's idea." She laid the folded carriage opposite the entryway door.

Hope pushed a paper bag into Beth's hands.

"For baby Olivia." Erin handed a second bag. "To borrow, not keep."

"Thank you." She gathered in the bags. "And I have something for you."

"To keep?" Hope held out her hands.

Beth waved a *follow-me* gesture. "To keep in your bellies." She routed her company to the guest room to deposit the baby bed, and then steered them to the kitchen. "We're having a tea party." Setting the bags on the counter, she eyed the place settings with pride: gold-rimmed plates, dainty cups and saucers, and coordinating burgundy napkins. More china plates loaded with cheese and crackers, red and green grapes, and kid-sized snickerdoodles and monster bars filled the center of the table. Her favorite floral teapot rested on a circular bamboo trivet.

"China?" Zoe raised her eyebrows.

Heat rushed to her cheeks. "Did I go overboard?"

"Well..." Zoe glanced at the table. "This will be China One-O-One."

"We'll be careful, Mommy." Erin put her hands on her hips.

"Yeah." Hope climbed onto the chair closest to the cookies.

Zoe swooped in and helped her kneel. "I'd ditch the saucers, though."

"Gotcha." Beth lifted the girls' cups and saucers. "Would you like tea, hot chocolate, or apple juice?"

"Hot chocolate." Erin clapped twice.

"Me, too." Hope leaned against the table and stretched a hand toward a monster bar.

Zoe curled her fingers around Hope's hand. "Wait—"

"Go ahead and dish up." Beth nodded toward the food.

"Thanks." Zoe held her gaze. "Tea?"

"Please." She carried the china to the counter. Reveling in the background chatter, she made a mug of hot chocolate. She breathed in the rich cocoa aroma and filled the teacups half full, spilling only a little. *I have a lot to learn.* She rejoined her guests and placed the cups beside the girls' full plates—turning the handles for easy access. Then she served herself and tucked in.

"We brought five baby books and lots of toys…" Listing their offerings, Erin showed her dimples.

Will we have a tea party someday, Olivia? A familiar mix of regret and anticipation constricted Beth's throat. Thousands of days with Emma could never be recovered, but she hoped for years of memory making in the future.

"*Goodnight Moon* is my fravrit." Hope reached for her hot chocolate.

"Two hands, Hope, like this." Erin laced her fingers around her cup. "Plus, you like *Mommy Hugs*."

Beth smiled at Zoe. *Chip off the old block.* She

brushed her fingertips against the cool metal of her bracelet. *You too, Emma?* Savoring the floral flavors of the herbal tea, she wondered if her daughter was doing the same…then she quieted a wish to learn *everything.*

As the party wound to an end, Erin drained the last of her hot chocolate and slid from the chair. "We'll fix the toys."

"Yeah." Hope wriggled side to side.

Zoe stood and wiped Hope's hands and mouth before helping her down.

Erin distributed the bags between herself and her sister.

"Let's put the books and toys on the coffee table." Beth ushered the trio into the living room.

"You fix your things, and we'll set up the bed." Zoe tilted her head toward the door.

" 'Kay." Erin knelt beside the short table.

Hope set down her bag and reached inside.

Walking down the hall, Zoe slipped a hand behind Beth's back. "How're you doing?"

She exhaled a whoosh of air. "Changes minute to minute. Sometimes, I can hardly believe Emma and Olivia are coming, and in the next breath, I want them here *now*." She flashed a wry smile. "I have a lot to learn."

"But China One-O-One was a success." Zoe grinned, rubbing Beth's back before following her into the guest room. "Five more days—I'm so excited for you." She unzipped the carrying case then opened the bed and cinched its rails. "You won't need this bassinet next time but for now it's perfect." She added a mesh sling.

"So are the stroller and books." Copying her

friend's lead, Beth tightened one side of the bassinet. "Your girls are adorable."

"Thanks. They had fun picking out books, and then Erin started on the baby toys." She handed Beth a pair of tubes. "Slide them like this."

Beth followed directions—threading the outer ends into the bassinet and fastening the tubes in the center. She surveyed the bed with a satisfied smile.

"Easy peasy." Zoe added the mattress. "The toys will be better—"

"All done." Erin burst into the room.

"You're fast workers." Kneeling, Beth opened her arms.

"We are." Erin melted against her.

Hope snuggled in, too.

Enfolding them in her embrace, she nuzzled their heads and inhaled the scent of berry shampoo. "*They're darling*," she mouthed, giving the pair a final squeeze.

Zoe nodded and grinned. "Time to go." She rested hands on the girls' shoulders.

"Aw, can't we stay?" Erin frowned and crossed her arms.

"Yeah…" Hope pursed her lips.

"No." Zoe reached for their hands. "What do you say?"

"We'll come back and see baby Olivia." Erin flapped a hand between herself and Hope.

Flicking her head, Zoe met Beth's gaze. "How about 'thank you for the tea party.' "

"Thank you," chorused the sisters.

"You're welcome…" In the entryway, Beth enveloped them in another hug.

"Call if you need anything." Zoe clasped her hands

then shepherded the girls out the door.

As she passed the living room, she glanced at the treasures arranged on the coffee table. Her stomach tensed. *Will I know what to do with you, Little Bean?*

****

Four days later, Beth tore open a letter on her way into the house.

Dear Beth,

Thank you for your thoughtfulness regarding our upcoming visit. I can't think of anything else we need you to do, nor could Bennett when I ran your offer by him. In terms of food and drink, nothing has created gastrointestinal havoc for Olivia. I'm continuing my see-food diet—I see food and eat it. All systems are go...and by the time this letter reaches you, we'll be on the cusp of our arrival. I Can't Wait.

Much Love,

Emma

She held the letter to her chest. New guest room pillows were cased and waiting, the cupboards, fridge, and freezer were well stocked, and the house was spotless... She wanted to twitch her nose like Samantha on the TV show *Bewitched* and conjure Emma and Olivia here *now*.

The following morning, she arranged bouquets throughout the house: trollius and iris in the kitchen and dining room, roses in the bedrooms, and bachelor buttons and lily of the valley in the bathrooms and office. The entire house smelled like springtime. *Like love.* Before leaving for the airport, she surveyed her home, and her skin tingled all over. She paused in the guest room and caressed the rose petals between her fingers—yellow then red. In the office, she studied her

352

reflection. So much had changed over the past eight months. *Mom. Grandma.* She straightened her scarf. *Friend.* Beth smiled, and the woman in the mirror smiled back.

Driving to Missoula International Airport, she gripped the steering wheel and forced her concentration on the road. She scored a space in short-term parking close to the terminal. Her heart thumped out of control, seeming poised to jump out of her body and lead her by the hand. She strode inside and wound past the ticket counters, scarcely noticing the assortment of luggage, passengers, and the people that would be left behind. Tunnel vision propelled her to the arrival doors and flight status board where she zeroed in on Flight Four Eight Nine Four. *Eleven more minutes.* Unsure whether to sit or stand, she scanned the waiting area. Yielding to her lurching heart, she slipped into a front row seat kitty-corner from Arrivals.

A steady stream of people passed between Baggage Claim, Jedediah's Restaurant, and the restrooms on the left and the ticket counters and Security on the right. Their faces created a slide show of joy, indifference, melancholy, and anticipation.

None of them had *any idea* of the magnitude of this day.

I'm meeting my baby and grandbaby. The words crept into her mouth. After craning her neck for the fourth time, she stood and claimed a space in front of the arrival doors. She positioned herself near the wall, staring past the pair of doors to the stairs beyond where Emma would descend from a second-story gate. Struggling to relax, she brushed her palms against her khakis in a surreptitious attempt to dry her hands and hide telltale nerves. Then she straightened her scarf—its silky caress a visceral reminder of Kate and Therese. She ran a thumb over her bracelet. *Joy*.

A passenger appeared on the steps.

All at once, the air seemed too thin to breathe. Beth nearly slid to the floor but braced herself against the wall to protect her suddenly flimsy, unreliable legs. Then the dizziness vanished—its exit as rapid as its onset.

Laughter and exclamations filled the air as travelers pushed through the doors and greeted their people.

Where are you? She wrapped a hand around her wrist. Her pulse skittered beneath her fingertips. Squeezing hard against her bracelet, she imprinted *Joy* in the palm of her hand.

A pair of slender legs, bare below the knees, and a car seat appeared.

She lunged forward and sidestepped left, dodging but barely seeing.

Her baby and grandbaby were off the stairs and inside the revolving door then another half turn and they were out.

Emma smiled, glancing at her baby then back at her mom.

You're beautiful. Beth beamed a smile bigger than her face. She took four steps then two, drawing in a hungry intake of air and reaching for her daughter. "Welcome." Her single word was as moist as her eyes.

Snugging the car seat's handle with the crook of her arm, Emma slid her free hand to the small of Beth's back.

Her daughter's touch was both tentative and firm.

Beth reached beyond Emma's shoulder bag with one hand and cradled Olivia's downy head with the other. Tears ribboned her cheeks. She clung to her daughter then shifted for a breath and another look.

Emma buried her face in Beth's hair. "I've waited so long to meet you…"

Her voice quavered then broke. *And I you.* The words clotted in Beth's throat. Her heart beat calm, steady, and strong. A rush of peace enveloped her and she held on tight, wanting never to let go.

Two hours later, she sat beside her daughter on the couch. Heat from Emma's leg warmed her own, and images from a long-ago spring break sparked a tightness in her chest.

Detaching Olivia from her breast, Emma closed then blinked open her eyes.

Beth rested a hand on her leg. "Why don't you go lie down?"

"You wouldn't mind?" Emma held her gaze.

"Not at all." Smiling, Beth opened her arms.

Emma placed Olivia and her afghan in her grandmother's embrace then draped a burp cloth over Beth's shoulder.

A happy-sad tug flowed through her veins. *So many feelings, Little Bean.*

The baby quivered her eyelids between open and shut.

Emma glanced away, her lips trembling. She stood and crossed the room, casting a backward glance before heading out the door.

Beth skimmed her nose against her grandbaby's neck, drinking in her scent. Chasing an elusive burp, she patted her back more for comfort than purpose it seemed. After a final nuzzle, she cradled Olivia in the crook of her arm.

Her grandbaby wrinkled her brow then curled her lip into a half-smile. "Ah." She eyed her grandma.

Beth held her wide-eyed, searching gaze. "I'm your NanaBeth." Her singsong, new voice squeezed air from her lungs. She traced a fingertip along Olivia's forehead, cheeks, and nose, brushing feather-soft figure eights.

Olivia fluttered her eyes closed.

An ocean of happiness, joy, sorrow, and regret washed over her. She snuggled her grandbaby, drowning in her milky breath, innocence, and warmth. Three nights of restless sleep pulled at her eyelids. After stretching out on the couch, she arranged a pillow under her head and another to cocoon them in. She enveloped Olivia in her arms, heart to heart, and blanketed them both with alpaca softness. "I love you." Her words were soft as air. Tears rose in her throat, and she closed her eyes. *I'm so sorry.* Thirty-six years of sorrow broke open as she spoke to the baby girl she never knew. Then she breathed in her grandbaby's pureness and wept, holding both babies in the quiet of her heart.

That evening, Emma nursed Olivia then passed her to her grandma, seated on the couch. "Time for your momma to pump." Straightening her shirt, she stood. "I started pumping every night to have milk on hand when I return to work. I won't be long."

"Take your time…" Nestling Olivia on her lap, Beth reached for *Goodnight Moon.* "I hope we read together for years…" Her words fell muffled in her grandbaby's flyaway hair. She settled against a couch cushion and opened the book.

Olivia wriggled her arms and legs, opened and closed her fists, and moved her mouth in and out of fleeting smiles and coos.

Beth shifted her focus between the baby and book. She read in a lilting voice, and relished every wiggle and sigh. "Goodnight noises everywhere." She bent for a kiss. "The end, Little Bean." Laying her grandbaby on her lap, she slid her arms under Olivia's body and lifted her close. *Lighter than a sack of potatoes.* She brushed her lips against baby-soft cheeks. "Over in Killarney, many years ago, me mother sang a song to me—" Her voice broke. After a slow inhale and exhale, she started over and sang to the end.

"Beautiful." Emma stood in the doorway. "May I take a picture?"

"Sure." She turned Olivia toward her momma.

Emma shook her head. "The way you were."

She returned her grandbaby face-to-face and was overcome again by awe and delight.

Olivia smiled.

I'm your grandma. Beth leaned in and kissed her forehead.

"Bennett's been singing to her for months." Emma slipped onto the couch. She stroked Olivia's hair, grazing Beth's hand with her fingertips. "He sang during labor, didn't he? Hush, little baby don't say a word…"

Gripped by the sweetness of her daughter's voice coupled with memories of her dad's tenor, she bit the inside of her lip.

When the song ended, Emma kissed Olivia's cheek.

Beth kissed the other—first a touch with her lips then a fingertip caress. She met Emma's gaze. A galaxy of words hovered in the air—thirty-six years' worth. *I want to hear everything.* But this territory was uncharted. "How was your labor?" The question came out hesitant and soft.

"Labor was hard like you said it would be..." Emma tipped her head and raised her eyebrows.

Just like Ian. She looked away, stifling the gasp caught in her throat.

"Not that I didn't believe you, but I've always had a high pain tolerance, so I thought I'd rock labor. That thinking was misguided. I didn't have pain medication, but I came close." Emma leaned in for another kiss. "Bennett was awesome, and Jennifer helped a ton, too. Whenever I wanted an epidural, I'd chant my new affirmation..." She closed her eyes. "I can do this like my momma."

A four-four monotone, she enunciated each syllable. *Momma.* A hot flush coursed through Beth's body—the glow bearing both sorrow and joy.

"I told myself you'd be my role model this time, but with my second I'd be off the hook. My other affirmation was 'epidural—next time.' " Emma crossed a leg. "Knowing natural childbirth would be a one-off was huge...maybe I'll change my mind." She worked a little finger into Oliva's fist. "I don't know how you got through labor. All that pain and you didn't see or hold me..."

The ache in her voice wrenched Beth's heart. She stroked Olivia's forehead with her thumb. "The social worker's name was Cynthia...I'll never forget her." The words tumbled out. "She turned my lunch tray sideways to make room for the relinquishment papers. I had no appetite, so my food just sat. She held my hands…" Stifling the tremor in her voice, she closed her eyes. "She told me I wasn't giving away my baby… 'You're giving your baby *a way* to a better life right now. You're loving your baby unconditionally.' I didn't read the papers—I couldn't—but I forced a nod before she showed me three places to sign…" Sucking in a ragged breath, she exhaled long and deep. "I scribbled my name, hoping if no one could read my signatures they wouldn't count. Then I shut my eyes and waited for her to leave." She cast a sideways glance. "I thought you were a boy…"

Emma covered her mother's hand with her own. "Did thinking I was a boy make things easier or harder?"

"Easier," she whispered, pricked by the sting of a truth she never allowed herself. "If I knew you were a baby girl, I would have scoured faces for hints of my own."

"I can't imagine." Emma dipped her head.

Neither can I. "Cynthia asked if she could share a verse before she left. I just wanted her to leave…" Beth swallowed hard. " 'The light of stars surrounds you, the love of stars enfolds you, the power of stars protects you, and the presence of stars watches over you. Wherever you are, stars are. And all is well.' Her voice was so tender and soft… I didn't open my eyes, but I heard every word."

Emma squeezed Beth's hand, her lower lip quivering.

The rawness on her face broke over Beth like a thousand bits of glass. Glancing down, she wanted to take back her words and bury every speck of their shared pain. She held Olivia's gaze, absorbing the newborn's wisdom that intimated *tell her.* "Cynthia left a copy on my table…" She struggled past the tightness in her throat. "I've breathed that prayer for you every single day."

"Will you write the verse…"

Tears laced her words. Beth gave a single nod, blinking against the burn in her eyes.

Following a quiet stillness, mother and daughter talked long into the night, unfolding the years between them.

The next morning, Beth filled a pair of water bottles and set them on the counter.

Emma carried Olivia into the kitchen. "Bennett sends his love. The house is too quiet, so he's singing loud enough for us to hear."

"I bet your daddy has a beautiful voice." She stroked her grandbaby's cheek.

"He does. We were planning a video call so you could kind of meet him. But on the way to the airport, he backed out. He feared his new-dad hormones would turn him into a blubbering mess if he attempted a call with three generations of beauty." Emma held her gaze. "I told you he's charming… He'd like to do a video call with you after we get back."

Her pulse pounded in her ears. "Can we shop for a phone before you leave?"

"Absolutely." Emma held up a hand.

Beth tapped a high five in reply. "But now we're going to Greenough Park." She nuzzled her face in Olivia's silky hair.

After loading the car, she drove up Higgins

Avenue, pointing out University of Montana's South Campus: Lewis and Clark Village, Dornblaser Fields, and South Campus Stadium. "The women's soccer team plays there—UM doesn't have a men's team." She turned right onto South Avenue and wound around the stadium. "Do you play soccer?"

"Mm-hmm. I started in kindergarten." Emma shot her a glance. "That field is gorgeous. Bennett and I play co-rec soccer in the spring. I missed this year…"

I've missed thirty-six years. Regret knotted her stomach. *Be present.* She waved a hand toward UM's golf course and additional student housing, and then turned left onto Arthur Avenue. Driving through a residential neighborhood, she quieted. When she reached the west edge of campus, she resumed the mini tour. No one was behind her, so she slowed and gestured to the right. "Beyond that bronze grizzly is The Oval—three acres of lawn—then Main Hall. The mountain in the background is Mount Sentinel." *Where I sprinkled Reid's ashes.*

"Missoula is beautiful." Emma gazed out the window. "Do you ever pinch yourself to make sure you're not living in a dream?"

"I do." Her heart tugged, and she glanced to her left. The patio outside Liquid Planet Grille spun a reminder of leisurely weekend breakfasts with Reid. She shifted her focus straight ahead. Crossing the Madison Street Bridge, she highlighted the section of the Kim Williams Trail that snaked beside the Clark Fork River. Spring run-off flowed over the banks frequented by summer floaters and fly-fishers.

"Gorgeous." Emma let out a low sigh.

Beth nodded. *I'd like to see your home someday.*

Now, though, she reveled in every second with her daughter and granddaughter. Minutes later, she pulled into Greenough Park's south lot.

Emma placed Olivia in the stroller and reversed the handle. "Would you like to be the operator?"

"Yes." Heat radiated through her chest. Beaming, she leaned toward Olivia. "This is one of my fravrit places." The baby talk rolled off her tongue.

Opening and closing her fists, Olivia gurgled in reply.

Emma stopped on the apex of the curved, wooden footbridge. She photographed Rattlesnake Creek, adding a video of the swollen, babbling water. On the other side of the bridge, she choreographed a selfie of the three of them backdropped by the creek and Mount Jumbo.

I am a grandma. With her grandbaby in one arm and her other arm tucked around her daughter, Beth sighed, her heart feeling as full as the rushing creek. When she returned Olivia to the stroller, she fumbled with the safety belt, deflating a bit at her inexperience.

"Do you come here often?" Emma aimed her cell phone camera at a squirrel scampering across the path. "Twenty minutes from your house…I'd come every day if I could."

"I used to walk over on my lunch hour and arrive in about ten minutes—longer if I was stopped by a train. We have choo-choos over there." Smiling at Olivia, she waved an arm to her left.

"Ten minutes from your office…" Emma loosened a water bottle from an over-the-shoulder strap and took a drink. "Do you miss your job?"

Beth studied Olivia's bright eyes. "I miss the life

we had. Reid died so soon after I retired..." She let go of the handle, lifting her shoulders in a reflexive shrug. "Separating the two has been hard."

"Dang." Emma slipped an arm around her waist.

She met her gaze. "Our relationship recharged my life." Placing a hand over her heart, she flashed a shy smile.

"Mine, too." Emma smiled back.

For a moment, Beth rested her head against Emma's then continued the stroll. After the second bridge, she veered right, leaving the wide, pedestrian-only pavement to navigate the narrower footpath east of the creek.

The bump and sway of the stroller lulled Olivia to sleep.

Emma captured photos of rock cairns and interpretive signs, plus assorted trees and bushes—their furry and feathery occupants both visible and elusive. "I..." She toyed with her phone.

Slowing, Beth held her gaze.

"If Reid were still alive, I wouldn't have written." She glanced away. "I wanted to find you and see if you were happy. Not wreck your family if they didn't know. Then I found his obituary and..." She scuffed a shoe along the path.

You learned I was a family of one. The happy-sad rush of emotions banded around Beth's lungs. "Thank you for writing. Twice." The word came out whisper soft.

"I debated whether or not to send the Valentine's Day card." Emma tipped her head.

She couldn't see her face but could picture her eyebrows.

Birds serenaded them from all four sides.

A Yellow Warbler flew in front of them.

Emma looked from the bird to Beth. "Do you ever think he's up there working his magic?"

Tell her. She swallowed hard and squelched the words.

"Did he know?" Emma rested a hand on her arm.

Her tone was intuitive and accepting. Beth glanced at the sky. "No." The truth fell heavy as stone. A distant train whistle emphasized her remorse, and she completed the final steps in silence.

That evening, Beth scooted a chair closer to the kitchen table. She took a slow, deep breath, delighting in after-dinner tea with her daughter.

"I want to buy more Missoula tea while I'm here." Emma ran a thumb along the gold-rimmed cup.

"Deal." Beth savored a sip of the hot, herbal drink. She glanced at the baby monitor, whose silence confirmed a sleeping beauty down the hall. *Ask her.* Her heart fluttered. Curling her hands around the china cup, she absorbed its warmth. "When you found me, did you think I was happy?"

"I thought you had a bank of happy memories...and I hoped you found more joy." Emma nodded toward Beth's wrist. "Your bracelet is lovely."

She stroked a thumb over the etched word. "This is about you, Bennett, and Olivia." Fighting the burn in her belly, she took one breath then another. "Did you find Ian?" The thick, uneven words scratched her throat.

Emma nodded and straightened her placemat. "I didn't get in touch."

Beth hesitated. "Do you think he's happy?"

"I think so." Emma raised her eyebrows and tilted her head. "Do you want to know what I found out?" She rested a forearm on the table.

"If you don't mind telling me, I do." Beth hitched in her chair.

"He's married, has two sons and a daughter, and is a financial planner in San Francisco." Emma gave a half-shrug. "So, I assume he's happy."

Plus another daughter... Guilt stabbed at her gut and she looked away.

"Thanks for sharing his name." Emma tapped a fist against her heart.

"I almost didn't. Then I thought about your mom giving Doctor Z your address..." She stared into her cup. "Her bravery paved the way."

Emma tucked a strand of hair behind her ear. "I'll tell her. She was afraid if I located you when I was a teenager, I would have flown the coop. But when Doctor Z asked, I was already married. Plus, she knew our love was solid by then."

"You've had a good life." The words were part question and part matter of fact.

"I have." Emma nodded, her eyes glowing. "Thank you."

Her daughter's words hovered above a whisper. She managed a slight nod.

"I checked social media every month after Doctor Z sent the note." Emma fiddled with a cloth napkin. "I hoped to find your maiden name and get a glimpse of you..." She drew the napkin to her lips.

The cotton didn't conceal her muffled sob. Beads of regret broke open inside Beth's chest, smothering her breath. *I didn't know.* She clasped Emma's hands, and her grasp expressed what her voice could not.

Two hours later when she climbed into bed, she wrapped her arms around a pillow and buried her face in its fluffy softness. Revisiting Emma's words, she contemplated her vehement doggedness to avoid social media. Did divine intervention keep her from plunging in to online networking? Would she *ever* stop second-guessing her life?

Chapter Twenty-One

The following morning, Beth cradled Olivia on the edge of Emma's bed. "Are you ready for your bath, Little Bean?"

Olivia curled her lips into a half-smile.

"Bennett calls her Little Bean, too." Emma removed a hooded towel from her suitcase. "Would you like to bathe her?"

You wash and I'll dry. The ghost of pre-dishwasher days with Reid raised goosebumps on her arms. She shivered. Camouflaging her chill, she swayed Olivia side to side. *Ssshhh.* "How about you wash and I dry?"

"Perfect. Bennett and I tag-team sometimes..." Adding a diaper to the pile, Emma brushed the comforter with her knuckles. "Babies love black and white."

Her voice hinted a question. "I've had this set for years...now I love it even more." Beth ran a hand over the two-tone paisley comforter.

"She'll see more colors when she's about five months old." Emma gestured toward the red and yellow throw pillows.

By next time. She gazed into Olivia's blue-brown eyes. *You're beautiful.*

"Will you please grab a bath towel?" Emma bundled the supplies inside a small flannel blanket.

"Sure." She shifted Olivia into a one-armed carry.

After kissing her cheek, she detoured into the master bath. "Your grandma's getting the hang of this football hold. This towel"—she grazed a corner across her grandbaby's forehead—"is the color of cinnamon."

Olivia wrinkled her brow.

"Will your eyes be brown or blue?" She marveled at her rapt gaze and talked in a singsong voice all the way to the kitchen.

To the left of the sink, Emma layered the bath towel, blanket, and hooded towel. She held a wrist under a stream of water and adjusted the handle. "Do you want to feel the temperature?" She fastened the sink stopper.

"Sure." Beth dipped a wrist under the flowing water then into the sink. "Feels nice and warm, Little Bean."

"Mm-hmm." Emma removed Olivia's sleep sack and diaper. Glancing at the bath, she flashed a thumbs-up.

Beth reached over and pressed straight down then rotated the handle toward the empty sink on the right.

Supported in her spa, Olivia twisted and kicked.

The warm water and constant motion of her arms and legs fueled memories of baby gymnastics, the gush of amniotic fluid, and one tiny mew... A flood of dizziness buckled Beth's knees. She braced her elbows on the counter and leaned her chin against her fists, struggling to transform her vertigo into attentiveness.

"She loves her bath..." Emma washed Olivia's face and body then scrubbed her hair with a rectangular brush. "Time for your rinse." She glanced up. "Will you please turn on the water?"

Straightening, Beth gripped the counter's edge and

paused to confirm her legs were steady and strong. She opened the faucet. The water on her wrist was a smidge cooler than before, so she eased the handle to the left. *Perfect.*

"I'll protect her eyes while you rinse." Emma gestured toward a cup then curved a hand on Olivia's forehead.

She poured cupfuls of water with one hand and ran her fingers through Olivia's hair with the other. When no suds remained, she added one final rinse for good measure.

"Okay, baby girl." Emma transferred the dripping beauty from the sink to the layered linens. "Your turn." She smiled and stepped aside, keeping one hand on Olivia's belly until Beth moved into position.

Beth draped the hood around Olivia's head. Nesting her in the soft cotton, she dried her from head to toe. "You look like ET, except you're much cuter." She bent and kissed Olivia's wrinkled forehead.

"Bennett tells her 'phone home' when he dries her hair." Emma tapped Olivia's nose. "Time to ditch your hood for a dry blankie."

For two seconds, Beth lifted her grandbaby away from the wet towel. She lowered her onto the blanket and draped the flannel around her warm, wiggling body.

"We'll massage her together." Emma poured dime-sized dabs of oil into their hands.

Apricot scent filled the air.

Emma started on Olivia's abdomen, sliding her hands up her belly and chest and rounding to form a perfect heart. She gave one little pat then lifted her hands. "Now you…"

Beth modeled Emma's lead and skimmed her fingertips over the half-innie, half-outie belly button that mimicked her own. *Your belly button is perfect...* She didn't care now whether Emma had the innie that seemed so important all those years ago. Beaming love into her touch, she glided her hands over Olivia's thrumming heartbeat and velvet-soft skin.

Her grandbaby grunted and cooed.

She moved to an arm and leg—both wriggling nonstop.

Emma worked the opposite limbs then turned Olivia onto her belly. "You can do her back...it's her favorite part." She poured oil into Beth's outstretched hand.

Soft as a baby's bottom. A mixture of joy and sorrow hollowed her lungs as she started on Olivia's shoulders. Grounded by newborn softness, she stroked down her grandbaby's back then dipped to her bottom—belly soft.

Olivia raised her head and continued to wriggle her arms and legs.

"You're a sweet little yogi." Beth massaged her tiny toes.

"She's working on her commando crawl." Emma smiled. "I'm glad she's breaking us in before then."

After a final rub from Olivia's shoulders to her feet, Beth turned her onto her back. She slid a diaper under her bum, her fingers tingling at the newness of diapering and dressing a baby. "When will she crawl?"

"Probably between seven and ten months..." Emma sifted her fingers through Olivia's hair. "Some kiddos start earlier."

"Will you, Little Bean?" Beth wiped her hands on

the towel then cinched the diaper tabs and checked its fit. Snug. Not tight.

"I start with her arms." Emma proffered a koala sleeper. "Bennett starts with her legs."

Clumsy and slow, Beth threaded Olivia's arms then legs—all moving targets. "I wouldn't win any races." Affixing the final snap, she flushed with pride.

"Neh." Olivia scrunched her face.

"You have time for a five-second hairdo." Emma passed the brush.

With the still-damp bristles, Beth styled spiky accents.

"You are beautiful." Emma scooped up her baby and headed out the door.

You both are. Beth held the flannel blanket close to her face and inhaled the lingering scent of apricots. After scrubbing the sink and countertop, she gathered bath supplies then dropped off the toiletries in Emma's room. Grinning at the room's new name, she hurried down the hall to deposit the wet linens. Then she rerouted to the living room to join her daughter and grandbaby.

"She was a hungry girl." Emma patted Olivia's back.

"All done?" Beth slipped onto the couch.

"Mm-hmm. Bath time worked up an appetite." Emma kissed Olivia and handed over the baby. "Would you mind if I went shopping for a bit?" She arranged the burp cloth on Beth's shoulder. "We could all go, or maybe you'd like—"

"More cuddle time…" Beth nestled Little Bean against her chest.

"I should be back before she's ready to eat again.

Just when I think I have her figured out, though, she reminds me who's boss." Emma stood. "Be right back."

Tiny lines creased Olivia's forehead.

Her serious expression prompted a smile. Beth brushed butterfly-soft kisses on her grandbaby's forehead and cheeks.

"If she gets hungry, a bottle's in the fridge." Emma stopped in the doorway. "Two minutes in a bowl of warm water and she'll gobble the breast milk, according to Bennett."

"Gotcha." She snugged Olivia with one arm and joined Emma in the hall. "Downtown and city maps are in the door pocket."

"Thanks. I have my navigator, too." Emma pulled her phone from her purse. "I call her Georgette." She flashed a smile. "Where did you get the tea?"

"Rockin Rudy's." Beth retrieved the car keys then opened the garage door. Sunlight streamed in.

Emma tapped on her phone. "Which one?"

Rockin Rudy's topped Rockin Rudy's Record Heaven, followed by a place in North Carolina, and a street in New Hampshire. *Your birthplace.* She wondered if Emma noticed the latter. "The first one…" She pointed to the store less than five miles away per Georgette. North Carolina and New Hampshire's mileages were blank.

"Perfect." Resting a hand on Beth's shoulder, Emma kissed the crown of Olivia's head.

The casual touch wrenched her heart. Beth hugged Olivia a little tighter then turned her toward her momma. Averting her gaze from Reid's neglected hatchback, she focused on Emma. "Take your time."

"Thanks." Emma folded into the car. She started

the engine, blew a kiss, and backed out of the garage.

"It's just you and me." On the way to the couch, Beth fingered Olivia's hair and neck and the sleeper's cotton softness. She picked up the infant key ring and grazed the base of her grandbaby's palm.

Olivia opened her tiny fingers and curled them around the yellow ring. She wiggled and stretched, and the multicolored plastic keys tinkled.

"Hush, little baby don't say a word…" Stroking her forehead, cheeks, and nose, Beth sang the entire song without a single choke.

The baby flickered then closed her eyelids.

In Emma's room, Beth skirted the bassinet and monitor and collected the afghan. She stretched out on the couch, nesting pillows and covering her and Olivia with her handiwork. An ambush of emotions wrapped around her chest. She drew in a deep breath and exhaled long, slow, and deliberate. Twice more she repeated the cycle, purging the ragged remains of shame, guilt, and remorse. Emptied, she paused. Then she filled her lungs with gratitude, joy, and acceptance—every molecule teeming with her granddaughter's perfection. Little Bean's soft breath brushed her neck. Inhaling the scents of apricots, baby wash, and *love*, she closed her eyes. She yielded to Olivia's newborn innocence, allowing her granddaughter's weight and warmth to mend the slivers of her fractured heart.

Three hours later, Emma returned. "I didn't expect to be gone so long." She deposited her bags on the coffee table. "How did she do?"

"Her daddy has her pegged. She glommed onto her bottle like a baby bird." Beth traced a fingertip along

Olivia's jaw. "Tell your momma you burped like a champ."

"That's what Bennett says." Sinking beside them, she slipped an arm behind Beth and bent to kiss Olivia's cheek. "I missed you, baby girl."

Beth rubbed the heel of a palm against her chest. *I missed you, too, for thirty-six years.*

"And I was a champion shopper..." Emma displayed her purchases: a sundress and Montana onesie for Olivia, a Rockin Rudy's T-shirt and Draught Works pint glass for Bennett, and a bagful of Huckleberry Chocolate Bars and Missoula tea. "I shopped for myself, too." She extended an arm.

A slim, silver bracelet hugged her wrist. *Joy.* Beth glanced at her own, and a tingle ran along her spine.

"I hoped to find a bracelet like yours..." Emma donned a handcrafted hat made from pre-worn sweaters then turned side to side. "We'll be stylish together, too, Olivia Elise." Upside down *Joy* glinted from her wrist. She scooted off the couch. "I'll be right back."

Drawing Olivia to her chest, Beth nuzzled her downy hair. "You have a sweet momma." She closed her eyes, committing to memory every minute with her daughter and granddaughter.

Emma returned with a gift bag balanced atop a large, wrapped box—both creamy white. "I shopped like a champ in Maryland, too." She slid the gifts onto the coffee table and reached for Olivia.

Her pulse thrumming in her temples, Beth opened the card.

WITH
HEARTFELT
THANKS

The words overlaid a background of big and little hearts: pink, red, and violet. She turned her attention to the inside.

FOR
EVERYTHING
ALL MY LOVE,
EMMA

Her daughter's handwriting filled the blank card. "*Thank you.*" The words were as full as Emma's *EVERYTHING*. Beth held her gaze then shifted her focus to the bag. She pulled out tufts of purple tissue paper and a violet canister with scripted gold lettering. After fumbling with the lid, she removed a cut glass vase. "Beautiful—thank you." Gliding her fingertips along the etched diamonds and wedges, she spoke past the thickness in her throat.

"You're welcome." Emma smiled and rearranged Olivia on her lap. "Reading about your garden, I thought a vase would be a perfect gift."

"You were right." Beth positioned the canister and vase sentry beside *Mommy Hugs* and used both hands to pick up the box. She loosened the tape then undid the paper and turned over her gift. *Our Family Grows With Love*. The script wove around a collage frame. *Family.* A cry rose in her chest. She trailed her fingertips across the frame and counted the openings. *Nine.* Words caught between her throat and mouth. Struggling to still the quiver in her lips, she summoned a small smile.

Emma nodded, her lips trembling, too.

The softness in Emma's eyes sent a surge of warmth through her core. Beth set the frame on the coffee table. She stood and drew her daughter and granddaughter into an embrace, wanting never to let go.

That evening at The Pearl Café, Beth snuggled Olivia and savored a final bite of flourless truffle torte. "Mmmm. Did the aromas of chocolate and French press coffee wake you?"

Emma lowered her chin. "Are you a momma's girl? Our bison and halibut would've wakened your daddy—they smelled and tasted *delicious*." She met Beth's gaze. "We love sharing entrées, too. I'm pretty sure Bennett's never had bison, either…"

Glancing down, she stroked Olivia's cheek. "You'll have to bring him to Missoula someday." The words' smoothness belied their magnitude—they felt huge.

"He's already placed a request." Emma fastened the convertible diaper bag bassinet.

"Anytime." Her belly fluttered. "Tell him the Jorgennson Bed and Breakfast is open for business…"

"Will do." Smiling, Emma lifted her coffee cup. "He'll be thrilled."

I am, too.

Exiting the restaurant, Emma carried Olivia into the sun-kissed evening air.

"Wait until he sees what else is in store." Beth beeped open the car, parked on Front Street steps from the café. She retrieved the stroller, unfolding it in one fluid motion. After setting the brakes, she tucked the diaper bag in the storage pouch and congratulated herself on her grandmotherly ease.

Emma buckled in Olivia, rotated the handle, and stepped aside.

She piloted the stroller along Front Street then turned left onto Pattee Street to the Riverfront Trail. "The Kim Williams Trail is on the other side." She gestured to the left then leaned forward. "We're on the north side of the Clark Fork River now, Olivia."

Her grandbaby grunted in reply.

On the cusp of summer, the trail hosted a plethora of walkers, runners, bicyclists, and dogs.

Emma stopped for photos of the river, Caras Park, and the Old Milwaukee Depot on the opposite riverbank. Overlooking the man-made Brennan's Wave, she videotaped a river surfer and a kayaker. "Bennett will *love* Missoula."

"Does he kayak?" Beth resumed stroller duty.

"No…maybe someday."

"I bet he'll take a pony for a spin, Little Bean." She turned toward the lively music drifting from A Carousel for Missoula. The roll-up accordion doors offered sneak peeks of the hand-carved horses as they circled inside the brick building. "Your momma will unbuckle you, and I'll be right back." She parked Olivia next to the band organ then veered to the gift shop to buy tokens. The price menu captured her gaze. *Seniors—55 and over.* She *never* claimed a senior discount…

"What can I get you?" A white-haired man smiled and rested an arm on the counter.

She drew back her shoulders. "I need one adult and one senior plus a lap baby." Her status slipped out as though she announced it for years. After sliding a five dollar bill, she studied the man's lined face and age-spotted hands. *I'm happy to join your club.*

He returned two tokens and change. "Enjoy your ride."

"Thank you." Beth smiled and curled her fingers around the Carousel coins. *I will.* She escorted her daughter and grandbaby to the end of the line.

Two teenaged girls waited up front.

Behind them stood a man with a preschool-aged boy and a school-aged girl.

The boy waved to a woman seated in a chair along the perimeter.

Holding up a cell phone, the woman turned it sideways then raised a thumb.

A family. Beth reached over and stroked Olivia's hair.

"Photo op." Emma placed Olivia in Beth's arms. She tucked in close, draping a hand around her mom and baby before snapping a selfie of all three.

The multicolored Carousel horses whirled behind them.

"Would you like me to take some?" The man extended a hand.

"Sure." Emma passed the phone, and then drew closer than before.

Smiling, Beth tightened an arm around her waist.

He turned the phone. "Three generations?"

"Yes." His words buzzed in Beth's head. For a breathless moment, she braced herself against her daughter. She filled her lungs to overflowing, dazed by a profound joy that threatened to engulf her heart.

"Beautiful." He snapped horizontal and vertical views then returned the camera.

Happy squeals and organ music filled the air.

A smattering of kids and adults queued in line.

"Is the Carousel different than twenty years ago?" Emma spoke into her ear.

"The horses are still fast." The memory muscled back.

She had *not* wanted to go.

"*Please*. The Carousel will be really fun." Rachel's four-year-old son, Brendan, argued each of her excuses.

Finally, she agreed.

Loading Farmers' Market purchases into her car, Rachel shot her a smile. "I owe you one."

"He's persuasive." Beth bit her lip.

Brendan skipped ahead.

"For the past two years, Jeff professed Brendan would be a good lawyer…"

"Hurry up!" At the corner of Higgins and Pine, he waved both arms.

"I told ya." Rachel caught her son's hand and held on until reaching Caras Park.

People of all ages milled under and outside the giant white canopy. Beyond the open air pavilion, the week-old Carousel sported a rope of patrons that stretched out its doors and around the building.

Brendan sprinted to the end of the line.

The weight of ten thousand bricks crushed Beth's chest, and she wanted to bolt. When the music got too loud to talk, she fought for air instead of words. Then she mounted a sleek, black horse—Sweet Sue, according to the brass nameplate—and fastened her seatbelt. As the ponies spun at a dizzying pace, she acknowledged why she wanted to dash home. Being around a mass of kids had been *too damn hard*.

Now, as the gate opened, she leaned in. "We'll take a chariot. You go for the brass ring."

"I'll try." Emma tipped her head and raised her eyebrows.

She deposited her token and edged left, claiming the rear-facing Eagle Chariot. After settling onto the seat, she tucked Olivia in the crook of her arm.

"Bicycle Built for Two" boomed in the background.

Scoring the outside horse behind them, Emma pointed overhead. "Columbia Belle."

She spoke above the music. Beth gave a thumbs-up. She worked her index finger inside Olivia's tiny fist and examined her granddaughter. *Should I cover your ears?*

Olivia kicked, opening and closing her lips.

The little sucking motions contained no visible signs of distress. She leaned back. Their chariot for two, Olivia's random bicycle kicks, and the melodic tune triggered a smile. *A trifecta.*

Repeat customers from the previous ride trickled in. Some pony choices seemed deliberate while others appeared random.

Two boys lapped the Carousel twice.

They must be looking for an outside horse. She couldn't see where they landed.

Three rows back, a mom seated her toddler on a middle horse and climbed on behind, winding the seatbelt around both.

"You and me someday, Little Bean?" Beth buried her face in Olivia's hair.

Checking seatbelts, the pair of platform workers circled in opposite directions.

Then the ponies were off.

Beth angled sideways to watch the riders in front of and behind her vie for the brass prize from the ring-dispensing dragon.

When Emma grabbed her first ring, she flashed a grin then smiled again when the Carousel reached top speed.

Certain catching no amount of brass rings could be more thrilling than cradling her precious grandbaby, Beth tightened her arms around Olivia. "Glad we're in a chariot, Little Bean."

Two rows ahead, a school-aged boy snagged a ring on his first attempt, but it flicked away, ricocheting off the platform. He didn't reach for another.

The young girl in front of Beth stretched three times, and then caught a ring on the fourth revolution.

A teenaged girl rode the outside horse two rows back. She kept her hands in her lap, glancing at the dragon and Emma's growing collection of rings.

The music hushed. "Congratulations to the rider on Prairie Rose..." A worker's voice rang over the microphone.

Beth grazed her lips against silky baby hair and contemplated the analogies between merry-go-rounds and life. Parallels aside, had anyone predicted she would ride this Carousel with her daughter and granddaughter, she would have considered the prophecy *nuts*.

Leaving the building, Emma cradled Olivia in her arms. "You can ride after we stop for another photo..."

Alongside, Beth steered the empty stroller and scouted for a setting.

"Here"—Emma flicked a hand—"with the river and mountain in the background." She passed the baby then asked a twenty-something girl to take a picture.

Beth glanced southeast across the river to Mount Sentinel and the whitewashed M. The tug in her gut kept her from looking higher. Turning her grandbaby, she shushed the memories and smiled for the camera.

After buckling in Olivia, Emma straightened. "Will

you do a video call from here? Not the first time but after a while? We do *not* have mountains like this in Rockville." She tipped her head. "One from Greenough Park, too?"

"Sure." *Let's video call every day.* Beth wanted to singsong her wish to the wide-eyed beauty facing them.

A preschooler in a lime green helmet approached on a tiny, matching bicycle. Using her feet as pedals, she propelled forward. "Watch, *Abuela.*" She lifted her legs and coasted past.

Grinning, her dad and grandmother followed.

Beth smiled at their palpable pride.

"What did you call your grandmothers?" Emma slipped a strand of hair behind her ear.

"Nana and Grandma…how about you?"

"Yaya and Gram. We all called Mom's mom Gram—even Mom and Dad. Mom's sticking with Gram, and Bennett's mom wants Nonna. When I read Mamaw"—Emma slowed, holding Beth's gaze—"that name seemed perfect for you."

Mamaw. The word tingled on her tongue.

"Bennett and I could call you Mamaw, too, like with my gram." Emma rested a hand on her chest.

Her daughter's tender gesture tugged at Beth's heart. She shifted her smile between the two beauties. "Mamaw sounds perfect."

Three hours later, she sank into Reid's recliner and pulled out her journal. *What would you have felt, Reid? Anger? Betrayal? Disappointment?* Her silent words took hold in the dark of night. *I'll never know.* His reaction might have varied, depending on when she spilled the secret she guarded for years. The word's irony struck her. *Guarded.* Containing her longing with such fierceness, she turned into a prisoner of her own accord.

How would you feel now? Meeting Emma and Olivia both broke and mended her heart. If he were alive, might not he feel the same? *Did* he possess the power to see life after death? If so, did he embrace her joy? *They're beautiful, Reid.*

After he died, she was certain—bone deep—he was never more than a breath away. Learning about Emma changed things, though, and the thought of him realizing her pretense was unbearable. Isolated by the messiness of her deceit, she refused to acknowledge his closeness. But she longed for the sweetness of shared memories and the comfort of his presence, both tangible and imagined. She caressed her wedding band. *I miss you.*

She acted brave twice before—giving her baby *a way* to a better life and telling Emma her birth father's name. Garnering strength to chip away the space between lies and truth, she sucked in a deep breath. She exhaled and rolled remorse, regret, and resolve into one. By the muted light of a solitary lamp, she rallied her courage and uncapped her pen.

June Fifth

Dear Reid,

Thirty-six years ago, I gave birth to a baby girl. Emma. I thought she was a boy. Garrett, not Genevieve—names I held in my heart. I expected to carry this story to my grave but if I knew what lay in store, I would have told you the truth.

In New Hampshire, I gave my baby a way. My roommate, Lucy, and her mom knew. No one else did. I didn't see or touch or hold my baby, because if I said hello, I could never say goodbye. When they carried her out of the delivery room, my heart broke into a million tiny bits.

Hot tears rolled down Beth's cheeks.

Emma looked for me years ago, but she didn't know my married name. She found me last fall. "Reid married the former Elizabeth Gail Vicenza on May twenty-second..." Your obituary led her to me. I had such a hard time wrapping my head around that fact.

She's sleeping down the hall right now—at least I think she's asleep—and her baby girl is beside her. I'm so sorry I never told you I was a mom. Now, I'm a grandma. You're a grandpa. My lie was never intended to deceive you...ever. The charade was my best effort to stifle the unrelenting yearning I buried for years.

I loved you. We had a wonderful life together, and we would have made beautiful babies. I trust we would have been good parents...but falling in love with you after surrendering Emma seemed my destiny. I wish you were here to see them, Reid. They're stunning.

Words fall short in conveying my remorse for twisting our love into a façade. If only I could rewind time, mend what was broken, and speak unuttered words...but all I can do is express my sorrow with every ounce of my being and ask for your forgiveness.

I miss you and love you more.

Years of ache gave way to piercing sharpness. When she felt dry as sawdust, she wrapped her arms across her chest. Would she ever feel relief?

Chapter Twenty-Two

The following evening, Beth parked the car midway down the block from Therese and Kate's home. The outside temperature display read eighty-two degrees—the predicted high. When she opened the door, a blast of heat competed with the car's air-conditioned interior. She rounded to the sidewalk and waited for Emma.

"You get the honors." Emma smiled and handed over the car seat then raised a corner of the blanket draped along the top.

She secured the seat with the crook of her arm and peeked inside.

Olivia slept, and long, dark lashes brushed her cheeks.

Beth smoothed the blanket then led the way, her heart skittering. A quartet of purple and gold helium balloons with matching ribbons rose above the mailbox, static in the still air. Handwritten signs and the sounds of laughter and happy chatter steered her to the backyard.

The guest of honor ran across the lawn, barefoot. "Thanks for coming." She threw her arms around Emma. "I'm Kate." Stepping to her left, she captured Beth's hand with one hand and pushed aside the car seat's sunshade with the other. "O M G. She's adorbs…"

"You look adorbs, too." Beth nodded at her black floral dress.

"I'll put on my heels in a little bit so you get the full effect." Grinning, Kate wagged a foot. "Some peeps are waiting to meet you…"

"Thanks for having us." Emma gestured between herself and her baby.

"Anytime. C'mon…" Kate tugged Beth's free hand then linked Emma's arm. Skirting a group of teenagers gathered on the lawn, she guided them to a large rectangular canopy.

Six round, white-clothed tables sported mortarboard centerpieces and purple and gold *CONGRATS GRAD* and *SHS* confetti.

Kate stopped at a middle table. "Look who I found."

"Welcome." Therese stood and reached for Emma's hands.

"My mom—Therese—and Corrine, Zoe, and Maria." Kate motioned toward each of the seated women. "AKA Perimenopausal Women with Power Tools, as I'm sure you've heard." She folded back the blanket, uncovering the car seat. "Plus Emma and Olivia…"

"Nice to meet you." Emma smiled, sweeping a face-up palm.

Beth glowed at her daughter's room-lighting smile. Eager to showcase her grandbaby, too, she placed the car seat sideways on a folding chair. Then she braced the seat with her legs.

"You have a beautiful baby." Zoe flashed her dimples, giving Beth a one-armed hug before drawing Emma into an embrace. "Next?" She scooted aside.

"Welcome to Montana." Corrine leaned in and kissed Emma's cheek.

"Thank you." A pink flush spread across her face.

After studying Olivia, Maria met Beth's gaze. "She's perfect."

Pulse pounding in her ears, Beth gave a single nod.

Maria clasped Emma's hand between hers. "I'm so happy for all of you."

"So am I." Emma dipped her chin.

"Who do we have here?" Frank edged alongside Maria.

"Don't wake the baby…" Helen extended a hand. "We're the delighted grandparents—Helen and Frank."

"Pleased to meet you." Emma grasped their proffered hands. "What a wonderful day for Kate."

Two tables over, Kate stood next to an unoccupied chair, gesticulating to a pair of adults and three kids.

"She's a gem. Looks like you have something to be proud of, too." Frank gazed at Olivia.

"We all do…" Beth patted her chest.

Helen smiled a nod then waved an arm to the right. "The deck is loaded with food and drinks. Shall we move the baby so you can get a bite to eat?"

"Sure." Beth set the car seat next to a nearby tent leg then accompanied Emma to a trio of umbrellaed tables. After adding a graduation card to a basket adorned with purple and gold, she segued to the food. "Save room for Kate's world-famous pretzel salad." She picked up a spatula.

"Pretzel salad…sounds interesting." Emma glanced up, hovering a spoonful of pulled pork.

Beth smiled. "Kate's specialty is delicious." She filled her plate, poured a glass of wine, and followed

Emma to the table.

"Operation Stealth is underway. One at a time, check out the guy in the plum shirt behind me." Zoe signaled with a stiff thumb. "Our mission is to determine if SN—Scrawny Neck—is a fair name…"

"Anyone voted yet?" Beth cast a furtive glance.

"Mm-hmm. Three to zero." Zoe leaned in. "We're waiting on you and Therese."

She studied him out of the corner of her eye. "Thus far, is the consensus his nickname still stands?"

"Yep." Corrine stroked the front of her neck.

Beth gave a slow nod. "Four."

"Plus one." Emma held up a hand and splayed her fingers.

"If I may be so bold as to project the outcome"— Zoe rested her chin in her hands—"I predict a landslide."

Quiet laughter rippled around the table.

Beth took a bite of pretzel salad, which tasted as rich and satisfying as she remembered. *So many changes since Christmas…* She glanced from Emma to Olivia.

"They're beautiful."

The softness of Reid's voice brushed her ear. *Thank you.* A wisp of a caress lingered on her neck, and she reached for him, grazing nothing but air. *I love you.* Weightlessness swept over her, and she flickered her eyes closed.

"I'm serious." Kate's words carried from across the lawn.

The teenager's voice reined in her thoughts, and she focused her gaze on the graduate.

Kate gestured between her mom and Miles.

He grinned and slipped a hand into his pocket.

Shaking her head, Therese arched her eyebrows.

She's probably telling him to give her mom a call. Beth reached for her glass. *Well played, Kate.*

"This salad is scrumptious." Emma raised a forkful of pretzel salad. "I'd love the recipe."

"So would I." Zoe folded her napkin. "I'll be in charge…"

Tucking into her food, Beth registered bits and pieces of conversations. When she noticed Olivia's searching gaze, she excused herself and gathered her grandbaby from the car seat.

Maria opened her arms.

Beth passed her the baby. Luck, too, she hoped, grazing her friend's hand.

"You're darling." Maria sifted her fingers through Olivia's hair. "So are your momma and grandma."

"The rest of the crew is right here…" Kate opened her palms. "Here's your catalyst." She motioned toward Miles, standing behind her.

Beth gestured toward the empty chair. "Have a seat."

"Time out." Kate formed her hands into a *T*. "I want a picture of the *Perimenopausal Women*."

Her stage whisper made Beth smile.

Grasping her mom's hand, Kate kissed her cheek. "They'll keep you sane after I'm gone. You can miss me once in a while but no fair crying every single day…"

"Every other night?" Therese sniffled and pulled her into a hug.

"Once a week, tops." Kate wriggled out of her embrace. "You'll keep her honest, right?"

"Tough duty, Kate, but we'll try." Corrine raised an eyebrow.

Zoe curled a thumb and index finger into an *O*.

"Good. But first, head to the lilacs…" Kate flicked a heel-clad foot. "You get in the middle, Mom. We'll make copies, right?"

"Whatever you say, Boss." Therese brushed a two-fingered salute.

Beth circled by Kate and nodded at her shoes. "The full effect is stunning."

"Thanks." Kate lifted a foot and turned her ankle. "I'm glad these aren't my woodworking shoes."

She grinned. *I'll miss you.* Looping toward the others, Beth drew in a deep inhale of the lavender and white blossoms—*of friendship.* She joined Maria on Therese's right.

Corrine and Zoe flanked her on the left.

"Take a baby step toward the house." Kate tipped her head.

With an arm around Maria's waist, Beth sidestepped to the right.

Turning her cell phone sideways, Kate nodded. "Gorge." She counted to three before snapping several photos. "Now, some with your 'Kate-MacCaffert-is-the-best-furniture-maker-in-the-land' faces."

Miles whistled behind her.

Beth bugged her eyes and gaped, clapping in slow-motion.

"Perfecto." Kate took horizontal and vertical shots then held up a hand. "Hang on. I'm making sure your eyes are open."

You've been my lifeline. All of you. Beth wanted to announce her truth, but the words stuck in her throat.

Kate gave a thumbs-up. "C'mon, Emma..." She waved an arm. "Now some with you, me, and Olivia." She handed the phone to her grandpa.

"You trust me with this?" He gave an open-mouthed wink.

"With my life." She bumped his hip, and then slid in between her mom and Corrine.

Cradling Olivia, Emma crossed the lawn.

A wave of heat washed over Beth, bathing every molecule with tingling warmth. She realized she *was* selfless, and her beautiful Emma and Olivia affirmed an unequivocal truth. *Life gives us second chances.*

"Here, Mamaw." Emma smiled, her blue eyes twinkling.

Thrilling at the new name, she grasped her grandbaby. *I graduated today, too, Little Bean...from the School of Perpetual Guilt.* She nuzzled Olivia's downy hair and shifted to the right.

Emma slipped in between her and Maria and wrapped her arms around their waists.

Mamaw turned Olivia toward the camera and steadied her with one arm. Her upside down bracelet glinted in the sunlight. *Joy.* Curling an arm around Emma, she tucked in close. She beamed for the camera, knowing just where her photos would go.

Acknowledgements

Twenty-four years ago, a newspaper notice beckoned me to a Missoula Women Writers' Guild meeting. Eileen Kennedy was a newcomer that night as well. The critique group we joined morphed, years later, into our writing partnership of two... I am beyond grateful for her wise counsel, valued input, and friendship that remains strong despite the now fifteen hundred miles between us.

Thank you to Amy Knutson, whose group, "Menopausal Women with Power Tools," inspired my title five years before I wrote the first word. Brenda DeGrazio, Certified Nurse Midwife extraordinaire, answered my questions about perimenopause and primary ovarian insufficiency. For feedback on early drafts, thanks to Karin Knight, Kathleen Snow, Jan O'Hara, and Bev Reiner. I am blessed to call all of these formidable women my friends.

Like Beth, I knew nothing about power tools prior to taking a women's woodworking class. I am indebted to Andrew Oberg, Home ReSource, and The Lifelong Learning Center for the class's fortuitous timing. Stan Mast and Bryan Tipp familiarized me with home workshops, and Industrial Arts teachers Jim Swofford and Chip Rinehart provided glimpses into the world of high school woodworking. Habitat for Humanity employees and volunteers offered lessons and mentorship as I worked alongside.

I owe heartfelt gratitude to a host of family, friends, and colleagues for their encouragement and support and for words and phrases that are woven throughout the book. Special thanks to my parents, Kay and Dan Antonietti, who raised me to be a reader and have been my biggest fans. As the late author John Francis Kieran proclaimed, "I am a part of all I have read." My mom sifted through numerous drafts of this novel, praising each one. Though my dad passed away during this years-long endeavor, he, like Reid, makes his presence known from the heavens. I imagine him raising a glass in celebration.

Thank you to my editor, Leanne Morgena, for her belief in and championing of *Perimenopausal Women with Power Tools*. Her patience and guidance fostered a deeper story. Thanks, also, to The Wild Rose Press team of Rhonda Penders, RJ Morris, and Lisa Dawn MacDonald, as well as to my cover designer, Kristian Norris. The 2017 Pacific Northwest Writers Association conference introduced TWRP to me and presented instructional pearls that made this a better book.

Thanks to James Dillet Freeman for the 1943 "Prayer for Protection," and to the anonymous songwriter for the mid-twentieth-century tune, "99 Bottles of Beer." The Agatha Christie quote is from "The Last Séance" in *The Hound of Death and Other Stories* (Odham Press, 1933). Finally, thank you to my hometown of Missoula, Montana, for providing a rich tapestry for Beth's story.

A word about the author…

Born in Missoula, Montana, Karen Buley credits her roots to Butte, Montana, birthplace of her parents and her home throughout much of her childhood. She is the author of a novel and a collection of nurses' stories that was chosen a "Best Books 2010" Awards finalist by *USA Book News*. Her work has appeared in a number of publications including *Family Circle*, *American Nurse Today*, *Working Nurse*, and four anthologies.

After years of caring for new moms and babes, Karen traded the magic of birth for the magic of books. She is a high school library media assistant in Missoula where a river runs through.

Visit her online at:
http://www.karenbuley.com,
on Twitter @karenbuley,
and on Facebook at karenbuleybooks.

Thank you for purchasing
this publication of The Wild Rose Press, Inc.

For questions or more information
contact us at
info@thewildrosepress.com.

The Wild Rose Press, Inc.
www.thewildrosepress.com